YOU OUGHTA KNOW

SUE PHILLIPS

Sweetbriar Creek Publishing Company
PO Box 92683
Henderson, NV 89014-8845

https://www.SuePhillipsAuthor.com

Publisher's Note: This is a work of fiction. Names, characters, places, and incidents are a product of the author's imagination. Locales and public names are sometimes used for atmospheric purposes. Any resemblance to actual people, living or dead, or to businesses, companies, events, institutions, or locales is completely coincidental.

Book Cover Design © 2020 Sandra Paul
Editor: Julia Ganis—www.juliaedits.com

In Memory
My husband, my best friend, my soulmate,
DON PHILLIPS
June 18, 1951 – December 24, 2016

Thank you for being my biggest fan and always believing in me.

*I wish I would've finished this novel while you were still
with me so we could celebrate with a glass of champagne.*

*Thank you for asking Mindy to urge me
to get this book out there in the world.*

Thank you for 42 great years together.

Thank you for showing me you are still watching over me.

I will always miss you.

I will always love you.

*P*ictures of new mothers holding their tiny babies covered half the wall of the examination room. Ten years ago, Megan Fisher had watched her photo go up on the bulletin board and had told Dr. Ames that she planned to add several more to his collection.

"At least eight kids," she had said.

"On a policeman's salary?" her doctor had asked. "Or is your husband still holding on to the hope of being the next Michael Connelly?"

"Writing is Stewart's dream. Mine is babies. Lots of them." She recalled the conversation while staring at the array of adorable babies. *At least one of us got our wish.* A twinge of sadness swept past her before her thoughts were interrupted by a deep, soft-spoken voice at the foot of the table.

"You probably only suffer from stress-related amenorrhea." Dr. Ames sat on the stool as he pulled on a pair of white latex gloves. His medical assistant silently stood by, waiting for him to begin his exam. "Not surprised either. It's probably hard enough being married to a detective, never mind a big-name author. I suppose he's either tracking down bad guys or writing about them."

"Or flying around the country to promote his latest novel." Her voice sounded a little too lighthearted, too cheery. "I don't mind. I've got a classroom of sixth graders to keep my mind from worrying about Stewart. But Jason misses the days when his dad was more available."

"Hard to believe I delivered your boy ten years ago."

Faintly aware of the doctor's movements, she let her eyes remain on the photos. The metallic click of instruments unnerved her. She tried to take a calming breath without being obvious. It was only an exam, for heaven's sake. Dr. Ames gave her no cause for this skittishness. Still, she hated this feeling of being so vulnerable.

"Despite your symptoms, there is no sign of pregnancy."

"But I'm over a month late. I've heard of IUDs failing at the end of their use."

"Yes, but stress is probably the reason for your missed periods. There are other choices for birth control." He paused, looking up. "Unless you're ready to have that little girl you've always wanted."

Megan forced a weak smile. "Stewart thinks we're too old to start over again."

"At thirty-three? Hardly. But if that's how he feels, he should make it permanent." Getting up from the stool, he peeled off the gloves and threw them away. "You can sit up now."

Clutching the paper gown, she made an awkward attempt until he took one elbow and steadied her, then stepped back and leaned against the counter, folding his arms across his chest. Dr. Ames was in his late thirties, with a California tan and a gentle manner that made most of his patients fall a little bit in love with him, including the white-haired ladies. Even Megan had entertained a small crush on him during her frequent office visits while expecting Jason.

"As soon as your body is back on track, the tenderness in your breasts and the edema will take care of themselves. Give it another month." He gave her a smile of encouragement that she tried to return. "Meanwhile, enjoy this heat wave we're having and take the rest of the day off. If I didn't have a full schedule, I'd be hitting the beach myself. Go home and relax—doctor's orders."

~

SEVERAL MINUTES LATER, Megan left the medical building near Memorial Hospital and drove her Lexus down the streets of Long Beach toward the ocean, turning from Second Street onto the narrow streets of her Naples Isle neighborhood. Her three-story house looked more like an Italian villa, towering over the sidewalks surrounding their pie-shaped corner lot one block from the circular canal.

Five years earlier on Christmas Eve, Stewart had given her a velvet jeweler's box. She had expected a ring. An emerald, hopefully. Her birthstone. Instead, she had found a house key tucked inside.

"To our new home," Stewart had said with the enthusiasm of a little kid, never realizing that she might have wanted to share in the enormous decision to buy a multimillion-dollar house.

But Stewart wasn't that way. He made decisions for himself, not her. Sometimes Megan wondered why she hadn't once questioned this behavior when they were dating. Back then, he joked about being her knight in shining armor, someone who wanted nothing more than to take care of her, slay her dragons, treat her like a princess. Never once had she considered that he was incapable of thinking of anyone else but himself.

Megan pulled into the garage, cut the engine, and punched the remote button, shutting out the afternoon sun. Tossing her keys into her purse, she tried to shake off the feeling of unease that had plagued her since this morning.

Her sixth-grade students had picked up on it, acting out more than usual before she had left for her appointment.

She dropped her head back against the headrest and closed her eyes, half wishing for a physical reason behind her symptoms. Something simple. Something treatable. Not cancer, God forbid. And definitely not a pregnancy.

Opening her eyes, Megan took a slow, deep breath and exhaled, wondering how Dr. Ames would have reacted if he'd known that her charming and handsome husband hardly noticed her in recent months, making love to her as if it was an appointment penciled into his busy schedule somewhere between calls from his personal publicist and emails from his editor.

Despite his notoriously sexy crime novels, Stewart left passion to the pages of his books. Not that her husband wasn't good in bed. On the contrary, he knew exactly how to satisfy her. His technique was flawless.

But completely devoid of emotion.

The words seemed to have a voice of their own, taunting her with the pathetic truth behind their perfect marriage. She'd loved Stewart almost from the first moment they had met in college. Even though he said he loved her, he was not the type to show it. Orphaned at fifteen, he'd shut down his emotions, which served him just fine in the police force, he'd once told her, firmly closing the door on the subject.

Get over it, Megan.

Mentally pushing aside the quiet loneliness, she went through the door leading into the kitchen. As she entered the house, she left her purse and school papers on the counter adjacent to the back stairwell, then paused at the first step to slip the high heels off her swollen feet. With shoes dangling from one hand, she slowly climbed the two flights to the third floor where the melody from a jazz saxophone drifted to her ears.

A renewed feeling of dread swept over her.

She slowed, listening.

Initially, she thought the music was coming from somewhere beyond the open windows at the end of the hall. But as she approached her bedroom, she heard a weather report, then another song being introduced.

It's only the clock radio, she realized with relief. She must have forgotten to shut it off in her morning rush.

Unbuttoning her silk blouse, she decided Dr. Ames was probably right about her stress level. If something as trivial as a radio could shoot her heart rate sky-high, she needed to learn how to relax. She would start with a nice long soak in the Jacuzzi tub, then curl up with a good book until Jason came home from school.

Struggling with the one-handed approach, she looked down at the stubborn button as she walked through the doorway.

Stewart's chuckle brought her head up. Across the room, the floral bedspread rippled and shifted with movement.

"Stewart?" His name rushed past her lips so softly Megan wasn't even sure she had spoken until she heard a muffled curse coming from the bed.

She watched him scrambling beneath the covers, tangling himself in the sheets. Panic etched his face as he glanced down at his partner, then back at her. Her gaze fell to his companion.

Recognition rocked her back on her heels. A cherished member of their extended family for longer than she could remember. Someone she trusted. Her trembling hand cupped her mouth as she stared at the one person she never dreamed would betray her in this way.

"Maxwell?

~

STEWART SCRAMBLED TO SIT UP, throwing his legs over the edge of the bed, purposely blocking the view between his wife and his lover. "I know you're upset, Meggie, but—"

She held up her hand, momentarily halting his words. Her mouth moved, yet she didn't speak. Her eyes blinked back glistening tears.

"I'm sorry, Megan…" Ignoring his own nakedness, he went to her, but she backed away as if repulsed by the sight of his body. "Let me explain."

She shook her head, then turned and ran from the room.

Dashing to the other side of the bed for his pants, Stewart couldn't bring himself to look at Maxwell.

"What on earth are you going to say to her, Stew?"

"I don't know." He was having a hell of a time getting his foot through the pant leg. "I can't lose her though. Not now."

"It's too late, I'm afraid. For once in your life, you can't smooth talk your way around Megan. She'll leave you, you know."

"No, she won't." He finally got into his pants, zipped them, and grabbed a T-shirt from the floor. "I won't let her," he said, pulling the shirt over his head. "There's too much at stake. You know that as much as I do."

"You haven't much choice now."

"I will not walk out on my family like her father did. She never got over that. I'll talk to her. I'll explain."

"For God's sake, this is not as if she caught you with another woman. She can't very well forgive you just to avoid losing a father for Jason."

Stewart finally brought himself to glance at the man he had loved long before Megan had entered the picture. Maxwell had become a highly respected professor at the state university in town. Even though it didn't matter if anyone knew his sexual orientation, Maxwell kept his private life private. The last thing either of them wanted was a public scandal over their longtime relationship.

"Wait for me," he said, pausing at the threshold to make sure he was heard.

Bare-chested, the sheet draped discreetly at his waist, Maxwell shook his head solemnly. At thirty-nine, he had become only more distinguished with his salt-and-pepper hair and fine lines at the corners of his gray eyes. There was a gentleness in him unlike any man Stewart had ever known.

"I don't want to lose you," Stewart admitted.

Maxwell gave him a smile that might have been meant to be encouraging, but seemed more sad than anything else. In one instant their private paradise had been shattered. Nothing would be the same again.

"I'll find my way out without Meggie seeing me," Maxwell said.

Stewart nodded with resignation, then turned and raced toward the back stairs.

~

MEGAN HAD STARTED to leave but made it only as far as the kitchen. Keys and purse in hand, she stared at the door to the garage, suddenly realizing she had nowhere to go. She couldn't fly to Florida and show up on her mother's doorstep. Not without Jason, anyway. And not without her son knowing something was desperately wrong. Besides, this wasn't something she could tell her mother, a crusty old woman embittered by her own ancient loss. She had refused to accept that Megan had found a man who wouldn't abandon her. Instead, her mother stayed away, even from her own grandchild.

Megan didn't have any close friends to take her in, except other teachers at school. Considering Stewart's notoriety as a famous author, the last thing Megan wanted to do was air their dirty laundry to someone outside the family. She couldn't risk it. One leak to the wrong person…

It wasn't Stewart she wanted to protect. Or herself. Jason was the one she needed to shelter from this ugly truth.

Images of her husband with Maxwell flooded her mind. Numb from the shock, she sat down hard on the last step.

Her own husband had been having sex with another man. The big-shot detective, the macho crime novelist, the man who declined marriage proposals from female fans on a weekly basis was living a lie. And she was caught in the middle of it.

How could she not have known? Especially about Maxwell?

"Megan?"

The sound of her husband's voice came from behind her. He was standing on the landing above, though she didn't turn to look at him. Instead, she clutched her purse to her chest and rose to her feet.

Stewart came down the stairs. "Where are you going?"

"Back to work," she said. Even if it was the truth, which it wasn't, she still wouldn't have been able to meet his gaze without seeing him and Maxwell together in bed. She reached for the doorknob.

"We need to talk."

"Jason will be expecting me."

"Not for two more hours." He reached for her arm. She pulled away. He reached again, slowly this time, taking the purse and placing it on the nearby counter. "Give me a chance to explain—"

His cool handling of her was too much for her to bear. She wasn't a murder suspect who needed to be worked by some compassionate detective. "How could you?" she demanded, her voice escalating. "Here! In our house? In our bed?"

"It's not like you to get hysterical, Meggie. Calm down."

"Don't tell me to calm down when I have every right to act any way I please. And for once in my life I'm not going to pretend to be your mild-mannered Megan. Damn it, Stewart, answer my question. How long? How many others besides Maxwell?"

"No one else. I swear that's the truth. As for Maxwell, it's just something that happened out of the blue. You and I both knew about his…background, so to speak. This afternoon he and I got to talking about it and, well, one thing led to another in our conversation and—"

"And I don't believe for one second that this…this *thing* with Maxwell just accidentally happened this afternoon." She was shouting now. It was the only way she could keep from dissolving into a mess of tears. "God damn you, Stewart. You owe me the truth."

"The truth is that I love you, Megan. I didn't do this to hurt you. I was curious. You know how I am. I'm a writer at heart. Always open to new experiences to enhance the writing."

"Bullshit."

His eyes registered shock. She never used such language. Ever.

"This isn't like going to a sushi bar for research, Stewart. Or scuba diving with sharks. Don't insult my intelligence."

His shoulders slumped. A minute ticked by as he stared forlornly at his feet.

"How long has this been going on?"

His head jerked up. His mouth opened and closed.

"How long?" she repeated.

He closed his eyes, unable to meet her angry gaze. "Fifteen… years." Her sharp intake of breath drew his eyes up in panic. "I made a mistake, Meggie. But I don't want to make the same mistake your father made. I don't want to disappear without a trace. I don't want to abandon you or Jason. Please forgive me."

~

Several mornings later, Megan reluctantly opened her eyes and glanced at the digital clock on the bedside table. She'd managed to finally fall asleep around sunrise, and now it was almost noon. Dragging herself out of the bed in the guest room on the second floor, she went into the adjoining bathroom.

Avoiding her desolate reflection in the mirror was impossible as she methodically washed the sleep from her face. Her eyes were more red than brown, with dark circles beneath them. Her long brown hair was dull and tangled. She looked as bad as she felt.

The past few days were a blur, a self-induced fog of functioning on a normal level as a mother and a teacher, pretending nothing was wrong, while shutting out the sickening reality of the nosedive into hell that her life had taken.

As far as their son knew, his parents were sleeping on separate floors because of an unresolved argument, nothing more.

If only that was all this was about.

There was no argument to resolve. After Megan had discovered Stewart with Maxwell that afternoon, she'd barely heard him begging for her forgiveness. But nothing in the world could make her forgive. Or forget.

I wish I could forget.

But all she could do now was to pretend her perfect world was not shattered. She had to do it. For Jason's sake.

"Mom? Are you up yet? It's Sunday. Did you forget where we're going?" The soft voice of her ten-year-old came through the closed door of the bedroom. "We gotta be at the camp by two- thirty."

"I know, honey." She slipped into her pink cotton robe and cinched the sash at her waist, then picked up her hairbrush as she walked toward the door. "I'm running a little slow lately."

Brushing through her hair, wincing at the tangles, she opened the door to find him holding her coffee mug.

"Bless you, sweet child."

Her corny endearment widened his lopsided grin. Dressed in shorts and a T-shirt, he was starting to develop a deeper tan from the early summer sun.

As they walked over to the bed together, she sipped the coffee and sighed contentedly. "You remembered the cinnamon."

"Dad did it."

Her step faltered, and she nearly spilled the coffee. Stewart was supposed to be at a book festival in Denver the entire weekend.

"Your father's home already?"

Jason nodded. "He came back early 'cause of you. But he's sure you'll be feeling like your old self real soon."

"He said that, did he?"

Megan wondered how her husband could possibly believe that she could go back to being her "old self." Her old life was over. Their life as a family was over. But Stewart didn't see it that way at all, especially after she'd agreed to hold off telling their son of the inevitable divorce. Only temporarily though. Just for a few weeks. Just until school was finished for the year. Then she would tell him.

"Dad says until you're better I'm supposed to be extra good to you."

With the mug in one hand, she dropped the brush on the bed and reached out to him. "Jason, you are always extra nice to me. I couldn't ask for a better son. Please, honey, don't think that any of this is your fault. Your dad and I have some differences right now."

"Is that why you want to send me away for the summer?"

Her heart ached. "We're not *sending* you away. We're giving you a chance to have some fun rather than hanging out with boring grownups during your vacation. The Flying K Camp is supposed to be a terrific place, Jason. And the two of us will have a great time visiting it today. You'll see."

"Make that the *three* of us," added her husband, standing in the open doorway of the guest room.

"Stewart." Megan jumped up, sloshing the coffee over the rim of the cup and onto her robe. "What do you mean *three*?"

He slouched against the door jamb with his hands in his front pockets of his jeans. In his black blazer and white sports shirt, he could have been posing for his publicity photo on the back of his crime novels. Just as dark and moody too.

"I caught an early flight so I could tag along with you." He gave her the slight smile that his female fans found so sexy. So had she. Now it reminded her of how easily she had been fooled by him for so long.

"Cool, Dad!"

Megan turned to their son. "Jason, take my cup to the kitchen, please. Your father and I need to talk."

After a minor protest from his son, Stewart stepped forward. "Do what your mother asked, Jase."

"Yes, sir." Scuffing his bare feet on the white carpet as a final show of disgruntlement, he left the room.

When he disappeared from view, Megan closed the door and turned to her husband. "You're not going with us, Stewart."

"Let's not fight, Meggie." Despite his placating tone, an undercurrent of warning emanated from him.

"Don't do this." Closing her eyes and covering her ears, she wished she could make him disappear. Better yet, make their entire life together disappear. Except for Jason.

"I'm still his father," he said softly as if talking to a child. He lightly grasped her arms, but she shook him off, unable to bear his touch. "I don't intend to be shut out of his life. We can work this out if only you would—"

"Stop it, Stewart." She retreated to the far side of the room before turning to look at him again. She fought to control the quiver in her voice but failed. "How can you possibly expect me to put aside my feelings, my hurt, my anger at you? I can't possibly act as if nothing has happened."

"But you can't walk out on me. Not now. What about all we worked for?"

She had always known he was the center of his own universe.

But blaming her for the damage he'd done to their marriage was more than she could take.

"Leave. Now."

He didn't move. Instead, he watched her in silence.

"If you don't go downstairs and tell Jason that you have a sudden emergency and have to leave, I'll tell him about Maxwell."

"You'd never do that."

She was bluffing and she knew he knew it. There was no way she would ever reveal the truth to Jason. Not the whole story, anyway. Not about finding his father in bed with his beloved Uncle Maxwell. But she had no other cards to play. With any luck, Stewart would back down. She counted on it.

"I never said 'never,' only later. But I won't tolerate your Happy Threesome charade. It's only going to make it that much harder on Jason when he finally learns the truth."

His eyes narrowed. "This isn't over, Megan."

No, of course not. It would never be over. But at least she'd won this particular standoff.

As he closed the door behind him, she leaned back against the wall to steady herself. She could feel the drop of adrenaline like the sudden free fall of an elevator. Her knees weakened and buckled. Slowly she slid down the wall until she sat on the floor.

And the tears came again.

TWO HOURS LATER, driving north along the congested Pacific Coast Highway through Malibu, Megan regarded her son's silence with an edge of concern. She attempted to carry on a conversation with Jason, but it was mainly one-sided.

She knew he was disappointed that his father hadn't come along with them. Stewart had waited until the last minute before backing out, claiming he'd forgotten about some important business he needed to tend to. At least he hadn't blamed her for his change in plans. But then, she also saw how easily he'd fabricated the lie. He sounded so believable, so honest. How many times had she looked into those brown eyes and been more than willing to accept his excuses for working late, for not coming home to her?

She glanced at Jason.

He had changed in the last several months, withdrawing into sullen silences. Could he have already found out about his father's relationship with Uncle Maxwell, the man he'd known his entire life as if he was the patriarch of their little family?

She thought about the previous weeks, trying to remember if ever there had been a time when Jason might have come home unexpectedly from a friend's house and stumbled across a similar scene with his father as Megan had done.

She hoped not.

Her eyes focused on the northbound traffic on the highway. Certainly she would have sensed his anguish over something as huge as this. She didn't want to believe she could have missed the signs of such a traumatic experience.

She didn't believe his recent mood swings were severe enough to cause alarm, but then what did she know? She hadn't known about Stewart.

No, that was a bolt out of the blue. Or was it?

God, she was so confused. And hurt. Her whole world was shattered, and yet she'd forced herself to act as if nothing was wrong. For Jason's sake. Maybe even for her own.

She'd returned to her sixth-grade classroom to wrap up the final weeks before the end of school. But it'd been so hard to focus on anything. Nearly impossible.

Her son's silence this past week mirrored the tension at home with Stewart, not to mention her own anxiety over the tests she'd taken on Friday to find out if she'd contracted any diseases from her husband.

Her gut clenched as she thought about the possibility of an

STD. Yet if she spent too much time dwelling on it, she would crack. And she had to be strong for her son.

Despite Stewart's reassurance that he had been careful, she would be holding her breath until she heard from Dr. Ames. Her fingers immediately tightened on the steering wheel as she fought back the shocking image of her husband in their bed.

"Slow down, Mom! You're going to miss the turnoff."

Jason pointed out the pitted metal sign for Yerba Buena Road. A mile beyond the Los Angeles county line, the narrow two-lane road looked like all the others that branched off the coast highway into the Santa Monica Mountains.

"Thanks, honey." She reached over and lightly patted his shoulder. His head snapped around. His body tensed. But as quickly as he'd reacted, he relaxed.

Megan frowned. *What was that all about?*

Jason gave her a grin that was halfway between forced and genuine, as if to say, *I'm okay. Let's forget about it. Please?*

Megan hoped her own reassuring smile was more convincing.

CHAPTER 2

*S*am Kempton stepped out of the shower and toweled off with a vigorous rub. He picked up his watch, checked the time, then buckled the leather band across his wrist. Twenty minutes to shave and dress before his meeting with Megan Fisher down at the camp's office at the bottom of the hill.

When the woman had called earlier in the week about registering her son for the entire summer at the Flying K, Sam had invited her to tour the facilities after his weekenders left on Sunday afternoon.

Although the last car had pulled out over an hour ago, he'd lost track of time while handing out payroll checks to his staff before they'd headed home.

Now he had to hustle as he lathered the heavy stubble on his face. He stood naked in the breeze coming through the open window. Privacy was one of the advantages of living most of the year alone on a hilltop in the Santa Monica Mountains.

After the shave, he grabbed clean underwear from a pile of laundry spilling from a basket on the floor. With a snap of the waistband against his flat stomach, he felt damn proud of getting back into good shape. Five hundred sit-ups. Every morning. So what if he was addicted to them like some people were addicted to coffee? Or booze?

Better than being dead-ass drunk.

It had been eight years since his last drink. Eight years, two months, three weeks. He could count off the minutes if he didn't have to get his butt in gear.

He pulled on his jeans and slipped a white polo shirt over his head. The cotton fabric fit snug, stretching the winged-K logo above the left pocket. He'd shrunk more damn clothes in the dryer. Jesus, it was hard not having a woman around the house anymore. It'd been five years since he and Maryann had split, four since their divorce. Not nearly that long since they'd last slept together though. Still, he would never get used to living alone.

Several minutes later, Sam parked his old stake-bed pickup by the office and got out, whistling for his oversized mutt to do the same. "End of the ride, Riley."

The shaggy-haired cross between a Saint Bernard and Golden Retriever refused to budge, his black muzzle hanging open in a ridiculous canine smile. Sam was about to issue a stern order just as the sound of a car drew his attention to the entrance gate. A pearl-white Lexus passed under the Flying K sign posted on a high wooden cross-beam, then slowly maneuvered around a pothole in the asphalt.

Leaving the dog in the open truck, Sam walked a few yards and stopped to wait for the visitors. Feeling a canine nose poking his palm, he grinned and stroked Riley's enormous head.

While the car parked beneath a eucalyptus tree, Sam glanced down and chuckled at the dopey-eyed bliss on Riley's face. Looking up, he watched the dark-haired woman slide out of the driver's seat. From her amused expression, he wondered for an instant if he looked as dopey-eyed as Riley.

"Welcome to the Flying K Ranch," he said with his usual casual exuberance, closing the distance between them while her young boy came around to stand by her. Despite the dark European elegance of her olive skin and sable-brown eyes, this woman didn't seem to fit the mold of a pampered socialite who could afford to send her kid to camp for the entire summer.

She wore little, if any, makeup. Her hair, the same color as those eyes, was loosely drawn back in a braid. Other than the white leather running shoes, her clothes were suitable for the dusty rural ranch. Her slightly faded jeans looked loose enough to be comfortable, but tight enough to be appealing. Same with the tank-top beneath her open shirt. At the moment, he couldn't imagine anything sexier than the faint outline of lace just below her neckline.

"I'm Sam Kempton."

She grasped his outstretched hand. "Megan Fisher," she said, then withdrew her hand and placed it on her boy's shoulder. "And this is my son, Jason Fisher."

"Nice to meet you, Jason." Sam was impressed with the young man's firm grip and polite response. When Riley demanded his own introduction, Sam obliged. "You might say this here is *my* son. Riley, shake hands with Jason."

"Hi, Riley." Small for a ten-year-old, Jason knelt down and found himself in direct line with a sloppy lick of the dog's tongue. The more he laughed, the more Riley licked.

Watching her son with the dog, his mother seemed to relax a notch. "He's in seventh heaven already."

So am I, thought Sam. She had a voice that was just the slightest bit low and husky in a way that made a man think of hot, sultry summer nights.

"Was the Sunday afternoon traffic bad?" he asked, making polite conversation when he realized the silence between them had grown a little too long.

"Unbelievable." She rolled those eyes and his insides rolled right along with them. "Warm weekends have a way of turning the coast highway into one long parking lot."

He glanced at his watch. "When we finish this tour in about an hour, you'll be headed south right in the middle of the beach-goers headed home. You might consider stopping for dinner to give that traffic a chance to thin out."

For a brief moment he thought of offering to join her and Jason. But despite the innocence of the three of them sharing a meal together, his conscience intervened before he made the grave error of overstepping his bounds.

"Thanks for the suggestion. Now if we can just pull Jason away from your dog long enough for that tour." She gestured at her son with her left hand.

Then he saw it. The wedding ring. Strangely simple, the thin, unadorned gold band seemed out of place on a lady who drove a luxury car and intended to send her kid to camp for the entire summer. With mild disappointment, Sam realized he had jumped to the wrong conclusion about her. She wasn't a single mother, even if he had hoped that was the case.

"Let's start at the small animal compound." After a nod toward the enclosure adjacent to his office, he looked back at her for approval.

Damn, those eyes could drown a man.

$\sim$

"LEAD THE WAY." In a voice that sounded too chipper, Megan tried too hard to mask her sudden and inexplicable shyness.

Jason obviously noticed it too, flashing her a quizzical look before he marched ahead with Riley in tow.

Following close behind, she stared at the wide space between Sam Kempton's shoulder blades, wondering what it was about him that made her feel ill at ease. It wasn't necessarily a bad feeling, as if there was something wrong. She couldn't quite put her finger on it. Was it because he reminded her of Stewart? Admittedly, they were both built like athletes with much the same "Good-old-boy" mannerisms.

A real man's man. The thought surfaced in her mind before the irony truly registered.

Her stomach lurched. The phrase conjured up questions about Sam Kempton she had no business wondering. She stole glances at Sam as he pointed out the goats and sheep. He certainly possessed all the features to qualify as attractive, even for the vanity coast of dark-tanned surfers and aspiring actors. His hair was dusty blond and in need of a trim. His eyes were a deep shade of blue.

But was he the kind of man who could betray a woman as Stewart had done? She'd been duped for twelve years by her own husband, how could she know about a complete stranger? Was he the type to lie? Was he only pretending to be warm and friendly in order to sign up another kid for summer camp?

Watching him talking with Jason, she mentally shook off the doubts. Observing the camaraderie between the two of them, she chastised herself for questioning his sincerity. All because she'd started comparing him to Stewart. Would it always be like this? Questioning her own instincts? Never able to trust her gut?

She finally conceded that her mind had been dulled by the exhausting two-hour drive to the ranch. Following the worst week of her life. It was probably safe to say that she could chalk up her unfair judgment to "just plain stress," as Dr. Ames would say.

After seeing the usual array of barnyard animals plus an orphaned mule deer and two llamas, Megan and Jason climbed into Sam's truck for an inspection of the rest of the ranch. As he'd promised, it didn't take long to check out the horse corrals and the odd assortment of bunkhouses. Although the camp itself, including a recreation hall, a pool, and other activity centers, was spread out over a large area of mountainous terrain, it was only a small portion of the entire Flying K Ranch.

Thirty minutes later, Sam led them back to the office in the small adobe, one of the original buildings on the property. He swung open the screen door, then unlocked the office door and pushed it open. Inviting them to sit down while he grabbed some sodas for them, he disappeared through the other doorway while Megan called out, asking if it would be too much trouble for a glass of water instead.

"Not at all," he responded from the other room. "I keep bottled in here too."

As she entered the pleasant coolness of the dim room, Riley nearly knocked her into the desk when he pushed past and parked his carcass on the sunken cushions of a worn-out love seat.

Following suit, Jason squeezed into the narrow space between the dog and the frayed arm of the couch, grinning from ear to ear as the dog flopped his head into the boy's lap with a grunt.

"Isn't he great, Mom?"

Watching her son wrap his arms around the massive neck in a bear hug, she smiled weakly. "Just be careful around him."

Almost as if reading her mind, Riley turned those limpid eyes on her without lifting his head. He had more character in that reassuring look than most people she knew.

Refusing to believe she was under close scrutiny by some kind of psychic mutt, she glanced around the room. Books and small cardboard boxes were stacked in no particular order on top of metal file cabinets and shelves. Papers cluttered the desk. Obviously, Sam Kempton had a filing system that was uniquely his own. But she couldn't discredit the man for it. He came highly recommended for his expertise with children, not his efficiency with book work. As evidence of this, she spotted a framed diploma among the arrangements of photographs on the wall above the love seat.

Leaning closer for a better look, she read the certificate—a PhD from UCLA. In child psychology? Somewhat surprised, she never would have guessed from his laid-back attitude that he had the tenacity to earn a degree in child psychology. Although he seemed content roaming this ranch, she wondered why someone with his background didn't have a lucrative private practice. From the ease in which he drew Jason out of his shell, he would have been in great demand, especially with the escalating number of messed-up kids out there.

Her gaze wandered to a wedding picture of a younger Sam Kempton. A mocking inner voice challenged her assumption that he was happily married, reminding her of her own marriage. The photograph of marital bliss on the wall was merely an image. It wasn't flesh-and-blood reality. She didn't know the real Sam Kempton any more than he knew her.

But she wanted to learn more about him. After all, she was placing her son in his care for the entire summer, she told herself, trying unsuccessfully to drown out deeper, more complicated reasons.

She didn't like this new side of her—skittish and shy in the presence of a man. She hadn't always been this way. She used to be strong and independent. Then Stewart came along and she gradually and willingly gave away her autonomy, only to be left with this constant questioning of herself and others. She hated this self-doubt that haunted her, surrounding her like a black veil.

"How do you like my pride and joy?"

She swiveled her head around to see Sam step behind the desk, a bottle of water in one hand and two unopened cans of soft drinks in the other. It was nice to hear a man speak so fondly of his wife.

"She's really beautiful." Megan accepted the water and passed the cola to Jason. When she turned back to Sam, she watched him down several gulps from his can before he lowered it and stared thoughtfully at the pictures.

"Yeah, she was in bad shape when I first found her. But then, so was I."

Megan didn't quite know what to say so she made a sound that she hoped sounded sympathetic and let it go at that.

"I tell you, every spare minute, and every dime, I spent on her." He was beaming with pride, yet almost wistful. "I really don't get to take her out like I used to. But when I do, you should see the guys drool."

By now Megan had an odd feeling about the direction this conversation had taken. With a second look at the cluster of photos, she noticed a classic red Thunderbird which appeared to be in mint condition.

A car. He's talking about a stupid car!

She felt a little foolish for misinterpreting his passion. Choosing to drop the subject altogether, she looked down at her son. "Jason, why don't you take Riley outside while Mr. Kempton and I talk over boring registration stuff?"

"You mean it, Mom? I really get to stay here the whole summer?" To her optimistic nod, he added, "Awesome. Come on, Riley."

Despite the boy's best efforts, the lethargic dog refused to budge. Even when his master issued a warning, Riley pushed his limits, engaging in a stare-down to the rhythmic thump-thump of his shaggy tail.

"Outside." Sam motioned with a jerk of his head. Riley gave a sad-eyed look of defeat, then dragged himself off the couch.

Megan watched in mild amazement as the dog butted his head against the screen door with enough force for it to open, then trotted off with Jason close behind. She allowed herself a moment to enjoy this rare glimpse of the carefree boy her son used to be. If this was the result of a brief visit, she could easily imagine the benefit of several weeks here in the mountains.

In a way, she envied him. She would give anything to be able to be a kid again, to have the opportunity to ride horses in the fresh air and wildflowers, and leave behind that house, that bedroom.

And those nightmares.

"I'd like to come up here for the summer myself," she said without a moment's hesitation.

~

SAM CHOKED on his soda and sputtered. Swiping at his mouth, he chuckled nervously then paused, realizing she was dead serious. "If you're worried about Jason being away from home for the first time, I assure you this will be a very positive experience for him. You'll be surprised how well he'll do without his parents."

"I'm sure Jason will do fine without me." She stared at the half-empty water bottle in her hands, then she looked up at him. "But this isn't about my son. It's about me. I need a summer job."

"Would you care to run that by me again?" Sam set his soda can on the desk and leaned forward.

"I need a short-term job, preferably one that would take me out of town for a while. I teach sixth grade at Saint Mary's Catholic School in Long Beach. You said during our tour that your camp counselors are often teachers on their summer breaks. I'd like to apply for one of those positions here at the Flying K. As far as Jason is concerned, I can see by the way he's behaved here today he'd do fine without me. Better than fine, actually. You seem to have quite an effect on him."

For some reason, her praise meant a great deal more to Sam than he wanted to admit.

"If anyone has won over your son, Riley should be the one who deserves the credit," he said.

A single, soft noise indicated her amusement as she glanced toward the door, then back at him. "You may have a point there. But *my* point is that Jason won't interfere with my job. In fact, it'd be best if he was assigned to a bunkhouse under another counselor's authority. If you'd give me a chance, I know it can work."

"Oh, it *can* work. Some of my staff often bring their own kids up here." Sam reached for a pencil and tapped it lightly on top of a stack of camp applications. "But I also know how rough it is on a marriage to be up here six to seven days a week for the entire summer."

"I appreciate your concern, but…I, um… That is, Jason's father and I are separating. The reason we're sending Jason here for the summer is to give us time to figure things out before we tell him."

"Are you sure he doesn't already suspect?" Sam was accustomed to perceptive children who knew more about what was going on at home than their parents gave them credit for.

"He's been moody lately, but I think it's just a reaction to tension between his father and me. That's all. Really."

He saw the way her hands twisted, the way her gaze skittered away. She was trying hard to convince him. Probably harder to convince herself.

"As a teacher yourself, you must understand that I need to be prepared to deal with problems that may come up while your son is in my care. If you say that's all there is to this, fine. But if there's anything going on at home that would disturb Jason, such as drug abuse or physical abuse—"

"No!" She blanched. "I mean…that is, his father wouldn't do anything like that. And as for me, I may joke about getting my Irish up, but I'd never lay a hand on Jason, or do drugs, for that matter."

It was Sam's turn to let out a long breath of air. His impulse was to gently turn her down, especially after he'd learned about her impending divorce. Plain and simple, he wanted to date her, not hire her. And in his book, he couldn't do both.

His business sense warred with his personal feelings. There was something about her that was nurturing. Maybe it was those eyes. Maybe it was the way she looked at her son. Whatever it was, he had to admit she seemed to convey a special maternal appeal that would be good for his youngest camp kids.

And yet he wanted to keep his options open for that lobster dinner he'd considered on her arrival. Given a few weeks to settle her divorce, she might accept his invitation. Then again, she might not. Where would that leave him? He'd be lucky to catch a glimpse of her once every two weeks when she came to visit Jason.

In silence, he reached into the bottom drawer of the old mahogany desk and withdrew a blank application. She seemed hesitant to take it, as if she was having second thoughts about her decision.

Take it, he silently prodded. *Take it before I change my mind.*

Almost as if she read his thoughts, she lifted her gaze from the paper to him and reached across the desktop, the corners of her mouth curving slowly into a victorious smile.

Even though his insides twisted so tight he had to stifle a groan, Sam figured he'd do just about anything to get her to smile like that for him again.

Good or bad, the decision had been made. Good or bad, this was going to be one hell of a summer.

~

Two weeks after handing Megan Fisher the job application, Sam still wondered if he'd done the right thing.

As it had turned out, the routine background check revealed her excellent teaching record. But that hadn't surprised him. His gut instinct rarely steered him wrong, especially when it came to his counselors, all of whom would soon be arriving for the first summer session.

The desk chair's steel spring squeaked as he lowered himself into the upholstered seat that molded to his butt. Leaning back, he hooked his heels over the edge of his cluttered desk and rested his head against the cool adobe wall behind him.

Reflecting on his impromptu interview with Megan, he'd discovered that the husband she was about to divorce was the well-known crime novelist Stewart Fisher. That interesting bit of information *had* surprised him, albeit mildly. Even though he'd read a few of the "Collin Quinn" books, he hadn't made any connection to the Fisher name.

Sam couldn't help but wonder what caused the breakup of her marriage. Maybe fame and fortune had claimed another victim. Change could do that to a couple.

He looked across the room at his wedding photo. He and Maryann had shared the dream of a perfect marriage while she built her own production company and Sam built his practice as a therapist. But when the ranch was left to him after his parents' deaths, he had become as obsessed with the camp as his mom and dad had been, destroying his marriage in the process. Thankfully, he and Maryann were still friends, and sometimes lovers, which was why he'd never gotten around to taking down their wedding picture.

Was the split between the Fishers also amicable? After questioning her about drugs, there was no reason to suspect a problem in that area. Nevertheless, he was curious why any man would let a woman like Megan get away. Then again, his own friends said the same thing to him about Maryann.

The low rumble of a bad muffler announced the arrival of one poorly maintained Toyota coming down the entrance road. It was as familiar to Sam as the bleating sheep and grunting pigs in the small animal compound. He didn't need to stick his head out the screen door to know that four of his staff had just arrived.

Karen and Mario were both single and in their mid-to-late-twenties. Teenagers Taylor and Griffin were counselor's assistants, or CAs. All from the South Bay area, they drove up together every weekend.

As Taylor sauntered into his office, Sam turned his attention toward the door. "Hi, kid."

"Hi!" She dropped her army surplus bag by the door and perched herself on the corner of the desk, whistling Riley over to her. Her blonde hair was spiked into a style that made Sam think of some kind of windblown explosion.

"Love the look, Taylor," he said, halfway between amusement and warning at her all-black outfit of a biker's jacket, jeans and boots.

Despite her hardened appearance, she knew not to cross Sam on any of the rules, including the dress code of a white staff shirt and plain blue jeans.

She cracked her gum and rolled her eyes. Beneath the layer of black eyeliner and thick mascara, there was still a twinkle of childhood playfulness in those blue eyes.

The sixteen-year-old had been a spoiled, tough-talking summer resident at his camp until three years ago when she found her niche with the littlest kids, filling a gap left by her parents' divorce. Both of them were too busy for Taylor—her mother as a designer, her father as a television writer.

"I've got, like, a *total* change of clothes right here, okay?" She hiked a thumb toward her bag.

With his own background as a counselor at a continuation school for teenagers, Sam had the edge over Taylor. She wasn't the first to challenge him and she probably wouldn't be the last.

He nodded toward the door that led to the only bunkhouse attached to the office. "Better get a move on before the kids show up. I don't want their parents to think we've got hardened criminals teaching their children how to stab each other in the fencing class."

When Taylor stood, Riley returned to his comfortable cushions.

Even as she left the room, Sam knew she would conveniently forget about changing out of her silver-tipped cowboy boots.

He shook his head, smiling to himself. One of these days she was going to get all that rebellion out of her system, and she'd do fine. He only hoped he could help her find her way to that promising future.

He called out, "Lose the black eyeliner while you're in there."

"Yeah right," she groused. "One clean-cut California surfer girl coming up."

Karen, Mario and Griffin entered laughing and joking around. Riley eyed the threesome with his head still resting on his paws, obviously deciding that possession of the couch was tantamount to a fleeting scratch behind the ear.

"Here, Griff." Karen handed her sports bag to the fifteen-year-old. "Toss this on my bed for me, please."

Sam thrust his arm out in time to block the doorway. "Hold up a minute there."

Griffin pulled up short. "What's the matter?"

"Taylor is changing clothes."

A momentary grin lit up the young man's reddened face before he sheepishly nodded, said "Oh," and took a step backward.

Mario teased, "Aw, come on, Sam. What's the harm in a little nudity among family? You're getting to be a prude in your old age."

Mario had been a CA at the K during Sam's wilder days before inheriting the ranch. At twenty-nine, six years younger than Sam, he was more like a kid brother, often reminding Sam of his own older brother. Like Bill, Mario could tease and joke at Sam's expense. No offense taken. So he got away with needling his boss about one of the serious subjects of rules and regulations: no swearing, no smoking, and no sexual misconduct.

Sam said with a warning smile, "Careful there, Mario. Griffin here knows you're joking, but Taylor might call your bluff and come out naked just to shock you."

"She'd do it too," added Karen, using a jerky treat to coax Riley out the door so she could claim the couch.

Griffin joined her while Mario took the corner of the desk. "Did you read the *LA Times* this morning?"

He didn't need to elaborate for Sam to know that he was talking about the teacher accused of child molestation. "The whole thing is so fu—" Sam caught his slip. "Fouled up. Who are you supposed to believe? Even if those kids *are* telling the truth, the lawyers are going to get that teacher off on a technicality."

He shook his head, aware of media hysteria and his own vulnerability to such an accusation. He'd warned his staff repeatedly that one wrong move—however unintentional—could close the Flying K. In everyone's best interests, they had to refrain from hugging or touching the children in any way that could be misconstrued as malicious intent. Although they still managed to nurture the children in a positive manner, it was frustrating to deny them a simple, non-threatening touch of reassurance.

"A-hem." Taylor stood in the doorway, hands on hips, waiting to pass inspection. True to her word, she looked fresh-faced and wholesome. Sam grinned, then lifted one eyebrow disapprovingly at the sight of her tight black jeans.

CHAPTER 3

Stewart stared at the blinking cursor on the computer screen for over twenty minutes while he listened to Megan moving around in the guest room next to his writing study.

She hadn't set foot in the master bedroom in nearly three weeks, except to remove her clothes and personal things. But never while he was home.

Propping his elbows in front of the keyboard, he rested his chin on his folded hands. It was no use trying to breathe life into his fictional detective, Collin Quinn, when his own life was falling apart all around him.

And he had no one to blame but himself. With his rising popularity as a novelist, he couldn't risk being seen too often in public with Maxwell, never mind slipping off together to a remote motel in another town. Yet the neighbors knew Maxwell as a family friend. No one would suspect anything unusual about the occasional afternoon visit. If ever the subject came up, Stewart would say Maxwell loved to talk about writing and discuss new plots for the Collin Quinn novels.

Lately, though, the visits had become more frequent than

once a month. Stewart had been careful to monitor Megan's schedule, but had somehow missed the date of her doctor's appointment.

"Subconsciously, you *wanted* Megan to find out," Maxwell had pointed out the following day in a superior and testy tone.

Bullshit, Stewart thought to himself. He had worked too long and too hard to have a family and a career only to blow his future with this one mistake. He had a professional image to maintain as a damn good police detective and as a best-selling author. He loved his son and needed a family. Why in hell would he screw that up?

The question sparked another surge of self-condemning anger. He pushed himself to his feet and paced the same worn strip of carpet between the balcony and a bookcase.

At the sound of Megan moving around the house, he glanced in irritation toward the open door. He knew she was packing her suitcases. And he knew she'd be leaving for camp with Jason in another hour.

What he didn't know was how in the hell to stop her. He stepped out onto the balcony and braced his palms on the low stucco wall. They had come so far from that filthy studio apartment over a garage on the west side. Only one burner worked on the two-burner range, but Megan never complained. She only wanted to be with him, and nothing else mattered.

Consumed by guilt, he had worked to give her everything she could ever need. First, a place of their own in a safe neighborhood. Then, the baby she'd wanted so badly. Finally, this million-dollar mansion.

He couldn't imagine not having Megan around anymore. Maybe he was just scared of change. Maybe he was afraid of losing Jason's love. He just didn't want either of them to leave him.

Not now.

Not ever.

He walked back into his study and took a poetry book from the shelf. She had been reading from a copy of this same book, he thought, remembering the day he had first approached Megan in the college library. He had impressed her by reciting the Eugene Field poem from memory. That was twelve years ago, yet he still knew the verses by heart.

But it hadn't been the first time he had noticed her. A few weeks earlier, Maxwell had pointed her out at a local coffeehouse known for its soft jazz.

"There's a pretty one for you," he had said with a subtle nod toward the bookish student in line for a cappuccino.

"Quit picking out potential wives for me," groused Stewart.

"Now really, Stew. You must reconsider my suggestion. As much as it simply kills me to admit, it would be best for both of us if you kept up your straight image."

Maxwell had brought up a concern too important to ignore.

After moving to California to live with his aunt during high school, Stewart had focused on sports, becoming a hometown hero. In his junior year, there was a substantial betting pool among the cheerleaders to be his first sexual conquest. His teammates pressured him to do something to kill the growing rumors about being gay.

During a drunken homecoming victory party, Stewart reluctantly allowed himself to be locked in a room with five of the cheerleaders. From that infamous night, he was treated like a goddamn hero by the guys. The girls were worse, blatantly propositioning him in the halls. He had created a no-win situation. Every Saturday night from then on, he got drunk enough to give another girl a notch in her bedpost. As for Stewart, he wasn't keeping score. Christ, he couldn't remember half their faces or names. He just used them to keep anyone from knowing his real secret. Nobody knew how much he hated himself for what he was doing.

Nobody, that is, until Mr. Maxwell Hamer was his summer

school Civics teacher at Poly High. After graduation, Stewart abruptly cut himself off from his classmates, entered college on a scholarship with the help of Maxwell, and shortly afterward, they began their private relationship.

Two years later, Maxwell had finished his degree to teach at the same university where, from all outward appearances, the two men were a professor and student having coffee after class when they spotted Megan. It had taken several more weeks before Stewart had finally decided to act on Maxwell's advice and ask her out on a date.

When he began to recite the poem about a childhood cut short, she'd turned her head and looked up at him, clearly annoyed at first, then confused, and finally flushed pink with embarrassment as she glanced around to see if anyone else was watching the two of them.

The instant she looked up at him with those deep, brown eyes, he had thought he'd found the one woman who might change him. If leading a normal life had been his dream, then Megan had been his dream come true—until the day he woke up to the reality that he couldn't be happy without Maxwell in his life as well.

He had kept the truth hidden from her because he didn't want to hurt her. Whether she believed him or not, he really did love her. Just not the way a husband loves a wife. She deserved that much, he knew. But knowing it didn't change his fear of losing his family.

The book of poetry that had brought them together might do the trick again. He jotted a few words on a sticky note, pressed it onto the printed poem, and closed the book.

As he entered the guest room, Megan paused only a moment over her open suitcase on the bed, then stuffed a pair of socks in the corner.

"Please don't start in with me again," she warned, taking a smaller makeup bag into the adjacent bathroom.

"I won't." With her back to him, he tucked the book into her suitcase, then walked up behind her and looked at her reflection in the mirror. The pain he saw in her eyes tore at his insides, and he hated himself even more for being the one who put it there. "I didn't mean for you to be run out of your own house."

She rummaged through the top drawer without taking anything out of it. "I thought I made it clear that I was not going to stick around while Jason went to camp."

"I didn't think you'd leave town, for Christ's sake." The last shred of control was slipping through his fingers—control of his life, his wife, and worst of all, his temper. "Just when do you think we're ever going to talk this out?"

When she turned to find him defiantly blocking her exit, she marched silently straight at him, daring him to stop her. He stepped aside as she brushed past him, her own anger clearly at the boiling point. She shoved some clothes around, making room for her cosmetics bag.

"Megan!" He grabbed her arm and turned her to face him. "Talk to me, damn it!"

She slapped his face. "You have no right to make demands on me. Not anymore!"

His impulse was to strike back in anger. The violence of his father flashed through his head. Never had he been brought so close to inflicting the same brutality he had endured. Surprised and horrified with himself, he released her arm. "I do have a right to try to salvage this marriage. If you don't stay home and make an effort to see a counselor with me, you'll regret it. I swear to you."

This time he saw her hand come up, and caught her wrist in a vise grip, grabbing the other as well.

"Let go of me."

"Not until you listen to me."

"I don't want to hear about how sorry you are. I just want out.

I don't want to remember how much I loved you all these years while you lied to me."

The harder Megan fought, the more his fingers tightened.

As her tears flowed, she stumbled over her words. "What do you want from me?"

"I don't want to lose everything we've worked for." He let go when he saw the fight drain out of her.

~

RUBBING HER REDDENED WRIST, Megan marched away, still fuming, unable to stop the tirade of hurt and anger.

"Our marriage was the perfect front for you, wasn't it? First, there was the police officer's image to worry about. Then came your image as a macho detective living the life he writes about in his crime novels." She spun around, throwing her hands up in the air. "God forbid the tabloids would get a hold of your little secret. This isn't about salvaging our marriage. This isn't about how much you want us to remain a family. It's about you and…and *Maxwell*."

The memory of seeing the two men made her feel sick. She dropped onto the edge of the bed, toppling the suitcase to the floor.

Clutching her stomach, she sobbed, "All these years he has sat at our table for holidays and family parties! All these years he's been Uncle Max to Jason! All that time you two were lovers, weren't you?"

Stewart knelt in front of her but didn't dare touch her. "I prayed this day would never come. This is why I couldn't bring myself to tell you the truth about me. I can't stand hurting you like this, Meggie. I only wish you knew what it feels like to be me."

"Why does everything have to be about *you*, Stewart? I have given you twelve years of my life. *Twelve years!* Only to find out it's all been a lie. All because of you. And you think I care about what it feels like to be you? I don't. Because the only thing I can feel right now is *my* pain, *my* humiliation."

Without offering a word in his own defense, he got up and walked toward the bedroom door. With his back to her, he paused for a moment and turned his head as if he was about to say something. The handsome profile that had once caused butterflies in her belly now made her ache from the emptiness inside.

He left without another word.

A few minutes passed before she realized Jason would be coming home soon from riding bikes with his friends. She couldn't let him find her this way. She couldn't begin to explain why she'd been crying.

After splashing water into her burning eyes, she lifted the overturned suitcase and put it back on the bed. Turning to the pile of clothes left on the floor, she recognized the book of poetry poking out of the disarray of her belongings. Gingerly, she picked it up, turned to the poem, found the scribbled message, and began to cry all over again.

~

AT TWO IN THE AFTERNOON, Jason and his mom pulled up in front of the camp office. From the looks of things, none of the other kids had gotten there yet, which was fine with him. He wanted time to get used to everything. He wanted to look like he really knew his way around. He didn't want anybody seeing him all excited like a little kid or something. It was important to be cool about these things, especially around older guys. All this was on his mind when he'd bugged his mom to get to the ranch early, only he didn't tell her any of it. Instead, he let her think he couldn't wait to see Riley again. It was partly true.

Jason unbuckled his seat belt and threw open the car door, slammed it and headed around to the trunk, eager to get his gear.

"Hi, Sam!" he called out, waving as Sam stepped out of the shade of the porch. "What bunkhouse do I got?"

His mom came up behind him. "Do you *have*, young man."

"You're in number three, sport," Sam answered before Jason had to repeat the question right. "Let me show your mom to her cabin, then I'll take you down to yours."

"I know where it is! Can I go right now?"

"By yourself?" his mom asked. He knew that look she got. The one that was unsure.

"Aw…Mom. It's not like we're in the city or nothin'."

"Anything," she corrected him. "I'm not sure if Sam wants you running around unsupervised."

"Sam?" Jason pleaded.

"Go ahead." Sam grinned. "I'll send Griffin down to help you get settled."

"Cool." Jason grabbed the huge green duffel bag stuffed with his sleeping bag, pillow and clothes and started down the hill, eager to show his mom that he was big enough to handle something as simple as finding his bunkhouse.

Carrying the bulky canvas bag turned out to be a lot harder than he'd expected, especially when the road got real steep. His feet slipped once in some loose gravel, but he managed to stay up somehow. After that he was real careful to watch for other dangerous spots.

Standing in the doorway of the empty bunkhouse, he dropped the duffel bag onto the cement floor and wiped the sweat off his forehead.

The room looked a lot bigger than he remembered from his visit. For one thing, there wasn't as many bunk beds crammed into it now. Only four were lined up along the far wall and another four along the wall by him. The only other stuff besides the hanging lights was a bunch of different chests of drawers, all of them the same color of blue.

Which bed was his, he wondered.

"You must be Jason."

Jason nearly jumped right out of his skin. His head swiveled around just enough to see a guy with light brown hair pulled back in a ponytail.

"Y-yeah, I'm Jason," he croaked, wishing his voice was deeper so he didn't sound so much like a wuss.

"My name's Griffin." The guy put his hand out for a shake.

Jason looked down at the callused palm like it was an alien. He wasn't used to this kind of polite stuff between guys, especially coming from somebody who was in high school. Cameron, the older brother of his babysitter, only acted that way when adults were around. But there were no adults around now. So who was this guy Griffin trying to impress?

Jason shrugged, figuring it wouldn't hurt to just shake his hand. When he did, he suddenly wished he'd wiped the sweat off his palms. But Griffin didn't seem to mind since he didn't make a face or anything.

"I'm the CA for this cabin. That's a counselor's assistant. And Mario's the counselor." Griffin stepped over the duffel bag in his path. "Don't just stand there, come on in."

"What's Mario like?" Jason asked hesitantly, still at the door.

He knew it was dumb of him to be worried about Mario. Or Griffin. But Jason already knew that lots of people weren't always as nice as they pretended to be.

"Mario is the best there is." Griffin leaned his shoulder against the frame of the doorway to an area that looked like somebody had moved in already. "When I was coming here as a camper like you, I was one of Mario's boys. He's lots of fun, but he won't let any kids break the rules. You don't mess with him."

Jason swallowed hard, then asked quietly, "Does he ever hit anybody?"

"No way!" From the shocked look Griffin gave him, Jason instantly regretted his question. But almost immediately Griffin behaved as if it was nothing and changed the subject. "Since you're the first one here, you get to pick any bunk you want."

Jason looked around the room once more. The windows were just square frames covered with screens and a hinged piece of plywood propped open with short, wooden poles. A fly buzzed around the dark light bulb hanging from the middle of the ceiling. If he wanted to read his sci-fi books before he went to sleep, he should take the upper bunk near the light. But then he wouldn't get much privacy, especially if he got singled out by some older kid who wanted an easy target to hassle.

That's not gonna happen here, he told himself, trying to stop thinking all those dark, creepy thoughts.

This place was nothing like back home in Long Beach. It was dusty and dry and…safe.

Knowing he was taking way too long to make up his mind, he sheepishly glanced over at Griffin. The guy just stood there and lifted his eyebrows as if to say, Take your time, I got all day.

He was kind of starting to like Griffin. There was something about the CA that was real nice, maybe because he didn't treat Jason like a little kid. Or even worse, like a spoiled rich kid.

He tossed his gear on the bunk next to the doorway where Griff was standing. "I guess this will be okay."

Over the next several days, Jason decided Griffin was pretty okay, even if he was kind of quiet compared to the other teenagers Jason knew, which was only Cameron and his buddies. Oh, Griff laughed at jokes and stuff like that, so it wasn't like he was boring to be around. But the only other things Jason found out about his CA was that Griff was fifteen, had parents who were still married to each other, and a kid sister that he liked a lot.

Griff was a good listener too. He got Jason to talk about more stuff than he'd ever told anybody in his whole life. He even admitted how hard it was being a teacher's kid and a cop's son. And now that his dad's books were selling so good, someone was always saying how lucky Jason must feel to have a dad who was a big-time celebrity. If only they knew how much he really hated it. He knew it was the real reason Cameron liked to come over when Melissa was babysitting, just so he could brag to his friends. And Jason also hated how everybody always expected him to be polite and perfect. It was like his parents would lose their jobs if he messed up, or nobody would buy those stupid books if he even picked his nose in public. Sometimes he just wanted to be a nobody so he could do anything he wanted.

The first time that Griffin heard about how Jason felt, he had said, "Here at the ranch, none of the other kids know who your dad is unless you tell them. And your mom's just another counselor, not a teacher who's gonna give them an 'F' in English or something. So you can be a nobody like the rest of us for the whole summer."

When Jason had heard that, he sat back and grinned. He was beginning to wish he could live at the Flying K forever.

~

THE FIRST SESSION break came on the second Saturday in July. Shortly after sunrise, Sam stepped out of his ranch house that was perched out on the edge of a narrow plateau, overlooking the bulk of his sprawling acreage. An early riser, he enjoyed the quiet serenity before the rest of the camp awoke, before the canyon echoed with boisterous voices.

He was about to whistle for Riley, who was sniffing around somewhere nearby, when he spotted Megan across the dirt road leading down the steep hill to the office and bunkhouses.

Not quite ready to make his presence known, he lifted the ceramic mug to sip the hot coffee, then winced as he burned his tongue.

Silently watching her, he noticed something didn't seem quite right. She stopped beside the painted plank fence and rested her hands on the white railing. When she dropped her chin to her chest and closed her eyes, he could see she wasn't there to admire the breathtaking panorama of the canyon spread out before her.

Normally, he would have walked over and offered a sympathetic ear. That's if she was one of the hundreds of teenagers he'd counseled over the years. But she wasn't a teenager—not by a long shot, despite the youthfulness of the thick braid that ended below her narrow shoulders.

His gaze drifted down her bulky, white sweatshirt, pausing momentarily on the curve of her bottom, then continued down her jeans to her white leather running shoes, now scuffed and dusty. And she didn't seem to care the least little bit.

Not bad for a city girl, he admitted to himself.

Cautiously testing the coffee again, Sam recalled another pleasant surprise he'd discovered about her. She had a laugh of pure, uninhibited enjoyment when she was with the children.

Both she and her son fit right in without a hitch, just like she'd promised. She was also a damn good counselor. Despite his attraction to her, he wasn't willing to risk losing a valuable employee. Besides, he didn't need a complicated relationship right now. And, he guessed, neither did she.

As he watched her head tilt back and her shoulders lift in a long, drawn-out sigh, he saw a woman who appeared to be carrying more than her share of problems.

He carefully sipped more coffee, determined to turn away from the temptation to poke his nose in where it didn't belong.

Leave her alone, Kempton.

Do I look like I'm offering a shoulder to cry on?

Stand here long enough and you will.

I'm not stupid enough to cross that line.

Oh no? Get one good look at those dark eyes of hers and watch yourself sink.

At that moment, she turned and caught him watching her.
Damn.

~

MEGAN WONDERED how long he'd been standing there. No doubt
he was curious why she'd hiked clear up here at the crack of
dawn. There was no reason for him to know that she'd needed to
escape the quiet bunkhouse in order to clear her head of another
horrible dream. Only it wasn't really a dream, but the same gut-
wrenching flash of memory played over and over again in her
head. She'd gotten to the point where she was afraid to close her
eyes, knowing that her mind would recreate the afternoon her
life had crashed down around her.

He lifted his mug high as if toasting her. "I make a pretty
mean cup of coffee. Care for some?"

"Sure," she called back, masking her raw emotions.

As she approached him, she struggled to rid her mind of the
uneasiness that seemed to settle over her whenever she was
around Sam. She tried to tell herself it was the result of a defense
system gone haywire. Megan didn't need a psychoanalyst to tell
her it would take time to trust her own judgment again.

Trust.

That was the crux of the matter, even with something as
simple as friendship. At its best, trust was as fragile as a delicate
figurine.

And yet Stewart had carelessly destroyed her trust. She had
placed herself in his hands, despite her ideology of independence.
For years, she had blindly loved a man who, she now knew,
considered her a display piece. He'd broken her, shattered a trust
that he simply assumed could be patched with apologies and
excuses…and gifts.

Stewart had a way with gifts, she mused. It had been five
years since he'd surprised her with that elaborate Naples house

he'd bought without consulting her. Not long ago, he'd done the same with the Lexus, passing the key across the dinner table to her. Each time he'd given her a gift, she'd tried to tell him she didn't need expensive presents, she needed him—his time, his attention. All too aware of his overwhelming work schedule, Megan never considered the possibility of an affair. Nor did she see his gifts for what they really were: signs of a guilty conscience.

Megan mentally shook herself to ward off the inevitable attack of remorse. How long would it take to forget the pain? How long before she could finally feel she could trust again?

Within ten feet of Sam, she was startled by his overgrown mutt as it noisily lumbered out of the bushes next to her. She greeted Riley self-consciously. Even though she'd been around the amiable dog quite a bit, she still found it difficult to be at ease around the enormous animal.

"Take off, boy," Sam commanded softly. To her surprise, his order was promptly obeyed.

"I'm impressed." Turning toward the aromatic scent of his coffee, she added, "Will I be as impressed with your coffee-making skills?"

"See for yourself."

When she held up her hand to refuse the cup, he pressed the warm mug into it, then made a deliberately humorous effort to wrap her fingers around the ceramic handle. His hands cupped hers, lingering a little longer than necessary, then dropped away.

"Careful," he warned.

She looked at him for a moment. Careful? He couldn't possibly know the impact of that single word. It was as if a disembodied voice had whispered in her ear. Of course she knew it was only Sam, and of course she knew he was referring to the hot coffee.

Megan forced a smile and found it wasn't quite as difficult as she'd expected. But when she met his blue-eyed gaze, her cheerful resolve faltered. Taking one sip, she complimented its good taste, then tried to return it to him.

"Finish it. When that's done, we can go inside and I'll get us both a fresh cup." Without waiting for her answer, he nodded toward the canyon. "Did you get up early to see the sun rise over the ridge?"

"Yes," she lied, risking a sideways glance to see his gaze intent upon the distant mountains. "This is a beautiful place. No smog. No traffic. Room to roam free. You must've loved it when you were growing up."

"In some ways, it was every boy's dream come true. Like living in one of those old Hollywood Westerns."

"In some ways?"

He shrugged. "See those green patches that look like steps in the hillside across the way? My older brother and I used to ride out there and let our horses graze while we stretched out in the tall grass and wished my folks never owned a camp."

"Why?"

"Because we were jealous. We wanted to be the center of attention. We wanted to come first. But here at the ranch, the camp kids came first. Ma and Pop didn't have time to come to Little League games or high school football. There were lots of days when Bill and I would get our chores done early and take off on long rides, dreaming of the day we'd turn our backs on this place. And I did just that. Now here I am again, walking in my old man's footsteps."

"You're not happy about that?"

"Happy? Hell yes, I'm happy. I love what I'm doing. I love the idea that there are hundreds...no, thousands of kids out there who will look back as adults with terrific memories of this place." He turned and gazed down at her, his expression almost self-mocking. "Strange how we start out as rebellious teenagers with arrogant ideals, determined to be nothing like our parents. Then we wake up one day and see them in our bathroom mirror."

Megan shuddered inwardly, seeing a similar pattern evolving in her own life. As an eight-year-old, she had idolized her adoring father, only to wake up one morning to find that he had left his family and run off with another woman. Some time later she had heard he was in the Midwest, a pillar of his community, deacon of his church, and had put his three boys through college.

Pushing aside thoughts of her three half-brothers who had the luxury of an all-American childhood, she asked Sam about his own brother. "So while you're here carrying on the family business, Bill's out there somewhere pursuing his lifelong dream?"

"Yeah, he's out there somewhere," he answered thoughtfully, then invited her into the house for that second cup of coffee, leaving her wondering about his obvious diversion from the subject of his brother. A few minutes later, he led her from the kitchen and motioned to the nine-foot couch in his living room. "Have a seat."

She lowered herself onto the black leather cushions, jostling the coffee as he took the easy chair. His vast living room was a sharp contrast to the cramped adobe office. It was difficult for her to imagine one man rambling around alone in such a large place.

The same could be said about Stewart in their palatial home in Long Beach.

Don't forget about Maxwell.

In her mind's eye, she could see the two men sharing meals in the formal dining room, or watching television in the second-floor family room. Trying to block the agonizing vision was futile. Caught in her thoughts, she told herself she never should have accepted the invitation for coffee.

~

SAM WAS near the brink of frustration. Each time he felt as if she was finally beginning to relax, she'd retreat somewhere behind those dark, haunting eyes. He tried to fill in around her silence with polite compliments of her skills with the children. "You have a special knack with your students."

"Thank you," she said in that low, throaty voice of hers that once again conjured up images of rumpled sheets and soft skin.

Although it was clear she no longer wanted his company, he was still babbling like a schoolboy trying to impress the teacher. Why? Damned if he didn't already know the answer to that one. And it wasn't anything as innocent as an adolescent crush.

"Megan?"

"Hmm?" She looked up, her mind obviously elsewhere.

"Session breaks are slow around here. Until the new group arrives, there's only ten full-time kids to worry about. We usually just kick back and relax. So…"

Why don't we go for a drive and you can talk about whatever's bothering you?

Weighing the possible consequences of voicing those words, Sam sat forward in the chair and braced his elbows on his knees, toying with his empty mug. He couldn't look at a wounded person and not want to analyze, to ease the pain. And this woman was definitely wounded.

"So…?" she prompted.

"So why don't you take Jason somewhere for a few hours. Spend some time together. Just the two of you."

It might not have been what he wanted to say, but Sam knew by the smile on her face that it had been the *right* thing to say.

CHAPTER 4

The Recreation Hall was the hub of mealtime at the Flying K, as well as evening activities. Built on the same plateau as the ranch house, the Rec Hall was designed with an open-beam ceiling and two opposite walls filled with windows that created the feeling of being outdoors.

After a breakfast of pancakes and sausage, Sam left his dirty dishes in the camp's kitchen, then paused in the adjoining alcove and gazed out the west windows. He recalled the many times he'd climbed up that bank of red clay to pick blue wildflowers for his mom, who'd then scolded him for the dirtied knees while unceremoniously arranging the scraggly bouquet in a metal one-pound coffee can.

Turning toward the east-facing windows, Sam took in the view, thinking about a more immediate memory from early that morning.

Behind him, water rushed from the tap and metal pots clinked as his staff cleaned up the dishes with practiced efficiency. The noises droned on, blending with the voices of the counselors sitting at the tables next to the windows.

Sam's gaze settled on Megan. With her back to him, she

reached up to the nape of her neck and briefly massaged it, letting her head tilt a little to the side. The movement was unconsciously sensual, which made it all the more disarming.

From the back of the room, Sam studied the thick line of dark braid that traveled down between her shoulder blades, accentuating the curve of her spine.

Assessing the chassis, Kempton?

Sam glanced surreptitiously around the room. Satisfied that he hadn't been caught, he made a conscious effort to look past Megan to the kids outside. His eyes met Taylor's. Sitting at a picnic table with her five- and six-year-old kids, she stared at him as if she had voiced his inward reprimand.

Sam smiled, hiding his guilt. Taylor returned a half-hearted grin before her attention was drawn away by one of the younger children.

If he kept this up with Megan, he was going to see more trouble than a kid busted for joyriding in a stolen car. Although his own exploits had never quite crossed that legal line, he'd counseled enough juveniles with police records to know that the penalty for such an impulse far outweighed the adrenaline rush of the challenge. Right now, he had to remind himself that his current situation wasn't much different. For the time being, that wedding band meant she still belonged to someone else, and he was not about to steal—or borrow—another man's wife for the thrill of it.

With that decision made, Sam went over to the double doors, swung one of them open and invited the kids inside for a while. In the tradition established by Sam's parents, the children ate outside not only to allow for the inevitable spills but also to give the counselors a quiet meal.

After he stepped out of the way, the mass of kids shuffled in. A few grumblers wanted to go back to their bunks and sleep until noon. From the lethargic movement of the crowd in general, it seemed as though most of them were of the same mind. While some went directly to the second-hand sofas that formed a horseshoe around the brick hearth, others took a spot on the twelve-foot-square carpet remnant.

As Sam passed Megan's table, he overheard her ask Jason about taking a drive.

"We gonna go see Dad?" the boy asked hopefully.

"No. He has a deadline coming up for his next book. But you can call him." The empathy in her voice tugged at Sam.

He glanced over his shoulder to see the two of them sitting on the bench as she brushed back a lock of her son's hair, then pressed her forehead to his. From somewhere inside Sam rose a deep-seated envy.

Sunshine streamed through the window, bathing mother and son in light that reflected softly in their hair. Both of them had hair the same deep, rich shade of brown.

In that fleeting moment, he felt his world shift. Up until now he could only say that lust ruled his thoughts about this woman. But now there was something more.

Curiosity. Intrigue. Caring. A deep caring that was beginning to get under his skin.

And that scared the hell out of him.

Thankful Megan would soon be out of his sight—if not his mind—for the day, Sam turned his attention to the sleepy-eyed kids awaiting him.

IN THE MID-AFTERNOON, Taylor wandered into the Rec Hall in a red swimsuit with a beach towel draped around her neck. Mario and a few others sat at the back table playing cards. In the corner next to the fireplace, the Navajo blanket that usually covered the TV was lying in a crumpled heap on the brick hearth. The original *Iron Man* was playing on the DVR. Even though Taylor had seen it a dozen times, she didn't feel like losing at cards and she didn't feel up to adult company at the moment.

Eyeing the movie, she slipped through a gap between two of the sofas—one covered in puke-orange flowers, the other in a dark green pattern that looked like protozoans from biology class.

Griffin was stretched out on the green couch, his head propped against the arm. He was so totally into action movies. It seemed like he couldn't get enough of them. Sex scenes were a different matter entirely. She remembered his embarrassment during a steamy hot-tub scene in another film.

Passing in front of him she reached out and tousled his hair. "How's it hanging?"

"Taylor," he groaned. "Do you have to say that?"

"Say what?" she asked nonchalantly as she plopped down on the orange sofa and tucked her legs beneath her.

When he lifted his head and looked at her, she smiled with wide-eyed innocence. She loved doing this to him, then watching his face get pink and his Adam's apple bob up and down with a hard swallow.

"Never mind," he muttered, turning his attention back to the kind of action he could better understand.

Grinning, Taylor gave up the idea of taunting him further and focused on the tube. She knew she shouldn't tease him, but he was such an easy mark. Even though he was fifteen, he still had the boyish ignorance of most nine-year-olds. She was just a year older than him, but she was so extremely beyond his naive little mind that it was ridiculous. Besides the fact that he actually liked wearing those lame staff shirts, his biggest problem was that he had "virgin" written all over him. It was so obvious that he came off as kind of a nerd.

From firsthand experience, Taylor had learned that sweetness and innocence got you nowhere, especially if you were a girl with a body that wouldn't quit. Her mom had called her an "early bloomer." Ha! God, as if that made her feel any less of a freak. She'd done more than bloom. She had exploded from a boyishly flat-chested toothpick to a big-boobed male magnet. The guys who'd once been her tree-climbing buddies became drooling idiots.

But it had been the older high school boys who attracted her attention. Even though she wasn't allowed to date, she managed to sneak around with a few of them—that is, until they found out about her age or her virginity or both. At that point, they either dumped her or tried to seduce her, without success.

Sick of playing by their rules, Taylor had simply made up her own. Her age was easily fixed with a fake ID. Then, after a few dropped hints, she convinced everyone in her school crowd that she gotten laid by some college jock, which was a lie.

It was all a matter of survival. Before she perfected her sex-kitten act, she been cornered too many times by those perverts who lived to nail virgins. Even her mom's old boyfriend had tried messing with her. She had only been eleven years old. He hadn't gotten any further than a kiss when she puked all over his silk shirt.

The memory of that gross mess brought a smile of satisfaction. The asshole had gotten exactly what he'd deserved.

Griffin's voice brought her back to the movie showing Tony Stark's cliffside mansion. "What I would give to live in a house like that."

"I'll trade you," Taylor offered.

"Yeah, right." Griffin didn't even bother looking up. "I can just see you mowing our front lawn some Saturday afternoon. It'd take you two seconds before you were wishing you could be laying around your pool with some guy rubbing suntan oil on your back."

Griffin came from a blue-collar family with a little house down in some middle-class neighborhood of Long Beach, which was why he knew jack about where she was coming from. In her opinion, she was leftover baggage from a failed marriage. After her parents split, her mom now made mega-bucks as a costume designer and her dad did the same as the brains behind four network sitcoms. When Griffin had learned about their hotshot careers in the business, he'd assumed she lived some kind of glamorous Hollywood life.

And she would let him keep right on thinking that. No way would she admit she envied Griff's normal family. She had to admit that her mom and dad had everything they could possibly want and more. So did she. Still, they acted like it was never enough; they were always going for the ultimate thrill.

But then, so was she.

"I wouldn't let just any guy rub oil on my back." She purred in a deliberately sexy voice. "Liam Hemsworth would do quite nicely, thank you."

"He's taken," Griffin mocked, his eyes on the action-adventure. It bugged her that she couldn't hold his attention.

"Hey—Griff. My mom's having a big party. I could get some stars' autographs for your kid sister if she wants them." Even if he was interested in one for himself, he'd never admit it.

"Unless it's Shawn Mendes, forget it."

"How about Jennifer Lawrence? Katy Perry?"

Now he was interested. "How you gonna get 'em?"

Looking around, she half whispered. "It's supposed to be a secret. But you won't call TMZ."

This time he was the one to roll the eyes, mocking her with his own disbelief.

"Mom's got this big talent agent for a boyfriend, see. And she's, like, letting him use our house for a top-secret wedding for one of his people."

"And she's going to let you hang with all those big guys? Ri—ght," he drawled. "And I'm going to come in a stretch limo with two awesome brunettes, one on each arm. Get real."

"Mom said I could, like, hang out on one condition—I could

not wear my black mini. So she took me shopping and found this hot-pink fifties-type dress. Oh my God, Griff, you should've seen it on me."

From his bored expression, he'd rather be watching *Iron Man* than listening to a fashion report. But when Taylor stood up and dropped the towel from her shoulders to describe the dress, his attention escalated.

"It has this halter-style bodice and it, like, pushes me up real high." With her palms beneath her breasts, she demonstrated as if he was just some girlfriend and not a fifteen-year-old guy with his eyes glued to the straining red spandex of her swimsuit. "And then it's real tapered all the way down to the waist that's dipped in front."

Her gestures followed the imaginary flow of the dress.

"There I was in the dressing room and my mom—God, she's so lame—she says it makes me look 'mature.' Can you believe her? I looked like my boobs were gonna pop right out in some guy's face!"

~

"Leave the poor guy alone, Taylor," Sam scolded with just enough firmness to make his point. "Can't you see Griffin's trying to watch the movie? Besides, your suit's getting the couch wet. Why don't you hike down to the bunkhouse and get changed."

She looked at Sam. "How about giving me a ride down?"

"I'm not your personal chauffeur." He gave her an I'm-not-buying-it grin. "Get going."

With a sigh of resignation, she exaggerated a pout as she passed by him. "I can't believe I thought spending the summer here was better than going to Hawaii. Sometimes I'm totally amazed that I let you talk me into being a CA. You have, like, more rules than my dad, y'know."

Sam mimicked, "I thought you were, like, totally impressed with all the buff dudes who work here, y'know?"

Erupting into chuckles of laughter, Griffin rolled onto his back, his arms crossing his stomach.

"Cute, Sam. Real cute." Taylor punched his arm and retreated before he could respond.

Turning his attention back to the fifteen-year-old, Sam sat on the edge of the same couch Taylor had vacated. "Your folks left a message on the phone machine, Griff. They'll call back at eight tonight. If you want, you can take it up at my place instead of in the office."

"Thanks."

"The door's unlocked so just go on in and make yourself at home, watch TV while you're waiting."

"You're not gonna be there?"

"As a matter of fact, Karen's going to hold the fort for a few hours tonight."

Mario interrupted, launching himself over the back of the couch and landing on his butt on the other side of Sam. "Hot date?"

"Maryann called," he lied.

Actually, he'd called her for some female advice. She was more than happy to serve as confidante as long as she didn't have to serve dinner. All she had on hand was a six-pack of diet soda. He'd offered to deliver her favorite pizza and the "date" was set for seven.

Griffin was too immersed in the movie to notice Mario raise one dark eyebrow, wordlessly indicating the direction of his thoughts. "I suppose you two are getting together to talk about the good old days."

"Something like that." Sam chafed under the knowledge that his friend was one of the few who knew the sordid details of his past.

Mario knew about the good and the bad, about the great sex

with Maryann and the drunken orgies with the bottle. There was a time when Sam couldn't resist either one. For several years he'd managed to get by without both. For the most part, anyway. Although he hadn't fallen off the wagon, the same couldn't be said about his relationship with Maryann. A few times since their divorce they'd ended up in bed together. Not exactly a common practice between them, it was more like a no-strings-attached silent agreement to enjoy the sexual pleasure that had always been so good between them.

And without Sam uttering a single word about the night with Maryann, Mario had always seemed to pick up on it, claiming to have a sixth sense about such things. Although he long implied that he'd inherited psychic abilities from his Romanian ancestors on his mother's side and sexual sensitivity from his full-blooded Greek father, he finally confessed that he could read Sam's restless behavior better than his own. The longer Sam went without sex, the worse it got. Until he got laid again. Then the lines of tension on his face eased and he was a hell of a lot easier to live with.

As if reading Sam's mind, Mario stretched his legs out in front of him and dropped his head back, closing his eyes. "Save me the effort of staying up late for tomorrow's forecast, Sam. What's it gonna be—more of the same or are we in for a mild spell?" He opened one eye, waiting for the answer.

"Plan on a cold front," he muttered, getting up from the edge of the cushion.

~

AFTER TAYLOR CHANGED into a pair of jeans and a tank-top, she put in the earbuds to her phone, selected her favorite playlist and closed her eyes with a smile. Instant relief from the quiet world. She pumped up the volume of the hard rock and gritty guitar, then aimlessly wandered around the empty cabin.

Other than one six-year-old boy, her group of kids had gone home. Eight more would arrive tomorrow, but she had plans to be at her dad's house until Monday. Megan would have to handle the little munchkins' first night by herself, calming down the homesick criers. She was good at that. It was almost like magic the way those kids acted with her.

Taylor still hadn't made up her mind whether she liked Megan or not. For an adult, she wasn't too bad. Not too nosy or too talkative. Thank God for that, Taylor thought, recalling cutesy counselors who wanted to be summer buddies. Megan kept to herself mostly—reading books and listening to her music on her own phone.

Finding herself back in the counselor's area, Taylor stood beside Megan's bed, looking down at a few personal articles left neatly arranged on top of the dresser. The pink brush was clean but for a couple dark hairs. If for no other reason, Taylor should hate the woman only because of that beautiful hair. It was so thick and long and shiny that it made Taylor sort of wish her own hair didn't look so dried out like straw.

While the pounding rhythm of Hollywood Undead beat against her eardrums, she picked up the poetry book she'd seen Megan reading from time to time. The two of them had something in common after all, though she'd never admit her own interest to anyone. What Taylor wrote was a bunch of garbage that no one would understand, let alone appreciate.

As she turned the pages to the first poem, she sat on the mattress, immediately drawn into the world of the poet by his eloquent words and phrases, some understood, some not. It didn't matter.

After a while, she came across a yellow sticky note hidden in the middle of the book—

Megan,
I NEED you in my life.
Your Little Boy Blue,

—S

PUZZLING OVER THE CRYPTIC MESSAGE, she remembered Sam watching Megan at breakfast. As she removed the paper to read the poem beneath it, she wondered if the "S" was Sam. The rhyming stanza told of a little boy who had put his old toys away before going to sleep. Then an angel came and took him away.

Blinking back tears, she finished reading about the faithful toys waiting for their Little Boy Blue to come back.

Sitting on the bed and staring at the words, Taylor mulled over the note from Sam. Maybe he knew Megan from some other time in their lives. Had he been faithfully waiting for her to come back to him? No, she decided, they didn't act at all like long-lost lovers.

Then again, that look at breakfast hadn't been the first time she'd seen Sam staring at Megan. She also remembered that Megan hadn't been in her own bed when Taylor awakened early that morning. There was only one conclusion—Megan must have snuck off to meet Sam.

Suddenly, the poetry book was snatched from her hands.

Her head jerked up. "Sam!" As the note fluttered to the floor, she rocketed to her feet, yanking out her earbuds. "You scared the shit outta me!"

"God damn it, Taylor," he swore, despite his rules against it. "What the hell are you doing here going through Megan's stuff?"

Refusing to admit guilt, she crossed her arms and spun away from him so fast that she almost lost her balance.

"I'm not accusing you of taking anything," he said in a calmer voice.

"Oh, gee, thanks for the vote of confidence." Turning halfway around, she tipped her chin up and watched him through narrowed eyes. "Do you know where she went this morning before anybody was up?"

"What? Why? You're not making any sense."

She dipped down and scooped up the paper. "This didn't either…until I read that poem it was stuck on."

Taking the note in one hand, he lifted the book that was in his other. His thumb was still wedged in the same place in the book where he'd grabbed it earlier.

~

SAM READ THE MESSAGE, then scanned the page of poetry. Momentarily stunned by the desperate plea, he could only see that Megan had obviously left a husband who deeply loved her, and who didn't want the divorce. Was she the kind to cut and run without consideration for those she left behind? Somehow he couldn't imagine her as the type to be so coldhearted. There had to be a good reason for her to leave her marriage.

"Yeah, just as I figured," Taylor said petulantly.

Snapped from his thoughts by her sharp remark, he hadn't a clue what she was talking about. Carefully reattaching the sticky note to the page, he asked, "Mind filling in the vowels, Vanna?"

She eyed him defiantly before she broke off the contact, turning away again.

"Just blow it out," she mumbled.

"No, I'm not going to 'blow it out.' I want you to tell me exactly what's going on upstairs."

She whirled around. "Quit playing dumb, Sam. It's pretty obvious where Megan was at six o'clock this morning."

"She was with me."

"No kidding, Mister 'S-is-for-Sam.'"

"You think I wrote this note to her?"

"Good job, Sherlock."

"That's what you meant about whose bed— You think— How could you possibly come up with an idea like that?"

"I'm not a space cadet when it comes to sex, Sam. Just because

I'm still a virgin I—" She clamped her mouth shut, then dropped her gaze.

Masking his mild surprise at her accidental revelation, he lifted her chin with the crook of his finger, coaxing her to look him straight in the eyes. "Listen to me, young lady. First off, even though that bit about your virginity is nothing to be ashamed of, it will never leave this room. Got that?"

She nodded, her blue eyes large and vulnerable.

"Second, Megan and I are not sleeping together. She was out for a walk and I invited her in for coffee. That's it. She happens to be going through a rough time with her husband, Stewart. He's the 'S,' not me. Clear?"

Again she nodded, but moisture pooled in the corners of her eyes as her face flushed pink. Obviously embarrassed by her mistake and mortified by her confession, she shifted awkwardly and stared down at her feet.

In the four years he'd known her, Sam rarely saw Taylor cry. Despite his own regulations, he couldn't stand by and let her wish the earth would open up and swallow her. To him, she was the closest he would ever come to having a daughter.

"Come here." He wrapped his arms around her in a big bear hug.

"I'm sorry, Sam."

"No kidding."

CHAPTER 5

Sitting with his mom at McDonald's after seeing a movie together, Jason swirled a french fry around in some ketchup, then sucked on it as he shrugged, avoiding her eyes.

"Griffin's nothing like Cameron," he said, referring to his babysitter Melissa's older brother. Melissa was a freshman in high school and real pretty. Cameron was a senior, but he liked to come over to the house and sometimes even filled in for Melissa. "Cameron's got his own Jeep and lots of money and stuff. Griff's not like that."

"That isn't quite what I meant, honey. I just thought…that is, at home Cameron takes you and Melissa to the beach and to the movies. From the way you get along with Griffin, I thought perhaps he reminds you of Cameron."

"Nuh-uh." He wished his mom would stop asking him dumb questions, like if he missed Cameron. He didn't miss anything back at home, except maybe his dad.

"So Griffin doesn't have a car or money. I guess you two talk about a lot of things."

"Yeah."

"Does he like the same things you do?"

"I guess."

"Does he talk about his family?"

"Only if I ask him." Jason knew it was bugging her that he wasn't saying much. But how do you tell your mom that there's some guy-talk you just don't feel like talking about?

He knew Griffin would really be bummed if anyone else knew about his mom and dad having a hard time with their jobs. Kids weren't supposed to know those things. Just like Jason wasn't supposed to know that his own mom and dad were probably busting up. That's the kind of stuff that Griff and him talked about. And they didn't have to make stupid promises about not telling anybody else. It was sort of understood between them.

That was partly why he liked Griffin—he didn't tell you to keep your mouth shut like Cameron did. Cameron did lots of junk that you weren't supposed to tell anybody—like hanging his bare butt out the window at some dumb high school girls, and speeding down the side of the freeway when it was all backed up with stopped cars. He didn't really like Cameron, but he *did* like getting all those cool things like trips to the movies with Melissa and to Disneyland and places like that.

Maybe Griffin was broke, but being with him was still better. But Jason didn't feel like trying to explain all that to his mom. It wouldn't change anything. When summer was over, him and his mom would go home, and he wouldn't see Griffin again.

Jason offered a lame excuse so his mom wouldn't feel bad.

"I guess I'm kind of tired," he said, leaning back against the plastic seat. He finished the last of his chocolate shake and listened to the airy sound of the straw sucking the bottom of the cup.

"Hard to believe that one movie can tire someone out so much," she teased. "Come on, let's go. Do you want to help me out by pumping the gas for me when we stop at the station next door?"

Happy that his mom had given up, he lifted his gaze to hers and smiled. "Sure. No prob."

It was no problem, all right. That is, until his mom's credit card got refused.

Several minutes later, Jason slouched down in the car with the window open as his mom practically yelled over the cell phone.

"How could you cancel my cards, Stewart? That's the lowest —" Her words broke off, probably because his dad was yelling back at her. "If your wallet was lost, why didn't you at least call me?" Again a pause. "No, I don't happen to believe you. Yes, I covered it… No… I've got Tuesday off. I'll be down then… Fine."

Jason noticed she hung up without saying goodbye or anything. Things were worse than he'd figured. Of course, maybe she was just too steamed to say goodbye.

"Are we going to go see Dad on Tuesday?" he asked when she got back in the car.

She blew out a long breath, then turned and looked at him like she was real sorry. He knew what was coming.

"I'll have to leave you at the ranch, Jase. I've got business to take care of and your dad's going to be too busy. It's just not a good idea for you to go along, okay?"

"Yeah." He nodded reluctantly, then glanced out the window.

"Tell you what," she said in a happier tone. "How would you like to keep me company on the ride down, and when we get home I can leave you with a babysitter."

"No!" he snapped, then instantly regretted it. "I'm not a baby and I don't need no babysitter."

"I never said you were a baby, Jason. I just thought you might like to see Melissa. Maybe even Cameron. I'm sure they'd love to see you."

The only thing left to do was whine. "Do I have to go? I hate sitting for two boring hours in this car listening to that strange music. It's not fair when all the other kids get to go swimming and junk."

His mom buckled her seat belt and started the engine. "I swear you'd move to that ranch permanently if Sam would let you."

How does she know?

~

SAM SAT BACK on the white leather sofa as Maryann perched on the edge of the cushion next to him and opened the pizza box he'd placed on her coffee table.

"You actually remembered the pineapple this time," she remarked with surprise, lifting two slices onto a delicate china plate.

She handed it to him, then turned back to get one for herself. While he went at the food with a normal approach to eating, Maryann seemed to make it a sensuous art form. With the plate on her lap, she carefully leaned over it as she brought the wedge of pizza to her lips and bit off a tiny corner, leaving strings of mozzarella stretched between. She pinched off the cheese and popped it into her mouth, sucking the grease from her fingertips.

When she caught him watching her, she paused, then impishly grinned. "You always did get off on watching me eat, didn't you?"

"I always got off on watching you do anything."

"So…who are you watching *these* days?"

"One of my counselors." After a gulp of milk, he set the crystal tumbler on the end table and polished off the first slice of pizza.

"Convenient," she said without the slightest hint of jealousy, then added with a twinkle of mischief in her eyes, "It's a given that we're talking female and over twenty-one."

His mouth full, he grunted affirmatively as she drank her white zinfandel.

"Good answer. Now tell me, Thor, when do you plan to club her and drag her off to your cave?"

His eyebrows shot up as he made a muffled noise that remotely sounded like a question.

"Don't look so stunned," she said. "If you'd already done it, you wouldn't be sitting in my living room right now, salivating over my eating habits."

He finally managed to swallow. "If I *had* already done it, I'd have made one hell of a mistake."

"We're talking about sex, not marriage."

"And I'm talking about complications—like she's my employee, for Christ's sake. I can't have an affair with one of my staff."

"Beats celibacy. Take it from me."

"You? Celibate?" He flinched at the incredulous tone in his voice. "I didn't mean for that to come out the way it sounded. It's just that you—"

"Calm down, Thor. I understand what you're trying to say. God, what happened to your verbal skills? Did *she* do this to you?"

Critical of his fumbling remarks, Sam devoured the second piece of pizza like a Neanderthal. Maryann shook her head in amusement, then patted his knee. He spared her a quick glare but she only chuckled as she got up and walked into the kitchen with her plate. Although she'd allowed herself only one slice of pizza, he knew she'd raid the refrigerator in the middle of the night. He was more than a little familiar with her dieting routine as well as her lingering guilt the next day.

It felt comfortable being with Maryann. No surprises. Playful teasing and easy talk made him relax, as it always had. As she walked back into the room with a second glass of wine in her hand, he remarked wistfully, "I miss being married."

"So do I."

"Do you regret marrying me?"

"No, I regret losing you to that ranch," she answered quietly, standing before him. As she took a long sip, his eyes traveled down her neck and over her petite body. Without any food in his mouth, he swallowed hard, thinking of Mario's comments earlier in the day.

Forcing his eyes off her, he reached past Maryann and loaded his plate down with more pizza. If he couldn't satisfy one craving, he'd at least satisfy the other.

She settled on the cushion next to him, closer than before. "So tell me about this new talent who's got you drooling."

He smiled at her show-business slang. Sam always knew she'd be the successful producer that she'd become. Looking at her now in her neatly pressed safari shirt and mid-thigh shorts, it was easy to picture her in a fashionably casual blouse and slacks. Her chin-length soft-brown hair would be pulled back. Her reading glasses would be either on the bridge of her nose, or in her hand when she gestured passionately about a point she wanted heard.

She thrived on the organized chaos of the television business. The "business" was not only in her choice of words, but also in her blood—so was her knack of going straight to the heart of a problem. She went after what she wanted, which right now was information, and she did whatever it took to get it. The woman was shrewd. And sexy as hell.

In between mouthfuls of pizza, Sam told her about Megan Fisher, ending with his frustrating decision to maintain his strict standards regarding the staff.

"I don't buy it," she said, returning to his side with her third glass of wine and another glass of milk for him.

"What? I spill my guts and you don't buy it?"

"Get your brain out of your pants for half a second, Thor. You want her. What you *don't* want is someone who'll walk."

"Maryann—"

Abruptly stopping him with her hand held up, she lowered the Waterford glass from her lips, leaving them wet and glistening.

"We're both scared, Sam. Christ, look at us—we go forever without any sort of relationship, always falling back to each other, the tried-and-true buddies that we are. As if STDs don't make us paranoid enough, our own fear of another failure leaps in there to keep others at arm's length."

"I don't see it as scared, Mare. Cautious, maybe."

She set her glass down, then took his plate and put it on top of the pizza box. Wordlessly, she took his hand and stood, bringing him to his feet.

When she started toward the bedroom, Sam gently pulled her back until they stood face-to-face. Gazing down into her green eyes, he knew theirs was an intimate friendship that was neither weakened nor strengthened by sex. Yet guilt assailed him.

"I don't think—"

Her fingertips touched his lips. "Then don't."

An hour later, Sam rolled onto his back and wished to God he had a good stiff belt of whiskey to wash away the recriminations seeping deep into his gut. All the other times they had both enjoyed a romp in the sack just for the pure physical pleasure of it.

But not tonight.

Not for him, anyway. Tonight he had run his fingers through Maryann's hair with his eyes closed, envisioning Megan's long dark hair. With each touch, each movement, he'd thought of Megan. The more his mind wandered the more he drove himself, believing his unleashed passion would satisfy Maryann and make up for using her as a substitute for the woman he really wanted beneath him.

Lying on her back next to him, Maryann rolled her head to the side and smiled. "That was one hell of a performance, Thor."

He chuckled, masking his dark mood. "Not too shabby yourself, Xena."

She stretched her arm across him, reaching past the empty

foil packet on her bedside table, then tossed a couple unopened ones onto his chest.

"What do you think I am—Marathon Man?"

With a laugh, she moved away from him, got up and slipped on her silk robe, cinching the sash at her waist. One corner of her mouth tipped up in a cocky smile. "Just in case you finally get around to asking Megan out."

As she disappeared into the bathroom, he picked up the condoms and shook his head. After he dressed, he tucked them in his wallet, still amazed at her brassy insight. By the time he was dressed, she was back out in her living room as if nothing had transpired between the two of them.

He joined her on the sofa, brushing his lips across the top of her head as he sat down. She looked at him affectionately as he eyed her refilled wineglass.

"I know my limit, Sam. This is sparkling cider." She gestured toward the cluttered coffee table where another glass waited for him.

He picked it up and raised it in a toast. "To one special lady," he offered as the glasses clinked. "May you find that knight in shining armor."

"To the Lone Ranger—"

"If you say 'May he find his Tonto,' I'm going to wring your pretty little neck."

"Okay, okay. All joking aside." She lowered her hand and gazed at him with compassion in her eyes. "Sam, you have tried and convicted all of womankind on the basis of our failed marriage. Just because I refused to live out in the sticks on a ranch, and I couldn't revolve my life around your camp, doesn't mean Megan will feel the same way. She's a teacher. She loves kids. You haven't given her a chance. Using this excuse about your strict rules is a bunch of crap and you know it. You set those guidelines for the Flying K so those hormone-hopping teenagers won't jump each other's bones when no one was looking, not so you would remain a bachelor the rest of your life. If you really want to pursue a relationship with this woman, I'm sure you can do it discreetly."

When she had finally finished, he asked lightheartedly, "Is the sermon over, Reverend?"

"Amen."

~

As Mario poured a cup of coffee the next morning, Sam entered the noisy kitchen and grabbed a mug out of the cupboard. The moment of truth had arrived.

"How is it?" Sam asked, never certain what to expect with the morning brew.

Grinning smugly, Mario turned around and took one long look at Sam, who had hoped his charade of nonchalant innocence was working. "Oh…I'd say it's hot." He winked. "Definitely hot."

"I'm talking about the coffee," Sam muttered under his breath, barely loud enough for Mario to hear.

"And I'm talking about your sex life," he countered in a whisper. When Sam glared, Mario stepped back in mock surprise. "My lips are sealed, boss. I swear—"

"Hey-hey-hey, Sam." Karen popped up next to the two men. The stupid grin told everything. "Late night at Maryann's, hmm?"

Mario defended himself. "I didn't say a word. Honest. Come on, Karen, tell him you figured it out all by yourself."

~

During the rest of the week, most of the older staff members ribbed him with inside jokes about his sexual prowess, much to his chagrin. Immediately following one particular incident overheard by Megan, Sam couldn't help but notice a chill wind coming from her direction. He had no idea what she was thinking about him, but he knew it wasn't good—and that bothered him more than the endless remarks he'd ignored.

Waiting until her group of kids went into their cabins for the afternoon rest period, he poked his head in the door and asked Taylor to take over while he spoke with Megan in his office.

In silence, he led the way, all the while wondering what he was going to say that could somehow dissipate her cold front. Stepping aside, he allowed her to enter the office first, then came in and closed the door behind him, leaning back against it as she turned around.

Her dark eyes were full of disbelief yet inquiring. "You wanted me?"

Do I ever. "Something's bugging you and I think I know what it is."

"You do?"

"It's about some things that are being said about me. And I gather you don't approve."

"It's not my place to approve or disapprove."

"Maybe not. But it still matters."

"To who? You?"

"Yes, me. I care about you, Megan. A lot. Maybe more than I should. I don't want to, but I do."

"I seem to have that same effect on Jason's father," she shot back. "You care about me, and yet you don't want to. If that's supposed to make me feel good, you missed the mark."

"No, wait. I didn't mean—" He was scrambling for the right words but seemed to be digging himself in deeper. "When you came here on that first visit and I learned about your impending divorce, I had actually considered asking you out. Then out of the blue you asked for a job. Once I got a look at your résumé, I couldn't lie and say you weren't qualified just so I could keep you to myself. So, I made a deal—with the devil, you might say—that I wouldn't jeopardize our working relationship with my personal feelings for you. But it hasn't been any picnic."

Megan had not moved during the entire time he talked. Instead, she stared at the wall of picture frames, her face silhouetted by the single light bulb overhead, which did little to reveal her emotions.

"If I'm supposed to be flattered, I'm not." Though her voice remained level, her arms crossed tight beneath her breasts. "I find it hard to believe you're attracted to me while you're still carrying on with your ex-wife, according to certain counselors. And even if I was interested in you, I can't risk any kind of romantic involvement until after I've received complete custody of Jason."

Sam didn't need to guess about her feelings of fear. They were written all over her face. No doubt she was also harboring a whole lot of bitterness and resentment, if her comment about Stewart was any indication. Now his own confession had dumped one more thing in her lap to deal with.

Maybe a smarter man would've packed up and run. Maybe he was just plain stupid for wanting to help her through this tough time. But something urged him to stay. To him, there was no other choice.

It seemed like they'd stood silent in the cool, quiet adobe office for more than just those few brief seconds before Megan spoke again, this time with a trace of uncertainty in her voice.

"I saw a lawyer on my day off last Tuesday. I saw Stewart too. And I feel like I've already lost the fight before I've even begun. So much is in Stewart's favor—his money, his power, his...reputation. Once the press gets hold of the story, he'll be portrayed as the misunderstood genius, and I'll be the hardened, social-climbing bitch sucking him dry."

Sam stepped forward, gently put his arms around her, and felt her weakened defenses falter. Despite her best efforts, the tears flowed.

Like Taylor, Megan needed him—if only for the moment, but

that was enough for now. Yet these feelings inside him were nothing like the fatherly compassion he felt for Taylor when she'd cried in his arms.

It wasn't long before the soft weeping subsided. But when Megan started to move back, he couldn't bring himself to let go, though he would've done so if she'd insisted. Instead, she looked up, her gaze searching his face. Gripped by the pain he saw in her eyes, he responded with a tentative kiss—one of emotional intimacy rather than sexual desire.

His lips touched one corner of her mouth, then the other, brushing across the fullness of her lips. Far more exotic yet no less intoxicating was the scent of her perfume. When he finally claimed her mouth with his own, she seemed to give in to the tenderness, tilting her head, leaning her body into his. He gently pulled her closer. He felt her hands rest lightly on his waist. Sensitive to her touch, his skin warmed beneath her palms as they slid up his back.

Lightly tracing the outline of her lips with his tongue, he felt the slightest pressure from her fingernails, urging him on as her lips parted. One taste of her and he knew he wouldn't be able to stop.

He wanted more.

As if they both realized the same thing at the very same time, they each broke away. In the awkward moment that followed, there was no denying the tension.

They tripped over each other's apologies.

"That can't happen again," Megan said, stammering over her words.

"It won't," Sam promised, opening the door and exiting before either of them could say any more.

CHAPTER 6

Opening a letter from his dad, Jason hiked alongside Griffin as they returned from the mailbox on the main road. It'd been a month since summer camp started, and at least once a week he'd gotten something from his dad. His dad never wrote more than a page but Jason didn't either. He was just happy to get anything 'cuz most kids didn't. Like Griff. And even if he'd been old enough for his own phone to text or FaceTime, none of the kids were allowed to bring them. They were told cell service was really bad in the mountains, anyway.

"My dad's comin' on Sunday," he read excitedly. "Do ya think I can show him how good I can ride Brownie? Huh, Griff? Do ya think so?"

After wiping the sweat off his forehead with the back of his hand, Griffin glanced down, grinning. "Yeah, I suppose. Nuthin' fancy though. Got that?"

"He's gonna be so totally blown away that I can flip-mount and all."

"Totally? Blown away? You're starting to sound like Taylor."

"Oh, gross. I don't sound like a *girl*."

"Not any girl. Just Taylor."

Although Jason didn't see the difference, he figured out that Griff didn't mean anything by it. Still, talking about girls was dumb, so he decided to talk about something else.

"Are you gonna finally get to see your mom and dad this Sunday?" Jason asked.

"No. They…uh, can't afford the gas."

"Don't you miss them?"

"Sure. It's just…well, I don't have a ride to go see them on my days off. And now my mom's laid off and all, so money's real tight."

"Oh."

"Besides, they don't need me scarfing up all their food. At least if I stay up here I can eat all I want and not have to worry about my folks having enough money to buy groceries."

"I never think about money when I eat."

"Why should you? Your dad's rolling in it."

"Don't get mad at me, Griff. If I could, I'd give you a whole bunch of my dad's money. He's got more than he needs."

"Thanks, Jase." He chuckled, ruffling Jason's hair. "And I'm sorry. I'm not mad at you. Honest."

"Are you mad at your folks?"

"Naw, it's not their fault that the aerospace industry is cutting back. It's just scary is all. I mean, I read all this stuff about real nice families who ended up on the streets. And I can't help but think maybe we could end up there too."

"No, you wouldn't. Sam would let you stay here. I know he would. Just tell him. He'll help you and your family."

Stopping in the shade of a huge eucalyptus, Griffin knelt in the pungent dried leaves, dropped the stack of mail at his side and gently grasped Jason's shoulders. "*If* that happens, I can't tell Sam. I can't tell anyone. You've got to understand what will happen if the wrong people find out."

Jason was scared but refused to show it. Griff was starting to sound like Cameron and that made Jason's stomach hurt.

"If certain people learn that my folks aren't taking care of my sister and me, we might get taken away and put into foster homes."

"They do that to kids for real? They take them away?"

"Yeah, if some know-it-all can prove that the mom and dad aren't good parents. I mean, like, say a kid is in some kind of danger and the parents don't do anything about it. Then the kid gets taken away so he won't get hurt anymore."

"Did somebody tell you that?"

Griffin shook his head. "I picked it up from different places. I'm not a lawyer so I don't know all the legal stuff about it. But I know one thing—I'm not gonna take any chances. If my family has to live on the streets, I can't tell anybody. And neither can you."

"I won't, Griff. I promise."

If anyone knew how to keep secrets, he did.

CLOSE TO NOON ON SUNDAY, a blue Corvette pulled into the dirt parking lot of the Flying K, passing the departing white limousine in which Taylor was the sole passenger.

With Stewart due to arrive soon, Jason had dragged Megan away from her last-minute duties before the third-session kids began to flow into camp later that afternoon. Though her son had insisted his reason for bringing her up to the parking lot was to see the limo that had been sent for Taylor, Megan knew his real intention was to stage his own happy family reunion.

"Oh wow, check it out, Mom," Jason exclaimed as the two of them watched the sleek new convertible approaching them. His excitement multiplied tenfold when it pulled up in front of them with his father in the driver's seat. "It's Dad!"

"Stewart?" Megan couldn't believe it was her husband

opening the door and unfolding himself from the black bucket seat.

"Hi, troops!" He scooped up his son for a quick hug before he set him back on the ground and turned to his wife.

Feeling uncomfortably awkward, she nodded at his car. "Is that yours?"

"Yes. And is that any way for a wife to greet her lonely husband?" Stepping toward her, he lifted the aviator glasses from his eyes and hooked them on the low yoke of his yellow tank shirt, then gathered Megan into his arms.

Instinctively, her hands pressed against his chest, poised to resist his embrace if he took this ruse any further. All too aware of Jason's presence, she struggled to maintain some semblance of calm. After all, to her son, the two of them were still a married couple in every sense of the word.

Even though she had long ago memorized every line and angle of Stewart's face, she studied him a moment. His impeccably styled hair was still thick and full, and black as midnight—just like his mustache. Years of sailing had etched tiny lines across his forehead and around his light brown eyes where the sun itself seemed captured in tiny flecks of gold. At five ten, his hundred and seventy-five pounds were packed into a solid body.

Not unlike Sam Kempton, her mind unwittingly added.

Shocked by this sudden and unwelcome comparison, she knew she had absolutely no business thinking of Sam in the same context as her husband. Or a soon-to-be ex-husband, she hoped.

Seeking to obliterate all thoughts of the camp director from her mind, she placed a quick obligatory kiss on Stewart's cheek, a kiss that lacked the intense passion she had once felt for him. Still, she couldn't deny a tiny spark of something that might have once been love, or might have been misconstrued as love. She just didn't know anymore.

To her dismay, Stewart moved his head to capture her lips with his own. Knowing Jason would surely notice her resistance,

Megan acquiesced reluctantly. Her confusion and anger escalated when Stewart deepened the kiss. This was more than an act for the benefit of their son. Was this his way of proving he could still perform as a husband?

He might be perfectly capable of fulfilling her sexual needs, but she now knew that it was Maxwell who fulfilled his. That final thought drove her to step back. Unable to voice her thoughts in front of Jason, she wordlessly glanced away. Thankfully, their curious son was too preoccupied to pay them any mind, his body now teetering over the driver's door, his beat-up tennis shoes bouncing in midair.

Stewart moved in and lifted Jason off the glossy finish, gently dropping him to his feet. "Just got it day before yesterday. Thought I'd give it a good workout this afternoon. How about it, Jase? Want to take off with your old man for the afternoon?"

"Cool! Can I, Mom?" He gazed up at her with pleading eyes.

She felt the competition between divorced parents starting already. Even though Stewart could afford the most expensive toys to impress Jason, she knew deep down their son couldn't be bought. And neither could she.

"We could squeeze in all three of us," coaxed Stewart, even though it would be impossible to take her without breaking the seat belt laws.

"I'm going to be busy with the new kids." She looked down at her boy. "Besides, you two probably have lots of father-son stuff you can do without having me tagging along."

The look in Jason's eyes seemed to be reluctant to agree, as if he was afraid of hurting her feelings.

"It's really okay with me, Jason," she said.

Stewart opened the driver's door as his son headed around the front bumper for the passenger's side. "You're always welcome to come."

"Thanks." She waved goodbye, trying so hard to act as if everything was as normal as ever. "Have fun."

Flashing a wide grin, Stewart shifted the car into gear and maneuvered a U-turn, then kicked up some dust as he sped out of the parking lot.

Megan started back to the bunkhouse. She could feel the tension drain from her muscles as if her whole body had been clenched as tight as a fist. Stewart had a lot of nerve laying a kiss on her like that. It had come as much as a surprise as the one Sam had given her.

But without the same effect. This realization sent a shockwave deep and low, leaving behind a tingling warmth. Stewart might have accosted her. But Sam had aroused her. There was no denying it.

And it scared the hell out of her.

~

THE SUNDAY AFTERNOON wedding at the home of Nicole Bradley in Rancho Palos Verdes was considered a small, private ceremony by Hollywood standards. Sworn to secrecy, the hundred or so guests were all involved in the entertainment world in some form or other.

Taylor was somewhat surprised that no one had shot off their mouth to an envious associate, or traded a hot tip for some fast cash. But an hour into the party there still weren't any helicopters buzzing the trees for aerial photos of the famous newlyweds.

The wedding couple looked totally gorgeous, and they knew it. Romantically linked at one time or another with almost every leading woman, starlet and wannabe, the pretty-boy rock star had finally succumbed to the seductive Oscar-winning actress.

Unlike the other guests, the best man seemed to be paying more attention to Taylor than to the bride and groom. Whenever she looked over at him, she always caught him checking her out.

Seeking relief from the heat outside, she glanced around the front foyer to make sure no one was watching her, then lightly flipped the skirt of her dress as she sat down on the tiled step where the cool Italian marble sent an icy thrill from her bare butt to the backs of her knees. Leaning back on her palms, she tilted her chin up and closed her eyes, savoring the rush of chilly air pouring down from a ceiling vent, drying the sweat between her breasts.

Although she hadn't intended to draw anyone's attention, least of all the best man, she was mildly pleased with herself when he chose that moment to finally speak to her.

"You *are* one of the lucky ones now, aren't you?" he said in a British accent. She opened her eyes to see that he was talking about her envious position beneath the air-conditioning vent.

Trying to act indifferent while her palms started sweating, she managed a shrug. "I suppose."

"I'm Anthony Thorndike. Maybe your mom's boyfriend Bernie mentioned me. I'm part of his agency."

"Yeah, he's talked about you," she lied, nodding, hoping to keep him interested in her.

"All good, I assume."

"Oh, of course." She crossed her legs at the knees, drawing his gaze to the hem of her skirt riding up a little higher on her thighs.

Enticing him gave her a cheap thrill of excitement, but she didn't care. It was only a harmless game. She had to admit it was more fun than teasing Griffin.

She let her sandal dangle from her foot as she asked him more questions about himself. He claimed to be an old rugby "mate" of the groom's, even going so far as to say that he'd been the one to discover the singer and bring him to Bernie's attention. The way he saw it, he was the golden boy of the agency. His bragging didn't surprise her. From what she'd already seen of her mom and dad's business deals, nobody got anywhere in this town without steel balls—women included. Anthony wasn't any different. She knew he had to play the game if he wanted to be a success.

"May I get you something?" he asked after he seemed to have run through his entire life story.

"To drink? To smoke? Or to snort?"

Her flippant response made him laugh, but she couldn't help sensing those blue eyes watching her with a hint of amusement were weighing her answer, wondering if she was really seriously into drugs.

"I'm sure I can get you whatever your pleasure."

He's baiting me. She didn't doubt for one second that he could probably supply her with anything she wanted.

But no matter how tough she acted at school or how sophisticated she acted at these parties, she drew the line at hard drugs. Partly because of Sam being totally against the stuff. And partly because of her parents' own experiments with everything out there. Both her mom and dad had been through rehab, even though they thought she didn't know. Taylor sometimes wondered if their drug abuse before she was born might have screwed up her own chromosomes, or genes, or whatever. Maybe there was a scrambled genetic program inside her, ready to go off like a damn time bomb. The thought of someday having cancer or a deformed baby scared the hell out of her.

"I really don't need anything," she said, deciding that a vague question deserved a vague answer.

"Allow me to be the judge." The mischievous half-smile on his lips sent a nasty message through her mind and a thrill down her spine.

She knew she was playing with fire but she figured she was safe. Nothing could go wrong with the wedding reception happening a few feet away.

"I assure you," he continued while standing up, "that you will thoroughly enjoy a particular drink I have in mind."

A few minutes later, he returned with a tall glass of something that looked more like red fruit punch. Suspicious, Taylor tasted it with a bit of caution, surprised to find that it didn't taste bitter like any kind of alcohol.

She smiled. "What's in it?"

Obviously amused, he avoided her question. "A little of this and that. Quite refreshing on such a hot afternoon, wouldn't you say?"

She nodded.

As she sipped, Anthony eased down next to her while making casual conversation about the various other guests. He pointed out a famous Hollywood director and his actress wife, commenting that this was a rare appearance for the couple who preferred private family life over glitzy parties. He added that he'd seen them earlier at a poolside table with a well-known author and her husband.

As he dropped names, Taylor gave her own sterling performance of one who was only slightly interested. Behind her bemused smile, however, she was completely mesmerized—not only by her fascination with the elite, but also by the silken voice of the Englishman. Despite the presence of the other Hollywood power couples, Anthony Thorndike became the only one in her universe.

"Tell me about you, pet," he prompted, lightly skimming the back of his index finger up her bare arm. "What sort of work do you do?"

"I'm a counselor—" She made a conscious effort to delete the title of assistant. "At the Flying K camp in the summer and on weekends."

"Only summers and weekends? And I suppose that leaves you available to laze around your mum's house all week long. How delightful."

Watching him turn toward her, she tried not to pay attention to his thigh resting practically on top of hers. Even though she figured anyone passing by probably wouldn't notice, to her it was intimate in a daring sort of way.

"I still go to—" She stopped. His distracting nearness had almost made her forget Bernie's strict instructions.

Keep your age to yourself, he'd said, worried that the wedding guests wouldn't relax with a nosy teenager hanging around.

If anyone asks, you tell them you attend a small private college and you work part time at that camp, he'd told her.

"I…attend a small college. Private. Very private."

"My, you do sound like the busy one. You must have a very understanding man in your life."

"No." She lifted the glass to her lips, pausing long enough to say, "No one at the moment anyway," then took a long drink, eyeing him over the rim.

God, this is so fun.

~

AT AN ICE CREAM stand on Santa Monica Beach, Stewart paid a small boy for two cones, amused at the grinning kid standing on a wooden crate behind the counter alongside adults who were likely the parents.

As he and Jason walked toward the carousel building at the foot of the pier, he marveled over the work ethic instilled in the youth of the Asian immigrants—some of which spilled into the drug trade, invading his own territory down in Long Beach. From his jaundiced viewpoint, he eyed all but clean-cut high school jocks as probable gang members.

If someone told him that the ice cream vendor was a runner, he'd no doubt believe it. And why not? That was the kind of world he worked in. Which was why he wanted to know more about this fifteen-year-old buddy of Jason's. Who was Griffin? Where was he from?

Though Stewart didn't openly admit it, he didn't like the

looks of the kid mentioned in the rare text that his son had sent from Megan's phone earlier in the week.

"Tell me more about this guy—Griffin, is it?" The two of them climbed the cement steps to the pier level.

Jason seemed more engrossed in the double-dip strawberry than the conversation. "He's totally great, Dad."

"From the picture I saw, he doesn't look like the kind of boy I imagined you would strike up a friendship with. He looks a lot older than you."

"That's 'cuz all the guys my age don't stick around more than a couple weeks. Griff's always 'round, even on his days off."

"He never goes home to visit his parents?"

"Nuh-uh." Jason quickly added, "But he talks to them lots on the phone."

"So you've never met his mom and dad."

"Nope."

Stewart wondered what kind of kid went for weeks without seeing his parents, or for that matter, what parents went for weeks without seeing their child? He discounted his own circumstances because Jason had his mother living at the ranch with him.

Calliope music drifted in a breeze scented with sea salt and frying oil from a fish-and-chips vendor. They skirted tourists spilling out the doorway of the carousel building. Momentarily separated from Jason by a passing Japanese tour group, Stewart frantically glanced around. He finally spotted his son wandering in the midst of the smothering crowd, his eyes fixed on the arcades and souvenir shops.

Stewart zigzagged through the sea of bodies and stepped up behind Jason, gently catching him by the shoulder. His son ducked evasively before recognition dawned in his eyes. The detective part of Stewart admired the boy's defense system; the father in him puzzled over that flicker of fear on his son's face.

"Are you okay?" he asked, sliding his hand to the back of Jason's neck and giving it an affectionate squeeze.

"Yeah, sure. Fine. I just thought you were up ahead of me so I didn't know it was you grabbing me at first."

By the time they reached the end of the pier, they'd nearly finished their ice cream. A long, single line of fishermen edged the iron railing. Out over the water, gulls hovered on the air currents, screeching at each other. Jason tossed them the last bite of his waffle cone, cheering as one bird swooped down and caught it in midair.

Stewart wished his life could always be this simple.

~

WITHIN AN HOUR, Taylor finished her second glass of punch and wanted Anthony to get her another, but didn't know where he'd gone. After asking around, she found out from an old guy that the two men had passed each other in the hall.

"Which one?" she asked, trying hard to concentrate. Her head was a little fuzzy but not so much that she couldn't remember there were at least four different halls in this ridiculously huge house. The man waved his hand toward the east hall which led to three guest rooms and her own bedroom.

Halfway there, she stopped one of the bridesmaids—a gorgeous model who reminded Taylor of a sleek cat.

"Have you seen the best man?" she asked.

Almond-shaped eyes appeared suspiciously glassy as the Jamaican beauty drawled, "Last I saw him, sweetie, he was headin' into the last bathroom on the left."

"Thanks." When Taylor started to walk by, the woman pressed close and slung an arm around Taylor's neck.

Giggling, she whispered in her ear, "I wouldn't go down there if I were you."

Not sure if the woman was stoned or gay or both, Taylor

slowly pulled away, careful not to do anything that would draw attention to either one of them, especially like this. She would just pretend they were old friends and let it go at that.

"Thanks…uh, Amber."

"Autumn."

"Right. Thanks for the advice. I'm just going to deliver an important message to him and I'll be right back out."

With a little smile, the bridesmaid cocked one eyebrow and gave Taylor a quick up-and-down scan.

"Any-ting you got to tell him, sugah, ain't nearly as important to him as what he's doing right now. Believe me, I know." She reached up with one finger and skimmed it down Taylor's nose, then hooked it under Taylor's chin and lifted it. Their eyes met. "Don't go messin' with stuff you can't handle."

The model glided away, leaving Taylor dazed and confused. She closed her eyes and tried to shake off the muddied haze in her brain.

Heading toward the end of the hallway, she couldn't seem to keep from bumping her shoulder into the wall. Her legs felt wobbly too. She paused at her bathroom door and raised her hand to knock. Muffled voices came from the other side, then the sound of glass clinking, like bottles being knocked over. And finally, a thump.

She wondered what was going on behind the closed door. In her blurry mind, she imagined a small group of people sneaking a fix, getting high with powders and needles and pipes. The thought of her very own private bathroom being trashed by a bunch of wasted party guests made her sick. Could Anthony be one of them?

Don't go messin' with stuff you can't handle.

Her curiosity finally pushed her to tap softly on the door.

"Yeah?" Anthony's voice was raspy. Was he smoking a joint?

"It's me. Taylor."

"One minute, pet."

But it was longer than a minute. When the door finally opened, a drop-dead-gorgeous redhead in a blue sequined dress preened in the mirror for a moment longer, then walked out without a backward glance.

Feeling a bit woozy, Taylor only vaguely noticed that the woman didn't act like she was spaced-out on drugs.

"One of the bridesmaids," Anthony explained nonchalantly. "I was waiting outside the door, you see, and she asked me to step in and unsnag her zipper."

"Oh." She craned her neck into the room beyond him, sniffing for any signs of smoke. Nothing. Maybe Autumn was too wasted to know what she was talking about.

Anthony leaned back against the marble vanity. "Was there something you needed?"

His ruffled tuxedo shirt was open partway, exposing a thick mat of dark blond curls. Taylor swallowed, embarrassed to think she'd almost accused him of doing drugs when all he was really doing was fixing that girl's zipper.

"I wanted you to…"

What *was* it she wanted from him? Why had she come looking for him? Her arms and legs felt funny. A strange warmth started low in her stomach and radiated out until her face felt flushed.

"*Wanted* me, you say?" One corner of his mouth lifted into a toe-curling smile. "I quite like the sound of that. What exactly"—he lightly shoved himself off the edge of the counter and came over to her in the doorway—"do you want me to do?"

Taking her hand, he led her into her white tiled bathroom, closed the door and locked it.

"I, uh…can't remember." He turned her toward the mirror and stood behind her. She stared at their reflection—both of them blond, blue-eyed and tanned. They looked perfect together.

"I suppose some fortunate fool has already had the honor of telling you that you look bloody beautiful in this dress."

Her head slowly shook side to side. Through the soft-focus

haze in her brain, she eyed the familiar curves of her body, then watched his hands travel lightly up her bare arms. A small, dreamy sigh escaped her lips as his fingertips slid over her shoulders and gently scooped her long hair up behind her head, leaving wisps of soft curls around her face.

"Mm…mm—lovely. Lovely, indeed. Have you ever worn it this way before? No? You should, pet. Makes you look quite sophisticated…in a sexy sort of way."

The heat in her body doubled.

"I would wager that you and your mum are often mistaken for sisters. Am I right on that one?" She gave him a single, silent nod. "Bet your mum eats it up, mature lady that she is. No doubt she worries about crow's feet and all that." Another nod. "You, on the contrary, have a long time yet before you need to be worrying about such things."

His fingers glided down to her elbows, then rested lightly at her waist. Aching to feel his touch on her bare skin, Taylor had a sudden wish that her confining taffeta dress was history. But that would never happen. Not here. Not now. Anthony wasn't like those oversexed jerks who'd tried to wrestle her in a parked car so they could cop a feel. Unlike them, Anthony was a gentleman, mature enough to simply enjoy flirting with her. If she kept his attention long enough, he might even ask her out. With any luck, she'd get to meet some of those rock stars he claimed to know.

Suddenly the reflection of the two of them blurred and her knees felt like rubber. She swayed a bit but his hands steadied her against him.

"Take it easy, luv." She heard his deep voice in her ear, felt his warm breath on her neck. "You're not going to nap-out on me *now*, are you?"

Shaking her head, she giggled at the rumbly way his words seemed to vibrate through her back where she felt the soft curls of his chest against her skin.

With her eyes closed, she had a vague awareness of being

turned in the circle of his arms. Then he kissed her. It was soft and wonderful and deliciously warm like hot cocoa thick with melting whipped cream. One of his hands cupped the back of her head, the other the curve of her bottom, pulling her tight against him. Everything felt so good. Too good to stop him even if she wanted to.

An incredible rush shot through her when his tongue parted her lips. French kissing wasn't new to her, but nothing compared to the way Anthony did it. This was the way it was supposed to be…just like in the movies.

Only this was the real thing.

In her drowsy euphoria, she was only vaguely aware of the soft shush of her zipper being opened, and of the muted rustle as her gown fell to the floor.

"No bra. No slip. You truly know how to dress for a man," he whispered in her ear, then moaned as his hand cupped her breast. "Absolutely ravishing. *Every* inch of you is absolutely ravishing."

Wearing only a black thong, she felt hot and cold at the same time. Her mind swirled as he gently twisted her nipple between his thumb and forefinger.

Tantalizing excitement mingled with growing fear. She wanted him to do more while at the same time she knew she should ask him to stop. But it'd be so easy to let him introduce her to sex. Real sex. Adult sex. He could teach her more than any guy at school could. He wouldn't be able to brag to the other kids. Doing it in here was better than the back seat of some car.

In her present state, all the reasons why she should let him make love to her made sense. Age didn't matter—his or hers. Even her best friend was fooling around with a boyfriend.

"Dare I say what another one of those drinks would have done to you? My guess is that we'd probably be doing this on your mum's sofa in the middle of the whole damn wedding party."

They both chuckled.

"I should've known"—with mock anger, she waggled a finger at him—"there was something in that punch. That's why I feel so…so wonderful."

"I'm afraid my ego would be tremendously bruised if I were to learn that my skillful touch hadn't contributed to your giddiness."

He kissed her again.

In her inebriated state, it was impossible to concentrate on anything. She was too busy experimenting with her tongue—touching, tasting, thrilling under his murmured approval. So she hardly noticed when his hands left her body and slipped his slacks and briefs just low enough to make himself available to her.

"I hate to be a boor and ask, but are you—how shall I say it?—all right by all this?"

She nodded.

With a sigh, he nuzzled her neck. "Good girl. I am ashamed to admit that my little tête-à-tête with that bridesmaid a few minutes ago has left me a bit unprepared. But it's all your fault, really. Had I known of your…availability, I would never have considered settling for second best."

With his mouth moving over her, he hooked his thumbs over the ribbon-thin sides of her panties and began to pull them down. But Taylor pulled away with a short, startled gasp.

"Shhh, luv. There's nothing to fear. I promise I won't hurt you. Just say the word and I'll stop. Though you may regret not finishing what we've started here."

"It's just—" She was afraid to tell him about her virginity, afraid he would laugh at her innocence, or worse, walk out on her, leaving her aching to know about the secrets of lovers. She couldn't make herself stop now. Nodding to the adjoining door to her bedroom, she suggested, "I think we'd be more comfortable in there."

In her lavender and white room, Anthony went over to her

queen-size bed and peeled off the rest of his clothes while Taylor checked the lock on the door.

This is it, she thought when she came up behind him and wrapped her arms around his waist. He nodded at the teddy bears on the lace-trimmed bedspread.

"Looks like your mum still treats you like a little girl," he commented, unaware of the accuracy of his remark. Right now, any reference to her mother was the last thing Taylor wanted to hear. She stepped around him and pulled him down with her onto the bed.

Smiling victoriously, he shifted his weight onto her. Suddenly another wave of panic swept over her. She pressed her hands against his chest, trying to resist him. His heartbeat pounded against her palm.

"I—I'm sorry." Her voice was a grainy squeak. "I can't go through with it."

Anthony released a frustrated sigh as he rolled onto his back. She watched him stare thoughtfully at the ceiling.

"Taylor, my pet. Tell me now…" His head turned toward her on the pillow. "Do you *want* me to make love to you or not?"

"Yes, but—"

"But what?" When she winced, he apologized, then softened his words. "Tell you what—while you keep your panties on and your legs together, I'll just duck into the loo and get dressed. If you don't want to see this old sot cry, you best stay out here until I'm gone. What say, pet? Deal?"

Seeing the twinkle of mischief in his eyes, she giggled at his dry humor. He was so irresistible. The stirring deep inside began again, stronger than before. Her undeniable attraction broke down the last of her barriers and she drew him to her. His fingers played with her hair as his mouth moved over her. In a low, throaty voice, he talked of a man's needs and a woman's duty to take care of them.

In her haze, she believed him, allowing him to press her

deeper into the soft pillows. She believed him when he promised not to hurt her.

After he removed her black lace panties, his palm trailed up her inner thigh. Their kisses deepened, becoming rough and urgent. In the midst of her sweet torture, Anthony whispered naughty little encouragements as she spiraled higher and higher, almost reaching her own private heaven.

There was no warning. No slow, careful introduction. Only his sudden, loud grunt as he plunged deep into her with such brutal force that she gasped in pain.

His hand clamped down on her mouth to silence her cry as he let loose with a stream of profanities and pulled out of her.

Tears streamed down into her hair. He'd promised not to hurt her, but he'd lied.

His eyes narrowed. "Why didn't you tell me you were a goddamn virgin?"

"I'm sorry, Anthony. I was afraid if I said anything, we wouldn't do it. And—" *And I'm tired of being a kid. And I wanted to see for myself if sex was everything I'd heard about and read about and saw in the movies.* "—you were the only man who ever made me want it so badly."

Turning his head away, he closed his eyes for a moment and she was afraid he was going to decide to leave.

"Please," she begged, cupping his face, kissing his chin, his cheek, his ear. "Don't go. I want this. I want *you*."

He looked at her with renewed interest. The corner of his mouth tilted up. "You are a naughty little tease, aren't you?"

She only shrugged her shoulders seductively. "I wanted you to be my first fuck."

He snorted at her vulgarity but seemed impressed by it as well. "One more question."

She caressed his thigh. "Later."

"How old are you, Taylor?"

She slid her hand higher. "How old do you think I am?"

"If there is a God, you will tell me you are twenty-one and I am not in jeopardy of arrest for statutory rape."

"What would you say to nineteen?"

A grin widened on his face. "Not great, but I think I could get it to hold up in court. I say we get on with it now, pet. If your mum comes sniffing around, the two of us will likely be caught in a most embarrassing circumstance."

Giggling, Taylor nodded in agreement, taking him into her arms with surprising ease. When he entered her the second time, it was with a gentleness that her body welcomed, responding to his movements like a longtime lover.

He was done in five minutes, if even that.

Taylor masked her disappointment as he abruptly hopped out of bed, telling her to wait there and he'd bring her dress back to her when he returned from the bathroom.

She pulled the sheet up over her naked body. Smoothing a wrinkle in the white bedspread, Taylor wondered when she would share a bed with him again.

After a while he came back into her room fully dressed, carrying the dress she'd left on the bathroom floor and tossing it casually onto her bed.

"I must say, you are a hell of a good sport, luv. Dare I add that you gave me one smashing good go-round once we got cooking."

He lounged against the low country-French dresser near the door and pulled a silver case from inside his tuxedo jacket. He drew out one cigarette and popped it in the corner of his mouth.

"Take my advice—" A cigarette lighter emerged from another pocket. The flame flared as he sucked on the filter. "Don't let anyone hand you a drink if you don't know what's in it. You can't handle your alcohol, if you know what I mean."

Anthony tilted his head back and blew a long stream of smoke toward the ceiling, then looked back down at the cigarette in his hand. Shaking his head, he let out a small chuckle.

"I do believe I've had more fucking fun this afternoon than the groom will get tonight."

Shamed by his strange behavior, Taylor couldn't bring herself to look at him. Trying to act as if nothing was wrong, she clutched the sheet to her chest and leaned over to grab the dress from the end of the bed. Very much aware of the dull ache from her first taste of sex, she slipped the dress over her head and down her body, letting the sheet fall away.

Turning to sit on the edge of the bed, she kept her eyes downcast, afraid to look at Anthony, knowing he was watching her as she wriggled the hem under her bare butt.

Reaching behind her, she was zipping up the back of her dress, staring down at the carpet, when she saw his feet in polished black dress shoes walk up and stop in front of her. Her gaze traveled up the tuxedo slacks, the white shirt, bow tie.

With a deliciously decadent smile, he tucked the cigarette in one uplifted corner of his mouth, freeing both hands.

Her stomach fluttered nervously. Maybe he hadn't meant to hurt her feelings. Maybe it was just his warped sense of humor, and she was just being too much of a child about it.

Assuming he was going to help her with her zipper, she smiled at him and turned sideways, offering her back to let him finish the job. But he didn't reach out to her. Instead, he withdrew his wallet and tucked two faded green bills into her hands on her lap. He paused a moment, then added two more before he patted her on the head as if she was a five-year-old.

With a numbness like she'd never felt before, Taylor watched him walk toward the door.

"You look a bit pale," he said as he stood with one hand on the doorknob and the other fingering the butt of his smoke. "Perhaps it would be best if you rest a bit. Give me some time to circulate before you come out. We wouldn't want to arouse suspicion, would we, luv?"

When she shook her head absently, he slipped out into the

hall and closed the door behind him. Without looking down, she crumpled the money and threw it toward the door, watching it flutter apart and drift to the white carpet.

Next came the silent tears.

Then came the far-reaching stab of pain that twisted in her gut until she doubled over. When her throat constricted, it was all she could do to roll into the center of her bed and curl up into a ball before the sobs overtook her.

"Taylor!" Her mother's voice barely broke through the black void that seemed to surround her. "What the hell is going on here?"

CHAPTER 7

Curled into a tight ball of pain and humiliation, Taylor wanted so much to jump off the bed and run into her mother's arms. More than ever before, she wished she could be a kid again, remembering how she used to climb into her mom's lap when things got hard. If she'd cry about another kid who'd hurt her feelings, her mother would hug her, and Taylor would believe everything was going to be okay.

Taylor held her breath as her mom's gaze dropped to the money on the floor.

"Four hundred dollars!"

Taylor cringed, hoping that the live band outside was loud enough to drown out her mom.

"Thorndike gave this to you, didn't he? I saw him come strutting out of the hall with that grin on his face, but I didn't think it was my goddamned daughter he'd just—" she sputtered. "You little slut! You got paid four hundred dollars for screwing him, didn't you?"

The dirty accusations grew louder until her mom yanked her from the bed. Her half-zipped dress barely stayed up. Face-to-face with those icy blue eyes, Taylor felt the open palm smack across her cheek with teeth-rattling impact. Trying to regain her senses, she clutched the top of her dress to keep it from falling down, and blinked several times, finally seeing the four bills waving in front of her face.

"Who *else* paid for you?"

"No one! I swear to God."

"You expect me to believe that?" Nicole screamed, throwing the money in Taylor's face, then slapping her. Again and again.

Stunned, Taylor cowered, covering her head. This wasn't her mom. It couldn't be. She tried to back away but Nicole kept hitting her.

"I've got eyes. Anyone who looks at you can see you're a tramp. I just never thought you'd stoop so low as to turn tricks with the goddamned wedding guests. And in my house!"

"Nicole!" shouted Bernie, running from the doorway then dragging her mom backward.

"Let go of me," Nicole demanded, struggling against his restraining grip. "This isn't any of your damn business."

"It is too."

"Why? Have you been doing her too? How much did she charge you? Or is it free for family?"

"Shut up, Nicole!" He shook her.

"Tell him about my last boyfriend, Taylor. I bet good ol' Neal got it free, didn't he?"

Seeing Bernie had a strong hold on her mom gave Taylor the guts to stand up for herself. "The only thing Neal got from me was a face full of puke."

"That's not what he said when I kicked him out. He told me you were sleeping with him, but I refused to believe him. He even said he'd knocked you up and paid for the abortion."

"I never did it with Neal. And I never had an abortion. I never did it with anybody until today. I was a virgin!"

"Yeah, right. I bet there's half a dozen drunk and horny bastards who shelled out for you this afternoon."

Bernie yanked on Nicole's arm to quiet her. "Don't say another word." Turning to Taylor, he said, "You better get out of here until she calms down. You got somewhere to go? A friend's?"

"I—"

"I'm sure Anthony would love to take you in," her mother said sarcastically. "Then again, at your prices"—she kicked at the money at Taylor's feet—"I doubt he could afford an all-nighter."

Taylor lashed out before she realized what she was doing. The slap echoed in the sudden silence. She only wanted to stop her mom from saying all those nasty, ugly things about her.

"Oh, God," she cried after realizing she'd actually hit her. "Mom, I'm sorry."

"Get your sleazy little ass out of my house. Now!"

Taylor brushed past the two adults. Instead of heading for the door, she crossed to the walk-in closet and started to take out a suitcase.

"I said now and I mean now."

"You better go, Taylor." Bernie nodded toward the hall, then silently mouthed the words, "Call me." He added a quick wink and a dirty grin.

You fucking bastard.

Standing beneath the closet's single light bulb, Taylor licked her swelling lip, tasting the saltiness of her own blood.

They were all a bunch of hypocrites, every last one of them—Neal, Anthony, her mother, and now Bernie. They *all* screwed around.

But I make one shitty mistake and I'm this major slut. Well, fine—if that's what you want to see, then take a good long look.

Without taking her eyes off them, Taylor reached behind her, unzipped the lower half of the zipper and let the dress fall to the floor. Bernie's eyebrows shot up at the sight of her nude body.

Ignoring her mother's swearing, she kicked the hot-pink taffeta aside and looked around for the cutoff jeans and tank top she'd worn home from the ranch. Finding them in the back of the closet, she yanked the cotton spandex shirt over her head then grabbed the faded shorts and, without bothering with panties, slid them up over her thighs. After pushing her feet into a pair of sneakers and leaving them untied, she went over to her bed and picked up the crumpled bills from the floor.

As she straightened and pocketed the money, she caught Bernie staring at the outline of her nipples. He disgusted her. They all did.

Without saying another word, she left.

Despite her effort to skirt the perimeter of the living room, Taylor saw the stares and forced herself to act totally cool and indifferent. She stepped into the marble foyer when the band outside finished a song.

In that moment of unexpected silence, a woman's loud voice continued into an echo. "Nicole's daughter *begged* him to have sex with her. Of course Anthony obliged…"

Taylor stopped. Hot blood burned her neck and cheeks. Part of her wanted to run for the door, leaving behind all these pompous jerks. But another part of her wanted to give Anthony a taste of humiliation. She pulled her shoulders back, determined to hide her nerves with false confidence, and turned around to scan the room.

Spotting him at the bar, she called out, "Hey, Horny Thorny."

He turned slowly, leaving one elbow hooked over the rolled edge of polished mahogany. "Excuse me, Miss, uh, Bradley, is it?"

Holding the cash up high enough for everyone to see, she mimicked his British accent. "Thanks ever so much for the 'blood money.' Dare I ask, do you always pay four hundred American dollars to have sex with sixteen-year-old virgins? Or am I the only one?"

"Miss Bradley." Anthony nonchalantly folded his arms over his chest, "You have had far too much to drink. I believe your little joke to be quite offensive, I assure you—not only to myself, but to these lovely guests. Please apologize at once."

Her chin tipped up and her eyes narrowed. "Go to hell, Thorny," she managed to say with a lot more arrogance than she felt, then turned her back on him and walked out.

Once she closed the door behind her, the smart-ass grin faded from her face as she ran down the steps and out into the night.

~

STEWART BROUGHT Jason back to the ranch after dark. He retrieved a flashlight from the small earthquake emergency kit in the back of the Vette. Walking together down the hill to the bunkhouse, he smiled at the way his yawning son automatically issued warnings of a pothole here and loose gravel there. Even half asleep, Jason knew the terrain like a seasoned camper.

Inside the wood-frame building, Stewart ignored the rustic squalor as he surveyed the roomful of curious young faces, nodding a friendly greeting.

When a dark-eyed man emerged from behind a plywood partition, Jason introduced him as his head counselor, Mario. From all appearances, the young gentleman passed Stewart's rigid code of acceptance. The same couldn't be said about the teenager who presented himself with a sullenness that reminded Stewart of the gang members he'd come across in the seedier parts of town. The light brown hair was pulled back with a rubber band.

A long-haired punk. Damn.

His son had picked one hell of a replacement for Cameron, who had the brains and the athletic ability to get into any university. This kid Griffin looked like he'd probably be lucky to get a few credits from a community college before he quit altogether for some menial blue-collar job, if he chose to work at all.

For Jason's sake, Stewart kept his opinion well masked as he made polite conversation with Griffin. There was too much going down in his life right now without fighting over his son's poor choice in role models.

Stewart turned to Jason. "I better be heading home."

A few minutes later, Stewart stood with Megan at the open bunkhouse doorway. "Walk me up to my car?"

He saw hesitancy in her eyes, then acquiescence. She called over her shoulder to someone he couldn't see, "Be right back, Katie."

"I'd hoped you would've stopped by the house on one of your days off," he began, noticing the way she crossed her arms as if the warm summer night had suddenly turned cold.

"One day a week doesn't give me enough time to fit everything in."

"At least you don't deny that you've been back in town."

She glanced at him with caution. "I have nothing to hide from you."

They walked several steps in silence. Stewart wondered if she had found his note in the poetry book yet, but he couldn't bring himself to ask. If she'd already read it, her lack of response was answer enough. Suppressing his own curiosity, he held out hope that his cryptic message might help persuade her to stay with him. It was a long shot and he knew it.

He looked back on the little boy he once was—as happy and unsuspecting as the toddler who'd had gone to sleep in the poem and never woke up. By the time he was twelve, he knew he was different, but he also knew older boys who were open about their sexuality and suffered for it. Beaten up after school. Thrown out by unaccepting parents. So he tried to be straight. He'd kept up the pretense, just like the dusty toys in the poem. Even though that little boy was never coming back, they would always be there, faithful and loyal to him to the end of time.

That's what Stewart needed now. He needed Megan and Jason to be there for him. He needed their loyalty. He needed to be who everyone expected him to be.

"Are you on the Stanford case?" Megan asked, interrupting his thoughts. Knowing she'd never been comfortable discussing his police work, he gave her credit for trying to make up conversation between them.

"No. Johnson's been assigned," he said, regarding the gang-related homicide at Stanford Place a week earlier. "Where did you hear about that?"

"*Press-Telegram* website. I'm looking for a place to rent and I want to know more about the neighborhoods I can afford."

Although the flashlight cast only a small circle of light on the ground ahead of them, Stewart knew she'd turned to look at him. Keeping his own eyes glued to the ground, Stewart pretended not to notice. He didn't need to see those dark eyes to know they were glaring at him, reminding him of the line she'd drawn, warning him not to cross.

"The house is big enough for all of us. I'll hire an architect to reconfigure the three floors into two units. It's the most practical solution. You'd have your space. And Jason wouldn't be shuffled back and forth between us."

"Don't use Jason to get me to stay." Her voice was calm but firm.

"But it's your house. I bought it for you."

"No, you didn't. I'd always dreamed of a beach cottage, but you couldn't hear me. You had to have that massive mansion."

"It's hardly a mansion."

"You're missing my point." Her mild rebuke hung in the air between them. He didn't mean to start a fight. "Keep the house or sell it. I don't care what you do with it. I'm going to rent a place until we settle our finances, then I'll find something that suits my own tastes."

At the car, he leaned against the fender, in no hurry to leave. Megan, on the other hand, was obviously anxious to say goodbye. She shifted from one foot to the other.

"It was nice of you to take Jason out today. He's missed you a lot."

"You make it sound like I was doing him a favor," he said softly. "I'm his father, Megan. I *wanted* to be here. I've wanted to be here every weekend but—"

"I know—your schedule."

He sighed, wishing the darkness didn't hide her expressive face. Did she think he was lying about his workload so he could be with Maxwell? He couldn't blame her if she did. Man, he'd really screwed up this time.

They both spoke at once.

"Megan, I—"

"Stewart, I—"

"Go ahead," he said.

"I've got to get back. Have a safe drive home."

"Wait." He grabbed her arm as she turned to go. "I...wanted to apologize about that kiss this afternoon. To be honest, I thought if I used my old MO, I might stir up some old memories...for both of us. Give you something to think about at night for the next few weeks. Then maybe you'd finish the summer here and come home and forget about the divorce. Pretty stupid of me, huh?"

She shook her head.

"Talk to me."

"Why? You haven't been interested in talking to me for months—no, make that *years*."

Accustomed to her Irish temper, he knew it wouldn't do him a damn bit of good to rile her any further. Still, he had too much at stake to walk away now. "I admit I've been a bastard to live with. But I had this secret I couldn't share with you and I was miserable."

"You mean you were miserable with me."

"Yes. No! Ah—hell," he muttered. "It wasn't you. It was me. Can't you see that? Don't blame yourself."

"I can't help it," she whispered, her voice breaking. "Damn you, Stewart, for making me feel so…incompetent. All those times in bed with you. That wasn't love. You were just going through the motions. Do you know how that makes me feel, knowing that your mind was somewhere else, *with* someone else?"

"Hold it right there," he gently interrupted, pulling her into his arms despite her weak resistance.

He was now glad the cloak of night hid her eyes. He was certain neither of them would've been this honest with each other under the revealing glare of daylight.

"I'll tell you where my mind was when I made love to you," he began, stroking her head. "It was right there in the bedroom, hoping and praying I was pleasing you. It was telling me that you deserved more than me, you deserved someone who got as lost in the passion as you do. When we made love, I won't deny how good it felt, physically. But when I saw the love in your eyes, I hated myself for not loving you the same way. You don't know how many times I wanted to run from the room, ashamed. But I needed to keep up the pretense of being straight."

His voice trailed off as he held her tight, his body stiff with the struggle to hold on to the last thread of control. He would not give himself over to the pain in his gut.

With each measured breath he took, he felt her breasts against his chest and wished the sensation could arouse him, if only to prove to her that she was sexually attractive. It was bad enough he had destroyed their marriage. He didn't wish to destroy her too. He loved her too much for that. The problem was, he just couldn't love her enough.

~

"I wish…" Megan paused, fighting the warring emotions of resentment and forgiveness, bitterness and compassion.

As much as she wanted to despise him, she couldn't. This was a glimmer of the sensitive young man who had once written poetry and discussed Yeats and Emerson with her. Gone was the brusque, aloof Stewart of recent years. This was the Stewart she'd fallen in love with.

"What do you wish?" he asked, cupping his hands around her face and tilting her head back. He lowered his head until his gaze locked with hers.

"I wish I could change you."

"You can't, Meggie." With a sad shake of his head, he pressed his lips to the corner of her mouth. "I'm sorry."

~

SLEEP DIDN'T COME EASILY for Megan. After several episodes with homesick children waking in the dark, unfamiliar bunkhouse, she could only lie awake as her mind wrestled with the divorce proceedings.

How would Jason understand her decision to break up their family if Stewart couldn't be truthful with their son about Maxwell? Maybe Stewart was right about staying together. She had managed to endure the weak excuse of a marriage in recent years, albeit unhappily. Surely she could sacrifice a few more years for Jason's sake. After high school she could leave. Maybe by then, Stewart would be able to tell their son the truth.

She rested her arm over her eyes, trying to block out the absurd idea of sacrificing any more years of her life for a man who was willing, however reluctantly, to fulfill her physical needs while having his own met by his male lover. The thought of sharing Stewart made her stomach reel.

She pressed a balled fist against her abdomen and rolled to her side. How could she even live platonically with Stewart while he continued his liaison with Maxwell? What about her? What about her own sexual needs?

As her mind drifted into that dreamy state between real and imagined, she thought of Sam. His laugh. His smile. His kiss. The sensation of lying naked beneath him was nothing more than an erotic image, yet her body responded with a sweet ache. She squeezed her thighs together, escalating her arousal. Though her body didn't move, she felt her fingernails dig into his back, her legs strapped around his hips, pulling him toward her until her muscles burned with the effort. She held her breath, waiting for that moment of pure pleasure.

Suddenly his voice filled her mind as if it was all around her...

"I can't."

Why, what's wrong?

"If your husband had left you for a woman, I wouldn't have a problem. But he left you for a man, for God's sake. And it makes me wonder what you did to him."

Stewart said it wasn't my fault. There was nothing I could've done to change him. There's nothing wrong with me. Please, Sam. Let me prove it to you.

"I can't make love to you."

Then he was gone.

Still in her dream, Stewart stood over her. "He can't, Megan. He can't do it with you."

More familiar faces appeared around her, looming larger than life. Floating. Circling. Chanting. "He can't. He can't. He can't. He can't..."

Gasping, Megan sat up in bed. Drenched in sweat, she rocked back and forth, stifling the moan straining in her throat.

It was only a nightmare, she reassured herself. And yet the gnawing doubt hovered around her in the dark, like wild wolves circling a dying fire.

Could she really be sure there wasn't some speck of underlying truth to the dream? Stewart had been her first and only lover. She had no idea if she was even the least bit arousing to another man. What if she was completely incompetent with someone other than Stewart?

Covering her face with her hands, she silently prayed that it wasn't true.

~

ALTHOUGH SHE FELT as if she couldn't possibly have fallen asleep, Megan instinctively awoke to the sound of someone attempting to open the latched bunkhouse door. In the pitch-black darkness, she held her breath. A lifetime in the city, as well as marriage to a police officer, had conditioned her to suspect the worst. Remembering her responsibility to the children in her care, she threw her legs over the edge of the bed and grabbed the flashlight from the bedside table.

It's probably only Sam.

But only an emergency would bring him down from the main house in the middle of the night. A faint tapping came from the door as she hurried barefoot across the cold cement.

With one hand on the latch, she whispered only loud enough for the person on the other side to hear. "Sam?"

"No, it's not Sam," snapped a petulant young voice.

"Taylor?" Megan unlocked and yanked open the warped door, then shone the beam of light into the girl's face.

"Je—sus." Taylor threw her hands up to block the glare. "Turn that thing off, will ya?"

Staring at the purple bruises on Taylor's forearms, Megan barely stifled a gasp of shock. Without speaking, she took Taylor by the wrist, escorted her past the sleeping children and into the bathroom, and closed the door. After turning on the light, she turned off the flashlight and set it aside. Under closer scrutiny, the battered sixteen-year-old sat on the toilet lid, her back rigid, refusing to make eye contact.

"What happened?" Megan wet a washcloth and wrung it out

before handing it over. "Let's see if we can get that swelling down."

"What's this *we* shit?" Taylor snatched the rag, then tentatively placed it on her swollen lip, wincing from even that slight amount of pressure. "I can take care of myself. You can go to…bed."

Although she barely knew the tough-talking teenager, Megan didn't think there was a real boyfriend of any kind, at least not one that would do this. "Were you raped?"

With an indignant snort, Taylor rolled her eyes.

Megan reached for the doorknob. "I'm taking you up to see Sam."

"No way. I'm not that bad off."

"Bad enough. Come on."

When Taylor stubbornly refused, Megan left her alone in the bathroom, nursing her wounds. A few minutes later, she returned and told the girl that she'd asked Mario to fetch Sam.

"Why don't you just wake up the whole fuckin' camp?"

"We're going to meet him in his office," she explained, ignoring the mouthy outburst. She snapped the wall switch off and turned on the flashlight. "While we're waiting for him, I'll check the first-aid kit."

Guiding with the narrow beam of light, Megan led the way down the center aisle of the bunkhouse, through the door to the adjoining storage room and finally into the office. While Taylor slumped onto the love seat, Megan searched through the supplies for a chemical cold pack.

Her teaching experience with children had never been higher than sixth grade, which made it difficult for her to deal with Taylor's tough facade. Adolescence was a foreign field to Megan. Fortunately, it wasn't to Sam.

"You really don't have to do this. I'll be fine by myself till Sam gets here."

"I don't mind staying here with you… Here it is." She held up the square blue packet.

"I'm not one of your little kindergartners."

She lobbed the ice pack onto Taylor's lap, effectively warning her that patience had its limits. "*Our* kindergartners. You're there as much as I am when they scrape their knees or get their feelings hurt."

"Just like a real, honest-to-God loving mommy," Taylor muttered, exchanging the damp, lukewarm washcloth for the ice pack. "It's all bullshit."

The sound of hurried footsteps and the creak of the rusty springs on the screen door preceded Sam's entrance. As the two of them turned toward the opening door, Megan watched Taylor's stoic composure vanish. In its place was the face of a frightened child waiting expectantly for her knight in shining armor to slay the dragons that haunted her.

His hand still on the doorknob, Sam glanced first at Megan, then down at Taylor with the ice pack held to her mouth.

"I charge extra for late-night office visits." One corner of his mouth was tipped up in a crooked smile on his otherwise grim expression. Taking a seat next to Taylor, he lowered the ice pack for his own inspection.

"Aw, Sam," she groaned, her voice cracking. "I really blew it this time."

He stroked her blonde hair and glanced up at Megan who could only lift her shoulders in bewilderment and shake her head.

"C'mon, spill it. Must've been pretty bad to bring you back here in the middle of the night. How *did* you get here, anyway?" He hastily added, "Scratch that. I don't think I want to know."

"I hitched a ride."

From the pained expression on his face, that wasn't what he'd wanted to hear. "Thank God you didn't hook up with some serial killer," he half joked.

"I wish I would have. I wish I was dead right now. Then they'd *all* be sorry, wouldn't they?"

"Who?" he asked as she broke into sobs. "Who did this to you, Taylor?"

She collapsed into his arms, burying her face in his shoulder.

He tried again. "Were you raped? You said *they*—was it more than one?"

She shook her head, continuing to cry. He held her, rubbing her back and rocking her.

"I want to help you but you've got to tell me what's going on. We've got to get the guy who did this to you."

"Not while *she's* here," she mumbled into his neck.

Sam gave Megan an apologetic look, saying to Taylor, "She's okay—"

"No! I'll tell you but not *her* too."

"All right, all right."

Megan offered, "If you need anything, I'll be in my bunk."

AFTER SHE LEFT, Taylor opened up. "I-I wasn't raped. I wanted it. We…did it…in my bedroom… But my mom found out. She started screaming and hitting me… She threw me out. I can't go back, Sam. Ever."

"Why?" He couldn't believe Nicole Bradley would do such a thing, but Taylor didn't sound like she was lying.

Sobbing and stumbling over her words, she poured out the whole story.

"But it wasn't what she thinks, Sam. I didn't do it for money. I know I let everybody think I screw around but I don't. It was my first time. And I never thought he was gonna give me money for it."

"Did you tell all this to Nicole?"

"I tried, but she wouldn't listen. Her old boyfriend even said he'd slept with me and paid for an abortion. But it's all a lie. How come she believes him and not me? She's supposed to believe *me*, Sam! I'm her daughter."

"Shh, it's okay. We'll work this out. I promise." He stroked her hair, allowing her to cry until she couldn't cry anymore. When she seemed calmer, he asked, "Was the boy someone you already knew? A boyfriend?"

She shook her head. "He was the best man."

Sam concealed his own shock. "Then I take it he wasn't your age."

"Hardly. He's twenty-nine. He works for my mom's latest boyfriend, Bernie, as one of the talent agents for rock groups and singers."

After hearing her sketchy details of the events leading up to the fight with Nicole, Sam managed to put together a pretty clear picture of statutory rape. While she blamed herself for being naive, Sam blamed the lowlife agent, though he sensed there was more to it.

Sitting on the sunken cushions, Sam left one arm around her shoulders and dropped the other arm across his knees, rubbing his thumb and index finger together. "Taylor...I need to ask... Did he use protection?"

She dropped her gaze to her lap.

His own disbelief and anger threatened to erupt, but he kept a tight grip, holding it just beneath the surface. "What about you? Any birth control?"

Silence.

Sam swallowed a curse and maintained a calm exterior. "Could you have gotten pregnant?"

"I-I don't know. My, uh...my periods aren't real regular."

Lowering his head, he closed his eyes and pinched the bridge of his nose, contemplating his next step. After a long silence, he twisted his neck just enough to eye her. "We've got to get you lined up for some tests, kid. But not until we talk to your mom—"

She interrupted. "Uh-uh. No way. She'll beat the shit out of me again."

"And your dad."

"Oh, God, no! I can't, Sam. He *would* kill me."

"Look, they'll *both* kill me if I overstep my bounds of authority with you. You're a minor, Taylor. They're your parents. I want to help you but my hands are tied. Unless I have some kind of temporary custody agreement from your parents, I can't act as your guardian. Hell, they could accuse *me* of sleeping with you. And then where would you be? Out on the streets?"

"Oh shit," she groaned, then glanced warily at him.

Giving her a wry smile, he half-heartedly chucked her on the chin. "My sentiments exactly."

CHAPTER 8

The next morning, Megan allowed Taylor to sleep in, and tended to the children, quieting them as they dressed and ushering them out into the sunshine for their walk up the hill to the Rec Hall for breakfast.

"I'll take 'em, Megan," offered Katie, a fifteen-year-old in her first summer as a CA. "Why don't you hitch a ride up with Sam when he comes down to get Mario's boys? It's their turn for a ride up."

No doubt Katie saw the dark circles under Megan's eyes. A little makeup had done nothing to conceal the wear and tear of the sleepless night. She probably looked too exhausted to crawl ten feet, let alone hike the steep dirt road.

"Thanks, Katie." It was not so much the free ride that Megan looked forward to as it was the opportunity to enjoy a little time with her son. "Save me some Raisin Bran."

A few minutes later, Megan stood outside her son's bunkhouse while the boys filed out.

"Hi, Mom!"

His bright smile lifted her spirits until he glanced at the other guys, as if suddenly embarrassed by her presence. As much as she wanted to give him a hug, she restrained herself, wishing she wasn't witnessing the disappearance of the affectionate little boy who used to crawl into her lap.

Instead, she stuffed her hands in the front pockets of her jeans much the same way Jason had just done. "I thought I'd catch a ride with you this morning. Do you mind?"

He shrugged. "Okay by me."

Walking alongside him toward the bench where the kids waited for their ride, she wondered if she had really seen the warmth in his eyes as he looked up at her, or if it had been just her wistful imagination.

"Did you have fun with your dad yesterday?"

"Uh-huh."

"That's some nice new car he bought."

"Yeah. It's real awesome."

"Did you two drive around the whole time?"

"Naw. We stopped a lot of places. Went to Santa Monica Pier and rode the old merry-go-round and the Ferris wheel. We walked around and ate ice cream and stuff."

"He's a pretty good dad, isn't he?" With the sound of the truck approaching, she realized their brief time together was coming to a close.

"Yeah. Except—" Jason paused just as the truck rolled up in front of them. Megan held her hand on the door handle, waiting. "I never did get to show him how good I can ride a horse now. I really wanted to show him."

His disappointment wrapped around her heart. "Maybe next time, sweetheart," she murmured quietly.

Jason's gaze darted toward the other boys clambering into the truck bed, all of them too busy talking and joking around to pay him any attention. When he looked back at her, he seemed so small and vulnerable. Her chest tightened.

Certain no one was watching the two of them, she silently

folded her arms around his skinny shoulders, kissed the top of his head, then gently shoved him toward the tailgate.

He glanced over his shoulder, giving her a little-boy smile that felt like sunshine streaming through a break in the clouds.

She swung open the passenger door of the truck and hopped onto the seat with a burst of energy.

"You're really good with him." Sam shifted the engine into gear and headed up the hill.

"Good enough to gain custody?" she asked impulsively, instantly regretting the invitation into her personal life. "I'm sorry, Sam. That was completely uncalled for. I guess I'm a little tired."

"Hell of a night, wasn't it?"

More than you realize, she wanted to say, recalling her humiliating nightmare before Taylor had shown up unexpectedly. Instead, she stared out the side window at the sagebrush growing wild along the narrow, rutted road.

Pushing the dream to the back of her mind, she went back to the subject of the teenager. "I didn't bother waking her up this morning. I hope you don't mind. Maybe I should have cleared it with you first since you are her boss."

"That's fine. You may as well know that I might be taking over as her temporary guardian for the time being."

"You really *are* her knight in shining armor."

The right tire hit a deep pothole, jostling them. The kids in the back let out a groan as their bottoms bounced on the hard bed of the truck. Through his open window, Sam hollered an apology back to them.

On smoother ground, he risked a curious glance in her direction. "Say again?"

"Last night when you walked in the door, I watched her look at you as if you were Sir Lancelot. She worships you, Sam. She'd probably do anything in the world for you."

"Let's see if she still feels that way when I take over temporary custody of her. She'll probably tell me to go to hell."

"I doubt it… Did you get her to open up?"

"Yeah," he said, shaking his head.

Whether it was a note of disgust or sadness in his voice, she couldn't be sure. Perhaps both, she thought, as he seemed to wrestle with a decision to continue talking.

"I've never betrayed a confidence of one of my kids, but I think you should know about what happened to her at the wedding reception, especially since you're her head counselor and you're around her more than I am."

In the short amount of time before the truck reached the Rec Hall, Sam summed up the events leading to Taylor's return in the middle of the night. Even though she had begged him not to contact her parents, he had phoned Nicole Bradley to let her know that her daughter had made it safely back to the ranch.

Even though she seemed to regret striking Taylor, she had refused to believe her daughter's side of the story. Despite Sam's suggestion, there would be no complaint filed against Anthony Thorndike. Nicole preferred to sweep it under the rug rather than parade her daughter up the steps of a courthouse where news crews would have a field day. Image was everything in Hollywood. Since her only child looked like a slut and acted like a slut, they had a snowball's chance in hell of convincing a judge that the little brat had been raped.

Washing her hands of any further responsibility for Taylor, Nicole told Sam that he'd better get in touch with Taylor's father, Joel, whenever he finally returned to town, though she wasn't sure when that would be.

"I've left a message to get back to me as soon as possible, but Nicole seems to think he won't take Taylor either."

Megan thought it was sadly ironic that she and Stewart were both determined to have custody of Jason while two other parents would discard their own daughter as if she was a defective possession like a broken radio or television.

Sam slowed to a stop, killed the engine and called out his window, "All out, fellas."

The truck jiggled and rocked from the dozen or so boys jumping off the lowered tailgate.

Though neither of them had any good reason to remain in the cab, they didn't move to get out. Instead, Sam stretched his arms out, resting them on top of the steering wheel. Megan sat watching him stare at some unseen point in the distance, knowing the burden that weighed heavily on his shoulders.

He didn't need to ask her to keep any of this information to herself. Just the same, she quietly said, "None of what you've just told me will go any further... But Sam?"

With a slight turn of his head, his troubled gaze settled on her, his eyes now a dark and cloudy shade of blue.

"Be careful with Taylor," she gently warned. "She's an imaginative teenager who might misconstrue your concern for her."

With a pronounced blink, Sam looked at her with confusion, then dawning realization, then a disbelieving shake of his head.

"Just be careful."

~

FROM THE LOOK of Taylor at dinner the next night, Griffin was dying to know what had happened to her. With all her big talk about the wedding reception at her house, he had it pretty well figured out that the "hottest Hollywood party of the decade" didn't go as great as she'd expected.

Still, he couldn't help but feel sorry for her once he got a look at her fat lip and banged-up face. Of course he didn't dare show any pity. So he just kept quiet about it when he worked next to her on the serving line, him dishing out canned corn, her handing out bags of potato chips.

The first kids through the chow line were the youngest ones. Afraid of dumping their food into the dirt, they never looked up and they always kept a death grip on their flimsy paper plates the whole time they walked by. The older campers were completely different—talking and joking with friends they'd only met the day before.

When someone did bother to look directly at Taylor, Griffin noticed they couldn't really see her face anyway. With her blonde hair hanging down like blinders on a horse, she kept her head lowered as if she was staring at something more interesting than the bright yellow bags of potato chips.

"What happened to Taylor?" Jason asked when Griffin finally sat down with a double cheeseburger of his own making. "Derrick says he woke up when he heard my mom and Mario talking real quiet. Something about Taylor. And needing to get Sam. And now today, she didn't even come out for breakfast or lunch or anything."

Griffin knew Jason looked at skipped meals as serious stuff, not yet aware that girls did it all the time.

"So what happened?"

Griffin shrugged. "Dunno."

"Aw, c'mon, Griff. Didn't you hear nothin'? Derrick bet me that you wouldn't tell even if you knew. He says Sam probably told you to keep your mouth shut. But you can tell me, can't you?"

With a half-smile, Griffin bit into the burger and shook his head, not as a form of an answer, but as a gesture of mild amazement that Jason was becoming more and more like the rest of the gang, picking up the way they talked and teased.

And gossiped.

Derrick was right about one thing—if Sam would've said to keep quiet, Griffin would've done exactly that. He'd do anything for Sam.

After a quick swallow, he paused, holding the burger over his plate. "Tell Derrick that Sam didn't tell me to keep my mouth shut. He didn't have to. 'Cuz he didn't tell me anything about what happened to Taylor. That's all there was to it, Jase." Seeing the disappointment in the boy's eyes, Griffin added, "I've never lied to you, so don't let Derrick start putting ideas like that in your head."

From the guilty look on his face, Jason was obviously embarrassed about listening to Derrick.

"Besides," Griffin went on, "friends shouldn't ask friends to blab about other friends. If Taylor had wanted to make a big deal about it, she would've said something already. Since she's not talking to anybody, we don't go butting our noses in where they don't belong. Got it?"

"Got it," Jason mumbled, his dark eyes downcast as he chewed on his thumbnail.

Watching Jason shift uncomfortably in his seat reminded Griffin of the time he'd got caught ditching school in the sixth grade. It wasn't the restriction and extra chores that had bugged him as much as his dad's disappointment in him. He felt real lousy about that. His parents never hit him, never called him names, never yelled or screamed. They always talked things out with him. Facing them when he'd done something stupid or wrong was always the hardest thing he had to do.

He reached over and ruffled Jason's hair like his dad used to. When the boy looked up with a shy, lopsided grin, Griffin had a glimpse of himself at that age. It was weird, in a nice sort of way.

A sharp stab of homesickness hit him unexpectedly. Griffin damned the sudden stinging behind his eyes as he turned back to his unfinished dinner.

Can't a guy miss his folks without getting choked up about it? Pissed off with himself, he sank his teeth into his burger.

But he didn't taste a thing.

~

"GRIFFIN'S HELPING Mario at the archery range right now, Mr. Hughes," Sam explained into the phone after checking his watch.

Something was wrong. Not only could Sam read it in the tired voice on the other end of the line, but also by the timing of the call. It was only Friday. And midmorning, at that. Griffin's weekly call from his folks always came in on Saturday evening without fail.

Sensing the urgency, Sam quickly offered to get the boy, then added, "If you can't stay on the line I'll have him call you back at work—"

"No!" he cut in. "Thanks for offering, but it can wait. I, uh, don't know what I must've been thinking, calling early like this. Should've known he'd be busy. What time's his lunch break? I'll catch him then."

"Twelve thirty. But if this is important—"

"No. Really," the man insisted. "I'd appreciate it if you'd just tell him I'll be calling."

Assuring Mr. Hughes that his message would be passed along to Griffin, Sam said his goodbye and slowly cradled the receiver.

"Go for a walk, Riley?" He levered himself out of the desk chair. Squeezing alongside the dog already positioned at the door, he patted its head and grinned a little, in spite of the lingering concern for Griffin.

There was nothing wrong with the boy's father checking in a day early, he told himself in an effort to shake the uneasy feeling.

Maybe the call was about some good news—like Griffin's family was finally going to make it up for a visit. It'd been six weeks since Griffin had seen his family. That in itself bothered Sam, considering how close the boy was with his parents and kid sister. But they had been having car problems and conflicting work schedules, which couldn't be helped. Still, he hated to see the effect it was having on Griffin. Although not many teenagers would admit missing their family, Sam figured this had to be the reason behind the sullen look in Griffin's eyes lately.

With Riley loping along beside him, Sam rounded the corner of the adobe office and headed down the service road to where it dipped into a wide gully. Down to the left was the isolated rifle range with tin cans staked to the top of a haystack at the far end of the clearing. It was deserted at the moment.

But on the right, beneath a weathered wood shelter that edged the road, a dozen boys sat on benches, facing another narrow clearing. On the other side was the paper target bull's eye for archery. Leaning against one of the posts, Mario kept one eye on them and one on Griffin, who demonstrated a proper stance, grip and shooting technique with the bow and arrow.

Sam hung back so the kids wouldn't be distracted from the archery lesson.

Riley loped a few more feet, stopped and looked back, wagging his tail. Sam shook his head, then pointed to the ground, signaling the dog to return. Instead, Riley flopped down in the dirt, his doleful eyes gazing up. Not sure if the mutt misread the silent command or just chose to ignore it, Sam was satisfied to leave him be so long as he wasn't disturbing anyone.

"Now just let the bowstring slide off these three fingers real slow…" instructed Griffin, drawing Sam's attention. The arrow shot through the air and hit the center of the target. As the raucous boys whooped and hollered, the young CA nodded somewhat modestly.

Allowing the fifteen-year-old to bask in the limelight for a minute, Sam applauded along with the rest of them, then noticed Riley lift his head, his ears picking up on something beyond Sam's range of hearing.

When the boys quieted down, Sam called out. "Griffin, your dad's going to call you at lunch. Make sure you get yourself near a phone, okay?"

The teenager gave Sam a puzzled frown, then shrugged and acknowledged the message with a wave as Riley trotted back toward the office. Sam followed.

From the purposeful manner in which Riley loped toward the screen door, it was a pretty sure thing that the visitor had gone inside.

"Heel, Riley," Sam ordered, still some distance from the porch. Mentally running through his schedule, he couldn't recall anything about a tour or an early pickup of one of the camp kids.

Surprisingly, Riley turned around and fell in step with him. But his command also brought a response from the office as the screen door creaked on its rusty hinges.

"Hello? Someone there?" Sam picked up a trace of accent in the male voice. "Ah, yes. There you are."

Maybe it was gut instinct. Maybe it was the intensive protectiveness he felt toward his kids. But something told him that this guy was the British bastard from Taylor's story.

It isn't. It can't be. No man would have that kind of balls. But all the rational arguments couldn't silence the suspicion.

As the tall blond Englishman quickly closed the space between them and extended his hand in greeting, Sam's own pace slowed.

"Anthony Thorndike here."

It *was* him. The son of a bitch. Sam felt as if a strange and eerie slow motion had overtaken him. Every muscle in his body tensed. His right hand curled into a tight ball until he could feel his fingernails dig into his palm. Even a simple breath took forever to fill his lungs.

"I wonder if you might tell me where I could find Taylor—"

His fist struck the bastard. Knuckles met jawbone. Slightly aware of a muffled crack, Sam didn't know whether he'd broken his own hand or the man's face. And he didn't care.

Still caught in the daze of distorted time, he watched Thorndike stumble back, lose his balance and land hard in the dirt. It was only when Riley stepped forward in a guarded crouch that a sense of normal time and space returned. And only then did he fully realize what he'd done.

"Back, Riley," he commanded with a harshness he hadn't intended, but which prompted immediate obedience. Returning to Sam's side, the dog sat on his haunches.

Sam cradled his right hand, carefully flexing his fingers. Nothing that an ice pack couldn't fix, he assured himself, wondering if the same could be said about the man's jaw.

Battling against sudden guilt, Sam glared down at him.

The bastard had it coming.

Unlike Taylor, Thorndike had gotten off lucky. Memories of her battered face refused to let him feel remorse over one single punch.

Thorndike gingerly rubbed his jaw, then moved it back and forth a bit, checking for damage as cautiously as Sam had with his own hand. Apparently satisfied that no major harm had been done, he slowly gathered his feet under him and faced Sam from a safe distance.

"I dare say you've got yourself one hell of a poker face, ol' boy. I never saw that one coming," he admitted with a sheepish lift of his eyebrows. "Might I add that I've never deserved it more."

The confession took Sam by surprise, but he hid it well.

"I am grateful"—Thorndike batted the dust from his slacks, then his suit jacket—"that you exercised restraint."

"Too bad Taylor couldn't say the same about you."

His ominous tone brought Riley to his feet and a low growl to his throat, which Sam silenced with a touch to its head.

The Englishman nodded toward the dog as it sat back down. "It seems Taylor has more than one avenging angel on her side."

"It *seems* you don't know when to walk away from trouble."

"If you are referring to last Sunday—"

"I'm talking about now."

"See here, Mister…Kempton, is it?" He took one step forward, glanced at the dog, saw it wasn't a wise idea and retreated. "I honestly don't wish to cause any further problems for Taylor. In fact, I came here today to personally apologize about the entire ordeal. It was a terrible misunderstanding…on both our parts, you see. Girls that age are so easily—"

"Manipulated?"

"That is hardly the word I would have chosen."

"No? How about *molested*? Or better still—*raped*."

"I beg your pardon? I'm afraid you've been dreadfully misinformed. She as much as begged for it—" He stopped himself, then looked away for a long moment, obviously struggling to regain his composure before turning back to Sam. "Clearly, this is a matter of poor communication between Taylor and myself. You must agree that it would be best for all concerned if I make my apologies."

Sam knew the kids would soon be switching activities. Taylor might come walking by any minute. And then what would happen? His first priority was to protect her.

Something told him that there was more to this grand gesture of Thorndike's than just an apology, which could have been done with a phone call or letter. Sam didn't like the idea of this guy showing up here to see Taylor. Whatever the reason, he sensed it was going to stir up a fistful of trouble.

"It would be best for all concerned," Sam repeated as he moved closer to the Englishman, "if you get back in your car right now and get the hell off my ranch."

~

WITH TWO LITTLE girls at each side, Taylor walked up the road, holding their hands and talking quietly about their favorite bunnies. Together, they led the rest of Megan's group of five- and six-year-olds toward their cabin for a potty break before the next activity.

Tugging on Taylor's right arm, Kelsey pointed at a black Porsche at the top of the hill. "Somebody's here! Can we see who it is? Huh, can we?"

Taylor smiled down at the little redhead in pigtails who was always asking questions. She'd never seen a kid so totally excited about everything, sometimes wanting to know stuff that even Taylor wasn't smart enough to explain. If Kelsey wasn't lifting up rocks to look under them, she was sticking her nose in everybody's face and expecting answers to real embarrassing questions, like, "How come your chest is so big?" Good thing the kid was only six, otherwise she might have been tied up and gagged with a sock, which was something Taylor would never do, of course. She adored her little kindergarteners, especially this Kelsey.

Taylor stopped dead when she saw who was talking to Sam.

Anthony?

She didn't want to know why he was here. She didn't want to ask. She only wanted the ground to open up and swallow her right where she stood. The only thing in her body she could feel was her heart slamming against her ribs. The frightening numbness spread. To her legs, her hands, her arms, her chest. Then her eyes played tricks on her, making the images of the two men look all wavy and out of focus.

Oh, shit...don't pass out. Don't pass out. Don't pass out.

Squinting, her gaze darted from Sam to Anthony before she realized they were watching her.

The other five-year-old at her side tugged on Taylor's hand, dancing and holding the crotch of her shorts. "I gotta go to the bathroom."

"Sorry, Jen. I was just catching my breath," she lied, forcing a smile she hoped didn't look bogus.

Grateful for the distraction, she willed her feet to move, somewhat surprised when they did. Just a few more feet to their cabin and—

"Taylor!" Anthony called out.

Her steps faltered. Her fingers tightened their grip around two little hands. Staring at the ground, she refused to look up.

"She's busy," Sam said in a low voice that meant he was dead serious. Taylor didn't dare look back, but imagined him blocking Anthony's path.

"I need only a few moments of her time, that's all I ask."

"I don't think so," Sam answered with tight politeness. "You see, Megan over there is in charge of this group. And she'd skin me alive if I let her assistant take off whenever some guy showed up looking for Taylor. Isn't that right, Megan?"

Taylor heard the senior counselor clear her throat. "Yes… right. I can't possibly handle these kids alone for even a second."

"That's what I figured." Sam added, "Why don't you and Taylor take the children to their next activity while I walk Mr. Thorndike to his car."

"I refuse to leave until I have a word with Taylor. She deserves an apology from me and I intend to give her one." His voice grew louder. "Hit me again if you like, but I'm *not* leaving."

HIT him? AGAIN? Taylor spun around.

Anthony tried to get past Sam, but Sam stepped back in front of him. Her quick glimpse of Anthony's face was enough to see the red mark just below his cheek. The idea of Sam hitting anybody was brain-blowing, but the proof was right there.

Her eyes caught the movement of Sam's fists clenching at his sides. Still feeling battered and bruised from her mother's attack, she wanted the satisfaction of Anthony getting a beating. But she never imagined Sam doing it. And not here. Not now. No matter how much she hated Anthony, she was scared what might happen to Sam. He could get hurt. And the camp kids would see it all! Then what? Would Sam be arrested? Would he lose the camp?

"Sam! Don't!" Breaking away from the kids, she ran up to him and grabbed his arm.

"I wasn't going to hit him," he assured her. Even though he still sounded pissed off enough to do it, she reluctantly dropped her hands. "Now stay out of this. Please."

"Taylor…"Anthony's voice was so soft and apologetic.

The sad look in his eyes made her think of all the times she'd done something really stupid and regretted it later. Maybe he wasn't such a total SOB after all. If he was, would he have come looking for her like this? He could've just forgotten all about her. But he didn't. He was here, looking at her like a little kid in big trouble.

"I only wanted to tell you I'm truly sorry—"

Sam cut him off. "Shut up, Thorndike."

"Stop it, both of you," she snapped in a loud whisper, then pleaded with Sam. "Let him say what he has to say. It won't hurt anything if we just talk. Please, Sam."

Waiting for his answer, she held her breath as he looked at Anthony. The muscles along Sam's jaw twitched. His eyes were narrowed. But when he turned back to her, his face softened and he sighed, shaking his head.

"Five minutes." He held up his five fingers, then turned his attention to Megan. "Go on ahead. She'll catch up."

Following a nod, Megan rounded up the children and led them into the cabin for the bathroom break before taking them to the next activity.

Taylor saw Mario and Griffin approaching with their group of boys.

"Sam…" she groaned, "do we have to stand out here where everybody can walk by and stare at us?"

Another cluster of kids was coming toward them from the tennis courts. Soon, the road around the adobe would be a swarm of noisy kids, passing each other and adding to the organized confusion.

"You can use my office," he offered reluctantly, "but I'll be right outside the door."

CHAPTER 9

Without another word, Taylor led the way into the office, walking fast enough to stay one step ahead of Anthony.

Inside, she flipped on the overhead light and moved as far into the room as she could. Hearing the door close and the shuffle of Anthony's shoes on the cement floor, she realized they were finally alone.

Her empty stomach grumbled, complaining more from nervous butterflies than from hunger. She wrapped her arms tight across her belly, trying to block out the sound.

"Is it a bit too chilly in here for you?" His sexy English accent sounded gentle and caring. "If you'd rather, I'll leave the door open."

"No. That's okay," she answered over her shoulder, still not brave enough to face him. She wished he'd just say he was sorry and get it over with.

"Oh, Taylor-luv."

The tender but unhappy way he said her name made her melt inside. But she couldn't let down her guard. She couldn't let him see this reaction she had to him.

"I was such a fool. Such a complete and utter fool." His words seemed to drift across the room, touching the back of her neck and sliding down her spine. "I can't begin to tell you how enchanting you are to me. Like my wildest dream come true."

Even while her mind warned her about getting burned again, her head slowly turned to one side, waiting to hear more, *wanting* to hear more.

"I'm certain you were aware that my, ah, performance was embarrassingly brief. Quite humiliating, actually. You must believe me when I say that I was overwhelmed when I learned—too late, I might add—that you were still a virgin. But when you insisted I continue, I couldn't resist you. You were so incredibly beautiful that I seem to have lost all control. Ah, Taylor, my pet… I had fully intended upon making your first experience a wonderful one."

His hand touched her bare arm. Its warmth spread through her until a fire started to burn down deep inside. As he spoke softly in her ear, the heat of his breath drifted down her neck.

"I was so horrified with myself for cheating you of that tender moment. I had assumed you'd be angry at me. Instead, you looked so confused, as if you'd blamed yourself for my own ineptness. I should never have left you feeling that way. But I'd allowed my blasted male pride to interfere by simply getting up and getting dressed."

When his lips brushed a kiss below her ear, her mind clouded with warring feelings.

Stop…

No, don't stop.

She whispered, "Go on."

"Standing there in your bedroom that afternoon, I had decided that I would rather you hate *me* than yourself." He slid his other hand along her left arm, then drew her against him. The pad of his thumb caressed her skin. "So I decided to act like a bastard."

"And you did, you know." Taylor was surprised at how out of breath she sounded.

"Oh, God, how I know it. And I *am* sorry, luv..." He nuzzled her neck again. "Especially about the money. I never meant for it to appear as though I paid you for sex. On the contrary, I meant it as an apology for mucking up everything."

"I should call you a liar."

"You should." He turned her around in his arms. "I deserve to be called that and more. But right now, at this very moment, I'm telling you the God's honest truth. I'm miserable without you. Considering the difference in our ages, I know it's wrong to be feeling the way I do. But if you'll find it in your heart to forgive me, I'll do anything...*anything* to make it up to you."

She gently touched the reddening mark on his cheek, then reached up and fingered his neatly clipped hair.

He really likes me.

No, he's messing with you.

Uncertainty swirled around her head like buzzing flies. She bit down lightly on her lower lip as she stared into his eyes.

He was so intensely gorgeous. Just looking at him made her insides get all hot and bothered.

We just got off to a bad start, that's all.

His sorry expression turned hopeful. "At the very least, I can see that you're no longer angry."

She loved watching the movement of his lips as he talked. The faint scent of mint on his breath brought back the delicious memory of his toe-curling kisses, making her wish he'd give her one right here, right now.

"I'm deeply grateful that you've allowed me to get this confession off my chest."

All she could manage was an insignificant nod.

The corners of his mouth tilted up ever so slightly. "Ah, that's my pet."

From inside his jacket he brought out a gray business card

and tucked it into the front pocket of her snug jeans. His fingers slid just the tiniest bit deeper, then slowly withdrew, sending a thrill to the depths of her belly.

While her knees nearly gave out on her, he rested his hands at her waist. "Don't lose that card now, promise? Ring me any time you want. Even if it's just for a chat."

She nodded numbly.

As he pressed his lips against her forehead, she closed her eyes, waiting for his next kiss to be on her mouth. Feeling the warmth of his palms through her shirt made her imagine his hands slipping under the material and—

"Time's up!" bellowed Sam from outside the door.

Taylor jumped back as if fireworks had exploded between them. "Okay, okay," she answered loudly.

Nothing ever worked out right for her. Nothing. In another minute Anthony would've kissed her for sure.

Watching him turn to leave, she felt panic spread through her. What if he thought she didn't forgive him? What if she'd acted too cool, too indifferent? Maybe he'd figure she didn't want him to bother her anymore.

When his hand turned the doorknob, she tried to keep her tone as casual as possible. "If things work out with my dad, I might be moving in with him after camp's over. He's got a pretty busy schedule—gone most of the time. And I'll have two whole weeks before school starts. So…if I get bored…maybe I'll pick up the phone."

"Splendid!" He grinned and her insides melted.

"No promises."

"None expected." His gaze lingered on her for a long moment. She wished it could go on forever. "Later, then?"

"Yeah. Later."

He opened the door and left.

～

SAM WATCHED Anthony Thorndike pass by. From the pleased look and silent nod, the Englishman was apparently satisfied with the way things went with Taylor. And that bugged the hell out of Sam. What he really wanted was for the bastard to come out with his butt dragging after Taylor knocked him down a few pegs. And he knew she could've done it. If she'd wanted to.

Rather than making sure Thorndike was on his way, Sam entered the office to see how Taylor was holding up. But the empty adobe told him she'd slipped out through the connecting door to her bunkhouse. Disappointed that she hadn't stuck around long enough to talk to him, Sam wondered if she was simply avoiding him, or if she was in the other room crying into her pillow.

Like it or not, he had to admit that his new role as her guardian had changed his relationship with Taylor. But not in the way Megan had warned him about. Before, he'd been a friend and advisor. Now, for the time being anyway, he was the parent.

The enemy.

~

ALL MORNING, Griffin dreaded the phone call. It wasn't going to be good news, he knew that much. Things just hadn't been going too good for his mom and dad for a long while. They said that it'd be okay, that their luck was going to change. But when Sam came down to tell him to expect a call at lunch, Griff saw that look in his eyes, the one he always got when he was worried. Even the smile couldn't hide it.

Now Griff held the receiver to his ear, both elbows resting on Sam's desk.

I won't cry, he promised himself as he pressed the butt of his palm against the bridge of his nose.

"I'm sorry you've gotta hear it this way. Maybe we should've told you before now, but I was really hoping that loan would come through at the last minute. Besides, there wasn't anything you could do anyway. Except worry."

"But it's our home, Dad. How can those people just kick you out of our home? What are you going to do? Where are you guys going to go?"

"Calm down, Griffin. Things will work themselves out, I promise."

Yeah, right. Just like he'd promised we'd always have a roof over our heads no matter how bad things got? Even though he didn't express his anger out loud to his dad, it almost felt good to be something other than scared. He wasn't really pissed off at his father, anyway, but at the hard times that seemed to be swallowing his family like a flesh-eating alien.

"I want to come home," he said with more control than he felt.

"No. Your mother and I agree you should stay up there. Keep your job."

"I could get Sam to give me a couple days off." He quickly added, "I can't just sit up here while you and Mom and Annie are down there going through all this. At least let me come home long enough to pack up my stuff."

"That's already been taken care of. Some fellas from work helped us move everything into George's garage. He says we can leave it there for as long as we need. But I told him we ought to be able to find something in a few months—just as soon as I have enough saved up for a first and last month's rent. Then there's the security deposit and cleaning fees."

"Are you saying the house is already empty?" Griffin couldn't even imagine not going back to his own bedroom with all his favorite things on the walls and shelves.

His dad sounded real tired. "Today's our last day here, Griff. I'm sorry. Like I was saying, I would've told you—"

"Please, Dad... Let me come home—" He faltered, realizing he didn't have a place to go home to anymore. "You don't have to come get me. I'll get down there on my own. Just tell me where I can find you."

"I don't know yet."

"But I gotta know where you're gonna be." Trying to keep the panic from his voice, he imagined this call being his last connection to his family. "What if something happens to you and nobody would know how to get a hold of me? What if you just disappeared?"

"Now take it easy." His dad paused, then let out a long sigh. "Okay, look here—tell Sam I'll call tomorrow night to talk to him about letting you come down for a day. Maybe you could cash your paycheck and hop a bus or something."

"Suppose he asks me why?"

"You can say it's Mom's birthday…and, uh…I want you to join us at some restaurant as a surprise… But I can't come get you or your mom might figure out that something's up. You got that?"

"Yeah."

"Now say it back to me so I know we won't trip each other up when I talk to Sam tomorrow."

Griffin repeated the story, mildly amazed at how easily his father pieced together one long stream of lies. Always admiring his dad's straightforward truthfulness, he wondered if this was how it was going to be from now on—little lies to cover up their shame. Would they ever go back to the way they were?

After he finished, his dad praised him. "Good. Real good. Okay, we're all set. I'll talk to you tomorrow, about seven thirty."

"Dad?"

He wanted to tell him he loved him but the words didn't come out as easy as when he was little. Back when his dad would come home from work carrying the same beat-up gray metal lunch box, Griffin would run down the walk to meet him, slamming into his dad's legs. His mom would come out about then and wait there on the porch, holding his baby sister in her arms.

The whole scene played back in his mind just like one of those sappy old movies. But no matter how lame it might seem to any other teenager, right now he'd give a million bucks to be able to go home and see his mom standing on that same porch with her arm around eight-year-old Annie.

His dad finally broke the awkward silence between them. "Mom and Annie send their love." He cleared his throat, then added, "Me too."

"Yeah. Same here. Talk to ya later."

Griffin hung up the phone and leaned back the same way he'd seen Sam do a hundred times, listening to the rusty spring creak in the otherwise quiet office.

Sitting there with his hands folded over his dusty white staff shirt, he might've looked as laid-back as Sam always managed to look, but he was a wreck inside. Unable to imagine Sam ever feeling this miserable, Griffin wished he could sit there surrounded by all Sam's stuff and soak in all his strength and confidence. Certainly his boss had enough to share.

Dream on, kid, scoffed a little voice inside as his stomach growled for its lunch.

"You in there, Griff?"

"Yeah, Jase." Embarrassed to be seen mimicking Sam, he jumped to his feet before the boy swung open the screen door.

~

JASON KICKED a dirt clod as he hiked up the hill beside Griffin. Sweat was pouring down his back but he didn't complain. Hearing about Griff's problems made him feel like he didn't have any right to whine about the hot weather.

After all, he wasn't the one wondering where he was going to end up when summer camp was over. He had that humongous house to go home to, with its three stories and rooftop Jacuzzi. Except for his dad's writing office and the guest room, the second floor was like his very own apartment with his bedroom, bathroom, game room and family room that had a mini-kitchen in the corner.

A whole family could live up there and you'd hardly notice, Jason realized, wishing he could talk his parents into letting Griffin's family move in for a while. Mr. and Mrs. Hughes could have his room and he could sleep in the guest room, which would make his mom move back in with his dad, which would be cool. And the game room would be great for Griff and his sister. Jason figured his own parents could use the living room on the first floor when their friends came over.

The best part of all would be having Griffin around all the time, just like a real big brother. And his parents wouldn't have to call anybody to babysit anymore. But even as he imagined the perfect solution to his best friend's problem, Jason knew he'd never be able to pull it off. Not without breaking his promise to Griff about keeping quiet.

Still, there had to be some way he could help Griffin.

LINGERING OVER COFFEE, Megan turned from her after-dinner conversation at the table as the children filed into the Rec Hall for the nightly songs and games. When her son slid in next to her rather than dog behind his CA, Megan offered him an appreciative smile. He sheepishly returned it.

She leaned a bit closer. "To what do I owe the pleasure of your company?"

Rolling his eyes in that boyish way of his, he reminded her of Stewart a long time ago when such innocent expressions could melt her heart. All too soon, her son would be turning that same charm on some unsuspecting teenage girl instead of his mother.

"I was wondering if there's any chance we could, like, go home on Sunday. Just for the day."

Puzzled by this sudden and unexpected request, Megan

chuckled in disbelief. "What? Don't tell me you're getting bored up here?"

"Nuh-uh. It's just…"

He lifted one shoulder and let it drop, his usual gesture to appear indifferent when in fact he had something eating at him inside. Like his father, he still exhibited certain behaviors that couldn't get past Megan, though those moments had become less and less frequent lately. For him to admit that he missed his own room and other familiar surroundings would be asking too much.

Taking him off the hook, Megan admitted, "It sure would be nice to get out of this heat for a while. Besides, I have this craving for a burger at the Hangout."

"Do you mean it, Mom? We can go?"

Resisting the urge to stroke his hair, she agreed to take the Sunday drive down the coast route to Long Beach, but only if she could get another counselor to take her five-year-olds. And then only if Sam would agree to those arrangements. Switching her day off with Karen was easy enough, especially since they were in the middle of a session. Had it been a week earlier or later, the arrival of a new group of kids would not have allowed such an impulsive trip back home.

Approaching Sam with the request might not be an easy task, however. After his run-in with Anthony Thorndike earlier that morning, his mood was downright surly. It didn't help matters knowing she'd warned him earlier about getting too involved with Taylor's problems. Considering his breach of conduct when he'd slugged Thorndike, he probably wouldn't welcome a private conversation with Megan, afraid she'd come to say "I told you so."

Later, as he dismissed the kids for the evening, she saw her chance to catch him for a minute. Working her way back through the sea of small bodies flowing toward the door, she instructed her little ones to wait on the couches with Taylor for a few minutes.

Satisfied they weren't going to take off without her, she looked across the room for Sam only to find Griffin had already stopped him. From the solemn expression on the teenager's face, she sensed another problem loomed ahead for Sam to deal with.

The man was forever slaying dragons, she thought in mild wonderment. Did he ever tire of being everyone's hero?

Not *everyone's* hero, she corrected herself, determined to solve her own problems and keep his status with her on the level of mere mortal.

She watched his head nod, then an encouraging smile break across his face. Whatever the concern, it appeared he'd resolved it easy enough, especially when he reached up and gave the CA's shoulder a reassuring squeeze.

"Thanks a lot, Sam," the boy said, then glanced nervously at Megan as he passed her on his way out.

She paused for a moment and watched him leave, then turned to see Sam's eyes on her. Unable to read him like Jason, she couldn't be certain if his guarded look was meant for her or Griffin.

She approached him. "I need to ask a favor."

"Seems to be the night for those."

His dark mood almost assured the futility of her request, but she tried appealing to his soft spot for kids, which seemed to be the best strategy.

"Jason asked if I could take him home for a few hours on Sunday. I guess he's finally getting homesick after all these weeks. To tell you the truth, I was wondering if he'd ever talk about going home again. He's so stuck on this place."

"I think Griffin has something to do with it."

$\sim$

SAM GUESSED that the sharp young boy might have picked up on his CA's troubles. The teenager and the ten-year-old were tight, no doubt about that. There was a good chance the two had talked about the surprise birthday party Griff wanted to attend. And the fact that the teen would have to find transportation. Why else would Jason suddenly become homesick and beg his mom to take him to Long Beach on the same day? It seemed to be too much of a coincidence to ring true.

"Yes, Griffin's a big reason why Jason loves it here," Megan agreed. "But so are you. Not to mention that dog of yours. He loves Riley."

"I'm flattered, but I wasn't talking about Griffin's influence in quite that way."

Puzzling over the odd bent to their conversation, Sam wondered how he could be so damned attracted to this woman when they couldn't even stay on the same wavelength. Hell, he had a hard enough time keeping his own mind on track when he stared into those eyes of hers, let alone following her train of thought as well.

After updating her on the teenager, he added, "My bet is Griffin's need for a ride to Long Beach is behind Jason's sudden need to go home on Sunday."

"He's beginning to sound a lot like one of your protégés—'All for one and one for all.'"

"That bad, huh?"

"That good, I suppose."

"Try to sound a bit more convincing," he said with a note of sarcasm after hearing her own dubious tone.

"Do I sound otherwise?"

"I think you don't like the idea of Jason helping out a friend." His pointed remark hit a nerve, forcing her to look away, her dark eyes narrowing.

Turning back to him, she kept her voice low. "Just because I warned you to be careful with Taylor doesn't mean I'm against the whole concept of human kindness."

"Then you'll drop Griffin off?"

"Wh—" She stopped in mid-thought, her lips slightly parted. Sam felt his own mouth go dry. Damned if his brain didn't zero in on her sexuality at the most inopportune times. She recovered quickly with a resigned shake of her head and a softening smile. "I guess there's no shame to be outmaneuvered by the best."

"Dealing with teenagers taught me to be ruthless," he answered, enjoying the humor in her husky voice.

She knew how to give and take, when to fight and when to concede. Or so it seemed. Admittedly, he had an unfair advantage as her boss. Would she be as acquiescent if the line between them wasn't so strictly drawn? God, how he wished he could rid himself of this self-imposed barrier with her.

But that was the paradox—having her near meant keeping her at arm's length.

THE FIRST SUNDAY in August drew the usual weekend crowds to the beach as well as the usual road congestion in the late afternoon. But by the time Griffin was picked up at the restaurant where he'd been dropped off earlier in the day, the traffic wasn't too bad on the 405 going north, or on the 10 going west.

Griffin sat in the back seat of the Lexus, occasionally catching bits of conversation between Jason and his mom. Once in a while one of them would ask him a question, like if his mom enjoyed her surprise birthday party. Except for a polite response, he didn't feel much like lying any more than he'd already had to.

Instead, he stared out the window in air-conditioned comfort, aware of the expensive soft leather around him. Here he was, sitting in this car that was worth forty or fifty grand, while his real life was waiting for him in West Long Beach. He couldn't enjoy the luxury. He could only think about the past several hours he'd spent with his family—

Griffin had said he was supposed to meet them inside the

fancy restaurant. To his relief, the bogus explanation had worked. If Megan had made a major deal about meeting his folks, he would've been busted for sure. Instead of meeting him inside, they had really planned to pick him up in the alley around back. He'd gone inside, told the hostess he was joining his party, pointing to a nice big family sitting by the kitchen. Then he'd walked right by them and straight on through the kitchen and out their back door.

As soon as he'd spotted the van, his mom had hopped out and hugged him, sniffling back tears. He still wasn't real sure whether she was happy or sad. Annie got into it too, wrapping her scrawny little arms around his waist. Afterward, he'd stepped over to his dad and stuck out his hand for a man-to-man handshake. But that only lasted about a second. His dad used his strong grip to haul him into his arms. Although Griffin had pretended to be embarrassed, it actually felt pretty great.

In fact, the whole day was great. They drove the short distance to Alamitos Bay and spent the rest of the morning and afternoon no differently than any other family on a Sunday trip to the beach. For a while anyway, they had all pretended everything was perfectly fine. Only at the end of their time together did the four of them talk about their crappy situation.

Even though his parents had assured him they had enough money to stay in a motel for a few weeks, Griffin had felt better when they'd accepted the money he'd earned at the ranch. At least it might help buy them a little more time. By then, he'd be back with them.

Griffin was glad to have his thoughts dragged away from his worries when Jason pointed out a hot-looking sports car cruising by them. He remembered how he used to get just as stoked as Jason about the same sort of things. It wasn't all that long ago. The first of summer, as a matter of fact. Might as well have been twenty years. That's how much he felt he'd aged since then, especially since Friday when his dad had called.

They passed through the tunnel at the end of the Santa Monica Freeway and started north on PCH. Although the sun had gone down, a few diehards on the beach played volleyball in the dwindling light. There were several joggers too.

And the homeless.

Some were more noticeable than others, like the ones pushing grocery carts with all their belongings, and the ones wearing layers of mismatched clothes no matter how hot the temperature.

On the road ahead Griffin noticed an old minivan pull off the highway and into a deserted parking lot along the beach, where it parked behind a closed-up hamburger stand. A man and a woman and two little kids got out and started picking through the trash bin.

As the Lexus passed, Griffin craned his neck, staring at all the stuff in the back of their car. It looked like all their worldly belongings were stashed in there. The sight made him feel sick, knowing his own family might be doing the very same thing some day soon. He couldn't stand the thought of sinking so low that he'd have to eat somebody else's leftover sandwich.

He turned his face away from the tinted glass window, hoping and praying that his situation would never get that bad.

CHAPTER 10

The last summer session passed with daily activities continuing in the same easygoing routine developed throughout the summer months. After the final group of camp kids departed, the staff packed up their own belongings. Some were eager to get back to their homes. A few were in no hurry at all, choosing to take their time with goodbyes. Nearly everyone would be returning the following week to spruce up the camp with a fresh coat of paint for the weekend sessions scheduled to begin after Labor Day.

Within a few hours, however, all but Megan were on their way, paychecks in hand.

"Hey, sport," Sam called out as he emerged from the office to find Jason wrestling a stick out of Riley's mouth. "Aren't you supposed to be helping your mom load the car instead of running my dog ragged?"

Jason kept playing tug-of-war with Riley, answering between grunts, "She's…still packing…her stuff."

The dog growled playfully, inching backward, gaining ground.

"What's taking her so long?" Sam glanced over his shoulder toward her cabin. "Everybody else is long gone."

"She's making sure everything's cleaned up." His concentration was momentarily diverted as he freed the stick and heaved it down the road. Watching Riley bound after it, he beamed with satisfaction, then turned back to Sam. "She even went through *my* cabin before the other guys left, getting after them to pick through all the clothes and junk."

Sam cocked an eyebrow. "Where was Mario during all this?"

"He was jus' standing there letting her do it. He says she could get work outta us boys he could never get us to do." Suddenly Jason looked guilty as hell, his eyes large. "I mean, uh…Mario's real good at being our counselor. He was just joking around is all."

"Don't worry. I'm not going to get on his case."

Obvious relief washed over the young boy's features. Amazing how much he took after Megan, not only with his facial expressions but also with his smooth olive skin and long dark lashes. He was almost too pretty for his own good.

Riley trotted up and dropped the stick at Sam's feet, taking his mind off his thoughts.

Sam shook his head. "Don't look at me with those pleading eyes. You got into this game with Jason, remember?"

The canine's mouth opened into a panting smile, eliciting a giggle from the boy.

Sam gave in, took the stick and hurled it considerably farther than Jason's throw. "Maybe I'll see if I can hurry your mom up. I bet you're eager to get home."

"Uh…yeah, right."

The odd hesitancy bothered Sam. He'd known kids to get attached to the ranch but not one so reluctant to leave, especially after a long summer. Usually they were more than happy to get back home again.

"Got any plans for your last two weeks of freedom before school starts?"

"I'll probably just hang around the dumb ol' house."

Shading his eyes with one hand, Sam kept his eyes on Riley nosing through the bushes. "Doesn't sound like much fun. Living at the beach like you do, there must be plenty of stuff to do down there—swimming, riding bikes..."

"Naples isn't exactly on the beach. It's just a little island on the bay with canals around it and really tiny streets. Cameron says the only real cool beaches are where everybody surfs and stuff."

Sam glanced down at the boy whose hands were stuffed into his back pockets while he rocked back and forth on the soles of his shoes. Despite the boy's physical resemblance to Megan, Sam could've been looking back nearly forty years into a mirror of himself. But that wasn't so unusual. He saw a little bit of himself in every kid who came through here. Some said that was the secret of his success. Every child was special to him. Jason Fisher was no exception.

"Is Cameron a buddy of yours back in Long Beach?" Sam asked.

Jason paused before he answered, "He's Melissa's brother. She's my *babysitter*." He wrinkled his nose as if the mention of the word *baby* left an awful taste in his mouth.

"Too old for a sitter, huh?" It was more a statement than a question, to which Jason simply nodded. "And I suppose your friends get to stay home alone when their parents are gone."

"No, but it's not the same as me. They got littler kids in their house that need a babysitter. Or else they got a big brother or sister who stays with them. I just wish—" He suddenly pointed down the road, giggling.

Tail-wagging Riley dragged a four-foot-long dead branch toward them, raking up a cloud of dust in his wake. Although it appeared as if the dog's antics had distracted the boy, Sam was almost certain Jason had already decided not to finish what he'd started to say.

More than just a little curious, Sam wanted to prod the boy, get him to open up. What was the wish? For a big brother? For his parents to let him stay home alone without a babysitter?

Whatever it was, Sam knew he'd lost the opportunity to find out. Now he had Riley to contend with. No way was he going to throw a stick the diameter of a baseball bat, and twice as long. Time for diversionary tactics.

"Why don't you get a dog biscuit out of my office before Riley lugs that thing all the way up here?"

Jason called out in his high-pitched, youthful voice, "Hey, Riley! Wanna bone?"

Enough said.

As the dog and boy disappeared into the office, Sam rounded the corner of the adobe building and headed for the bunkhouse. While he could have easily backtracked through the office and entered through the inside doorway, he decided against it. More than likely he'd catch up to Megan on her way to her car.

~

MEGAN METICULOUSLY FOLDED a Flying K staff shirt and placed it in her open suitcase lying on the mattress. Her sleeping bag had been rolled and tied and tossed to the end of the bed where it lay next to her pillow and a pile of clothes. She picked up a sports bra and carefully folded it.

She had done everything in her power to delay the outcome of this day—the inevitable return to the Naples house. Now she found herself resorting to the ridiculous task of meticulously folding her underwear so she could prolong the chore of packing.

She paused, staring at the plywood partition, painted blue like nearly everything else at the ranch. Would she ever look at that particular shade of blue without thinking of this camp? The summer at the Flying K had been a reprieve, giving her time to gather her strength to face her future. To face Stewart. And now the time had come to do just that.

"I'm going to be just fine," she said aloud. "Now take a deep breath and get moving, girl."

Three sharp knocks on the door echoed throughout the room, defining the hollow emptiness in a cabin without all the children and their belongings.

Sam asked, "Mind if I come in?"

"Not at all." Her own voice bounced off the bare walls.

Looking toward the opening door, she squinted at the brilliant August sunshine spilling into the dimly lit bunkhouse. But the harsh light was quickly blocked by Sam's silhouette in the doorway.

As the weeks had passed since the incident with Anthony Thorndike, Sam had mellowed considerably. He was easier to talk to. Easier to be around. Gone was the tense irritability of the protective guardian. The laid-back Sam had returned, much to Megan's relief. She enjoyed his company, his jokes, his laughter. Maybe too much, she realized. But as long as she was aware of the pitfalls she could avoid them. She *must* avoid them.

"Who are you talking to in here?" he asked as he came toward her.

"Myself."

"Just as long as you don't answer."

"And if I do?"

"Then I'd suggest a long session with a therapist."

"Know a good one?"

"The best. You might say I know him as well as I know myself."

"Is that your personal or professional opinion?"

"Both. I'm talking about me. I'm all ears. Any time you care to unload…"

Stopping at the foot of her bed, he glanced first at the open suitcase, then at her hands. Megan didn't need to follow his gaze to realize his attention had been distracted by the shimmery pink satin. A quiet but rapid heartbeat began to pulse in her throat. For reasons she didn't have time to analyze, she felt an intimacy in the moment that both fascinated and frightened her. And yet, when their eyes met, she was somewhat surprised to see that Sam's own expression remained amiably neutral.

As nonchalantly as she could manage, Megan tucked away her panties.

~

SAM SMILED to himself as he watched Megan fiddle with her perfectly packed suitcase, her long braid draped over her right shoulder. His impulse to unravel it had not lessened any more than earlier in the summer. Now he was forced to let her walk out the door without so much as a single touch. He couldn't cross that line again, much to his regret.

He felt little consolation that she'd be back in a few weeks for his annual Labor Day barbecue—along with her son and the rest of the staff and their families. And as always, it'd be hands-off between the two of them. Employee-employer.

Megan broke the momentary silence as she went back to her packing. "Taylor's dad came inside when he picked her up earlier. Seems like a nice guy."

Sam tried not to pay any attention to the way her yellow short-sleeved top clung to her slender figure, or how the hem of her tan shorts rode up when she bent over, revealing another inch of those long legs.

Megan continued, unaware of his wayward thoughts. "He's not as old as I had expected though."

"Two weeks with Taylor and he'll be showing his age."

Megan attempted to close the overstuffed suitcase, leaning heavily on it. "Do you think—" She paused in concentration until she managed to get the first of the two locks snapped shut, followed by the second. "Living with her father is going to work out?"

"Time will tell," Sam said philosophically.

When she struggled to drag the suitcase off the bed, he stepped over and reached for the handle. "Let me help."

Expecting her to protest, he was mildly surprised when she acquiesced so quickly. But it bothered him that she practically yanked her hand away, as if any physical contact between them, no matter how innocent, was forbidden.

"If you wouldn't mind carrying that to the car," she suggested, "I'll grab this stuff..." Her voice drifted off into a groan as the gray nylon sleeping bag uncoiled from its tight roll.

Hiding a smile, Sam set the suitcase on the floor. "Let an expert do this." He stepped up beside her and started to re-roll it.

"I don't understand. I *always* knot the string."

"Maybe you had other things on your mind at the time."

"I suppose."

The quiet yet soft, husky tone in her voice gnawed at him. He was going to miss the sultry sound of her words and the effect they had on him during the most common conversations. She could merely mention the weather and his blood raced through his veins like a hot Santa Ana wind whipping through the canyons.

Sam finished securing the sleeping bag and passed it to Megan. She thanked him, but neither of them moved to step apart nor turn away. Her dark eyes swallowed him with a thought-filled sadness.

The sleeping bag between them was a buffer of safety, keeping their bodies from touching yet allowing a closeness to one another they hadn't shared in weeks.

"Are you still going through with your divorce?" he asked.

She nodded slightly, her gaze not wavering from his.

"Does Jason know yet?"

She slowly shook her head. "No."

"Are you sure?"

"Yes, of course." Her light remark didn't tell him as much as the defensive expression in her furrowed eyebrows. "Stewart agreed we'd tell Jason together. Why? Has Jason said something to you?"

"Not exactly. But he seems reluctant to go home."

"He's going to miss Griffin, that's all. Those two were inseparable. Besides, I think he's disappointed that Griffin took Karen and Mario's offer for a ride home instead of waiting for me to finish up here."

"Just exactly what have you been doing the last few hours, anyway? You know good and well that almost everybody else is coming back to clean up this place."

"I wanted to do my share before I leave." Something in the way she dropped her gaze and gave a small shrug told him more than she was saying. She was being deliberately evasive. "I really am sorry that I can't come back to help out. But I need to prepare my classroom and—"

"Quit apologizing," he admonished gently, wishing he had the freedom to touch his fingertips to her lips to silence her. But he knew he couldn't stop there. Instead he would trace the outline of her mouth, then the delicate profile of her chin to her long, slender neck. Abruptly dismissing the fantasy, he answered simply, "I understand. Really, I do."

Though he didn't dare move, his gaze traveled over her suntanned skin. He watched her throat as she swallowed. He swallowed too.

"There's just so much I need to take care of."

Like divorcing your husband. How long would that take? Recalling her firm stand against any relationship that might risk losing Jason, Sam thought of waiting endlessly for Megan to be free, wondering if his self-control would hold on long enough. He wanted to kiss her right then and there. How the hell was he going to manage for the duration of a divorce and custody dispute?

He wasn't.

Sam cradled the back of her neck with his hand, and lowered his mouth to hers, holding her to him even after he realized she hadn't been struggling against him. The sleeping bag nestled between their bodies allowed only the touch of their lips in a kiss that felt like a tenuous lifeline between them. A gentle reminder of unspoken feelings he couldn't contain any longer, despite his promise.

His lips lifted from hers only enough to allow him to whisper, "Just a little something to get me through the next couple weeks."

Closing her eyes and shutting him out, she said quietly, "I don't think I can deal with something like this right now."

"Don't think of me as something else you have to deal with. Think of me as someone who cares about you, who wants to be here for you."

"I don't need a knight in shining armor to rescue me. I fell for that twelve years ago when I allowed myself to become dependent on Stewart. It's time for me to stand up for myself."

GRIFFIN PASTED on a carefree smile as Karen pulled her car into a gas station a block off the 405 freeway in Long Beach. He slid out of the back seat as the muffler rumbled even louder now that the door was open.

She twisted around, draping one arm over the steering wheel. "Are you sure I can't drop you off at your house?"

"Yeah, I'm sure."

He hefted the duffel bag onto the black asphalt of the Mobil station, careful to avoid a patch of grease that might soak through and wreck his junk. His mom would kill him if he ruined the bag or the stuff inside. Everything he owned was in that bag.

At least everything that wasn't locked up inside old George's garage.

"Dropping me here saves my dad the trip clear back to our house to get me so we can go to the home center for some plywood."

He felt sweat prickling his armpits but it wasn't from the heat. Lying about his house and his dad and going to the home center —that's what did it. This wasn't going to be easy covering up all the time. Being homeless sucked.

Mario warned lightheartedly, "Be careful lifting all that lumber. Don't want you pulling a muscle when we need you back to work next week."

Griffin tried smiling optimistically, hoping it didn't look too phony.

Karen added, "If you need me to pick you up on Sunday afternoon, you better give me directions to your new place."

"It's, uh, too complicated. I can't remember all the names of the streets or which way you gotta turn. I'll just have my dad drop me off back here. Okay?"

Almost certain they'd seen right through his excuse, Griffin held his breath, waiting for one of them to tell him he was full of shit. But they didn't.

"Suit yourself," Karen said cheerfully.

Mario added, "Catch ya later, Griff."

Only after they waved goodbye and took off did Griffin find he could breathe easy again, but not without feeling totally wiped out. He squeezed his eyes shut, wishing once more that when he opened them he'd be home again and everything up until now would've been a dream.

The dull drone of traffic hummed in his ears. He could hear some kind of metal rattling around in the bed of a truck as it pulled into the gas station behind him. The familiar smell of oil from the refineries hung in the salty breeze. Maybe this place wasn't as quiet and peaceful as the Flying K, but there was something real good about all the sounds and smells he'd grown up with. Standing here with his eyes closed, he could pretend he was waiting for a bus to take him to the Lakewood Mall, just like in the old days.

But it wasn't.

A horn honked. He opened his eyes, blinking at the harsh glare of the sun reflecting off the windshield of his family's van. He reached down and picked up his canvas bag as his dad pulled up.

"How's it going?"

"Fine, I guess." After tossing his bag on the floor in front of the passenger seat, Griffin climbed in and sank down into the seat.

~

STEWART HELD the cell phone against his ear with one hand as he opened the door to the caterer's delivery boy, then silently gestured toward the kitchen while speaking with Maxwell on the other end of the line.

"I know what I'm doing, Max."

"I'm sure you believe this plan of yours will work but I must tell you that I don't believe Megan will go along with it."

"There's no other acceptable alternative."

"Perhaps for you, but not for her." A long, heavy sigh drifted over the line. "Stew, we have always dreaded that something like this would happen. Now that it has, how can you possibly think she will settle for a marriage in name only? How can you expect her to maintain a charade of marital bliss?"

"Because I haven't been married to her all these years without learning something about how her mind works."

"Very well, then. Obviously your mind is made up and I'm wasting my breath trying to convince you to throw in the towel."

With one eye on the dark-haired young man setting the box

on the tiled counter and unloading foil-covered dishes, Stewart purposely evaded anything in his side of the conversation that could be overheard and used against him. "I always get what I want."

"But you don't want Megan." Maxwell paused, then quietly questioned, "Do you?"

"I'm strictly interested in security measures."

"Let her go, Stew. Let her find a new life."

"No, dammit!"

The delivery boy flinched but continued working without looking up.

Stewart shook his head and stormed out of the room, lowering his voice as he walked out of earshot.

"How can you blithely tell me to leave her?" he demanded in a harsh whisper, his fingers clutching the receiver. "You set this all up for us. You knew the stakes. Now you expect me to risk everything? My whole life? I can't do it, Max. I won't."

"You really have no choice any longer."

"I do so. I can make Megan stay with me. She won't leave if it means losing Jason."

"Don't use your own son as a pawn." His soft-spoken plea reached through the receiver. "I love your family, Stewart. And I'm simply a wreck over this whole tragic episode in our relationship. I don't want to see either Jase or Meggie hurt any more than you do. I know you're just letting your emotions get the better of you right now."

"Please, don't patronize me."

"I—I'm sorry." Maxwell's voice quivered with quiet desperation uncharacteristic of the professor. "I don't want to lose you. But I'm afraid that's exactly what is going to happen if you insist upon salvaging this marriage. She'll expect you to sever all ties with me. And I don't know if I could bear it."

Neither could I. Stewart squeezed his eyes shut, feeling the tension gripping his chest. He gathered the tattered remnants of his peace of mind. "I have to hang up, Max. Megan and Jason should be walking in the door any second."

"Will I still see you on the fourteenth?"

"I'll let you know."

"Perhaps it would be best if we didn't—"

"I *said* I'll let you know."

"Promise?"

"Whining doesn't become you, my friend."

"I have stooped quite low, haven't I?"

"It's understandable, considering the circumstances."

Stewart shifted from one foot to the other, growing increasingly uncomfortable with this side of Maxwell, a side that was too needy, too accommodating, too eager to please. He was accustomed to the gentlemanly manner with the solid confidence and quiet strength that Stewart had come to rely upon over the years. They were kindred spirits, attuned to every mood, every quirk. Likes and dislikes. Goals and dreams.

Distracted by the young man appearing in the doorway, Stewart abruptly ended his conversation. After tipping for the delivery, he didn't expect to receive a polite request for his autograph.

With a practiced smile, he reached for a memo pad on the kitchen counter. "I would think you'd be accustomed to celebrities on your route."

"Yeah, but I've been a huge fan of yours. Never dreamed I'd be standing in your kitchen someday. This is some house. Must've cost three mil or something."

"Or something," he answered, disturbed by the adoration in the compelling eyes that reminded Stewart too much of himself at a younger age. They were approximately the same height and weight, as well. Enough of a tan to be attractive. *Very* attractive. While there were no overt signs of his sexual orientation, there was something about his gaze…

Growing increasingly uncomfortable, Stewart wondered if

this delivery boy was merely a fan of the crime novels or drawn to Stewart for other reasons. Perhaps he was gay. Perhaps he was one of those seemingly normal fans who had become obsessed to the point of stalking.

Belatedly realizing he'd let himself become too distracted by the phone call with Maxwell, he now berated himself for not being more careful. He should have had his radar up long before this.

Holding the pen poised over the paper, he asked, "Your name?"

"Make it out to Wayne."

He scrawled a personal greeting to Wayne, signed his own name and tore off the sheet. "There you go."

Wayne accepted the paper with a wide-eyed reverence as if Stewart had handed over the keys to a Porsche. Maybe he was just an awestruck delivery boy. Still, Stewart would run a check on Wayne. Just to be safe.

CHAPTER 11

Megan turned left off Second Street and drove slowly through the narrow streets of Naples, dreading her return home. Beside her, Jason was silent and sullen in the passenger seat.

As she started down her block, a young man came down their front steps, gazing at a piece of paper in his hand. He appeared to be in his early twenties, fairly tall and good-looking. Stuffing the paper in the pocket of his slacks, he rounded the front of a minivan with almost a bounce to his step.

Megan might have gone with her first guess that this was someone who had dropped something off, or stopped to ask directions, or any number of harmless reasons for a handsome young man to be leaving her home. But she was no longer quite so confident in her guesses. Not anymore.

She watched him get behind the wheel, then pause and gaze up at the looming facade of the pseudo-Italian villa. She had seen so many people gawk at the opulent home that his interest should not have caused her to notice him. And yet she did.

The hair prickled on her neck. Her stomach suddenly felt queasy.

"Why are you slowing down, Mom?" Her son sat up straighter in his seat and peered over the dashboard.

She wasn't about to voice her suspicion. "That driver doesn't seem to have his mind on the road. I don't want him to cut me off when I turn into the garage."

"He's stopped."

"Yes, I noticed."

"In front of our house."

"Yes, Jase, I see that." Megan had stopped her car as well, watching the driver, her anxiety escalating.

"Do you know him?" asked Jason.

"No. He's probably just admiring our house." *I hope.*

"Maybe Dad knows him."

I hope not. Mounting suspicion intensified with the sickening feeling climbing up her throat.

His head pivoted. "You look funny. You okay?"

"Yes," she assured him with an uneasy breath.

Something inside her had set off alarm bells, warning her to stay away. To not go inside. At least not for a while. The memory of that one afternoon taunted her. She didn't want to catch Stewart making the bed or coming out of the shower, acting as if nothing had happened. She didn't want to see any circumstantial evidence that this young man might have just spent the day with her husband.

With no small effort, she masked her immediate panic with a sudden burst of enthusiasm. "How about burgers for dinner. At Hof's Hut in Los Alamitos. It's almost dinner time, and I really don't feel like cooking as soon as I walk in the door."

"Cool."

As the blue car started up and drove past them, she tried to avoid looking at the driver. But her morbid curiosity got the better of her. Squeezing by in the narrow lane, he was less than three feet from her with the window down when their eyes met and he nodded with a smile.

"Sorry if I was in your way," he said.

She mutely nodded back, all too aware of how gorgeous he was, even for beach standards. Of course, his looks did nothing to make her heart pound. Obviously, he was about ten years too young for her.

But not for Stewart, perhaps.

The thought crossed her mind, bringing with it another wave of nausea. She tightened her grip on the steering wheel and drove on, passing the short driveway in front of the four-car garage.

"Mom, you went right by! Aren't we going to get Dad?" Her son was craning his neck around to look back at the house.

"Jason…honey…"

"I don't want to go without him."

"He's probably not even home," she cautioned, aware that her son hadn't seen the young driver departing from the front door. "We *could* call to see if he's there, then ask him to join us."

"He's waiting for us. I talked to him last night."

"You did? Where?"

"From Sam's office."

"Why did you call your father the night before we were headed home?"

His eyes downcast, Jason shrugged. "I dunno. I…jus' wanted to talk, I guess."

"And you told him we'd be back by dinner?"

"Before that, even. I didn't think you'd take so long packin' the car."

Megan knew how much Jason idolized Stewart so she shouldn't have been the least bit surprised that her son had placed the call. But she remembered something Sam had said about kids knowing more than their parents might realize. Without a doubt, Jason knew of the tension in the air. Perhaps he was only needing to verify that his dad would still be around when he got home.

If nothing else, she knew one thing about that phone call. Stewart had been reminded of their return this afternoon. And if that was the case, surely he wouldn't have risked being discovered with that young man she'd seen leaving the house. He wouldn't be so reckless. Not when Jason might walk in any minute.

So maybe she'd been wrong about the young man.

"Don't be disappointed if he's too busy to join us," she gently warned, turning the car around and heading back the other direction.

"He won't be."

A few minutes later, Megan stood at the arched entrance to the dining room where the table had been set with silver and china saved for special occasions. Covered dishes of delicious-smelling food were set in the center around a crystal bowl of floating gardenias and candles. Soft music played in the background.

"Stewart, you shouldn't have done this."

"It's a welcome home celebration for you and Jason," he explained innocently. Too innocently.

Jason piped up. "Do I have to wear a suit and tie like at Christmas?"

"No," answered his dad. "Now scoot upstairs and take a shower. Afterward you can play the new Xbox game. I'll call you when it's time for—"

"A new game? Cool!" Jason headed toward the stairs, half dragging his oversized duffel bag behind him.

Megan pulled out a chair and sat down hard. "You don't play fair, Stewart. I can't compete with you."

"Who's asking you to compete?"

"Just forget it. I'm too tired to fight with you."

"Meggie…" His voice was too soft and consoling as he circled her chair and laid his hands on her shoulders.

She tensed and sat forward. "Don't."

"I'm only going to massage your neck." He grasped her shoulders again, gently pulling her back against the chair. She started to protest, but he shushed her. "Just sit and enjoy. No talking."

"I know what you're doing and it's not going to work."

"You were always a good mind reader."

"Obviously not good enough."

"Let's not go back to that. Just let me rub your neck for a few minutes, then I'll run a bath for you."

With a heavy sigh, she slowly pulled away from him and stood up. "I can't be pampered and spoiled like Jason. Not anymore. No matter what you say or do, I can't stay married to you. We agreed to tell Jason when the summer was over. Well, it's over. Tonight might be the best time to break the news of our divorce to him."

"I only agreed to let you take some time to think about a decision. Once you realize it's best for all of us—"

"Best for you, yes. For Jason, maybe. For me? No. Not unless you could become the husband I thought I'd married. Not unless you could actually say you love me and want me."

"But I *do* love you, Meggie."

She held up her palm. "Stop right there. I'm not buying it. Not for one second."

"It's not what you think—"

"Quit rationalizing, Stewart. You hid behind our marriage to keep your secret without any concern for me." Megan remained surprisingly calm. Detached. Almost as if she was watching some other woman with more strength, more poise than she'd thought herself capable of.

"I wish I could make you understand what it's like to be me. The *real* me. Here, inside." He lowered himself into the chair she'd vacated, sitting sideways. He dropped his elbows to his knees and hunched over, his shoulders sagging. "It's been a living hell, Meggie. And I loved you too much to ever want to drag you into it with me."

She stared down at the back of his dark head, wanting to believe his sincerity. But how could she? She had once given her complete trust to him, and he'd betrayed it. All the love in her heart hadn't been enough to stop the slow deterioration of their marriage.

Her chest suddenly ached with the emptiness of losing the husband, the lover, the man she had expected to spend the rest of her life with. And yet there was something in her that mechanically drew out another chair and sat down, knees to knees with this intimate stranger.

Aware of the shower running in a distant part of the house, she had intended to ask Stewart to tell her about his feelings now before Jason came back downstairs. But the words wouldn't form in her throat. She stared at him in silence for a long moment.

"I miss you." Her barely audible confession surprised even her, though it was Stewart who glanced up, his eyes so full of pain as if searching for forgiveness.

Years fell away as time seemed to roll back on itself. There he was—the handsome college junior she had met in the library so long ago. It seemed unimaginable that he had noticed her, let alone given her the least bit of attention. Yet he'd struck up a conversation over a book of poetry she'd held open in her hands, reciting the words on the page without once looking down. It had moved her that he knew the poem by heart. It moved her even more that he spoke it with such tenderness as if he knew the quiet anguish of the father who had lost his child—

THE LITTLE TOY dog is covered with dust,
But sturdy and staunch he stands;
And the little toy soldier is red with rust,
And his musket molds in his hands.
Time was when the little toy dog was new,
And the soldier was passing fair,

161

And that was the time when our Little Boy Blue
Kissed them and put them there.

"Now, don't you go till I come," he said,
"And don't you make any noise!"
So toddling off to his trundle-bed
He dreamt of the pretty toys.
And as he was dreaming, an angel song
Awakened our Little Boy Blue,—
Oh, the years are many, the years are long.
But the little toy friends are true.

Ay, faithful to Little Boy Blue they stand,
Each in the same old place,
Awaiting the touch of the little hand,
The smile of the little face.
And they wonder as waiting these long years through,
In the dust of that little chair,
What has become of our Little Boy Blue
Since he kissed them and put them there.

MEGAN REMEMBERED the look in Stewart's eyes at that moment, and had wondered then if he had lost someone he had deeply loved. It had been so clear that the poem touched a chord within him. Later, she had purchased a copy of the poetry book at the campus bookstore and given it to him as a birthday present.

And this summer it had shown up in her suitcase.

"The poem," she said now, her voice quivering. "Who is it about? For you, that is. Who did you lose, Stewart?"

"Me." He slowly lifted his head. "I lost me. My childhood. My innocence. My parents didn't die when I was fifteen. They kicked me out."

"Why?" Her question popped out before she realized she already knew the answer. "Did they find out about you?"

"Same damn exact way you did." He gave a short laugh of self-disgust. "My mom took off crying. My dad followed her out to the barn. God knows why she went there but it gave my friend the chance to get out of there."

Stewart paused, opening and closing his fist, staring at his fingers. Megan saw his jaw work as if he was trying to speak but couldn't. She reached out and gently grasped his wrist to comfort him.

He looked up, his eyes red with moisture. "He beat the shit out of me."

"Your dad?"

With a nod, he turned his face away. "Put me in the hospital. Fractured ribs. Punctured lung. Broken jaw."

"And he wasn't arrested for it?"

He shook his head. "The morning I was to be released I woke up in my room and found a suitcase packed with some of my clothes, a bus ticket to California, and a letter from my mother with a little cash to get me to her sister's place here in Long Beach. I tried to go home, but my dad stopped me on the steps of the front porch. Mom was standing behind the screen door, crying. I begged her to let me come in, but she didn't move. Just kept crying. So I left."

Megan's heart ached, trying to imagine herself turning their own son away, refusing to help. Refusing to accept him for who he was. But she could never fathom losing Jason that way. She would always be there for him. Always.

"I'm sorry, Stewart. I didn't know."

"How could you have known? It's something I've only shared with..." He let his words drift off.

"Maxwell?"

"I didn't mean to bring him up."

"He's been a good…friend," she said, for lack of a better word to use at the moment. She couldn't bring herself to refer to Max as anything else. It was still too hard to say it.

"You should know he doesn't want me to hurt you more than I…than *we* already have. He wants me to give you whatever you ask."

"Wise man," she offered with a slight smile of hopeful optimism.

"And, no, it's not about gaining my freedom to be with him. He genuinely cares about you. And Jason."

Putting aside for the moment his role in the deceit, she still had fond memories of Maxwell as a warm and caring gentleman with a quick wit and a generous spirit. He would drop anything to run to the aid of a friend. He gave time and money abundantly to anyone in need. He was perfect in every way, except one. He was her husband's lover.

Then she thought of the young man she'd seen leaving the house.

"I need to know the absolute truth, Stewart. In all these years, is Maxwell the only one you have been with other than me?"

Without batting an eye, he answered with a solid, "Yes."

"No one else?"

"No one else," he repeated without hesitation.

"This afternoon I saw someone leaving here—"

"That was the caterer. He was simply delivering our dinner."

"What about Cameron?"

He straightened. "Melissa's brother? What? Are you nuts or something?"

"No, I think he uses Melissa for an excuse to come over here, hoping to bump into you. I've seen the way he acts when you're around. You pour on the charm as usual and he hangs on every word. I just can't help but wonder now—"

"Jesus Christ, you think I'm some kind of pervert stalking adolescent boys?" Furious, he launched himself out of the chair as Megan shrunk back.

"You're awfully defensive," she muttered under her breath.

"Damn right, I'm defensive. That's one hell of an accusation. And it's typically ignorant assumptions like that one that make me want to keep this marriage intact. If my own wife can think I'm a pervert, how the hell am I going to keep anyone else from thinking it?"

"Getting a divorce doesn't automatically mean you have to tell anyone your sexual orientation, Stewart."

"But I don't want a divorce."

"Why not? You have hardly looked twice at me in twelve months. You're *married* to your career—both of them. There's no room for me anymore. Correction. There's never been room for me in this marriage. When are you going to realize that?"

"I do realize it. And I'll change. I swear I will."

"How? You said it yourself that you love Maxwell."

"I love you too!"

"Not in the way I need you to, Stewart." She threw her arms up. "God, why can't I get through to you? I want out. I want to find someone who wants to be with me because I'm a woman and not because I'm a convenient wife. I'm going to get my own place and—"

"What about Jason? I don't want him to grow up without a father. Or worse, I don't want him to think I don't want him."

"He'll never think that about you."

"Then don't take him away from here. From his school, his friends. Or me."

"Don't do this, Stewart. Jason needs to be with me. I'm his mother."

"And I'm his father. I don't want a custody battle. I want you here with us. Please. I'm begging you. Anything you want, just ask. I'll give it to you."

"I want a divorce."

"Anything but that."

The intercom in the kitchen crackled as their son's voice boomed from the speaker, "Hey, Dad! Somethin's wrong with the new game! Dad? Dad!"

"Patience is not his strong point," murmured Stewart, gazing up at the ceiling as if he could see his son at the computer terminal.

"Like father, like son."

He dropped his eyes to Megan. "I have all the patience in the world when it comes to Jason. You are the one who is acting on impulse with this divorce."

"I've had the entire summer to think things over," she said.

Until last June, she thought she'd known what love looked like, what it felt like, what a lover was. But she'd been so easily fooled into thinking sex was equivalent to love. Her brain knew it wasn't. But her heart had wanted so desperately to believe that this gorgeous guy had fallen head over heels in love with plain, bookish Megan.

Maybe it just wasn't meant to happen to her. She'd spent the summer thinking about going out on her own, and she believed she'd be okay. But if Jason remained with his father, she truly would be alone.

Footsteps pounded down the back stairs. "Dad?"

"I heard you, Jason," Stewart called out over his shoulder, his eyes still watching Megan. "I'll come up after dinner. Right now it's time to eat."

Megan glanced toward the kitchen, then back at Stewart. "I'm not really up to this welcome home feast. I'd rather go upstairs and lie down for a while."

"Please stay…for Jason's sake. Let him see us as a family."

His plea carried more meaning than just a request for her presence at the dinner table. She knew it. He knew it.

Jason came into the room, scuffling his feet, then stopped, looking first at his dad, then his mom. A youthful smile widened on his freshly washed face.

Megan was suddenly aware of Stewart's hand on her shoulder. She looked down at his fingers and a fleeting memory crossed her mind of a time when he had often touched her so tenderly.

"Don't go," he whispered, leaning close so his breath warmed her neck.

Goose bumps rippled down her arm. How could her body respond to him now, after everything that had happened?

For a brief moment she closed her eyes, wishing things were different, yet knowing they would never be the same.

"I can't do this, Stewart," she finally managed to say.

"Yes, you can."

"Mom?"

Megan stepped back to see Jason had moved closer. A frown of concern had replaced the smile. "I'm okay, honey. Just a little headache. And I'm tired too. Why don't you and your dad enjoy your meal together while I go upstairs?"

Her son's shoulders slumped. "Aw, Mom. Not tonight. I thought— Oh, never mind."

What Stewart couldn't accomplish, Jason did. She hated being the one to spoil the first evening home for her son. "Well, I suppose I could eat a few bites of something. Might even help my headache."

"Cool."

Stewart mimicked his son's response, "Yeah, cool. I'll bring in a bottle of wine for us and some sparkling grape juice for Jason. Be right back."

As she sat down at the table, Megan watched her son take a seat across from her.

A few moments later, with Stewart at the head of the table, he raised his filled glass in a toast. Jason giggled at the ceremonial solemnity in his father, obviously mistaking it as a humorous attempt at fun. But Megan didn't see it that way at all. Instead, she felt as if a cage door was clanging shut.

"Here's to my family," Stewart offered in grand style. "Welcome home."

CHAPTER 12

Jason lay awake later that night with earbuds in his ears, listening to a playlist that had been Griff's favorite. It reminded him of being back at the ranch and being with everybody else. At least at the Flying K he could pretend everything was okay when it really wasn't. He knew it the second he saw his mom and dad talking together before dinner.

They were talking too serious to be happy about seeing each other again. It looked like his mom was real upset. He guessed his dad was still in trouble for something, only he didn't know what it could be.

What if they got a divorce? What if he had to move away with one of them? Which one? And how far away? Not so far that he couldn't go back and forth between his mom and dad's.

He rolled over on his side and stared at the clock radio by his bed. It was past eleven and he still wasn't sleepy. He thought about sneaking downstairs to play the new game that his dad finally got around to showing him how to work. But he'd probably get caught. Both of them stayed up real late usually. Reading.

Always reading. And they were good at knowing if he was not in bed, like they had some kind of special radar.

He flopped onto his back. The music pounded in his ears. He kicked his covers off. But then his skin got all prickly and creepy. It wasn't like he was cold or hot or nothing like that. His window was open so the breeze felt sorta good. No, it wasn't something as simple as that at all. He just couldn't ever fall asleep unless he was under the covers. He didn't used to be like this. He used to just sleep any way he wanted. But not anymore. Not when he felt like he was just lying there all alone and anything could get him. The covers protected him.

Usually.

~

MEGAN FELT a hand on her shoulder, a tender touch that drew her out of her sleepy haze and made her realize she'd drifted off in the midst of her hot, relaxing bath. She lifted her heavy eyelids with no small effort and gazed at Stewart kneeling next to the tub with a bath sheet in his other hand.

"Come on, sleepyhead. Let me help you get into bed before you drown."

For a hazy, disconnected moment she felt as if she was drifting in a blissful memory of the early years of their marriage. The honeymoon stage she still cherished in her heart. He had been so sweet, so attentive, as if he could read her every thought. Always there when she needed something, always ready to please her.

Exhausted and groggy, she couldn't muster the strength to protest his presence in her bathroom, even if she'd wanted to, which she didn't. And this came as a mild surprise. Something had shifted in their relationship, but it was too new, too fragile to analyze it. Maybe it was nothing more than her exhaustion. She was simply too tired to care about her nudity in front of the one man who had seen her every morning stepping out of the shower and every evening undressing for bed. He knew her. Every inch of her. And apparently he wasn't the least bit affected by her one way or the other.

Slowly she drew her feet under her and, taking his hand, she let him help her stand. The soapy water sluiced down her body as she gradually became more awake to the fact that she was standing naked in front of her husband. For the breadth of an instant, she felt exposed and vulnerable. Then he placed the voluminous towel around her shoulders. Reverently. Silently.

The intense heat of the bathwater and the sudden rise to her feet gave her a slight loss of equilibrium, enough to waver a bit. He gripped her upper arms yet his concentrated gaze remained on the slippery porcelain edge of the bathtub.

Without looking up, he cautioned, "Steady there."

His words hung in the air. She gazed at him, her eyes filling with tears. His arms slipped around her and slowly drew her into a tight and desperate embrace. She clung to him, her body aching for the man she'd loved, the man she'd taken inside her.

Come back to me, she pleaded in silence, wanting to believe that somehow she could change him. Standing naked in his arms, she felt as if the room was spinning around them. Her mind swirled at a dizzying pace. Too much wine. Too much time spent in the hot bath. Too much happening in her life all at once.

God, help me. She turned her head and kissed her husband, long and hard, leaving no room for doubt about her motives. Just this once. Just this last time, she told herself, sinking to the floor of her bathroom and pulling him down with her.

She closed her eyes, kissing him, pushing away all thoughts or consequences. He touched her in familiar and intimate ways. Her body responded in a slow yet steady climb, ignoring the ache of sadness in her heart, longing only for one last physical pleasure. He gave her all she wanted and more. She cried out in climax. So did he.

He moved off her to lie next to her on his side. She opened her eyes finally, and found him watching her. His own eyes filled with moisture. "I do love you, Meggie."

Her fingertips touched his lips to stop any further conversation. She couldn't bear it. Not now. She was ashamed of dropping her guard, of giving in to the raw craving for sex. That's all it was, really. She'd glossed it over in her mind, believing she could somehow alter Stewart. Instead she had let herself down. She'd allowed him to prove that he could still give her what she needed in a husband. In the midst of the passion she had believed it herself. She had believed he had given her all she wanted and more. But he hadn't. He had merely gone through the motions. Just as he'd always done.

Megan sat up and pulled the towel around her.

∾

Stewart watched her, knowing the pain in her heart as surely as he knew his own. "Don't leave."

She glanced at him, skittish. Suddenly shy.

"Not yet. Not ever."

But she got up and wordlessly left the bathroom, walking away on slender legs that would have made another man go after her, take her into his bed and wrap those limbs around him again. But not him. His thoughts always drifted back to someone else.

Stewart dressed and went downstairs, dragging out a bottle of his best brandy. A half hour later, he was still cold inside. A physical chill like ice in his veins.

An hour later, he was warmer but still feeling the remorse of fucking Megan like a goddamned stud horse. He didn't blame her for instigating it. No, he blamed himself. Especially when he saw the guilt in her eyes afterward. He'd put it there. Every move was orchestrated to make her groan and gasp and reach out to him for more. He wanted her to see, to *feel* all that she would be giving up if she walked out on him.

He put down the empty glass and headed toward the garage, intending to take a drive along the coast highway to clear his head. But he wound up steering the Corvette around surface streets just a few short miles before parking in front of Maxwell's house in the College Park Estates.

He touched the display screen to call from the car. It went direct to voicemail.

"Maxwell, it's me. I'm parked out front. I didn't want to pound on the door and scare you to death at this ungodly hour. But I need to talk." He felt the brandy loosening his emotions and fought to tamp them down. "If you don't want me to come inside, I'll understand. I mean, if you're worried about the neighbors or anything. I'll, uh, wait here for a few minutes. And if you don't open the door, I'll just leave."

Not long after he hung up, the front door opened. Tall and slender and devastatingly distinguished with his usual poise, Maxwell stood for a moment, wrapped in a burgundy silk robe, a gift from Stewart last Christmas. One of so many throughout their fifteen years. Yet it seemed insufficient compared to all that this man had given to Stewart.

It had started out as merely a student/teacher friendship initially. Stewart was an eighteen-year-old football jock taking a required Civics class during summer school between his junior and senior year. Maxwell was the instructor who smiled easily at the outrageous flirtations of the love-struck girls practically throwing themselves at his feet. Of course, he was Mr. Hamer then. Six feet tall, single, mid-twenties with a killer grin and a hint of a British accent. Even the guys had to admit that Hamer was like an idol to them, the kind of man they could talk to, aspire to be, especially with the girls.

Stewart had found a mentor in Mr. Hamer. He was intelligent without being pompous. He would always put down his red pencil while grading papers after school and listen to a student who had "just dropped in to chat," knowing it was really a need to talk over something important. People were important to him. Even other teachers sought his advice. And yet they respected his privacy too.

There were a few curious whisperings about Mr. Hamer, those who wondered if he had a life outside the gates of Poly High. Some guys joked about the possibility of Hamer being gay, but nobody took it seriously. Yet the speculation planted thoughts in his own mind, thoughts he shouldn't have been contemplating as he went through his senior year, stopping by the classroom after football practice to shoot the breeze before heading home to his aunt's house.

Graduation came and went. Stewart enrolled in the state university on a scholarship. Academic, not athletic. Mr. Hamer had helped him get it after a blown-out knee killed a future in football. By then, Stewart had become immersed into a whole new world of great literature and music, thanks to his teacher.

Nothing else was supposed to have happened. Maxwell had certainly never intended or expected a deeper relationship. It had been Stewart who had initiated the first tentative step, the crossing over into forbidden territory, into the private life of his mentor.

After friendly discussions and meetings over lunch, Stewart admitted to Maxwell that his own feelings toward the man had grown deeper and stronger than he'd ever experienced before. He told him of his past with the boy in his bedroom, and his falling out with his parents. He told him about the pretense with the girls in high school. And, finally, he told Maxwell that he was in love with him.

Unable to keep his secret any longer, he had risked shame and rejection that night so many years earlier, arriving on Maxwell's doorstep just as he had done tonight. Alone. Troubled. Needing to be with him. Back then Stewart had been prepared for the worst, yet prayed it wouldn't happen again. Instead, Maxwell had not humiliated him as his father had done.

Now close to forty, Maxwell was still as devastatingly handsome as ever. His black hair had a bit of salt-and-pepper at his temples, adding even more distinguished charm. He was everything to Stewart. His whole world. The rest of it—the police force, the writing, his marriage, perhaps even Jason—seemed like a fictional stage play taking place out in front of the lights and audience while Stewart's real life hung back in the shadows, behind the velvet curtains and painted facades of props and canvas walls.

His real life was Maxwell. Maxwell the mentor. Maxwell the director. The playwright. The set designer. The choreographer. The musical director. Everything that Stewart was, Maxwell had been the guiding force behind it. He couldn't walk away from him any more than he could stop breathing.

Maxwell's face was solemn as he cinched the robe tighter, then cautiously motioned Stewart to come into the house.

"It's nearly three in the morning," were his first words after closing the door behind them.

"I know, and I'm sorry. I'm sorry for everything."

No words were spoken. No condemnation. No advice. No conversation whatsoever. Maxwell said everything with the compassion in his eyes. The softness. The sadness. Then he merely stepped forward and took Stewart in his arms, holding him and comforting him.

No one knew. No one could ever know the private moments between them. Yet Stewart could not imagine living a single day without them.

"I'm afraid you have to leave," Maxwell said finally.

"I shouldn't have come here in the first place."

"Nonsense. I'm always here for you. Always. And I absolutely hate to send you away."

"I know, I know."

"Tomorrow, then. Let's meet at that motel in—"

"I can't, Max. I just can't risk being recognized."

"Of course." A sigh of resignation. A slump of his shoulders. "How perfectly selfish of me."

"You're not selfish any more than I am. I want to be with you. I do."

Stewart should have left it at that. He should have turned and walked out. But he didn't. And Maxwell didn't insist he leave. So he stayed. Just for an hour, he told himself. Maybe two. He'd be gone before the sun was up for sure.

~

MEGAN COULDN'T THINK of her first night home with Stewart without cringing at the memory of the poignant desperation in their lovemaking, knowing all along that it was nothing more than his futile attempt to salvage their marriage. Yet she had initiated it, giving herself to him in the hope that she could have one last chance to love him the way she had once loved him. In the midst of the gentle passion, she had clung to him, knowing in her heart it would be the last time, knowing in her heart that it was her way of saying goodbye.

She never asked where Stewart had gone that night after she'd heard the garage door open and the Corvette rumble away into the darkness. In the past she had been too naive to realize he had been leading a double life. Now, however, she didn't want to know. She wouldn't allow herself to think of him with Maxwell.

Everything inside her shut down, refusing to feel the emotions that hovered near the surface of her skin like a demon hiding under the bed in a child's nightmare. She sank into the numbness, letting it wrap around her in a blanket of security.

As long as she couldn't feel the sadness, the fear, the panic, as long as she could keep from feeling anything, she could make it through another night, move through another day, push herself to the end of another week. This was grief, according to a clinical psychologist promoting her book on a morning news program a few days earlier. The death of a marriage triggered similar, if not the same, symptoms of mourning. The key was to feel the pain and sadness when it came up, not block it. But she wasn't there yet.

At breakfast, she told Jason that his father had been called into work, though she was certain she hadn't heard the phone ring before he'd left. Nor had she found any sort of scribbled note from him about any emergency. He had always left notes before.

But that was before she knew the truth.

"I'm going to be setting up my classroom for school to start in two weeks," she said over her morning coffee while Jason ate a bowl of Cheerios.

"I know."

"I didn't line up any kind of program at the Y to keep you occupied while I'm working."

"That's okay. I'll just hang out at school."

"Might be boring for you."

He shrugged. "I don't care."

"I suppose I could find some things for you to do. Maybe you could work on fixing up the bulletin boards."

"Yeah, I s'pose."

"Slow down. You're eating so fast you'll choke."

"I wanna play my new game."

"For just a little while. I'll be ready to go in about an hour."

As she skimmed the morning paper, sneaking a peek at the apartment rentals, Jason finished his cereal, leaving the milk in the bottom of the bowl as he got up from the table and carried it to the counter.

"Are you sure you don't mind going to the school everyday? Melissa will be at cheer practice, but said her brother will help out if we need someone to babysit—"

"No way!" The spoon clattered into the kitchen sink.

"Careful, Jase."

He turned on the water with an aggressive flip of his hand, rinsed his dish for two seconds and shut off the water with another slap of the hand.

"What's wrong with you?"

"Nothing."

"Then what's with the hostility?"

"I just don't need a babysitter is all. I keep tellin' you and Dad but you don't even hear me."

He hadn't looked at her at all, just stared down at the sink, his hands braced on the edge of the counter, his back to her, his posture stiff. Angry. Defiant. A glimpse of the teenager he would become? God, she hoped not. But she couldn't deny the bouts of moodiness that had already shown themselves. He was changing right before her very eyes. And she couldn't do a damn thing to stop it.

"Be ready to leave in an hour."

He only nodded, kept his eyes diverted, and walked from the room.

Over the next several days, Jason worked alongside Megan as she prepared her classroom for the opening day of school. More often than not he talked about the regulars at the ranch, especially Griffin and Sam, wondering how they were all doing with their own preparations for the weekend camp starting in mid-September. It was quite obvious that he missed everyone, missed the ambiance of the extended family. He was lonely for their company.

So was Megan. Thoughts of Sam constantly slipped into her mind from morning to night, showing up in her dreams as she slept. But as with Stewart, she wouldn't let herself feel anything for him, about him. She had enough on her hands at the moment with getting ready for school and dealing with her husband's stubborn determination to keep their marriage together. Thankfully, the subject of sex seemed to be dead and buried. For this she was grateful, unwilling to be some kind of charity case to him when he really didn't want to be with her at all. She didn't want to live this way.

~

ON THE WEDNESDAY before Labor Day weekend, she confronted Stewart again about breaking the news to Jason.

"Not now, Megan," he answered patiently, though his mind was obviously preoccupied. He had just walked in the kitchen door from the garage and had asked where Jason was.

"If not now, when?"

"I don't know. I'm not ready yet." Not his normal response; he had always talked about staying together as a family for the sake of their son.

Standing in the middle of the kitchen floor, she didn't quite know how to react to the possibility that he was actually giving in to her. "But I *am* ready. I'm going to the bank today to transfer money from our joint savings account into my own personal account so I can put down a deposit on an apartment in Belmont Heights."

He glanced at the ceiling, then at her. "Did you say Jase was upstairs?"

"I didn't say, but yes, he's playing his game." She felt a moment of relief that Stewart was ready to have the talk with their son together.

He pulled a packet out of the inside pocket of his blue sports coat. "Good. I can't wait to tell him the news."

"What are those?"

"Airline tickets. We're going to New York for a few days."

"We? But I can't possibly leave now."

His expression shifted from excitement to a wince of

awkward apology. "I only bought two tickets. Just him and me. A father-son sort of thing."

Before she could say a word, he launched into an obviously well-rehearsed speech about how he deserved to have some one-on-one time with their son, especially after he'd been forced to endure the entire summer away from Jason.

She didn't know why she felt hurt. Surely it had nothing to do with being left out of his travel plans. If anything, she was relieved to be off the hook. Spending time together as a family in public was becoming more and more challenging.

He had a right to be with his son. And God knew he wouldn't flee the country with him. Stewart was too well-known to pull a stunt like that. But she had not kept them apart as he seemed to imply. And that implication was the real core of her defensiveness, which she couldn't quite hide.

"There were plenty of opportunities for you to visit him at the ranch. Don't make it sound as if I had a restraining order against you."

"Now I've made you mad."

"Not quite, but you're getting there."

"Not my intention, I assure you." He sounded so much like Maxwell that goose bumps rose on her arms. His voice. The inflection. She had once teased him for picking up on his mentor's mannerisms. Now it truly unnerved her, knowing the close and intimate relationship between the two men.

"Will he be joining you?"

"If by *he*, you mean Maxwell, no. It will only be Jason and me. Aside from one meeting with my publisher, I'll have the rest of the time for the two of us to see the city."

Forcing herself to be fair, Megan stepped aside and gestured toward the back stairwell with a sweep of her hand. "I won't stand in the way."

A few moments after Stewart called their son to the kitchen,

Jason bounded down the stairs with loud thumps of footsteps that only a boisterous kid could make.

Stewart held up the tickets. "What do you say to a trip to New York?"

"Cool. When?"

"Tomorrow."

"Can we be back by Monday?"

"No, not until the middle of next week. You'll have to miss the first day of school on Wednesday, but I'm sure your mother can smooth things over for you."

"But what about the barbecue at the ranch on Labor Day? Sam's invited everybody, including us. Right, Mom?"

"Yes, but—"

"Griffin will be bummed if I don't show up."

As Stewart tried to sway Jason's decision, Megan told herself this trip might be just the remedy for their son's sullen mood. On the other hand, she'd been looking forward to the staff party probably as much as Jason, if she was being totally honest with herself.

She reassured him. "Considering how much Griffin always looked forward to seeing his own parents, I'm certain he would understand your situation. In fact, he'd probably be upset with you for passing up this chance to be with your dad."

"I s'pose you're right," Jason mumbled, then turned to his father. "Okay, I'll go."

"Good. There's only one thing I absolutely have to do while we're there, which is an important meeting about my books." He glanced at Megan, then at his son. "I've already talked to the hotel about arranging for someone to stay with you in the room while I'm gone."

"If you're just gonna be busy with meetings, I don't want to hang out in no dumb hotel room."

"It wouldn't be for very long."

Jason looked doubtful. "I dunno."

Megan spoke to Stewart. "He thinks he's too old for babysitters."

He looked at his son. "You do, huh?"

Jason stood a little taller as if to make himself look bigger and older. "Yeah. I don't need a sitter. If you let me stay by myself—"

"No," said Stewart.

"Out of the question," answered Megan at the same time.

In his defense, however, she questioned Stewart's decision to trust a stranger with their son. Even though he argued that the hotel hired responsible people, he reluctantly agreed to work things out so Jason could be with him, probably in an outer office under a secretary's watchful eye.

Noticeably victorious, Jason promised to be on his best behavior for his dad.

~

AFTER THE AIRPORT limo drove off the following afternoon, Megan spent a quiet weekend walking alone on the beach of Alamitos Bay. She tried to muscle her way through a thick historical novel that should have kept her mind off her troubles, but didn't. She had lunch with an old college friend without so much as hinting at the mess her life had become. As far as Lindy knew, Megan lived the life most people only dreamed about.

Waiting until Monday morning to phone Sam with her apologies regarding the party, she explained the sudden father-son trip to New York. "Jason really wanted to be there. He misses everyone, especially Griffin. Tell them all hello from us."

"I will," Sam said. "But there's no reason you have to miss the fun."

"I'm not very brave about driving in the beach traffic on summer weekends, particularly a holiday. I was only willing to tackle it for Jason's sake. Now that he's not here…well, I thought it would be best if I stuck close to home."

"By yourself?"

"Yes."

"Sounds lonely."

"I'll manage just fine."

"Be careful. You might turn into a recluse like me."

"A recluse is not even close to how I would describe you."

"And how is that?"

"A mother hen."

His laughter lightened her mood. "Gathering all my chicks around me?"

"Something like that."

"Well then, that explains it."

"Explains what?"

"My determination to gather my flock together this afternoon. You included. It's just my fowl nature."

"Sorry, Sam. This chicken isn't venturing across the road today, let alone the Pacific Coast Highway."

"Cluck-cluck-cluck."

She chuckled. "Have a good time without me."

"Impossible."

CHAPTER 13

"Get dressed. You're coming with me."

Megan stood at her front door in a satin kimono, her wet hair wrapped in a towel, not quite believing that Sam had driven all the way from the ranch to fetch her for his party.

"What in the world are you doing here?" It had only been two hours since their phone call.

"What's it look like? I'm gathering the stray chick."

His lopsided grin did things to her insides that she had no business contemplating. "I can't just leave. My hair—"

"Your hair is just fine. It'll get wet again in the pool, anyway. Run a comb through it and bring your swimsuit. C'mon. Time's a'wastin'. I've got a flock of hungry chicks waiting on us."

She laughed. He smiled. She felt her knees weaken.

"Now that I've risked my own neck by driving those freeways to spare you the trouble, the least you can do is come back with me. I promise to drive you home tonight after the party is over. Deal?"

She hesitated, but his look of determination melted away any and all reasons to protest. There was a part of her that wanted to be with him. Today. Tonight. Tomorrow. Though she tried to deny it, she was glad he'd showed up on her doorstep to drag her away from her self-imposed imprisonment.

"I'll just be a few minutes. If you want to come in and make yourself at home, I'll try to hurry." She gestured toward the living room to the right of the doorway.

He stepped into the foyer without a single glance at her opulent surroundings. His penetrating gaze made her feel as if she was the most important thing in his life at that moment. She tried not to look at his mouth. She tried not to remember his kiss. She tried not to pay any attention to the way her whole body responded to the predatory look in his eyes.

No one else was home. No one would ever know if she led Sam up the stairs to—

Images flashed through her mind of Stewart with Maxwell.

"Megan? Are you all right?" Sam moved closer, reaching for her, touching her arm. She couldn't bring herself to look at him.

No, I'm not all right. Hold me, Sam. Take me in your arms and make love to me. Prove to me I'm desirable.

As if her thoughts had penetrated the silence, he dipped his head and kissed her gently, testing the waters. She wanted this. She wanted him. She gave in to her need. Her need to be held, and touched, and caressed. Her need to believe that she could make him truly want her as only a man could want a woman.

Initiating another kiss, a deeper kiss, she slid her hands behind his neck, leaving no question in his mind that she wanted more, expected more. They were alone. There was nothing to stop him from untying her robe, from smoothing his fingertips across her waist, over her bottom, pulling her gently against him. He was aroused and ready for her.

She unfastened the waistband of his shorts.

He took her hands in his, then nodded toward the stairs.

"No!" She unzipped his zipper, unable to keep her voice from sounding a little too high, a little too scared. So much was at stake. So much he didn't know. "Right here. Right now."

He glanced down at the Italian marble beneath their feet, shook his head and began to lead her toward the stairwell. The memories she had wanted to escape slammed into her with the impact of a tidal wave.

"I can't, Sam." Pulling away from him, she closed her robe around her and cinched the belt tight. "I'm sorry."

"I understand."

"Do you?" Her head jerked up.

"Of course. You and Stewart. It's not over yet."

"Oh, but it is," she said too quickly, instantly regretting it.

"If so, you wouldn't still be together. Besides, you don't seem like the type to have an adulterous affair."

"I'm not. But neither do you."

"Then you don't know me well enough."

"Please don't tell me you cheated on your wife."

"No, not once."

"Then I'm to assume you've had affairs with other married women?"

"Guilty. But not proud of it. Not now, anyway. Those days are long gone. Or so I'd thought until now. You were right to stop us before it got out of hand."

Megan wanted to set him straight, to tell him that he was oh so wrong about her. She was more than willing to give herself to him. Shamelessly willing to forget that she was still married to someone else. But she couldn't tell Sam the truth without telling him everything.

And she could *never* do that.

"I...I'll be down in a few minutes," she said, repeating the very words she had spoken only minutes earlier.

"I'll wait right here."

She glanced over her shoulder as she ascended the stairs, watching him watching her.

~

TAYLOR BIDED her time in the lounge chair by the pool, soaking up some sun, trying to even out her tan, which was a waste. During camp swim sessions a one-piece Speedo was required "for discretionary reasons," Sam had called it, while all along her belly was staying as white as a baby's butt.

These last couple weeks working maintenance detail had given her a little time to herself after lunch each day to slip into her string bikini for an hour of tan time. Yet it still hadn't been enough to give her a nice overall bronze. Instead, she looked like a patchwork quilt, and her stomach looked…well, she just prayed Anthony wouldn't tease her about it.

Anthony.

The thought of him sent tingling anticipation from head to toe. It was all she could do to keep from pacing and checking the time again. But she couldn't give herself away. She couldn't let anyone know or even suspect that something was up.

For a while there, she'd been as nervous as hell while Sam was gone, afraid he'd return just when Anthony was driving up the road from PCH. Sam would've recognized the car for sure. Then there'd have been no way Anthony could park down the hill and sneak up to the barn to meet her. She didn't want anything to spoil her plans with him.

She hadn't seen him in person since he'd come to the ranch to apologize to her. Every time she had a free weekend, he had business to take care of or an out-of-town meeting. She was back living with Sam which meant the embarrassing curfew of eleven o'clock on weekends. Afraid to tell Anthony that she was practically being held prisoner, she always gave him a lame excuse when he suggested sneaking off to a motel in the middle of the night. His persistence only proved to her how much he wanted her. He told her as much through texting with her late at night without Sam ever knowing anything.

But today was the first time they would be together again. Alone.

Thank God Sam had got back okay. So what if he had Megan with him? So what if he had a stupid-ass lovesick stare every time he looked at the woman? No doubt he got laid. Probably been doing it with her for weeks, maybe even months. Didn't matter now though. Taylor didn't care. Not really. Not anymore anyways. She had Anthony now. He wanted her. He'd told her so a million times just how he was going to make love to her when they met again.

She could hardly stand the wait. In just a little while she'd be with him. And she planned to fulfill every last one of his erotic fantasies.

"Hey, Taylor."

"Hi, Sam. Hi, Megan. How come Jason didn't come?" She glanced up at the two of them, then back at some kids playing Marco Polo with Griffin in the water. She was trying real hard not to act nervous. The last thing she needed right now was Sam watching her like a hawk.

Megan answered, "He's with his father on a trip. But he says hi."

"Yeah, well, tell him hi back. I know he was real excited about coming to the barbecue. Talked about it all the time during the last week of camp. Was he going anywhere special-like?" *Or was it just a convenient excuse to get him out of town so you could fool around with Sam?*

"Stewart had a last-minute opportunity to fly to New York. He wanted to take Jason along."

"New York's cool. He'll probably like it okay for a kid. I like Tahiti myself. Anywhere that's hot and humid. The less clothes, the better."

She uncapped the suntan oil, dribbled it in a circle around her belly button, then spread it across her bare skin with the palm of her hand. It was one of those rare moments when she saw her body as totally perfect, totally appealing to every male eye within a mile of her. She was hot. She knew it. And she didn't need anyone to tell her so. Except Anthony. Soon he'd be whispering in her ear—

"Yo, Taylor!" Sam waved his hand in front of her face. "You're spacing out. Maybe you're getting too much sun. Your skin's pink."

Her head jerked up. "Sorry. You're probably right. I better go up to the Rec Hall for a while." She gathered up her stuff, grateful for the excuse to disappear from the crowd. Sam wasn't even aware of his helpful suggestion. Nobody would be the wiser if she wasn't around. For added security, she pretended to act a little woozy as she got up from the lounge chair.

Sam steadied her. "Maybe you should go up to the house and rest."

"Maybe I will. Too much hard labor these last couple weeks must've caught up with me."

"You can't work all week and party all weekend without suffering the consequences eventually. Take it from the expert."

"Who parties? You keep a tighter leash on me than both of my parents put together." She hated his eleven o'clock curfew, but she didn't want to get into it now. "I'll probably fall asleep, so don't start worrying about me if I don't come back down for a few hours."

Sam nodded. "Speaking of parents, I see Griff got here but I don't see his family. They didn't make it?"

"No, Mario brought him. He said his folks had other commitments. I gotta go."

Megan spoke up. "Are you sure you don't need someone to walk with you up to the house? I'll be happy to—"

"No." She didn't mean to snap. "I...uh, I'm just tired from too much sun like Sam said. Have fun. Swim. Eat." *Make Sam drool all over you, for all I care.* "I'll just be sleeping up at the house."

She liked the idea of letting them think the house would be

occupied. As long as they believed she was up there, they couldn't slip off by themselves to the privacy of Sam's bedroom. Meanwhile, Taylor would be in the barn with Anthony, having a private little party of her own.

~

THE SETTING SUN was still warm. The water in the pool still inviting. The ocean breeze just right. The ribs and chicken and all the other food was delicious. As Sam sipped from a bottle of Coke, he stood off by himself to watch the festivities.

He couldn't remember a recent time when he felt more contentment. Everyone was having a great time, including Megan, who seemed to blend into his extended family as if she had been born into it.

Watching her laugh at something Mario said, Sam smiled to himself. She belonged here. With him. He'd known it all along, from the moment she had walked into his life.

If only things weren't so complicated. If only he knew she felt the same way about him. One minute she could kiss him with such passion that he was certain she *did* want him as much as he wanted her. Then the next minute she was back living with her husband with no sign of separation in sight.

He refused to believe she could have lied about divorcing Stewart Fisher. From all that he'd seen of her over the summer, she had to be the most open and honest woman he'd ever met. He could see it in her eyes.

And yet, he saw with his own eyes this afternoon that she lived like a princess in a fairy-tale castle. Except her castle looked like an Italian villa. Not many women would walk away from such a charmed life without good cause. He wondered if Megan could.

Perhaps if her life was threatened. Or Jason's.

Somehow, though, Sam didn't think Stewart's polished public

persona masked a violent or abusive husband. Megan never gave any indication that she was in danger. It simply seemed as if the two of them had fallen out of love. Or at least Megan had. Stewart appeared to be fighting for their marriage.

Then why was she still living with him? Was it just easier for her to stay? The thought of her choosing to continue in the loveless marriage made Sam uneasy. He wanted her to choose to leave. No, it was more than that. He really wanted her to choose to be with him.

His thoughts drifted back to earlier that afternoon when he'd tried to take her upstairs. He hadn't driven all the way down to Long Beach only to walk into her house and jump her in the foyer. He hadn't planned to make love to her. Things just got carried away. She certainly didn't object.

Hell, she'd acted as if he could've taken her right there on the marble floor. A part of him was more than willing to oblige, take advantage of the moment, enjoy the excitement of raw, hot sex.

But another part of him could only see the damage it could do. He didn't want to just screw her like it was nothing more than a salacious affair behind her husband's back. He wasn't about to play the role of her lover while she continued to act as if she was happily married to the famous Stewart Fisher.

Today she had balked. Today she had chosen not to follow him upstairs. Perhaps he'd pushed his luck too far too soon. But someday…

Megan turned slightly, as if she'd known his thoughts were on her. She lifted a glass of lemonade to her mouth, eyeing him over the rim. After her dip in the pool, her braided hair was slicked back and she had covered up her body-hugging swimsuit by wrapping herself in a tropical-print sarong. His gaze drifted down and back up, catching her with a look of appreciation.

She smiled ever so slightly before turning her attention back to Mario and two others who had joined their circle. He was tempted to join them, for no other reason than to have an excuse to be near Megan. But he had to resist the impulse. The last thing either of them needed was to have him dogging her heels like a lovesick puppy, confirming any suspicions that there was something going on between them. Mario had already done his share of teasing and speculating. Sam didn't want to add fuel to the fire.

It was hot enough already.

~

FROM THE MOMENT Sam had picked her up for the barbecue, Megan had felt unsteady, a little off-kilter, as if the earth beneath her feet was just slightly off its axis. Without the role of mother and wife wrapped around her, identifying her, she was treading on unfamiliar territory and she wasn't quite sure how to handle it.

Or Sam.

The rest of the afternoon, she had kept a safe distance from him, afraid to say or do anything that might be misconstrued. Just because she was attracted to him didn't mean she had the freedom to act upon it.

After her dip in the pool, she had caught him watching her with a look that had been anything but subtle. She had almost glanced around to see if anyone else had noticed, but managed to maintain her cool and continue her conversation with Mario. Not for very long, however.

When her mind would not stop drifting back to what almost happened at her house, she had to find something more distracting than standing around in her swimsuit while avoiding Sam's gaze.

Pitching in to help take some empty food trays back to the kitchen, she joined Karen in a trek up the hill to the Rec Hall. A few yards from the door, two girls in the junior CA program were busy talking as they carried some trash bags to the garbage bins, unaware of anyone overhearing their dramatic discussion.

"She's been gone too long."

"She probably took off."

"Then we should tell Sam."

"Not me. If she found out who told on her, she'd kill me and you know it. Count me out."

"But what if something's happened to her? We gotta tell somebody!"

"She can take care of herself."

"But what if—"

"Look, she's a spoiled little rich kid who doesn't even have a clue how good she's got it. I'd kill to have her life. And all she ever does is get herself in trouble so Sam can come bail her out of it. Now she's *living* with him! I wouldn't be surprised if her parents let her *marry* him."

"That's sick, Pam. Real sick. Sam's not like that, and you know it. He just...*cares*. That's all."

"He cares all right."

"Yeah, he does. And that's why I'm gonna go and tell him that Taylor's missing."

Megan spoke up, "Taylor isn't missing, girls. Sam sent her up to the house to lie down for a while. She got too much sun."

The teenagers glanced at each other with expressions that said far more than their stunned silence.

Karen asked, "What gives? You two know something..."

One of them stepped back, shaking her head. "Leave me out of this. I've got work to do in the kitchen."

"Chicken!" the other called out after her friend heading off toward the doorway.

"Tracy?" Karen prompted.

After glancing over her shoulder at her retreating buddy, she hesitated another moment. "I, uh, might be wrong. Maybe she is up at the house. Maybe—"

"Maybe you just ought to tell us what you were going to tell

Sam," Megan said. "And if you're worried about Taylor finding out who told him, she can blame me."

"I'm not afraid of her."

"Of course not." But Megan could see a small sign of relief despite the girl's denial. "What makes you think Taylor is not up at the house?"

"I saw her taking the shortcut to the upper road. She glanced behind her a bunch of times like she was checking to see if anyone was watching her."

"She didn't see you?"

"I don't think so."

"When was this?"

"About two hours ago."

Megan realized Taylor must have taken off as soon as she had left the pool. Sam's suggestion had played right into the teenager's ploy to sneak away. "And you haven't seen her since?"

She shook her head.

The first thing Megan did was check the house, hoping in vain to find Taylor sacked out on the couch. Only after she came up empty-handed did she link up with Karen, who had tried the hiking trail in the remote possibility that Taylor had simply taken a long walk or had stretched out on a granite boulder for some nude sunbathing.

"No luck?" asked Megan as she approached Karen.

"I didn't find Taylor, but I found a Porsche parked off the shoulder. I have a sinking feeling that she and that sleazeball agent might be up at the old barn. If so, that's something Sam needs to deal with."

Megan hated to think of how Sam would handle it, but she had no choice in the matter.

Minutes later, as he stalked off in search of Taylor, Megan raced to keep up. She could only imagine the scene they were about to walk in on. As much as she wanted to catch up to him and beg him to calm down a little before they reached the barn, she didn't dare say a word. He was beyond listening.

He marched up the hill, past the Rec Hall, and up the well-worn rocky trail eroded away in some spots from the runoff of spring rains. Megan stumbled more than once, scrambling to her feet and panting heavily to keep on his heels.

At the top of the path where it opened onto the asphalt road, he pulled up short, taking Megan by surprise. She plowed into the back of him, startling him as well.

He glanced behind him as if it was the first time he realized he wasn't alone. The scowl on his face deepened.

"Stay here," he said, his voice barely above an angry whisper.

Megan looked past him. Several yards down the road, Taylor was wrapped in the arms of Anthony Thorndike standing at the open door of his Porsche. Their passionate kiss left nothing to the imagination. They were lovers saying goodbye.

"Sam, promise me you won't hit him again."

He glanced down at her hand resting on his arm. The muscle along his jaw twitched. Without saying a word, he turned and marched toward the car.

Megan followed. If anything went wrong, she didn't know how she could stop the two men from fighting, but she wasn't about to stand back as a spectator either.

"What the hell do you think you're doing?" Sam demanded as he approached.

Thorndike shoved Taylor away from him. She stumbled backward, catching her balance before she fell into the eroded ditch beside the car. Her mouth open in stunned disbelief, she stared at Thorndike backing cautiously toward the driver's seat.

Megan caught the teenager's expression of hurt and confusion from the blatant and rough rejection. Thorndike wasn't about to stick around for Taylor's sake. He only looked out for himself.

As he fumbled in his pocket for the keys, Taylor blinked, then saw Sam barreling down on them like a raging bull. Her gaze darted between the two men. In that split second, when she should have told Anthony to go to hell for taking off like a scared rabbit, she went from being hurt to being his defender.

Even though he didn't so much as look at her, she yelled for him to hurry, to get out of there while she handled Sam.

"Like hell you'll handle me!" Sam moved her aside and faced Thorndike. "I thought I told you to stay away from here."

"Yes, well… Perhaps you did."

"*Perhaps* I did? There's no 'perhaps' here, fella. You have asked for trouble and you're going to get it. Now."

"Stop, Sam." Megan grasped his upper arm with both hands, moving herself in front of him. "Please don't make this worse than it already is. You have too much to lose. You have this camp to think about. And everyone who works here. If you let things get out of control now, I know you'll regret it. Let him leave."

As Sam's hard glare shifted from Thorndike to her and back, she felt the muscles in his arm slowly relax.

"If you come back here again," Sam warned, "I'm calling the sheriff's department to have you arrested for statutory rape."

Thorndike shook his head, but kept his mouth shut. He raised his arms, palms up, as he backed slowly into his driver's seat.

Megan couldn't help but notice the physical similarities between the two men. Intentional or not, Taylor's infatuation with Sam might have transferred to Thorndike as a fill-in fantasy. Or maybe a means to get to Sam's attention.

The Porsche drove away slowly, likely to avoid kicking up pebbles or dust onto the pristine exterior.

Sam turned to Taylor. "In my office. Now!"

"You can't bully me around. You're not my father!"

"But I *am* your guardian as long as you are at the ranch."

"*Temporary* guardian."

"And that means I've got every right to come down on you for pulling this shit. Now get your butt down the hill and wait for me in the office. If I have to come looking for you, there will be hell to pay. I swear it."

Megan held her breath. She prayed Taylor would hold her tongue. The girl opened her mouth to speak, then snapped it shut and marched off toward the hiking trail that led back to the Rec Hall.

"Maybe you should go with her," Megan said quietly. "Make sure she doesn't run off."

"She won't." He stared at the trailhead as Taylor disappeared from sight. "She knows damn well that her parents won't take her back. I'm all she's got. She'll be waiting in my office when I get there."

"I hope so."

"Besides," he reached up and rubbed the back of his neck with both hands, gazing up at the sky, "we both need some time to cool off."

"I appreciate you not decking Thorndike again."

"I wanted to do more than that to the lying bastard." Dropping his clenched hands to his sides, he cursed the devious little Brit for sneaking around with Taylor. "I hope to God she's not pregnant...or worse."

"Sam, are you sure you're not in over your head?"

"What do you mean? I've dealt with plenty of troubled kids over the years. Taylor isn't any different."

"But I think this situation *is* different. You've put yourself way out on a limb by becoming her guardian. Temporary or not, it's the biggest risk you've ever taken with a kid. And I think...I think it may have been a mistake."

Especially if she's in love with you. She wanted to say it to him, but she held back, knowing she had no proof.

"You don't understand." Sam looked hurt, almost defensive. "I'm sorry that you have been caught in the middle of this mess."

"I should be the one apologizing to you for putting my two cents into it. You know these kids. I don't. Not really. I teach at a parochial school where the parents are involved and hardly anything of any significant magnitude happens to them. Not yet, anyway. I'm not like you."

"You're beginning to sound a lot like my ex."

"Sorry."

"Don't be. It's this exact same kind of involvement with my kids that led to our divorce," he explained, adding that Maryann resented taking a back seat to the children. "I had promised to make this day special for you, and it looks like I failed—in more ways than one. Give me some time to talk with Taylor, then I'll drive you home."

"Maybe it'd be better if I went with Mario. I know he's taking Griffin so he shouldn't mind driving an extra few miles."

"That's if he didn't have a full car already. You forgot Karen and her date." He pulled his keys from his pocket. "Here. Just take my car."

"But how would I get it back to you?"

"We can work that out later."

Megan hesitated a moment, wishing she had insisted on driving her own car to the barbecue. But it was too late now. She reached out and closed his fingers around his keys. "Keep them. We can leave after you've finished with Taylor."

"I'd better get down to the office. She might think I forgot about her."

"I doubt it."

CHAPTER 14

Taylor endured the lecture from Sam, letting him blow off some steam while he paced back and forth behind his desk. She was pissed too. Pissed that she got caught with Anthony. So she had sat there on the sofa in the office, listening to Sam but not really listening. More like pretending. Then he called her on it.

"Well shit, Sam. I'm sitting here, aren't I? I'm not talking, am I? So isn't *that* listening?" So what if she mouthed off at him? It's not like he was going to haul off and hit her. Sam wouldn't ever do that, no matter how mad he got. "So which one are you gonna call to come get me—my mom or my dad?"

Sam came around the desk and sat on the corner of it. His glare was gone. He looked at her with soft, kind eyes. "Is that what you expect me to do?"

She shrugged, unable to keep from acting cocky. "Why not? That's what they do. Neither one of them want me."

"They want you, Taylor. They just don't know how to deal with you."

"Mom says she already talked to Dad about some boarding

school in Europe if things don't work out here." Angry, she chewed on a hangnail.

"I take it you want to go."

Her head snapped up. "No way!"

"Then why mess up this last chance by sneaking around with Thorndike?"

She didn't like the way Sam said his name. "You don't understand. He cares! He…he loves me."

Sam didn't jump down her throat like she was expecting he would. Instead, he just sat there, not saying a single word. He didn't believe her. He didn't know how it was when she was with Anthony. Things were different now. Anthony was older, yeah. So what? What was a few years, anyway? There was so much about him that was good and wonderful and sophisticated but Sam would never see it.

"Taylor…"

Here it comes. He will send me away for sure.

"I am not about to play prison guard. If you are so determined to see this guy again, you'll do it come hell or high water."

She was surprised but relieved that he could see things her way. That was exactly how she felt. She loved Anthony. It was only a matter of time before she would work it all out so she could move in with him. Her parents didn't need to send her off to Europe. If they really wanted to get rid of her, they'd let her marry Anthony. Not that he'd asked her yet. But he would.

"Here's the deal," Sam said, leaning forward, his hands braced on his knees. "If I can do it, I'm filing a restraining order against Thorndike to keep him from coming onto my property. You know that if you sneak off to see that guy again, you've signed your own release papers from here. That means if you choose him, you choose boarding school."

"That's not fair!"

"Of course it is. I'm putting the responsibility of the outcome in your hands. You are underage, Taylor. And

Thorndike damn well knows it. I should report him for statutory rape."

"You can't prove it. I'll deny it. Besides, my parents care more about bad publicity than me. They'd rather sue you for slander than turn Anthony in for rape."

Sam shook his head in disappointment. "Cut me some slack, kid. I want you to stick around. But I'm not putting you under lock and key. Got it?"

"Yeah."

"Good. Now, with that said, I need to drive Megan back to Long Beach. Karen and Mario and a couple of others will be hanging around until nine, but then you'll be on your own until I get back."

Taylor couldn't believe Sam was really gonna trust her to be by herself. *I'm putting the responsibility of the outcome in your hands.* "That's cool. I'll be fine. No visitors, I promise."

"No phone calls either."

She chewed her nail again, then answered begrudgingly, "Okay."

~

THE DRIVE HOME was spent in long interludes of silence. Megan sat across from Sam, who was preoccupied with his concern for Taylor. Wishing she could say something to ease his mind, she knew she would probably not say anything he wanted to hear. They had already disagreed in his decision to leave Taylor cooling her heels by herself in her bedroom at the ranch house. Sam seemed to think she could be trusted to stay put and not run off to meet Anthony. Or worse, bring the man back to the ranch while she was home alone.

As far as trust went, Megan had to hope that Sam's judgment call was the right one. He had far more experience with troubled teens than she did. As a teacher, she was well aware of the child protection laws that defined "mandated reporters" legally oblig-ated to report abuse. Sam knew it would be the right thing to do. Tragically, Taylor's parents didn't think she was worth their protection. In all likelihood, Nicole would deny anything happened at her house. Her own Hollywood agent boyfriend wouldn't want his company tainted by the scandal of an employee. It was Hollywood, after all. With the "Me Too" move-ment, the tabloids would pounce on this.

Between small snippets of polite yet awkward conversation, she stared out the window and tried not to think of going back home to her own troubled life.

He pulled the car up to the curb in front of her house and cut the engine.

"Thank you for taking me to your barbecue, Sam," she said, adding, "And for the chauffeuring service."

"Hold on. My escort duty isn't done yet." He jumped out and opened her door for her. "I must see you safely inside, right?"

She glanced at the ominous dark windows of the house as she took his hand and stood. "I should have left some lights burning."

"Blame me for dragging you out of here so fast." He smiled. "I didn't want to give you a chance to talk yourself out of going with me."

Approaching her front door with Sam beside her, Megan fought her escalating anxiety about entering the empty house, still haunted by the afternoon she'd walked in on Stewart. She had thought the house had been empty then too.

Beneath the porch light on the warm evening, she unlocked the front door, hesitated, then pushed it open.

"Is something wrong?" he asked.

"No!" *Calm down*, she told herself. *Lower your voice.* "I…um, I'm sorry. Just skittish, I guess. Sometimes this huge house seems more like a haunted castle than a home to me."

"Ghosts in the closets?"

Only in the master bedroom. She tried to laugh a little to lighten the tension. "Phantoms. Ghosts. Burglars. Take your pick. I have a pretty good imagination."

Not good enough, apparently. I never imagined my husband leading a double life. With Maxwell!

"Megan?" Sam's hands closed around her upper arms. "You look like you're about to pass out. What the hell is wrong?"

She blinked a few times, trying to bring him into focus, trying to shut out the images in her head. She shouldn't have let Sam get out of the car. She didn't want him to see her fall apart.

"I can handle this on my own," she said before realizing she'd spoken her thoughts aloud.

"Handle what?"

Her mind scrambled for a plausible excuse for her behavior. "It's just that I'm not accustomed to coming home to an empty house. Well, it makes me think about the divorce, and what might happen if Stewart—" She cut herself off. "It's late, Sam. You have enough to deal with today without hearing about my phobias over my future."

"It's not late." He pushed the door open, took her hand, and led her inside. "And I'm not leaving until I know you feel safe, even if it means going through the house with you, room by room."

"That won't be necessary." She couldn't bear the thought of walking into the master bedroom again, let alone seeing Sam in the same room with those memories. "Really, I'll be fine. You don't need to do this."

"Maybe, maybe not." He walked her down the two steps into the living room. "But if you expect to get rid of me, you'll satisfy my urge to play the white knight one more time today. It's an obnoxious habit I've gotten myself into."

"So I noticed." Stalling, she straightened a pillow on the formal white-on-white couch. The room was a pristine portrait of the perfection Stewart had requested, down to the fine detail of the claw-footed mahogany side tables, the Chinese vases, and the sculpted marble figures. This room held his cherished possessions, not hers.

So stark. So lifeless. Frozen in time, waiting for Stewart to walk in the door with some important visitor.

Ay, faithful to Little Boy Blue they stand,
Each in the same old place,
Awaiting the touch of the little hand,
The smile of the little face.
And they wonder as waiting these long years through
In the dust of that little chair,
What has become of our Little Boy Blue
Since he kissed them and put them there...

WHAT *HAD* BECOME OF STEWART? The Stewart she had known was gone. Or rather, never existed. More importantly, what had become of *her*? Megan had lost herself somewhere along the way, somewhere between the college library and this Italian villa in Naples.

Her gaze went to an elegant antique secretary where Stewart kept a few glasses and bottles of liquor, the rest being upstairs in the wet bar of the family room.

"If you don't mind," she said, "I think I'll make myself a drink. Would you like something? Scotch? Brandy?"

"Soda, if you have any."

"In the kitchen. I'll get it."

He followed. After she handed him the last can of diet cola, she changed her mind about the hard liquor and pulled out a half bottle of merlot lying on its side on the lower shelf of the refrigerator. As she started to pour a small glass, her hands shook, clinking the bottle against the glass.

Sam stepped forward and silently took over, finishing the job.

"Thanks," she said, taking the glass. The sip she had intended to take turned into more of a gulp.

"Is it me?" he asked. "Do I make you nervous to be alone with me?"

"No. It's not you." She lifted the glass to her lips again, telling herself to slow down. But he was right. She was nervous. Jumpy, even. But not because of him.

He moved closer. His face hovered over hers. "It's time to get this over with."

For a long, breathless moment, she thought he was talking about making love to her.

"I...don't think I'm ready, Sam."

"Ready or not, I don't have a lot of time. I wish I could stay all night but—"

"Oh, no! I can't have you here in the morning. The neighbors would— Well, I wouldn't want Jason to find out. Or Stewart."

"That's not what I meant. I was talking about checking the rooms before I leave."

"Oh...of course."

She carried the wineglass with her as she led Sam up the back staircase. There was nothing to fear, she told herself. They would do a quick walk-through, and Sam would be on his way in less than twenty minutes.

Is that what you really want?

The voice taunted her. On the second floor, they checked Jason's room, neatly organized with his models and toys lined up on the shelves. Sam seemed mildly surprised by such orderliness of a ten-year-old.

"He's his father's son," Megan explained without thinking of the new meaning to those words. She didn't want to believe that Jason would turn out like Stewart—living with secrets and lies, deceiving the ones he loved. No, her son was not like his father.

She passed the guest bedroom without going inside.

"Didn't we miss one?" Sam asked, stepping through the doorway and flipping the wall switch to light the room.

He glanced around, then looked over his shoulder at her standing in the hallway. He didn't have to say anything. She saw it in his dark eyes. He knew this was her room from the hints of her presence. A framed photo of Jason on the dresser. Her toiletries on the bathroom vanity.

"All clear," was all he said before moving on.

They passed through the spacious family room decorated in big, cushy overstuffed furniture of browns and taupe.

Finishing the last of her wine, Megan left behind her empty glass on an end table, and showed Sam to the front staircase leading to the third floor.

She paused at the top step where the hallway angled toward the double doors. "I don't need to go any farther, Sam. I can see that everything is okay. There are no burglars hiding in the closets, waiting to pounce."

"We've come this far. No sense leaving the last rooms unchecked."

"No, I mean it. I think I made too much fuss over nothing."

"If you're worried I am going to pounce on you and throw you on the bed, you're mistaken." He might have meant it as a joke, but she didn't take it that way.

She hung back, practically clinging to the newel post at the top of the stairs.

He reached for her hand, and tugged her toward the bedroom door. "It'll be all right. Let me show you."

She pulled her hand away from him. "Please, don't."

"Megan..." His voice trailed off as he studied her. "All right then..."

She watched him walk toward the master bedroom before she went downstairs to the living room. He found her there, standing at the small liquor cabinet, a half-filled tumbler in her hand. She raised it in a half-hearted salute.

"This is a side of you I haven't seen," he said, coming up to her.

"It's new to me too."

"*Am* I making you nervous?" he asked again.

"No." Her answer was more like a sad sigh. "I'll be fine."

"I don't want to leave you this way."

After a failed attempt at a reassuring smile, she took another drink.

"No more knights to the rescue for me," she said after a quick swallow. "I've been that route. Look where it got me. Go home, Sam. Go back to Taylor. Slay *her* dragons. I'll slay my own from now on."

"Not this way." He gave a nod, indicating the glass at her lips. "Why are you so frightened of that bedroom? What happened in there?"

"I'd rather not talk about it, if you don't mind." She picked up the bottle to pour more liquor but only a drop plunked into the empty glass. "Damn."

As she set both the glass and the bottle down, Sam reached around her and gently grasped her wrists to keep her from grabbing a new bottle. "I know I can't really stop you if you're determined to get drunk—"

"Then don't," she said without a move, without struggle.

He dipped his head close to her ear. "I'm a good listener."

Her tense body relaxed into him, if only slightly, but she remained silent.

"Talk to me, Megan."

She turned in the circle of his arms and kissed him. No words were spoken. She gave in to her fear-driven desperation, allowing him to pull her into him, to hold her tight, to protect her. Her hands moved to the waistband of his shorts. He broke off the kiss and gazed down at her.

"Make love to me, Sam."

He shook his head. "As much as I hate to say it, I don't think it's a good idea. Not now. Not when you're feeling this way."

"Yes, now. Right here." She unbuttoned her blouse and started to peel it over her shoulders.

He grabbed the lapels of her shirt and yanked it over her lace bra. Her fingers closed over his hands, lowering them to her breasts. She pleaded with him again.

"Upstairs," he said.

"No!" She kissed him, then whispered. "Here. Now. Please."

~

GRIFFIN WENT LOOKING for Riley and instead found Taylor down at the small animal compound next to Sam's office. Dressed in cutoff jeans and a cropped T-shirt, she was standing in the llama's pen, her back to the entrance. He had sensed something was radically wrong ever since Sam got back to the pool party. He wasn't as loose and happy as when he'd left. Didn't take a genius to figure out that it must've been trouble with Taylor. Again.

Not too long afterward, Griff had heard from Tracy that the asshat talent agent had been sneaking around.

"Hey, Taylor."

She turned. "Hey."

It wasn't much of a greeting, but at least she didn't tell him to get lost. So he walked over to the pen.

Her gaze went back to the llama munching in the corner. "Do you believe the stories about this place being haunted?" she asked.

"Not really."

Griff knew the ranch property was used in a bunch of old Hollywood Westerns. The small adobe that was now Sam's office had been the sheriff's office and jail, which was why there were iron bars on the back windows. The movie history was no secret. But Sam didn't allow any talk of ghosts around the kids, not unless it was made clear that they were just campfire stories.

"Mario says he's seen things," she said.

"Mario likes to say a lot of things, especially if he's pulling a joke on one of us CAs."

She kinda chuckled a little, like she was agreeing with him. Then they fell into a long silence. Finally, she said, "Don't you ever wonder what it musta been like for those guys up here playing like real cowboys?"

"It would've been cool."

"I bet some of them are still here. I know if I died I'd come back here if I could."

"I didn't think you liked the ranch that much."

She gave him a sideways glance like she suddenly realized she'd been caught saying something she shouldn't have. But then she shrugged it off. "It's okay here. Sometimes. When it's not a prison sentence."

Griff didn't quite know what to say about that, especially when he thought she was lucky to have not one but two places to call home right now. He had a motel room. And there was no telling how much longer his family could afford to stay there. He didn't want to think about it. He wanted to change the subject.

"Missing a great party," he deadpanned, knowing she didn't give a damn about such things. Not when she had the big Hollywood bashes that her parents put on.

Ignoring the animals, she leaned back against the fence, hooking her elbows over the top rail, her gaze raised to the night sky. "I'm not the only one."

"I don't much care for parties myself."

"I wasn't talking about you. I was talking about Sam and Megan. He took her home, you know."

"Yeah, I know."

"I bet they're having their own little private party right now. Humpin' their asses off."

"You are so gross." He started to push away from the railing, more than ready to leave this conversation.

"You're still a virgin, aren't you?"

"And you're not. So what?"

"Don't you ever wonder what it's like?" She didn't give him a chance to answer. "It's awesome, y'know. Better than anything you could ever imagine in your whole life."

"I gotta go. Mario and Karen will be waiting for me."

She grabbed his hand as he began to walk off. "How about it?"

"How 'bout what?"

She rolled her eyes. "You. Me. Let's just do it. Now. On the couch in Sam's office." She smirked. "The ghosties can watch."

"No way." He yanked his hand back and pushed past her. She jumped around him and blocked his path.

"C'mon, Griff. Wouldn't you like your first time to be with an older, more experienced woman?"

"You're not that much older than me. And besides, you don't know it'd be my first time."

She closed the narrow space between them, skimming her hands up the front of his shirt. "I'm good, Griff. Really good. Let me show you how good."

He swallowed. Her breasts pressed into his chest. His dick hardened against her belly, making her smile with a real sexy, wicked smile.

He'd dreamed of something like this happening with her. And now that it was real, he knew he shouldn't do it. But he wanted to. God, how he wanted to.

Nothing else seemed to matter. Not her being mixed up with another guy who was practically twice their age. Not Sam's disapproval. Not Griff's own moral upbringing. Nothing mattered but following her into Sam's office and finally losing his virginity to the one girl who taunted and tantalized him nearly every day of summer camp, not to mention in his nightly dreams.

It seemed like only seconds before they were naked on the couch. She showed him how to touch her, where to touch her. She opened up a whole new world to him.

"Remember," she whispered in his ear, skimming her hands over his back. "We don't have a rubber. So you gotta pull out before you come."

"I will," he promised, barely able to hear her over the pounding of his pulse in his ears. He clumsily tried to enter her, frustrated that he didn't just plunge into her on the first try. Isn't that how it was supposed to go?

"Let me…help," she panted.

The feel of her fingertips drove him over the edge. "Oh, shit!" He groaned, trying to hold back, trying not to let go so fast, so soon. But he couldn't control it. Almost the second he felt himself inside her, it was all over.

As his body shuddered with the last of the climax, Griff gulped air as if he'd just run a mile in six minutes. Only it was a lot shorter distance and a lot shorter time, much to his shame. It couldn't get any worse than this.

Taylor slugged his shoulder with her fist. "You little shit! That's it? What about me?"

Mortified, he wanted to run like hell but he was too exhausted to move. He could only gasp for air, and murmur a pathetic apology.

"You could've lasted long enough so I could've gotten something out of it. You could've waited, damn you!"

No, he couldn't have waited. Not even if she'd held a gun to his head. "I'm sorry," he repeated.

"Sorry? Ha! Don't make me laugh. You're just like all the other high school boys—'Fuck 'em fast and leave em.' That's why I love Anthony. He knows how to treat a woman."

"If you love him so much, why did you do it with me?" he asked, getting up and grabbing his pants. He had gone from complete ecstasy to total humiliation in two seconds. It had to be a world record.

"I thought I was doing you a favor."

"Some favor." If anything, he was scarred for life. Shit, this whole thing was a nightmare.

"And you're a goddamn liar too. You promised you would pull out in time." She sat on the edge of the couch, not the least bit concerned about her naked body. Her fists pounded the cushions next to her. "Shit-shit-shit. If you knocked me up, Sam is gonna kill both of us."

Griffin froze. "You can't tell Sam!"

"If I'm pregnant, I'll have to tell him. Otherwise he'd go after Anthony."

"It was only once. You can't be—"

"The way my luck has been going, once is enough."

"But what about your boyfriend? If anybody is the father, it would be him. Everybody knows it. And besides, you were with him earlier this afternoon."

As soon as he blurted out the words, he regretted it. She bristled like nothing he'd ever seen before. Jumping up from her seat, she started yelling at him like it was nobody's business.

"Were you watching us in the barn? I just bet you were spying down on us, you pervert."

"No, I wasn't. Tracy told me that Sam caught you two up on the road."

"Well, for your information, Anthony has the smarts to use protection, unlike you."

"Me? What about you? If anybody should have been worried about getting pregnant, it should have been you. Why didn't *you* have a rubber? *You're* older and more experienced, right?"

She slapped him. Hard.

And he walked out.

The way my luck has been going, once is enough.

Between his own lousy luck lately and hers, he wouldn't be at all surprised if he had knocked her up. It would be a perfect ending to a perfect disaster.

What if she was pregnant? How would he face Sam? How would he face his own parents? They had enough troubles of their own without him messing things up even worse. He wasn't about to admit to anyone that he had let himself be seduced into losing his virginity. He would have to find a way on his own to pay for an abortion, or else he'd offer to marry her to give the baby his name.

Either way, it sickened him.

Christ, he was only fifteen! Owning up to his share of the responsibility was going to be the hardest thing he'd ever have to do.

CHAPTER 15

"We can't do this, Megan. You know it as well as I do." Sam looked down at her, wondering if he was crazy for not giving in to her. He wanted her, but not this way, not when she had so much at stake. He wouldn't.

She pushed herself away and stumbled back. He tried to grab her but she batted his hand away, managing somehow to keep from losing her balance and falling into the antique secretary. She eyed the few remaining bottles of booze.

"Don't do this to yourself," Sam said. "He's not worth it."

"No, Sam. The truth is *I* am not worth it."

"What's that supposed to mean?"

She spun around, tears in her eyes. "Am I attractive to you?"

"Of course."

"Sexually, that is."

"Yes." He shifted his stance, all too aware of his physical reaction to her. "You are most definitely sexually attractive. Probably more than you realize. You don't need to throw yourself at me."

"Words, Sam. Just words. If you really felt that way, you'd have been on me in a second. Instead you play the perfect gentleman.

Why don't you just say it straight—I have about as much sex appeal as a clam."

"A clam, huh?" He laughed at the absurd comparison, then regretted it when he saw the hurt look on her face. Abruptly grasping her hand, he led her toward the stairs.

"Where are we going?"

"Clamming."

~

Despite Sam's attempt to lighten the mood, Megan felt panic swell in her chest as they reached the third floor and started through the door to the master bedroom, then stopped.

The memory of her husband beneath the floral bedspread flashed in her mind. She could almost hear the music again. The sound of muffled voices. Stewart's naked body with tangled covers around his hips. The person beneath him moved into view. Maxwell. Their dearest friend all these years. Jason's Uncle Max.

Sickened by the vivid memory, she turned away, closing her eyes. Sam cursed under his breath and pulled her into his arms.

Until that moment, Megan hadn't realized that she had spoken every word aloud. And that Sam had heard every last, ugly detail. Mortified, she fled out the bedroom door.

He caught up to her at the top step. "Why are you so damn desperate to get away from me?"

"Not you. That room. This whole house. Me!"

"You? Why? You blame yourself for losing Stewart?"

She winced at the truth. "It would have been hard enough to deal with another woman. But he's in love with a man?"

"All the more reason to realize that Stewart's behavior has nothing to do with you." He traced the line of her jaw with his fingertip. "And you are a beautiful woman, Megan."

A tear ran down her cheek. "I wish right now that I could believe you but—"

"You asked me if I found you sexually attractive."

She groaned. "Much to my regret."

"Not mine. I happen to find you extremely attractive. Sexually and every other possible way. And unless you stop me, I intend to prove it to you."

"Here?" She sucked in a quick breath as he kissed her neck. "Now?"

"Right here. Right now." Turning the tables on her, he kissed her hard and deep, his hands moving quickly, taking off her blouse, unhooking her bra.

In their feverish rush of kissing and touching, they dropped to the soft carpet, only partially undressed before Sam entered her with a frenzied madness. She cried out. He stopped.

"Don't," she begged. "Don't stop."

She gripped his buttocks, pulling him deeper into her, urging him to take her harder. Their sweat-sheened bodies writhed and bucked. Primal. Raw.

WHEN IT WAS OVER and the last shudder rippled through his body, Sam dropped his face into the curve of her neck, gulping air, stunned at the ferocity of their lovemaking. Her sensuality rocked him to the core.

"Never—" He exhaled, then inhaled.

"Never again?" she asked, her voice shaky.

He chuckled. "Wrong!"

Rolling onto his back, he took her with him. Her legs straddled his hips as she sat upright. Her long hair fell over her shoulders and cascaded over her bare breasts. Her cheeks were flushed. And he couldn't seem to keep from grinning.

"I had *started* to say that I'd never had it so damn good."

"Ever?"

"Ever, sweetheart." He brushed her hair aside and cupped the back of her neck, pulling her down to him for another kiss. The movement of her body over his groin was painfully sweet. He slid his other hand between their slick bellies and stroked her, eliciting another soft moan.

Her lips curved into a smile. "Again?"

"Not yet. But I'm getting there a hell of a lot sooner than I would've expected. The way I feel right now, I don't know if I'm ever going to have enough of you."

The need for her was staggering. He felt like a goddamned teenager the way his body craved her, the way his heart raced. It made him want to be inside her body, wholly and completely.

When he made love to her again, it was slow and thorough, feeling her sweetness and tenderness seeping under his skin and entwining with his own soul.

Afterward, lying in one another's arms, he wondered in silence where this would lead. With her head resting on his chest and her hand splayed over his stomach, she seemed to doze off while he stroked her hair.

"Remember that afternoon when you brought Jason to visit the ranch?"

She didn't say a word. She didn't look up. She only nodded.

"I think I fell for you that day, only I didn't know just how hard until now."

"Please, Sam, don't make this any more complicated than it already is. You set out to prove a point, and you succeeded quite well, thank you very much."

"That's it?"

"Isn't that enough? You made me feel wonderful and sexy and beautiful. You made the earth move for me. I don't regret it for a second. Well, maybe a little. Maybe tomorrow morning I'm going to hate myself for—"

"Don't, Megan." He tried to pull her back into his arms but she straightened and turned, sitting beside him, gathering her discarded blouse to her chest, suddenly inhibited by her nudity.

He sighed heavily. "What about us, then?"

"There is no us."

"You certainly had me fooled." With the subtle intimacy of a lover, he gently tugged the blouse from her hands.

"You're not playing fair."

"I'm not playing, sweetheart." He caressed her nipple, rubbing it with the back of his hand, watching the way it puckered and her skin blushed.

With the slightest catch in her breath, she seemed about to give in to the sensuousness of his touch.

He leaned forward, trailing kisses from her navel to the valley between her breasts. "Trust me," he whispered.

"No!" Startled to her senses, her mood abruptly changed. Her walls went up. She moved quickly to gather her clothes and dress. "It's not you, Sam. I'm just not so sure I can trust myself to be the best judge of character at the moment. No, that didn't come out right. I mean, I fell fast and hard for Stewart. I don't want to make the same mistake with you."

Sam put on his shorts, then took the rest of his clothes with him as he followed Megan down the stairs, reminding himself that she was going through more than the usual emotional turmoil of divorce. After his split with Maryann he'd had a few of his own meaningless affairs to mask the loneliness and pain. Hell, he even went back to his ex for sex. But never again. Now he wanted only Megan. And he'd be damned if he let her write this night off as a mistake. Or worse, if she went back to her gay husband.

Leaving the rest of his things in an empty chair in the family room, he stopped Megan before she reached the door of the guest bedroom.

"I don't want to become a faceless lover in your blurred memory."

She dropped her gaze, unable to look at him. "This shouldn't have happened, Sam. I'm not even separated from my husband, let alone divorced."

"He's been sleeping with someone else for your entire marriage, and you're worried about…what, fidelity?"

She nodded. "It sounds ridiculous when you say it. But I don't want to do anything that will affect my custody of Jason."

Sam wrapped his arms around her and held her. "You are not going to lose Jason because of us. You're his mother. And that carries a lot of weight in custody cases. And I mean a lot."

"I know you're right. But I can't help freaking out a little bit. Jason is my life. I don't know who I am outside of being a wife and mother."

"You're a teacher too. You have your kids at school."

"If only you knew how I had to fight Stewart every year over 'that job,' as he calls it. According to him, my real career was supposed to be as a full-time wife, mom, hostess, and whatever else that fit into his life."

"So he's a self-centered SOB."

"True." She half-laughed, moving out of Sam's arms. "As bad as he looks, Stewart did have a good side. He worked hard so we had the best of everything, especially for Jason's sake. We didn't need my income from teaching. Stewart wanted to make sure that Jason wasn't neglected in any way, and wanted me to be around for our son. If anything, I should be glad that he loves our son so much. Even if that means he's willing to fight for custody. My father walked out on me. His father turned his back on him. He doesn't want Jason to feel abandoned like we were."

"Except you left out one very important detail."

"Maxwell." She couldn't keep the hurt-filled sarcasm from her voice. "Dear, sweet Maxwell turns out to be my husband's lover. God, how could I have been so blind? How could I have not known about them? I knew that Maxwell was gay, of course. But it never once occurred to me that Stewart…"

Sam realized she could very well talk herself into staying stuck in her loveless marriage. Where would that leave him? The question in his mind was as self-serving as Stewart's intention to seek sole custody of the son. But Sam couldn't help the way he felt.

He watched Megan pick up her empty glass from the end table. Even if she gave up everything Stewart had given her, Sam had nothing to offer but a remote ranch in need of constant upkeep, and a life of busy weekends and summers with dozens of kids. Not exactly the lap of luxury.

With her back to him, she continued to stare at the tumbler in her hand. "Stewart doesn't want a divorce. He's scared his high profile will draw attention to our split and expose his secret. Most importantly, I hate thinking of what this will do to Jason, having his father destroyed by the news media."

"So you'll sacrifice your own life."

"To protect my son? Yes. Right now, he's a happy kid. If this all blows up in the public eye, this house will be surrounded by reporters. The school too. Maybe even the camp. I don't know if I'm willing to risk the damage."

"I understand your need to protect him, but what happens when he does find out about his dad's affair? And he will. In a year or two or three. Then he'll know that not only his father lied to him. A lie of omission but still a lie. But he'll know you lied to him too."

She turned and faced him, first closing her eyes and then shaking her head. "I never saw it that way. Lying to Jase. And, if I have to face the harsh reality, lying to myself. I wonder who is this person, this Megan who is so wrapped up in being the wife, the mother, the teacher. Somewhere along the way I lost touch with just plain Megan."

"Just plain Megan?" he repeated.

"Well, I mean the Megan I used to be. The Megan who went off to college with wonderful dreams of traveling around the world, teaching in foreign countries along the way. The Megan who wanted to lose her inhibitions, dance naked in the desert moonlight, make mad, passionate love to a dark-eyed prince. I lost sight of her a long time ago."

"And I found her tonight."

"What you found was a very married woman who has too much to lose by having a tawdry affair. With her boss, I might add. I'd had too much to drink, period."

"Bullshit. Deny it all you want, but what happened upstairs was more than booze and a one-night stand. If you think for one second that I'm going to pretend otherwise, you're crazy."

"That's just it. Maybe I am crazy! I'd have to be to have done something so stupid as to throw myself at the first man who showed any interest in me."

"That's all it meant to you?"

"Oh God, no! I didn't mean any of that the way it sounded. It's just that…this isn't like me. I don't do these kinds of things."

"I didn't think you did," he said. "It's a little late to ask this, but could you get pregnant?"

"No! So, you are definitely off the hook as far as fatherhood is concerned. Even if I didn't have an IUD, I doubt I could conceive. I haven't had a period in months. My doctor says it's stress. God, I must be losing my mind for telling you all of this. I hadn't told a soul."

"Not even Stewart?"

She shook her head. "I was coming home from the appointment when I found him with Maxwell. Since then, there's been no reason to bring up the subject."

"No girlfriends to talk to about it?"

"No one I'm close to. There once was a time when Stewart was my best friend. We could discuss anything. We didn't need anyone else. Or so I thought. Now I realize he'd had Maxwell all along."

"I'm a good listener." Sam came up to her. The battle was over.

The tension between them vanished. "I won't even charge my going rate for therapy sessions."

"Therapy, huh?" She smiled a little smile, glancing up at the ceiling as if she could see the hallway where they had made love. "Is that what you call it?"

"Upstairs? Hardly!" His grin faded. "I'm willing to put sex on the back burner, if that's what you want. But I still want to see you."

"You'll see me every weekend at the ranch."

"Where I have to pretend that you are nothing more to me than another employee? I want to spend time with you. Alone."

"I don't know—"

"Tomorrow night."

"What about Taylor?"

He gave a heavy sigh. "I better not make it two nights in a row."

"I have school starting the next day. Then Jason will be coming home that night. Weekend camp starts on Friday…"

"Thursday night. Dinner."

"Are you forgetting Stewart still lives here? How would I explain to him that you want to take me out? I'm sorry, Sam. I can't. Not until I get a divorce."

"Then I say we'd better take advantage of tonight while it's still young. I know I promised no sex, but necking is allowed, isn't it? What about heavy petting?"

"The night won't be so young by the time you drive all the way home."

Glancing at his watch, he sighed in defeat. "Unfortunately, you're right."

After both of them dressed, Megan stood in the foyer, saying goodbye to Sam.

"No one will know about tonight," he said, guessing her fears. "If Mario gets nosy, I'll let him think I was with Maryann."

She tried to hide a surprising twinge of jealousy by dropping her gaze.

"Don't worry," Sam said, as if he'd read her mind. "I'm going straight home. Maryann is in the past. In truth, she knew it before I did. I haven't been with her since—"

Megan kissed him. He wrapped his arms around her, aroused and wanting more. She drew back, breathless, and aware of where she could take them in a blink of an eye.

"Like I said, no one will know."

"It's just that I have Jason to think about. I wouldn't want him to jump to the wrong conclusions and blame you for breaking up our family. He thinks the world of you, Sam."

"He's a great kid. I don't intend to do anything that would hurt him." He kissed her goodnight, holding her tightly to him.

As he nuzzled her neck, she fought the urge to let him stay a little longer, to make love to her one more time.

"Go, Sam," she whispered.

"I'll call you tomorrow night."

~

ON WEDNESDAY NIGHT, Jason got home from New York with his dad. His mom had made his favorite dinner of hot dogs, macaroni and cheese, and broccoli. He told her all about what a good time they'd had seeing stuff, and about staying at the Marriott Marquis right on Times Square, and how noisy it was in New York with horns honking and jackhammers going off early in the morning. They went to some Broadway shows; one he liked and one he didn't.

It was hard getting up to go back to school on Thursday, but the day went by real quick, and then Sam showed up to take all of them out to dinner. Except his dad couldn't go because he had some work to do on an investigation. His mom said she was just plain, old tired, and she was really sorry that Sam had come all the way down from the ranch. Jason didn't see why she had to go and say that. When he begged his mom to go she finally gave in, but she wasn't too excited about it. So it was just the three of them.

Sam let Jason pick the restaurant, so he picked Slice of New York Pizza in Seal Beach, just a little ways down PCH, saying it was just like the kind he'd had in New York City. He told Sam all about his trip, even though his mom had heard it all the night before. She pretty much just sat there real quiet through the whole thing. Something didn't seem right, but Jason wasn't quite sure what it was.

Later that night, as he was falling asleep he tossed and turned, thinking about his mom and dad, and how they both were acting real weird, and hoping it wasn't because of anything he did.

No, it wasn't him. It couldn't be about him. If they really knew, they'd say something for sure.

He pulled the covers over his head, and buried his face in his pillow, trying hard to stop thinking about the bad stuff he'd done, stuff that could get him in so much trouble.

It all started last fall…

"If you ask her," Cameron had said that one afternoon when he'd stopped by while Melissa was babysitting, "I know she'll do it for you."

Jason shook his head, getting all sick in the stomach. "I'm not asking her."

Cameron was sitting next to him and gave him a little shove against the shoulder. "Don't be such a wuss."

"I'm not a wuss." Jason swallowed hard and stared at the glossy pictures of the magazine that Cameron had pulled out of his backpack. His heart was pounding in his chest. He'd never seen anything like it.

"Gimme that!" Melissa grabbed the magazine from Jason's lap.

She was supposed to be downstairs talking on the phone with her girlfriend about algebra and boys, like she always did when she was there. He didn't expect her to come up like this and catch them.

She shook the magazine at them. "What are you two doing with this?"

Jason shrunk into the back of the sofa, wishing it would swallow him up. "Nothin'," he said.

"Not you. I was asking Cameron."

Her brother acted like nothing was wrong. "Just teaching little Jase here about the birds and the bees."

She glanced at the picture, wrinkled her nose in disgust and threw the magazine in his face. "Pervert."

"I am not." Cameron just had a big grin on his face. "He's curious like any other kid his age. Who's gonna teach him if we don't?"

"What's with the 'we' crap? I'm not in on this sick stunt."

"Why not? I was just telling Jason that he should ask you to show him the real thing."

"Shut up, you jerk. I could get in a lot of trouble if his parents find out you let him look at that shit."

"He won't tell. Will you, Jase? You don't want to get Melissa here in trouble, do you?"

Jason shook his head, but after looking at the pictures he couldn't stop looking at the front of her blouse, and feeling his face get hotter.

"See, Mel? He just wants one peek. What's the harm in a peek?"

"Get out! Now!"

Cameron turned to Jason. "Sorry, kid. I tried to help you out. Maybe one of these days I'll bring one of my girlfriends over to visit. When your folks are gone, of course."

When he left, Jason was so embarrassed that he went into his bedroom. Melissa followed him.

"I'm real sorry about my stupid brother," she said, fiddling with the end of her long blonde hair. "He's a real ass sometimes."

"It's…okay." Jason tried not to look at her so he sat down at his computer monitor. She sat on the edge of the bed, her knees nearly touching his hips. For a second or so, he thought maybe she was really gonna do what Cameron told her to do.

Her hand touched his shoulder. He gazed down at it, kinda scared and kinda wanting to see if she'd really do it. He licked his lips and shifted in his seat.

"Please don't tell, okay?" she asked. Her eyes were so pretty. So was her skin. She was fourteen, and was so beautiful and nice and Jason thought he couldn't do anything in the world that would ever hurt her.

"I won't tell."

"Good." She leaned over and kissed him on the cheek. Her lips were so soft.

His face got hot again. As she stood up and walked to the door, he touched his cheek where her lips had been. "Melissa?"

"Yeah?"

"Um…never mind."

She shrugged. "Let's just forget all this ever happened."

"Yeah, sure."

But they couldn't forget. Things changed after that. Cameron dropped in at the house a lot more often when his sister was babysitting. At first it was sorta okay, and they'd all play video games. But then he brought a girl and took her into a bedroom and locked the door.

Melissa would get real upset, but she couldn't seem to stop her brother from coming over, from using the bedroom, or from teasing and tormenting her about giving Jason a few lessons of his own. Pretty soon he stopped joking about it, and started bullying her to take off her blouse.

Jason tried to stop it. "Don't, Melissa. I don't need to see anything."

"Shut up, squirt. Sit down and enjoy this," Cameron said, gripping his sister's arm so tight that she yelped. "Stand right here in front of Jason and I'll tell you exactly what I want you to do."

"What if I don't?"

"If you don't, I'll tell his parents what you've been letting me do in their son's bedroom. I'll tell them you've been having boys over for the same reason."

"No! I'll tell them you lied."

"I'm the one they will believe, sis." He grinned. "And after Jason here has the time of his life tonight, I hardly think he's going to tell them what he got to do with you. He loves you, Mel. He's not about to get you into trouble. Hell, he'll be damn grateful to you!"

Melissa had tears running down her cheeks, but she did everything her big brother told her to do.

So did Jason.

CHAPTER 16

Sweating and crying and feeling guilty, Jason awoke with a muffled scream in his pillow. It hadn't been a nightmare though. All of it had happened to him for real. Things he shouldn't have done. Things that excited him and confused him and made him feel ashamed, all at the same time.

Dazed and afraid in the darkness, he felt his skin prickle with goose bumps. He thought he saw the shadow of someone standing on the balcony outside his window.

The house creaked and he nearly jumped out of his skin. Burrowing under the covers didn't help. It only made him think of the girls that Cameron had brought in here, and what they had done here.

Behind eyelids squeezed tight together, he saw Cameron's face looming over him. His heartbeat tripled, pounding away in his chest like maybe he was having a heart attack.

"Mom!" he hollered, throwing off the covers in panic.

He called out again, but she didn't answer. As he started across the hall to her bedroom, he heard the muffled sound of angry voices coming from the back stairs.

"Lower your voice, Megan. Do you want to wake Jason?"

"No, but he's going to find out soon enough. I can't go on living like this. I saw an attorney yesterday. I'm filing for divorce."

"On what grounds?"

"Irreconcilable differences. That should be vague enough to suit you."

"Don't do this to us, Meggie. Don't break up our family."

"You should have thought of that when—"

"Mom? Dad?" Jason stood on the middle landing between the first and second floors, looking down at the two of them facing each other in the kitchen.

He was trying real hard not to cry even though his eyes burned. His stomach hurt. His chest ached.

His dad hurried to the staircase, reaching his hand up.. "Come here, Jase."

Jason took forever to make it down one step, like his feet didn't even belong to him or nothing. He finally reached to his dad, who put an arm around his shoulder and gave him one of those "It'll be okay" squeezes. But it wasn't going to be okay. They were talking about divorce. And that meant everything was going to change.

He watched his parents glance at each other then back at him.

"I...don't want you to get divorced." His dumb voice cracked and went all high up like a girl.

His dad said, "I don't want it either. But sometimes...well... sometimes things just happen and we have to make the best of it. Your mother and I are trying to do that right now. But I don't think you need to be a part of the discussion. It's really between the two of us."

"But what about me? Where am I gonna go?"

Both of his parents said at the same time, "With me."

Then his mom came over to him and knelt down. "We both love you with all our hearts, Jase. That isn't going to change, even when I move out."

"Move out? When?"

"Soon. Somewhere nearby so we'll be close enough for you to see your dad whenever you want."

"So I'm going with you?"

His dad interrupted, "That hasn't been decided yet."

"Stewart—"

"Not now, Megan." His narrowed eyes meant business. "The discussion is closed for tonight."

That next weekend his parents did it. They went and split up. It was after him and his mom came home from the ranch. But his dad came up with an idea. Jase got to stay put at the house while his parents switched back and forth to live with him every other week. It was weird, but it meant Jason didn't have to go anywhere and still had his own bedroom all the time.

His mom didn't like it at first. Jase could tell she wasn't happy about it, but then she seemed okay. She wanted her own place, not one that his dad was paying for. But his dad said it would be dumb to get two different apartments and then let them sit empty every other week.

All this wasn't anything they said in front of him. It was part of an argument they'd had on Sunday night that Jase snuck down to hear. He was getting good at sneaking around to listen in on them. Except maybe not good enough. He was still trying to figure out what it was about Uncle Max that got his mom upset all over again.

~

At the Flying K, Megan spent Friday night and Saturday trying not to think of Sunday when she would spend her first night alone in the new place, a holding cell where her personal life stood still until she could be with Jason again. Stewart had moved out Monday night and into a two-bedroom Craftsman bungalow in Belmont Heights in the low rolling hills above the neighboring shoreline. Since Jason had spent the previous weekend at the ranch with Megan, it was his turn to be with Stewart.

"I don't want to go back there," she said to Sam, after telling him of the peculiar living arrangement.

Unable to sleep, she had taken a sunrise hike, ending up near enough to his house to bump into him walking with Riley. Somewhere in her unconscious mind, perhaps she had planned to bump into him all along, especially since he was the reason for her restless night.

"Stay here, then. Stay with me."

"No."

He reached out for her, turning her toward him, looking down into her eyes. "I've wanted to do this all weekend…"

He kissed her then and, God help her, she kissed him back, cautiously at first, trying to keep the walls from crumbling around her. Something in the way he touched her, held her, tore down her good intentions.

"Stay with me," he said again.

"I can't, Sam."

"No one will know. Leave when everyone else leaves. Stop somewhere for an hour, then come back. We can spend the evening together here."

"I have school in the morning."

"I'll send you home by seven. You'll be in bed by eleven."

She didn't go home by seven. Or eleven. By midnight, he convinced her that it was too late to drive home so he set the alarm for four thirty, promising to wake her so she could drive back to Long Beach before the commuter traffic bottlenecked the freeways. At nine a.m., with only a few hours of sleep, she faced a classroom of twelve-year-olds who didn't want to be there. She didn't either. She wanted to be back in bed with Sam.

~

Taylor swam naked in the pool at her dad's house just a few miles from her mom's place. Nobody was home but her. It was five o'clock on a scorching hot afternoon in late September. School always started out this way—too goddamn hot to think, let alone sit in a classroom and listen to a teacher drone on about the Civil War.

She rolled onto her back and kicked her feet, closing her eyes to the bright sunlight. The only thing missing from the deliciously decadent swim was Anthony. Just thinking about him made her ache for him.

Since her mom wouldn't take her back, her dad was guilted into buying a place nearby so she could start her junior year at her own high school. He didn't much like it though. So on Friday afternoons she went back to the ranch and stayed until Sunday afternoon.

Ever since Labor Day, there wasn't a chance in hell that Anthony would risk running into Sam again, so he stayed away from the camp. But it was a lot easier for him to visit her in Palos Verdes, especially since her dad wasn't around enough to keep track of her every move.

About once a week, she waited for a tap on her window between midnight and two in the morning, usually on Wednesday. Twice she blew off her afternoon classes so she could spend a few hours with Anthony. But she couldn't do that too often without getting caught.

No matter where they met, things always got hot and heavy real fast. They didn't have time to waste. Sex was unbelievable with him. Not anything like the disaster with Griffin. But that wasn't about love like she had with Anthony.

During that afternoon in Sam's office, she'd found out what it was like to be the one with all the power. Griff had done exactly what she told him. Well, almost. She got what she wanted from him, even if she made him feel like shit afterward. But she didn't have any choice. She couldn't let him find out that she did it on purpose, that she had set him up. He was perfect for her needs. No chance of any disease. Too young and horny to think about condoms.

Anthony was so damn cautious about protection that she'd never get pregnant if she left it to him. And a baby was her ticket out of here. It didn't matter anymore if her parents might have messed up her chromosomes with drugs before she was born. She wanted Anthony, and a baby of his would tie her to him forever.

Anthony was always telling her that he loved her, and she believed him. She really did. It was just that...if he really loved her...well, she just thought that none of this shit would've happened if he'd stand up to everybody and tell them all they planned to get married. In this day and age, it shouldn't be any big deal. The whole statutory rape threat was just that, a threat. If push came to shove, if she got pregnant and refused to get an abortion, her parents would hand her over to Anthony in a split second.

But her parents and Sam were so damn sure that Anthony didn't really love her. And she supposed it might look that way, considering that he didn't do anything with her but have sex. But that was only because they couldn't go out in public on a date.

Everything had gone exactly how she'd planned. Nobody would have found out that it was Griff, not Anthony, who had knocked her up. But two weeks ago her period came, dammit. She was pissed, but not ready to give up. She would get herself pregnant, even if she had to go back to Griffin again.

"Hey, baby."

Taylor gasped, sank under the water and came up sputtering, then squealing with delight. "Anthony! Ohmigod, you scared the shit out of me."

She scrambled up the pool steps and ran naked into his arms. "What are you doing here?"

"Well, after that little phone call from you about an hour ago, telling me about your plans for the afternoon, I couldn't stop thinking of you."

She started to unbutton his shirt. "Come in with me."

He shook his head. "Let's go inside."

"No, I want to do it in the pool. Please..."

He let her strip him down to his briefs, fondling her, exciting her. He let her drop to her knees and please him to the point of climax, then he swam with her. But when she tried to coax him to make love to her in the water, he refused.

Taylor pouted, but her mini temper tantrum only pushed him further away. He got out, gathered up his clothes, then pulled a foil packet from his pants pocket, waving it at her as if it was a piece of candy.

"You want it? Come get it."

"No, I don't want it. I want to do it *au naturel.*"

"Not a chance, luv." He nodded toward the house. "Your bedroom, if you please."

She crooked her finger, beckoning him to follow her. He stood firm, watching her stretch out on the padded chaise lounge.

"I'm using your shower," he said with no emotion. "Be waiting for me in your bed when I get out."

"If I'm not?"

"Your loss, luv. I'm fairly certain Amanda is available on a moment's notice. If not, there's Trudy. She's always good for a last-minute lay."

"God, you're crude."

"I know." His eyes twinkled with mischief. Or a touch of evil. Either way, it excited her to no end.

She knew he was teasing. He wouldn't dare go to all that trouble to screw some other girl when she was ready and willing, no matter how much she might act like she wasn't. Still, she didn't dare take any chances.

"You win," she said, getting up from the chaise.

"That's my girl." He handed his clothes to her. "Hang those on a hanger, will you, pet? I hate to go back to the office with wrinkles in my shirt and trousers."

"Of course," she said as he gave her a peck on the cheek, then ceremoniously dropped the foil packet onto the pile. "Don't worry, I'll take care of it."

"I'm not the least bit worried, baby." After a pat on her bare bottom, he walked buck naked into the house as if he didn't have a care in the world.

Taylor glanced down at the condom, thinking, plotting, planning. All she needed was a sewing needle to poke a hole in the foil, a hole that Anthony would never notice.

~

AFTER A FEW WEEKS, Megan had been forced to concede that Jason appeared to have adjusted to the situation far better than either of them had expected. Their son was more his old self again.

Sam had noticed too. "Kids are more resilient than parents give them credit for," he said, lying beside her in his bed late one Sunday night in October.

She kissed his shoulder, and wanted him to make love to her again, but resisted. This insatiable sexual hunger was so new to her. Almost frightening in its intensity. Never had she felt this way about Stewart. It was Sam she wanted. She couldn't get enough of him. And it was getting harder and harder to pretend that she didn't have these feelings about him when others were around.

Her fingers splayed across his belly, yet she drew her thoughts away from going any further. She would think of something else to say, something else to talk about, something other than how much she wanted to be with him day and night. She didn't want to feel this way. Not now. Not ever. She didn't want to give up her control to another man. Maybe Sam wouldn't be that way with her, but she couldn't be sure.

And yet the words were waiting there on the edge of every thought, words that were on the tip of her tongue when she watched him talking with his camp kids, joking with his CAs, playing with his dog. And whenever he touched her, even if it was only with his eyes in a quick glance across the room, she wanted to say it.

She wanted to say "I love you" but she didn't dare.

"Megan? You didn't fall asleep on me, did you?"

She chuckled. "Not a chance."

"Worrying about Jason?"

"Maybe a little," she answered, reticent to tell him the truth. Talking about her son was better than talking about what was really on her mind. "Kids may be resilient, but a separation in marriage is still hard on a child. I think he keeps hoping we'll get back together."

"Are you tempted?"

She shook her head, though not quite as adamantly as Sam might have wanted, and it showed on his face. She simply couldn't let him know her feelings. Not yet. Maybe not ever. For now she could only hold back, let him believe it was only a physical attraction for her. A temporary thing. This was best for both of them.

"Don't go back to Stewart."

The firmness in his tone startled her. She opened her mouth to speak but nothing came out.

"I'm sorry. I was out of line. But I'm just not cut out for these charades. Do you know how much I want to reach out and touch you when you're here with the kids? Do you know how much I want to call you in the middle of the week to tell you how much I miss you?"

"You already do that."

"Not without making a big production out of it like I'm in a damn spy movie. I can't just pick up the phone. I can't show up on your doorstep and carry you into your bedroom—"

Her fingertips touched his lips. "I need more time."

Her answer wasn't anything new. She had reminded him again and again until she wondered herself if she was making excuses. She was afraid to move forward, to take that chance. She wanted Sam but she didn't want to lose Jason if she pushed too hard. What if he resented her for the divorce and then refused to live with her? Right now, she still had both of them.

"I'll wait as long as it takes." He drew her closer. "But it's not getting any easier."

"I know…" She kissed him, and touched him, and slid beneath him.

In another part of the house, Riley began barking.

"Probably a critter outside the window," Sam said, trying to ignore the distraction.

"Shouldn't you check?"

"Now?"

"He doesn't sound like he's going to quiet down."

~

SAM DRAGGED himself out of bed and headed for the closed door. As he opened it, the barking grew louder, as did the sound of someone pounding on the front door.

"Damn. Who the hell could that be at nearly midnight?" He backtracked for a pair of cutoffs, put them on, and went out to the living room. "I'm coming!" he shouted across the distance, motioning for Riley to sit and stay. Of course the dog ignored him.

He glanced through the security peephole and saw Taylor standing under the glare of the porch light, carrying a pink bakery box. Her smile was broad and cocky, but her eyes told a different story.

He opened the door but before he could ask how or why she had come all the way up to the ranch, especially at that time of night, she sang in a wobbly voice, "Happy Birthday to me," while lifting the lid of the box and showing him a small white cake decorated in blue flowers and her name on it. "Hiya, Sam. Just thought maybe you might still be up and so I thought I'd come by to share my birthday with somebody," she rambled in her usual blithe manner as she breezed past him.

He caught her arm. "What the hell is going on? How did you get here?"

"Uber, of course. He's long gone so don't bother lookin' for him."

"That's just great. I don't suppose your dad knows anything about this little stunt."

Glancing down at his grip on her arm, she sighed in a pissed-off sort of way, but gave in to him. "Okay, fine. It's my goddamn fucking birthday and both my parents were too busy to bother with me. My mom's still pissed at me about Anthony, so she didn't even call. Dear Dad flew to Cabo for the weekend to nego-tiate some lame-ass deal. So there I was, sitting home alone, and finally I said, 'screw this' and came here. Now you know the whole story. Happy now?"

"No, not really." He took the box from her hands and put it on the narrow table in the entryway, then gave her a hug. "I'm sorry things didn't work out for you."

Her voice was muffled against his bare shoulder, but he could still hear the sadness and desperation. "They're my parents. They're supposed to like me, right? What's wrong with me? Why don't they like me? Why is it that the only place I fit in is here at the ranch?"

He pulled back and looked into searching eyes that were too old. What could he say about her parents? Neither of them knew how to love their wild daughter, let alone how to handle her.

"Maybe…" he said, cupping her chin, "these kids need you as much as you need them."

Her eyes rolled in disbelief. "And my parents don't need me at all. Never did. I've been excess baggage since the day I was born."

"I seriously doubt it." He knew both her mother and father were self-absorbed, highly driven players in the industry. Nobody made it without those kind of credentials. Despite their frustrations with a teenager who seemed hell-bent on making their lives miserable, they loved her in their own crazy-ass dysfunctional way. He'd seen this before. Sometimes there was reconciliation. Sometimes not. He wasn't sure which way it was going to go with Taylor and her parents. "As much as I hate to say this, you better call your folks and let them know you haven't run off."

"That's if either of them even answer their phones."

"If that's the case, you'll leave messages on their voicemail. Or text them."

"So I'm staying here for the night?"

Sam thought of Megan waiting for him in his bedroom, then shook his head. "I have to be somewhere early in the morning," he lied.

"I can hang out here while you're gone."

"No, I can't— That is, *you* can't— Ah hell, this is really awkward, Taylor. I…"

"You've got someone here, don't you? It's Megan, isn't it?" She didn't have it in her to be embarrassed. Instead, she just looked ticked off.

"No."

Mild surprise flickered across her face, leaving her momentarily without words. So was he. But she made a quick recovery.

"Then it must be Maryann, huh?"

"Taylor, you're walking a thin line right now." He guided her into the living room. "Wait here while I grab a shirt and some shoes so I can drive you home."

Returning to the bedroom, he held his finger to his lips to keep Megan from talking until he reached her side. He wasn't looking forward to explaining the situation. She wouldn't be too happy about it, but what other choice did he have? If Taylor stayed the night, she would find out who was in his bedroom. If he sent her away, she'd be left to find her own way home at midnight in the middle of the Santa Monica Mountains.

"I'll be back in a couple hours," he said to Megan, almost holding his breath, expecting her to be angry, expecting her to act like Maryann. "I know you have school in the morning, so I won't hold it against you if you have to leave."

Her hand slid behind his neck and drew him down toward her for a kiss that was deep and inviting. Intoxicating. Arousing.

"Take as long as you need," she whispered. No sign of resentment. Only sultry promises. "I'll be waiting for you."

Minutes later, on their way down the winding mountain road, Taylor broke the silence between them with an announcement. "I want to come back to live with you."

Sam glanced across the darkened interior. The instrument lights barely illuminated her youthful face, her mouth pressed into a thin line as if she regretted the sudden confession. Underneath all that brooding adolescent sexuality was one hell of a messed-up teenager. These were the ones who always tugged at his heart the hardest. Exactly why his first marriage had failed. And here he was back at it again. Would he ever learn?

Probably not.

"I wouldn't make it any easier on you. If you can't hack it, there'll be no more ping-ponging back and forth to your folks."

She nodded.

"No Thorndike either."

She didn't answer. He'd deal more with that subject later. Right now he had to deal with her father. If the man was home. If not…well, he'd take it one step at a time.

"Let's get past this first hurdle."

Pushing the speed limit, he shaved considerable time off the trip. The house lights were on, leading Sam to believe that her absence had been noticed. Perhaps even the police had been notified. Not that they would respond to a missing teenager in this city.

Taylor begged Sam to simply drop her off, but he wouldn't go for it. Instead, he insisted upon seeing her father. Apparently he had just returned from his own weekend jaunt and didn't bother to check his phone for a message. Or Taylor didn't send one. Either way, he hadn't realized his daughter was not asleep in her own bed, and now he was too tired to deal with her.

Escorting Sam to the door, he expressed his appreciation by trying to slip a large bill into Sam's palm. Sam pushed it back, said he would contact him later about Taylor, and left.

Between his anger at the father and his anxiousness to get back to Megan, he drove too fast and too recklessly on the nearly deserted freeway. He glanced up at the rearview mirror more than a few times, expecting to see flashing lights, almost daring them to show up. It was stupid and he knew it. But it was still a hell of a lot better than buying a six-pack.

Exhausted and defensive, Sam slipped back into bed with Megan, offering her an apology.

"Why do you do it?" she asked.

"She's one of my kids."

"No, why do you need to apologize as if I resent it?"

"Don't you?"

"No."

He must've looked surprised because she grinned in a way that made his chest tighten.

"I'm a teacher, remember? I spend more time with twelve-year-olds than with adults. You can't help but become emotionally attached to them."

"My ex-wife didn't feel that way. Maryann hated every intrusion. She was accustomed to having me to herself before I took over the ranch."

She traced a fingertip down the middle of his chest. "The funny thing is…the way you are with these kids? The way you love them like your own? That's what got to me."

"Really?"

She nodded, her hand moving downward. "That was the first thing. Eventually, I added a few more reasons."

"Let's see if we can add some more."

~

THEY MADE LOVE AGAIN, slow and passionate, then slept until the faint light of dawn crept through the bedroom window, waking both of them as if they were perfectly tuned into one another. Each with their heads on their own pillow, they opened their eyes, and their gazes met.

"God, how I wish…" Megan let her sleepy voice trail off, afraid to say how much she wanted to wake up every morning next to him.

"Me too," Sam answered, reading her thoughts.

It was too much to ask for, wanting him, wanting this life with him. She hated the thought of leaving in a few short minutes, going back to another life that didn't seem like her own anymore, wondering if it ever had really belonged to her.

Sam reached over and stroked her cheek with the back of his fingers. "Will you marry me?"

She blinked twice in disbelief, then frowned. "I…I don't think I can answer that."

"Yes, you can. Say 'Yes, Sam, I will marry you as soon as the divorce is final.' See? That would be easy enough."

"I can't. I mean, I can't make that kind of commitment. Not yet. I don't want it hanging over me."

"You make it sound like a guillotine waiting to drop." He

climbed out of bed and walked over to the open window, his body silhouetted in the early light.

Silently she came up behind him and slipped her arms around his waist. The scent of sagebrush and dry winds caressed her bare skin.

"I love you," she said softly, surprising even herself. He didn't move. "That's the best I can do right now. Please let's not spoil the little time we have left together today. I can hardly stand the idea of waiting another two weeks to be here with you."

"We can't meet like this again."

"Because I can't promise to marry you?" she asked, trying to hide any sign of hurt as she turned away from him.

"No, that's not it at all."

She picked up a T-shirt from the floor and pulled it over her head. It was big and roomy and draped to the middle of her thighs. One of his.

"I didn't want to bring this up yet, but it looks like I might be getting temporary custody of Taylor."

"Again?"

"Yeah, possibly as early as next weekend."

This latest turn of events pushed Megan to finally talk with Sam about her suspicions. As she had expected, he refused to believe that Taylor had anything more than a schoolgirl crush on him.

"It's Thorndike she wants," he argued.

"Only because she can't have you."

"That's ridiculous. I'm old enough to be her father."

"All the more reason Taylor is in love with you. Look at her environment. She's a child of Hollywood. Some of the men and women that her parents have dated are practically as young as Taylor. You are everything she wants in a guy. Anthony Thorndike even looks a lot like you."

"He does not!"

"You win. I'm wrong." She threw her hands up in the air in mocking defeat. "Just promise me something."

"And that is?"

"Try to step back and observe Taylor's behavior from an outsider's viewpoint. Pretend you are her shrink, not her boss."

CHAPTER 17

Two weeks later, on his weekend to have Jason, Stewart phoned Megan at the ranch. Called in on special assignment, he needed to leave right away and didn't know how long he would be gone. Usually he relied upon their sitter, but Melissa was only available for the next two hours, long enough for Megan to make the drive down to Long Beach to pick up Jason.

"I feel guilty as hell about this. I know this is going to be a huge disappointment to Jason. We had hockey tickets for tonight," he said, promising to make it up to their son and to her for interrupting her weekend. "Tell you what. If you'll drop Jason off at the house on Sunday, you can still have the night to yourself as usual. And I'll take him to his sports physical Monday afternoon so you won't have to rush out of your classroom when the bell rings."

He had thought of everything, Megan realized, holding her phone to her ear. Still, there was a wary part of her that suspected him of doing everything in his power to be the perfect father, to keep up his wholesome image so the courts would show favor to him. But another part of her wanted to believe she was wrong.

This was the Stewart she had known in college and during the first part of their marriage. He had come back. Only it was too late.

It had always been too late.

She checked her watch. On this hot October Saturday afternoon, the beach route would be slow moving with weekend traffic at a time of year when the rest of the country was getting the first cold snap of autumn.

"PCH will be jammed. It may take me the full two hours to get down there. Are you sure Melissa can stay that long?" She knew how much Jason hated the thought of a sitter these days. Yet she didn't want to appear as though she let her son call the shots. It was Stewart's decision. But still... "Maybe he could go to a friend's house."

"I don't have the time to make more phone calls. I'm late as it is."

"Fine. I'll be there in two hours."

JASON WAS SULLEN and subdued when Megan picked him up. Melissa had fallen ill with the stomach flu shortly after she'd arrived, but her brother Cameron had generously offered to pitch in. He was a tall, good-looking young man with an easy smile, almost too eager to please, but nothing that a little maturity wouldn't smooth over.

"I can't tell you how much I appreciate your help," Megan said, reaching in her wallet for cash to pay Cameron.

"No problem, ma'am. Jason is like the little brother I never had. We get along great together."

"I hope your sister feels better soon."

"Probably just a twenty-four hour bug," he said, waving off her offer to pay him. "Mr. Fisher already took care of it, ma'am."

"Well, thanks again."

"Sure. Anytime." He ruffled Jason's hair. "Hang loose, little bro."

"Yeah, okay," Jason muttered, then climbed into the car.

With a wave to Cameron, Megan pulled away from the curb, maneuvered the narrow streets of Naples, then turned onto Second Street.

"I don't blame you for being angry," she said.

He didn't respond. Instead, he sat slumped in the passenger seat, his arms crossed, his face turned away, his eyes on the passing scenery. The drive back to the ranch was nearly as long as the drive down, making for a decidedly uncomfortable and silent trip.

Throughout the rest of the weekend he almost seemed to be avoiding her, perhaps punishing her for his father's change in plans. Though he was still very much withdrawn, he did spend some time with Griffin. Once or twice she spotted them together, heading up a trail or returning from an activity. Yet neither boy appeared to be in any kind of for conversation.

Megan asked Sam to intercede, but not even he could tear down the wall that her son had put up around himself. Sam checked with Griff, hoping the teenager might have had better luck reaching the boy. But the story wasn't any different there either. Jason had built up a huge amount of anger and resentment that nobody seemed to be able to diffuse.

"Give him a couple days to cool off," Sam advised Megan in his office, moments before she was to leave for home on Sunday. "Obviously he's still mad, and probably not looking forward to going back to his dad's tonight. But that might be exactly what he needs right now. By next weekend he'll be back up here at the ranch, and I bet he'll be pretty much over this whole thing."

Megan wished she could be as confident as Sam sounded. "I hope you're right."

He stepped toward her, reaching out to take her in his arms to say goodbye. With Taylor now living under his roof, there would be no secret rendezvous tonight. No sneaking back to the ranch after everyone was gone. No more quiet Sunday nights together.

Startled by someone laughing and Riley barking outside the closed door, Sam and Megan both stepped back nervously.

Later that evening, Megan spent the quiet hours home alone in the small bedroom of the bungalow with too many thoughts going through her mind. Her custody of Jason and her relationship with Sam seemed so precarious, the outcome of both seemingly determined by circumstances beyond her control.

The only thing left in her hands was her teaching. She loved her job as a teacher, but something else was coming up more and more. Her work with the camp kids, her own son's behavior, even Sam's influence was beginning to make her think of a new direction in her career. A new path. One that would take a huge leap of blind faith.

Falling asleep that night, she found herself wondering if she could really do it, if she could start over again and go back to college for a degree in adolescent psychology.

~

JASON SAT in a chair in the doctor's waiting room, his heart pounding, his hands all clammy. He was sick to his stomach and was praying real hard that he wouldn't throw up.

She knows! She knows! She knows!

He had already seen Dr. Mead for his soccer physical, and he'd tried not to be nervous when she went over every inch of his body, especially when she looked down there. That's when she started asking all kinds of other questions, questions that he didn't want to answer, questions that got him more scared than ever.

He just knew she could tell he was lying to her, and he couldn't look her in the eyes. She was a real nice doctor.

She had been his doctor all his life, but that didn't mean he wanted her to look at certain places on him. She never did before when he had sports physicals. But this time had been different. Why now? Why today? Afterward, she asked him to wait out in the waiting room. Then his dad got called into her office.

She knows! She knows! She knows!

He put his hands over his ears, and closed his eyes tight, trying to stop the voice in his head. If she knew, then she was in there now telling his dad. A disgusting taste came up his throat. He swallowed a couple times to make it go away.

"Jason?"

His head jerked up. A nurse stood at the door leading into the hallway, her hand gesturing to him to join her. "Can you come with me, sweetie?"

He shuffled past her without a word, his eyes downcast.

"Dr. Mead and your dad are in her office. Just follow me."

As soon as Jason walked into the room, he wanted to turn and run back out, but he didn't. He acted as normal as he could, sitting down in a chair next to his dad. The doctor looked real worried. His dad looked upset too.

They know! They know! They know!

The words buzzed in his head, so loud that he could barely hear anything but his pounding heart. They both took turns talking to him, but he didn't want to hear them even if he could. He stared at a fuzzy little doodle-dog sitting next to a tin soldier on the doctor's desk.

"Jason, are you listening to me?" His dad knelt down in front of him, blocking his view of the tiny toy dog. He tried to look away, but his dad put his hands on both sides of Jason's face, holding it there. Not rough or mean-like. Just so's Jason would look at him. "Dr. Mead believes someone may have hurt you."

He shook his head as best he could with his dad's hands holding him. "Huh-uh."

"Who did this to you?"

"I told you, nobody did nothin'."

"Please, tell me. It's okay to tell."

"I don't need to tell 'cuz nothing happened." His stomach got sicker.

Dr. Mead came around the desk, and leaned against it. "There are many children who do things to their bodies out of curiosity or playing games with other kids. If that's what happened, no one will be angry with you, Jason. But your behavior and my examination lead me to believe that someone has touched you and perhaps hurt you, and I am obligated to inform your parents as well as the Department of Child Services."

"Nobody touched me!" Jason insisted, looking at his dad. "I swear, Dad."

"But Dr. Mead knows—"

"No, she doesn't! Maybe she just made a mistake or something."

"She wants to help you. She wants to protect you from whoever did it. Unless, of course, you did this yourself or let someone else because you were curious. If that's all, then say so."

The room fell silent. Jason fought back the urge to puke. His whole body felt hot and cold and sweaty and burning all at the same time.

Don't tell! Don't tell! Don't tell!

His mind searched for something to say, something that would make them stop asking him to tell what really happened. He couldn't tell them that. He couldn't tell them the truth.

"I did it," he said.

His dad glanced at the doctor and back. "Why?"

Jason shrugged. He refused to say anything else. He told them he was the one who had done it, and that was enough. Finally, he was excused to go out to the waiting room. Instead, he stopped at the bathroom in the hallway and threw up.

~

STEWART PUNCHED the doorbell of the rental house, then leaned on it, impatiently listening to the raspy buzzer. God help him, but he was ready to explode. If Megan didn't answer in two seconds, he would start pounding on the door. He knew she was home. Her car was at the curb.

She was probably taking a shower.

In the blur of intense anger, he remembered his own key, and reached into his pocket. Proprieties be damned. He was going in, even if he had to barge into the bathroom and scare her half to death.

"Stewart! What are you doing here?"

Noticing she was fully dressed, he strode past her. "Where the hell have you been?"

"The kitchen. Putting some groceries into the freezer. You didn't even give me half a chance to get to the door." She closed it and followed him into the middle of the living room. "Where is Jason? You were supposed to take him for his physical."

"I did. He's at home. With Maxwell."

"What's wrong?"

"According to Dr. Mead, Jason was sexually molested."

"Oh, my God!" Her hand clapped over her mouth as she staggered backward. Dropping her hand, she frantically glanced around her, then grabbed her purse. "I've got to go to him."

"Not until we talk." The finality in his voice pulled her up short as she was about to run out the door.

"About what? I need to see him."

"Why don't you ask *who*, Megan? Why don't you ask what happened?"

"I will. With Jason."

"He refuses to talk about it."

"Why?"

"I was hoping you might know."

"I don't! What makes you think—"

He had a hell of a time saying it aloud. "Dr. Mead has strong reason to think that Jason was molested. His rectum—"

"Oh, dear God…" Color drained from her face. She groaned, dropping back into an armchair, her purse falling forgotten to the floor. "My baby…my son…"

"*Our* son." Stewart stood over her, filled with anger, wanting to kill the bastard perp. "I want to know who was with him this weekend."

Her head lifted. Her eyes gazed at him in stunned disbelief. "This didn't happen at the ranch."

"How do you know?"

"Because I do. And you'll have to take my word on it. After he's spent the entire summer with all of those counselors, how can you jump to the conclusion that anything happened this weekend?"

"I doubt this was the first time." He backed up, shoving his fingers through his hair. "Dammit, Megan. You weren't with him every waking moment. You even slept in a different cabin. Admit it—there were plenty of wide-open opportunities."

She jumped to her feet. "Don't you dare point an accusing finger in my direction. Or did you forget that he was with you too this weekend."

"It sure as hell didn't happen under my watch!"

"You won't take my word, but I'm supposed to take yours?"

"There are a lot of people around that camp. Any one of them—"

"*None* of them, I tell you."

"Don't be blind, Megan. Someone has hurt our son, and I intend to find out before word of it falls into the wrong hands."

"Who? The press? Are we talking about Jason's welfare or yours?"

"This isn't about me. Dr. Mead is obligated to inform the Department of Child Services. We'll be lucky if they don't remove Jason into protective custody."

"They can't do that!"

"They can and they will if I don't come up with fast answers. And right now your boss Sam is at the top of my list."

"Sam didn't do it. Any more than Maxwell would be capable of hurting Jason."

"Maxwell? Not a chance."

"If you are going to suspect the owner of a camp based solely upon his interest in kids, then you damn well better suspect a gay man due to his homosexuality."

"That's crude and absurd."

"I'm just showing how crude and absurd you're being here. I want to know the truth as badly as you do. But I am sure as hell not going to destroy innocent people in my wake." She bent over and snatched her purse from the floor.

"We're not through here," he said.

"Yes, we are. I'm going to see Jason."

~

THE REST of the week was a blur to Megan, teaching through the haze and pain and shock during the day. She had tried and failed to coax Jason into opening up to her, but he had continued to stand by his weak excuse about an unnamed friend and curiosity that had gone too far. She had wanted to believe him, but his further withdrawal confused the issue.

During the evenings, she visited her son for short periods of time, always with Stewart close by, seeming to monitor her every move. How could he even think she could be involved? The possibility of being one of the suspects hurt her deeply.

"It's not you," he told her on Thursday afternoon when she dropped Jason off at the house. Stewart had taken an emergency leave of absence from the department so he would be a full-time father as well as his own private investigator.

Now, as she sat in the car with Stewart standing next to the driver's door, he had just informed her that Jason would not be going with her to the ranch the next day. "I have agreed with child welfare that he would not visit the camp during the ongoing investigation."

She threw open her door so fast he jumped back. Tamping down her temper, she fought to control her volume. "How dare you stand here and inform me that you have agreed to anything without my knowledge? Dammit, Stewart, I'm done with letting you call the shots. I have a say. I am his mother. Jason already told them that nobody at the Flying K had hurt him."

"They don't believe his story any more than Dr. Mead did."

"Or you."

"Or you either."

"I believed him when he said it didn't happen at the ranch."

"You are hardly an objective third party, Megan."

"No, according to your behavior, I am a suspect like the rest of them."

"I never said that."

"Of course not. You only watch me like a hawk, as if you expect me to hurt my own son."

"Hurt him? No. But I am concerned that you may, intentionally or not, say something to Jason that would make him feel he couldn't betray you or your friends up there."

"Betray me?!" She spun away from him to avoid slapping him. Shocked by her impulse, she turned back. "What kind of paranoia has gotten into you? Where is your perspective? You know me! You know I couldn't do anything like that to Jason. He's my own flesh and blood!"

"Don't forget he's my flesh and blood too. And I intend to do everything in my power to keep him from being hurt again."

"So do I! But I'll be damned if he's going to be punished by keeping him away from the ranch. He loves it there. You can't do this to him. He's going with me tomorrow, Stewart. I'll pick him up in the morning for school. And when we get home on Sunday, it'll be my turn to spend the week here, so I'll expect you to move back to the bungalow."

~

THE NEXT AFTERNOON, as Megan and Jason walked to her car parked on the street beside the side entrance to the school, a woman approached them on the sidewalk.

"Mrs. Fisher?"

"Yes?"

"You are *Megan* Fisher?"

"Yes, I am." Megan handed Jason the keys and her bag of books and students' papers, and sent him to the car. "May I help you?"

"This is for you." She handed Megan a large manila envelope.

"What is it?"

"Have a nice day, ma'am." The woman walked off without saying another word.

A sense of dread and doom sent a chill down her spine as Megan walked toward her car, opening the envelope and sliding out the sheaf of legal papers.

Skimming the words, she couldn't believe what she was reading. Her heart sank. She went over it again after she sat in the driver's seat. The letters blurred. The papers shook in her trembling hands.

"I don't believe this. How could he..."

"Mom?" Jason leaned over the center console, craning his neck to see what she was reading. "You okay?"

No, I am not okay. "Yes, I'm fine."

She shoved the papers back into the envelope, tossed them into the back seat with her purse, and drove straight to the house with a heavy foot.

"According to those papers, you are not going to the ranch this weekend, Jase," she said, clenching the steering wheel.

"How come?" For the first time since Monday afternoon he had snapped out of his dull monotone. He was angry, and she couldn't blame him. She was too. Why did Stewart have to protect Jason by taking away the one thing that meant something to him?

"Your dad—" She hesitated, trying to hold back the bitterness from her voice. She didn't want to rant and rave about Stewart's stupid stunt to keep Jason away from a sexual predator at the ranch, even though he was probably safer there than anywhere. "I'm sorry, Jason. I really am. I don't know how he pulled it off so fast." She glanced over at her son. "He filed for divorce to get temporary custody of you."

Jase shook his head, his lower lip trembling as he slouched in the passenger seat. "Why can't he just leave it the way it was? Why can't you trade off living with me?"

"I don't intend to let it end this way. I'm going to talk to your dad when we get back to the house." And call my own divorce attorney.

"But I want to go to the ranch. With you. Tonight."

"I'm afraid that's out of the question for right now. Your dad doesn't want you up there."

"Why?" Before she dared to explain Stewart's suspicions about Sam and the others, Jason seemed to read her thoughts. "Nothing happened at camp! I told him that! He doesn't believe me, does he? He just listens to that stupid, ol' Dr. Mead."

Megan pulled up to the curb, barely bringing the car to a full stop when Jason jumped out with his backpack.

"Jason, wait! I want to explain—"

He slammed the door and dashed toward the tall wooden gate leading into the courtyard off the kitchen. With little more than a pause to work the handle, he gave it a hard shove, knocked it open and ran inside.

She cut the engine and started to race after him, but something held her back, knowing she would only find him in his room, sullen and silent, pushing her further away.

Inside the kitchen, she placed her purse and the envelope on the tile counter, then slowly started up the stairs to his room. Stewart would have to wait until she checked on Jason.

"Hello, Megan."

Maxwell's voice.

She froze, her foot on the first step. She had not seen him since that afternoon in the master bedroom. Now he was here, in her house, in her kitchen! A rush of emotions raced through her. Anger. Resentment. Betrayal. Even, God forbid, jealousy.

"I suppose I can't really blame you for not wanting to turn around to look at me."

His words seemed to challenge her. She wasn't afraid of him. If anything, there was a part of her that wanted to walk over and slap him. No, slug him. Deck him.

She did finally turn around, however. Just to prove that she could.

"Hello, Maxwell," she said, barely able to maintain a tone of civility.

He was neatly dressed as usual, in a well-tailored gray suit. Handsome and distinguished gentleman, as always. Yet his eyes held nothing but a solemn softness that she didn't want to notice. She wanted to hate him for his role in Stewart's deception. She wouldn't let him off the hook.

"Stewart asked me to keep Jason company until he returned."

"How convenient for him." Her remark held a bite of sarcasm which did not go unnoticed. "He knows I won't stand for this stunt, but he doesn't have the guts to be here to face me."

"I assure you that he would have been here if it hadn't been for an untimely delay in some urgent matters."

It annoyed the hell out of her that Maxwell had the audacity to show up in her house to cover for her husband, to explain his whereabouts, and to look after their son—all at Stewart's request!

He acted like he was the wife, not her. He probably knew more about Stewart than she did.

The thought struck her as more than a possibility.

Hurt and angry, she refused to let him see her pain. "I thought he'd taken a leave of absence from work."

"He has." Maxwell moved into the kitchen with graceful elegance. "Would you join me in a cup of coffee? Kona?"

"No!" She held back the rest of the words she wanted to say. She couldn't risk being overheard by her son. He was her only priority now. "I need to speak to Jason."

"Ah, yes. Well, I did hear some slamming doors. He's upset then, is he?"

"Of course he is. And he has a right to be. Stewart went too far with this order for custody, but he really blew it by banning Jason from seeing his friends at the ranch."

"I advised him not to do this to you. Or Jason."

"I suppose you expect me to be grateful for that?" She turned to leave the kitchen, saying over her shoulder to Maxwell, "There's no need for you to stay. I intend to stick around until Stewart gets home."

CHAPTER 18

Griffin walked from downtown Long Beach along Ocean Boulevard, then Second Street through Belmont Shore, on his way to see Jason for the first time at his own house. Last weekend at camp, Megan had invited Griff to come over for dinner on Thursday night. He couldn't have said no, not when she looked so worried.

He had his own troubles, what with his family still living in the van, and the autumn nights getting colder. His mom had gotten a job as a hotel maid, but his dad hadn't found anything, mostly because he was too old or too overqualified.

Griff had temporarily dropped out of Poly High so he could work swing shift at the supermarket stocking shelves. He had lied about his age, and looked old enough to be eighteen. But he promised his dad that he would only do it through the holidays, then he'd go back to school for the spring semester.

"Something will come along soon," his dad had said more times than Griff could remember.

It never did though.

And then there was Taylor. As far as he knew, he hadn't knocked her up at the Labor Day party. Here it was the first of

November, and she hadn't said a word to him about it. So he was pretty sure he was off the hook. At least one thing had turned out okay for him lately.

But things weren't so great for Jason. The last time he'd seen the kid in October at the ranch, he'd heard about the divorce. Next thing he knew, Jase wasn't coming up anymore. Something about his dad taking over custody. Poor guy. Parents could be so screwed up. Not his own, luckily. Well, not when it came to their family anyways. And it really wasn't his mom and dad's fault that everything went to hell this year.

Griff ignored his sore feet as he walked past Taco Surf and several other small restaurants. It was getting close to dinnertime, and his stomach growled.

He had promised Megan he'd come over around four o'clock, giving her time to get Jason home from school. But it was almost five thirty now, and he wondered if she might have given up on him. He should've taken the bus but he'd thought he could walk the few miles easy enough and save the money.

He crossed the bridge over the main canal, passed yoga studios, nail salons, realtor offices, and turned at the corner by the drugstore. Checking the crude map drawn on the napkin, he followed the sidewalk as it curved up and over a smaller canal then back down to a little park and fountain with the road circling it.

Cars were parked everywhere. Every bit of space along the curbs was taken. He started across the street when a truck blasted its horn at him.

He jumped back to the curb, noticing that it was a Channel 7 Eyewitness News van. He watched it turn down the same street he was going.

As he rounded the corner, he saw the Fishers' house. The street was jammed with cars and more of the same kind of news vans. People were wandering all over the place, talking in clusters, hanging out around the vehicles. Neighbors were out on their front sidewalks, staring at the corner house.

Jason checked the napkin again. Sure enough, it was Jason's house in the middle of all the attention. He slowed his pace, not sure if he should leave or what. He didn't exactly want to go through that crowd to knock on the front door, even if he had been invited for dinner.

What if somebody's been murdered in there?

He shook off the chilling thought, telling himself there would have been cops everywhere if it was a crime scene. No, this was something else. But what, he didn't know.

He paused in front of a house where two women were talking together, hoping he could eavesdrop on their conversation. But the white-haired lady turned and glared at him.

"Do you know what's going on?" he asked.

The other woman—younger, blonde and with less suspicion in her eyes—answered him, "It's the Fisher house."

"Yes, I know. I'm a friend of Jason's and his mom. Are they okay? They aren't hurt or anything, are they?"

"No, but we sure don't need another scandal around here."

The sour lady added, "Like that one with the fella who chopped up his sister over their inheritance and stashed her body parts in trunks. God, that was grisly."

"What scandal?" asked Griffin, hoping the women wouldn't go on talking about some murdering neighbor.

"You say you know them, but you haven't heard? Where you been since yesterday afternoon? In a hole? First TMZ broke the story, then every camera crew parked themselves in our quiet neighborhood. Oh, good, here comes the police. It's about time."

Griffin turned to see three squad cars pull up. A phone rang inside the house. The older woman went to answer it.

The blonde took her eyes off the uniformed officers and glanced at Griff. "Only in LA."

"Excuse me?"

"The stuff they make movies out of." She counted off each detail on her fingers. "Son of the famous Stewart Fisher is molested. Daddy is a suspect. So is the mom. But so is the director of a camp for rich kids in the Malibu mountains where the mom and boy stayed all summer. Actually, the whole camp is under investigation. Oh, but wait, it gets even better. Turns out the dad is gay with a longtime lover, who is also a suspect!"

Griffin felt like someone had socked him in the stomach. He hadn't heard much past the part about Jason. Oh, God—Jason! He said he had secrets too. Just like Griff. Only this was way worse than being homeless.

"Are you Griffin?"

He snapped out of his dazed confusion, and looked around to see the older woman stepping back down off her porch and approaching him, a phone in her hand.

"Yes, that's me."

"It's for you. Mrs. Fisher. She's watching us from that third floor window. Says she'd like to speak to you."

He strained to view the windows, finally catching a glimpse of someone staring back at him. With a nervous swallow, he took the phone and slowly raised it to his ear.

"Griffin?"

"Yeah. Hi."

"I was worried you'd walk right into this, so I've been keeping an eye out for you. I'm glad you stopped to talk to Mrs. Maury long enough for me to catch you."

"Where's Jason? Is he okay?"

"He's here. Yes, he's…fine, considering the circumstances. I'm sorry. I tried calling you to cancel tonight."

His chest tightened. "You did?"

"Your number is no longer in service."

"Maybe you had the wrong one."

"No, Sam checked it for me."

He was sweating now. If Sam found out the number was

disconnected, he'd ask questions. "Maybe there was a mix up with the phone company. Maybe my dad forgot to pay it or something."

He didn't want to talk about this. He wanted to ask if all those things that the blonde lady had said were true about Jason, about the accusations, about the ranch.

"Listen, Griff," Megan said, "I'll have to drive the car out around the block because of all the traffic blocking the street, but I'll pick you up by the fountain in fifteen minutes to drive you home."

"No!"

"Why not?"

"I…uh…it's too far. And from what I can see, your garage is blocked too."

"Then let me call one of your parents to come and get you. Do you have a work phone for either of them?"

"No," he said truthfully. "I'll take the bus."

"I hate to make you do that. After all, I'm the one who asked you to come visit Jason, and…" Her voice trailed off. Griff glanced at the two women who were hanging on every word of his conversation.

Suddenly Jason's voice came over the receiver. "Griff? Hi, Griff! It's me, Jason."

He saw the ten-year-old waving from the third-floor window. "Hi, Jase." Not wanting to draw attention to himself, he hardly raised his hand at all when he waved back.

"Y'gonna come in?" Megan could be heard in the background, then Jason answered her sullenly. "That's not fair. I wanna go with you when you take him home. Lemme go with you, Mom. Please?"

"Hey, Jason?" Griff raised his voice, trying to be heard over the phone, then noticing an impatient glare from Mrs. Maury. "Tell your mom I gotta go, okay? Tell her I don't need a ride and that I'll call later tonight? Got that? Maybe you and me can make plans to see each other tomorrow or next Monday, okay?"

"Yeah," came the answer, although it didn't sound too happy.

"Listen to me, Jason."

A sigh, then, "I'm listening."

"We both got some pretty tough stuff to deal with right now, and we're both gonna get through it. I promise." He glanced at the women, wishing he could say more, knowing he couldn't. "I'll call you tonight at eight o'clock, and we'll talk then."

Jason seemed agreeable. Griff said goodbye, clicked off the phone and handed it back to the woman, thanking her, then turned and walked away from the whole scene.

Neighbors stared at him, probably wondering what to think of this long-haired teenager showing up in the middle of the cops and cameras. He didn't care. His stomach growled, reminding him that he hadn't eaten since noon, and probably wouldn't be eating much of anything tonight.

After crossing at the traffic light on Bayshore Drive, he passed the library on the corner and a restaurant next door with side-walk dining. He considered wandering around back to check the trash. The idea was disgusting and humiliating, but he was no longer above doing what he had to do. He glanced around to see if anyone was watching him just when a car pulled into the empty parking space at the curb. It was Megan.

"Get in, Griff. I'm taking you home." She had rolled down the passenger side window, and leaned over to talk to him. He hunkered down, his hands hooked over the opening.

"I'm grateful and all, but I can't let you drive me."

"No excuses. I'm here. And I want to do this."

He thought up a quick lie. "I, kinda, uh, had a bad fight with my dad, and I'd like to just sort of stay away for a couple hours. Give him time to cool off." It was the first thing that came into his head, but now he was regretting it. Not so much that he minded the lying as much as he hated making his dad sound mean or maybe even abusive.

"Your dad, huh?"

Griffin nodded, unwilling to dig himself any deeper than he had to. Then he realized he never should've used his dad as an excuse because now she would be wondering why his dad was off work so early in the day. He should've said it was a fight with his mom. Time for more fast-thinking. Time for more BS.

"My dad hurt his back, and he's off work on disability for a few weeks. I think he's just restless and sore and kinda taking it out on me is all. He didn't mean nothing by it. I just thought I'd hang out until later. So you see, you don't need to drive me home."

"At least let me give you dinner, then."

He hesitated, wanting so bad to say yes but not wanting her to ask any more questions about his family.

"Come on, Griff. I feel bad enough about tonight. Let me make amends. I asked you to come for dinner, and I owe you a meal. Get in, and I'll take you to the bungalow where I'm staying. No news media to hound us. Then I'll let you empty my cupboards and refrigerator. Pull out all the stops. All the food you can eat. Any teenage boy who can turn down that kind of offer has got to be crazy."

His stomach grumbled again. "Okay," he finally said, reaching for the door handle. "You win."

~

Sitting in his office, writing out payroll checks, Sam paused and rubbed his tired eyes. Riley let out a heavy sigh from his love seat.

"You and me both."

The dog's tail thumped.

Sam went back to his work yet his mind kept wandering back

to Megan. He hadn't seen her since all hell broke loose with the news media two weeks earlier. She was too afraid to return to the ranch so she'd quit. Not because she believed any of the accusations against him, or so she'd said. Despite his argument otherwise, she accepted the blame for bringing this nightmare into his life.

"Don't add another stone around your neck," he'd said in that final phone call. "We'll get through this together."

"No, Sam. I can't ask you—"

"I know you're not asking me. I love you. And I'm not leaving you."

"Take care of yourself. I'm sorry." She had hung up on him then, before he could tell her he didn't give a damn about anything the press had to say about him.

She hadn't given him a chance to explain that he'd already received overwhelming support from dozens of people who had ties to the ranch over the years. Some parents, some kids, and some of those now grown with children of their own who returned to the Flying K. None of them had wanted to believe the malicious headlines, and had said as much in cards, letters, texts, and emails to the camp's website.

Mitch Malcolm, the leading box office action hero, was organizing a press conference in support of Sam, Mitch's own childhood hero from his summers at the Flying K. He was finding plenty of other celebrities, as well, to rally around the ranch with its wholesome image dating as far back as the days when it was a movie set for Westerns. Vintage film footage would even be aired at a media event to be held at the Gene Autry Museum the day after Thanksgiving, four days away.

Sam hoped the publicity would kick the weekend camp attendance back up. This past weekend they had only had half the expected number of kids. Two church-sponsored youth groups had canceled after the news broke, one without explanation, the other with an apology and a request to book a date in late spring.

He couldn't blame them for avoiding this hot spot of paparazzi lurking in the hills overlooking the camp.

"Sam? Can I talk to you?" Griffin asked from the other side of the screen door. He had cut off his long hair since last weekend, hoping it would help him land a better after-school job. Sam suspected the boy's parents were still having some financial problems, especially after he learned about the disconnected phone.

"Yeah, come on in. Just let me finish signing these checks." He scribbled his last signature as the teenager entered the office. "What's up?"

"It's about Jason."

Sam wasn't exactly surprised, but he had anticipated something else along the line of asking for a raise in pay. He leaned back in the creaking chair. "Go on."

"I saw him last week. After school. When his dad wasn't around. Just Megan was there."

Sam didn't much like the idea of Griffin getting himself caught in the middle of the whole mess, but he couldn't blame him either. He'd do the same. "How's he holding up?"

"Not good." He obviously had more to say but he was struggling to do it. Sam waited. "He's real scared. He says nobody believed him before, and so he knows nobody will believe him now."

Sam leaned forward. "Now?"

Griff nodded. "I got him talkin', Sam, and he told me what happened. Not all of it, I s'pose. Only…"

"Only what?"

"Before he told me? I had to promise to keep it a secret. So I promised, see? An' I'm the only one he told. So if I tell his mom or dad, he'll know it was me. I know it shouldn't matter, but I feel like I gotta honor that trust. I know it's dumb—"

"No, it's not." Sam admired the boy's integrity. "It's my guess that you tried to talk him into going to his parents."

"Yeah, but you should've seen him freak out. He says worse stuff will happen. He says it's already all his fault that his mom and dad and you got all that bad stuff said in the papers."

"Like mother, like son," murmured Sam.

"Huh?"

"Nothing." Sam pushed himself to his feet. "You want a ride home?"

"Uh, yeah—no! I mean, I've got one, thanks anyways. What are you gonna do?"

"Don't panic, Griff. I'm going to pay a visit to Megan, and hopefully wrangle a talk with Jason. I won't let on that you came to me."

"He'll *know*."

"You haven't betrayed his confidence, and I'll swear to that. I think Jason will know I'm telling the truth." He paused, then asked again, "Are you sure you don't want to come along with me?"

"Yeah, I'm sure. Tell him hi though. Okay?"

"One more thing, Griff. I hate to ask, but is there something between you and Taylor I ought to know about?"

"No." The boy had hesitated just long enough to show his hand. "Why? She say there was?"

"Nothing direct. Innuendos. Just being Taylor, I suppose. I happened to notice her running hot and cold around you. No offense but it used to be she didn't give you much attention except to tease you."

"Yeah, she's good at that."

"There were a few times when I saw you two together this weekend and I couldn't help thinking that there was a little more to it. She's a handful, Griff. And I'm really concerned about either of you doing something stupid."

"Her maybe. Not me."

Sam's gut told him otherwise. There was guilt written all over the boy's face. *Shit.* First Thorndike. Now Griffin?

"She's my responsibility. I can't send her away, but I don't want to fire you either. If there's anything happening here, and I find out, I'm afraid it may cost you, Griff."

"I know, Sam." Averting his gaze, he looked down at Riley. "I know…"

"You're a good CA, probably the best I've ever had. Don't tell Mario though." He hoped his jest would lighten the tension. It didn't. "So much is on the line with this ranch right now… Help me out here, Griff. Promise me you'll steer clear of any extracurricular activities with Taylor, and I'll take your word on it."

His head snapped up, relief in his eyes. "I promise."

Mario came to the door, looking for his paycheck. Sam circled around the end of the desk, offered his hand to Griff who grasped it in a firm handshake. Then Sam tugged the boy to his feet.

"See you next Friday, then."

"Yeah, see ya."

"Almost forgot." He reached over the desk, grabbed the stack of checks, thumbed through for Griffin's and handed it over. "Don't spend it all on video games."

"Not a chance."

~

TAYLOR WAS WAITING in the shadows behind bunkhouse four when she finally spotted Griffin walking down the road, coming for his gear. She knew Mario was up at the office, and would probably hang out there for at least another twenty minutes, waiting on Karen who was always taking forever to pack her stuff.

She snuck into the cabin through the back door that led into the counselor's quarters, and came up behind Griffin, grabbing his butt with both hands. He jumped nearly a foot, and spun around.

"Jesus, Taylor! You scared the shit out of me!"

"Ooh…a bad word from you? I'm honored." She stepped closer.

He stepped back, bumping into his bed. "Knock it off, will you?"

"Not a chance." She reached up and ran her fingers through his short hair. "I like. A lot."

He ducked under her arm and out of her way. "Leave me alone. I don't want to play your stupid games."

"Believe me, this is not a game. I can't help it if I'm suddenly attracted to you again. It must be the new hair."

"Yeah, right." He pointed to his gear bag on the bed behind her. "Just let me have my stuff so I can leave."

"I don't think so. Not yet."

"Don't be stupid, Taylor. Sam's onto you. To *us*. He knows, and I wouldn't be surprised if you told him about what happened with us at his barbecue."

"Why would I? It was over so fast that I forgot it'd even happened. In case you were wondering, I was mad about that for weeks. But I decided to forgive you, and let you have another try. Longer, this time."

Her top was off in a flash, and his eyes fixed on her breasts long enough for her to strip off her jeans. She hadn't been wearing anything underneath, making it fast and easy. She pressed her naked body against him, kissing him like mad.

When he shoved her onto the bed, she thought smugly, *This is it.* She knew he couldn't resist her. God, he was easy. Too easy. But instead of unbuckling his belt and unzipping his pants, he stared at her. His breathing was ragged. He wanted her all right. He just needed a little more coaxing.

Using his bag of clothes as her pillow she stretched her arms over her head and arched her back, letting him have a good long look. "I'm ready and waiting."

He yanked his bag from under her, dropping her head hard onto the mattress. "Go fuck yourself, Taylor."

She blinked at his cruel slam, but refused to show any hurt. "I was hoping you'd do it for me."

"Never." He turned to leave.

"Never say *never*," she purred. "You'll regret it."

"Sam told me he's got his butt in a sling over all the crap about sexual misconduct here at the camp. Tell me something, Taylor. Do you even read what they're saying about Sam? Did you know that some papers are saying his temporary guardianship of you is under suspicion, and that it's just a sleazy arrangement made with your parents' approval?"

"Those tabloids are full of shit. Nobody cares about them."

"Obviously you don't care about them, or Sam, or anything but yourself. Otherwise you wouldn't be seconds away from someone walking in that door and catching you stark naked on my bed."

"Nobody's going to catch us, Griff. Come on." She climbed off the bed and cozied up to him again. "I'm horny as hell, and I won't take no for an answer."

"Grow up, Taylor. Acting like this while you're living with Sam is going to ruin him and close this ranch. Is that what you want?"

"No, I want this." She cupped his groin.

He pulled away. "I used to think you were just a tease, Taylor. But I was wrong. You really are a slut."

She smacked his face hard with the palm of her hand. "And you're a pompous prick!" She practically spit the words at him, "Get out! Get out!"

"Gladly."

~

After the door slammed shut, Taylor hurriedly dressed and fled out the back door and up the trail to the house. She called him every name in the book, but not one of them took the sting away. Dammit, she didn't want to feel the hurt of being called a slut. Two guys. That's all she'd ever done. Just two guys. And Griffin didn't even count. Not really. How could a two-second fuck count for anything? It didn't. She'd lost her virginity to Anthony, and he was the one and only guy who mattered. She wanted him and only him.

But she hadn't seen him in, like, forever. At least a few weeks. Her whole body ached for him, which was the only reason she went to Griff. She wanted sex, plain and simple. And, according to the book she'd read, it was the perfect time to get pregnant. She'd been certain that one more time with Griffin would do the trick. If only he'd taken the bait. The bastard. So damn paranoid. Any guy in his right mind would never have turned down such an offer.

Knowing that Sam was still down at the office, she walked through the cavernous living room, stripping off her shirt. Whenever he wasn't around, she pretended the place was her own private nudist camp. By the time she headed down the hallway, she was strutting her buff bod as if she was on a fashion show catwalk.

If only Anthony was here now. He adored her outrageous exhibitionism. She owed it all to him, really. Nobody, but nobody, knew about how he'd taught her to be a stripper for his entertainment. God, that was fun. Still was.

One time, though, she'd got a little drunk during one of their after-school marathons in a funky hotel room. He'd wanted to record her routine so he could watch it before he went to bed at night. Afterward they watched it together on his phone. She was pretty good. He offered to shop it around as an audition tape to some porn producers in the Valley. When she panicked, he swore he was only teasing.

Thank God for that!

She cruised into Sam's bathroom to use his shower, a secret little treat she gave herself when he wasn't around. It was bigger than the guest shower, which was only a small cubicle. This one had three shower heads: high, middle, and low—all adjustable too. Tons of light streamed through a big window where you could see the ridge across the canyon.

She let the water rush over her hot skin and took care of her horny little problem. Shutting off the water, she squeegeed the tile and glass, then reached for a towel and dried off before stepping out onto the floor, trying not to leave any evidence of her visit.

After tossing the towel in the direction of the open doorway, she stood in front of the vanity sink and reached for the aftershave for just one whiff. The musky smell was Sam in a bottle. She smiled, closed her eyes, imagining him in this same spot, finishing his shave. Probably buck naked.

A tingling sensation rippled down through her belly and between her thighs. *What would it be like with Sam?* she wondered.

Sam?!

No! It was Anthony she wanted. She loved Anthony. He was…

Sam.

No! Huh-uh. No way!

Sam.

Each time his name echoed in her head, she saw herself in his arms, in his bed. He wouldn't treat her like Anthony. He would be tender and warm and loving and…

With her eyes still closed, she sniffed the perfumed aftershave and sighed, "Oh, Sam…"

"What the hell are you doing?"

Her eyelids flew open. "Sam! I-it's you!"

He snatched the towel from the floor as he walked in. "For God's sake, cover up," he barked, holding the full length of the towel out between his outstretched hands.

His angry gaze fixed on her face, not showing even the

slightest hint of interest in her nudity. She felt like a little kid being scolded by a father. So much for her fantasy about Sam taking her to bed.

"Next time, close the damn door when you're in here."

He took the aftershave from her hand and motioned for her to leave. "I need to clean up and drive down to Long Beach."

Quickly recovering from her embarrassment of being treated like a child, she found her voice again. "Another fling with Megan, I presume."

"Don't start the cute mouth, Taylor. I'm in no mood for it. I plan to see Megan, but only to visit with Jason. It's not exactly a social call. Nuke a frozen dinner for yourself. I'll pick up something on the way home."

"When will that be?

"Early." He gently shoved her out of the bathroom and closed the door.

"How early?" she asked, raising her voice.

"Early enough so Thorndike doesn't have time to sneak up here before I get back!" The spray of water started, blocking out any further conversation.

"Let's see about that," she mumbled, walking down the hall to her room.

~

AN HOUR LATER, Sam was long gone and Taylor was curled up on the sofa watching TV with the phone clutched in her hand, waiting for Anthony to return her call. Another hour passed but still no word from him after she'd left two more messages.

She channel-surfed, pausing for a moment on an entertainment report.

Better than nothing, she decided, settling back to watch clips and gossip about Channing Tatum, then Miley Cyrus. She yawned over something about Matt Damon. Her stomach growled from hunger as the camera returned to the studio where a handsome host sat at a news desk with his cutesy blonde co-anchor. One more quick bit of gossip and they'd cut to a commercial. Then Taylor could head to the kitchen to hunt down something edible to nuke.

The perky blonde said in her perky voice, "Supermodel Shondra tied the knot in Vegas this weekend with her boyfriend, talent agent Anthony Thorndike. According to our sources, they have been secretly dating for over a year while she was married to one of Thorndike's clients—the bad-boy rocker Bobby Holloway."

A clip of the couple showed the ebony-skinned bride in a tight white minidress posing at the Bellagio as Anthony stood by her side, waving at the cameras, in his tuxedo.

Taylor watched in horror as he took his bride's hand and led her to the open door of an awaiting limousine, his hand on her ass as she ducked into the car.

Cutting back to the studio, the camera caught a smirk between the two reporters as Miss Blondie added, "Rumor has it that the happy couple will be jetting off to a honeymoon in Barbados where Shondra will be shooting her famous calendar."

Her co-anchor said with a grin, "They'd better make it a quick shoot. This much-sought-after black beauty from South Africa is already three months pregnant with their first baby."

"Unlike some Hollywood couples, it looks like these two plan to be traditional married parents. We send them our congratulations on both their marriage and their upcoming blessed event."

As the show went to a commercial break, Taylor sat there in shock and disbelief.

It couldn't be true. It was impossible. Not Anthony. Not *her* Anthony. He couldn't do this to her.

She thought of all the times he'd made love to her, telling her how much he needed her, how good they were together, promising to marry her.

But he married someone else! And she was going to have his baby—the one Taylor had wanted so badly. Now she knew why he was so stubborn about using stupid condoms.

God damn him!

She pounded the pillow beside her, then threw it at the television set. Leaping off the sofa, she screamed and screamed. Nobody was around. Nobody would hear if she screamed for hours, which was exactly what she felt like doing.

She wanted to smash everything in the room. She wanted to put her fist through the window. If she had a car, she would drive it a hundred miles an hour into Anthony—the prick!

So much hate and hurt and humiliation boiled up inside her. Pretty soon all she could do was stand there in the middle of Sam's living room, shaking like she was going to explode any second. She grabbed her head, as if that would do any good at all.

Shit, shit, shit!

Somebody somewhere was sobbing. The sound seeped into her skull like it was coming through a fog. It was her. She looked around at the empty room. Empty house. Alone. Completely alone.

Nobody gave a flying fuck if she lived or died.

Nobody wanted her. Not her dad. Not her mom. Not Anthony. Not Sam.

She'd had to *beg* Sam to take her in. He'd never offered. He'd been forced into it. He cared more about Jason and Griffin.

Shit, not even Griffin wanted her. She'd thrown herself at him and he'd shut her down. He called her a slut! Maybe she was. Maybe she always had been.

She thought of her mom's old boyfriend, and how he'd lied about being seduced by Taylor, and that her mom had believed him!

She remembered the wedding reception, losing her virginity to Anthony. She relived the moment he lit up a cigarette afterward and called her a tease, and left. The memory of the humiliation swept through her again, as fresh as the first time.

Then came that fight with her mom.

"God, Mom…why didn't you listen to me? Why couldn't you believe *me*? Why couldn't you love *me*?"

Taylor cried harder, her arms wrapping around her waist, hugging herself while the gut-wrenching pain ripped through her. Somehow the anger had vanished, leaving only the desolate agony swallowing her up into a black hole.

Her legs buckled. She sank down onto her knees, curling up into a tight ball. Her damp forehead rested on the musty rug.

If only she could make it all go away. If only *she* could go away. Far away. She didn't want to be here anymore. But she didn't know where to go, or how to get there.

"I want to leave." Her broken sobs racked her body.

Then leave!

Get out!

Now!

CHAPTER 19

Megan paced the living room floor of the bungalow, endlessly. Mindlessly. Waiting. Waiting for Sam. Waiting for Stewart and Jason. It had been nearly two hours since the phone calls. First one from Sam, then one to Stewart, who had balked at her decision.

"There's no way I am going to allow our son near him," Stewart had said.

"Sam believes he can get Jason to open up to him."

"How do I know he isn't trying to see our son so he can threaten him to keep him quiet?"

"You *don't* know. You have to trust me on this." His silence unnerved her. "Then trust your son. Do you really think he would've raved about how much he loved his summer up there if he'd been victimized while he was living there? Have you asked yourself why he was so upset when you refused to allow him to go back with me for the weekend camps?"

"He could have been covering up. He could have been afraid to show his relief. Afraid that if he did, it would be the same as admitting that any of it had happened."

"Fine," she had said in exasperation. "You have to see it your way. I see it mine. All I ask is that you let Jason know that Sam wants to see him. If he hesitates in any way, if he shows even a flicker of fear, then you can keep him home. If he doesn't act scared, if he really wants to see Sam, please bring him over here. Please, Stewart. Sam has dealt with kids in trouble before. He's a neutral party—"

"Hardly!"

"I really believe he could help."

Stewart had finally agreed, though Megan still wasn't sure if they would really show up. And Sam would have wasted his time driving down from the ranch.

Sam.

Just thinking his name brought up unwanted memories and feelings she couldn't deal with right now. The shock and emotional anguish of her son's ordeal overshadowed any feelings she had for Sam. Not that she believed he could be a sexual predator. No, not Sam. She was positive he was not a pedophile.

Again she remembered that she had once been just as positive her own husband was not gay. If Stewart had fooled her, so could Sam.

Groaning at the downward spiral of her thoughts, she covered her eyes and dropped her head back, wishing it all away.

When the doorbell rang a few minutes later, she couldn't help thinking that she wanted it to be Jason and Stewart rather than Sam. She didn't want to face him alone. She didn't want him to see any lingering questions in her eyes.

"Hi, stranger," Sam said as she opened the door.

"Hi," was all she could answer back, stepping out of the way so he could come inside. He didn't lean over to kiss her. But then she didn't exactly encourage him either. "Would you like a soda or a glass of water? Iced tea, maybe?" she asked.

"Just water…if it wouldn't be too much trouble."

Trouble? Water? Then she saw the slightest smile, and realized he was humoring her. He followed her into the kitchen which suddenly seemed too small for the two of them. But right now any room would be too small for all of them—the two lovers they had been, and the careful strangers they had become.

"You look good," he said as he took the tall glass from her hand.

She didn't believe him, of course, despite her feeble attempt to hide the dark circles under her eyes, and add some color to her sallow complexion. She hadn't slept well since she'd learned about what had happened to Jason.

"Thank you," she finally answered. "Would you like something to eat? I have cheese and crackers and—"

"Relax, will you?"

"Sorry."

"Not necessary." He paused, then asked, "Is Jason here?"

"Not yet, but they should be here any minute."

"Stewart agreed, then."

"Eventually." She nervously shifted from one foot to another. "Maybe we should wait for them in the living room."

He nodded. She sat in one chair. He sat on the sofa. They filled the silence with idle conversation. She asked about the ranch. He asked about her school. She asked about his counselors. He asked about her students. Neither of them asked about the wall between them.

"How is Taylor doing?"

"Better. She still has her wilder moments…" He hesitated. "I just don't know if things will ever work out so she can go back to live with one of her parents."

"Are you willing to keep her?"

"Of course. How can I not? She's a good kid, Megan. I know it. Both of her parents have finally agreed to family counseling, I'm relieved to say."

"With you?"

He shook his head. "I gave them the name of someone else. I'm too close to it."

"Wise decision."

He looked up from the glass he had been studying in his hands. "You still think Taylor has a thing for me?"

"I can't be sure. I haven't seen her for weeks." She watched him intently. "Why? Has something happened?"

"No…not really." He told her about his suspicions regarding his two young CAs.

"Griffin and Taylor?" she said, more than a little surprised. "Do you really think—"

"Let's just say I hope Griff has enough good sense for the both of them."

"Good sense? He's fifteen, and not immune to the way Taylor teases him."

"You're not telling me anything I don't already know." After a moment of silence, he added, "I had a talk with Griff. He knows how I feel. I trust him to keep a safe distance from Taylor."

At that moment, he looked as if he bore the weight of the world on his shoulders. Keeping the ranch going, dealing with Taylor, now facing the accusations from Stewart. How much more could he bear? "I'm sorry that you were dragged into the middle of this mess with us."

"Don't be. I can't blame Stewart for his feelings."

"I wish the whole world didn't have to know about it."

"You and me both. But it's happened and now the only thing that really concerns me is Jason."

"Do you really believe he'll talk to you?"

"It's worth a try."

"He told Griffin, didn't he?"

"That I can't say, Megan."

"You don't need to. Something in the way Griff acted as he left here, the way he looked, I was almost certain he knew. I prayed he'd go to you, and he did. I had hoped that this might happen if I brought the boys together again."

"That was a big risk, y'know. Going against Stewart. Not knowing if Griffin was the one."

"He wasn't. Any more than you are."

"Are you so sure?"

She opened her mouth, closed it, then nodded. He stared intently at her. She swallowed, regretting this moment. His gaze fell. Her heart sank.

"I understand," he said quietly.

But she was sure he didn't.

~

SAM STOOD BEHIND JASON, his hands on the boy's small shoulders, lending him the support he needed to face his parents.

"I lied," Jason admitted so softly that he had to clear his throat and repeat his words. "I lied about nothing happening before. I, um, did some stuff, and…well, I was afraid to say anything 'cuz if anyone found out, then a whole bunch of other people might find out, and I'd get in trouble and you might get in trouble and, and —" Jason broke into sobs.

Sam gently squeezed Jason's shoulders to calm him. "Slow down. Just tell them like you told me."

"It wasn't her fault. I swear it wasn't her fault."

"Whose fault?" both Megan and Stewart asked at the same time.

"Melissa's," he cried. "He made her do it. But she didn't hurt me. Honest!"

He sobbed a few more minutes as his parents both reached out to touch his hand, his arm, anything to reassure him.

"It's okay, sweetheart," Megan said, her own tears falling.

"Cameron said he was gonna tell on me. He said Dad was a big celebrity and so he'd pay a lot of money to make Cameron keep quiet, and not tell the newspapers about me and my babysitter."

Stewart said, "We wouldn't have let that happen."

Jason shook his head. "I told him I'd do anything he wanted me to do if he just wouldn't tell on me and Melissa. And he said, 'okay,' and from then on I had to do stuff to him."

"What kind of stuff?" his father asked.

"Touching, and…and, y'know, other…stuff!" He wailed, turning around and burying his face in Sam's chest.

Stewart started to ask another question, but Megan stopped him. "Can't you see he's had enough?"

"But this isn't about him doing things to Cameron. Our son was sodomized, for God's sake! I need to know what the hell happened."

"For once, quit being a detective. Quit interrogating him as if you're writing a damn book. Cameron is the one who hurt him, Stewart."

During the parents' angry exchange, Sam stroked the boy's hair, then knelt down in front of him. "You did great, Jase. I'm proud of you."

"They're mad at me," he whispered through sniffles.

Megan heard her son, and reached for him. "No, Jason, not at all."

Once the truth finally came out, Jason seemed surprised they believed him, yet still worried Melissa would get in trouble and that somehow Cameron would come back and get him for telling.

"The worst is over," Stewart promised.

Sam wasn't too sure about that, considering the legal testimony that was still ahead for them. But in a way, Stewart was right. The secret was finally out. The abuse had been stopped. And Jason had his parents in his corner now.

"I can't thank you enough," Megan said to Sam as she walked him out to his car.

Sam hadn't said more than a few words to Jason before the truth had popped out. Griff had laid the groundwork. The trust.

The ten-year-old had been more than ready to reach out for help. Sam merely lent his moral support so the boy could tell his parents.

"You can thank me by saying you'll come back to work. Not right away, I know. You have a lot ahead of you to deal with. But in a month or so, maybe? Bring Jason back too?"

"I promise to think about it."

At least that was something. He said a polite goodnight without touching her, without showing any outward signs of wanting to reach out and hold her. He couldn't risk it. Neither could she. If Stewart was watching them he could still make the divorce hard for Megan.

~

AT ELEVEN FIFTEEN, Sam drove up the long gravel road to the dark house. Riley met up with him at his car as he parked it in the garage.

"Hey there, buddy. What are you doing outside, huh? Did Taylor feed you?"

The dog buried his nose in Sam's hand.

"Well, we'll see about that." He walked into the kitchen, flipping on lights as he went along. No sign of an empty dog food can in the sink, which was as far as it usually made it if Taylor was doing the chore, no matter how many times he told her to wash it out and put it in the plastic bin for recyclables.

"Taylor?"

No answer.

"Taylor!" He called her name a few more times, wandering through the living room where the big screen television was streaming a movie. No sign of the teenager though.

He checked her room. Clothes strewn everywhere, bed unmade, but nothing else to tell him she was around. He began to suspect she had taken off again. Maybe with Thorndike.

No, not maybe. Probably.

"God dammit, Taylor," he muttered. "I swear I'm gonna tan your hide if you've snuck off with that bastard."

Not that he would, really. He wouldn't lay a hand on her, of course. But he was pretty pissed off at the idea that she hadn't stayed home as she'd promised, and getting more pissed with every passing second that he had actually trusted her.

Riley followed him down the hallway to his bedroom. There was one last place he hadn't checked. Sure enough, the water was running in his shower. At least she'd closed the door this time.

"Taylor!"

He could hear the voice of Alanis Morissette singing about love and betrayal in her song, *You Oughta Know*.

He pounded on the door, yelling louder. She didn't answer. "I know you can hear me!"

Something was wrong. He felt it in his gut.

"I'm coming in, Taylor!"

Opening the door a crack, he purposely kept his eyes averted from the glass-enclosed shower. His gaze fell to a box of extra-strength aspirin, torn open and lying on the counter, then to a plastic pill bottle left in the sink.

He charged into the room and grabbed the economy-sized bottle.

Empty.

"Shit! Taylor!" He threw open the door of the shower.

Shards of glass from a shattered vodka bottle were scattered around the drain.

In the far corner of the tiled stall, beyond the spray of cold water, Taylor lay curled up in a ball, blood trickling from the soles of her feet.

Sam shut off the water, slightly relieved to see that her wrists hadn't been slashed, though the painkiller cocktail might have been lethal enough. He scooped up her naked body and carried her to his bed.

How the hell she got her hands on the booze, he didn't know. But he could guess Thorndike might have had something to do with it.

"Wake up, Taylor!"

His hair and clothes dripped as he tried to waken her. She groaned. He reached for the bedside phone.

"How many did you take?" he asked, dialing 911. "How long ago did you take them?"

She tried to cover her face, but he pulled her hands away. They flopped back onto the bed. She was out again. Even when 911 picked up, it'd be faster to drive her to the ER than wait for paramedics racing up the windy road from PCH.

"Taylor!"

She seemed to come around again.

"We're going to the hospital." He kept talking to her as he ran back into the bathroom for the empty bottle of pills, shoved it into his pocket, then wrapped her in his bathrobe and carried her through the huge house.

"I'm sorry, Sam," she whispered, her words softly slurred. She was barely able to hold on to his neck. Her head lolled against his shoulder as he strode to the car.

"Come on, baby. Stay awake now."

"I just…wanted somebody to love me."

"I love you, Taylor.."

"No, you don't," she answered drunkenly, "but it's…okay. Doesn't…matter. Not…anymore."

As Sam buckled them both in his car, he kept talking to her, telling her that he loved her, begging her to hang on.

As the car sped down the dark and winding road, Taylor could hear Sam speaking to her in a loud but comforting voice.

"Don't go to sleep on me, okay? You're going to make it."

Make what? she wondered for a second, then blocked out the thought. She didn't want to think anymore. She only wanted to sleep. She'd think tomorrow.

Somewhere along the way to the hospital, she heard him on his cell phone, first with her dad, then leaving a message for her mom.

Shit, they are going to be so pissed off.

Horns blared, then a siren. Sam was pulled over for speeding and cutting off some other car. Or at least that's the story he was giving her. She could hear everything as clear as ever, even though she couldn't really open her eyes or talk. She was just too sleepy to talk.

"We're going in the squad car, Taylor," Sam said as he jostled her from the passenger seat.

"Leave me alone," she finally managed to say, but it came out all garbled. "Let me die, Sam."

"What did she say?" asked a man's voice. Probably one of the cops.

Sam answered him, "Dunno. She's slipping in and out."

When they were speeding off again, the lights were flashing and the siren was blaring. Someone from the front seat wanted to know if Sam was her father.

"No, I've called him though. He's meeting us at the hospital."

"What's your relationship to her?"

"She's living at my house under my temporary guardianship."

"Hey, wait one minute—I know who you are! Hey, Lewis, you'll never guess who we've got in our back seat."

The other officer answered disinterestedly, "Why don't you tell me?"

"It's that guy in the news."

"Oh, yeah. Uh-huh. Recognize him anywhere. Who the hell are you talking about?"

"You know that writer, Stewart Fisher?"

Sam adamantly clarified, "I'm *not* Stewart Fisher."

The driver said, "Hell, I know that. I read all his books, even got an autograph once. Mike, this is not Stewart Fisher."

"No, no, no. It's the *other* guy. The one with the kiddie camp. The one who's under investigation. Fisher's wife and kid spent the summer with him. On top of all that, he's got some Hollywood big shot's teenage daughter shacking up with him. Is this her?"

"Christ…" muttered Sam, his arm around Taylor as she leaned against him, drifting in and out. "I already told you—I am her guardian. Nothing more. I've been helping out the family."

"Doesn't look like you're doing too good of a job, if you don't mind my saying so."

"I do mind, officer."

Taylor whispered, "I'm sorry, Sam. I'm so sorry."

"It's okay. You're going to be okay."

～

SHE WOKE up again as she was strapped onto a gurney and raced through hallways. Despite the strange, drifting sensation, she was acutely aware of disembodied voices barking commands and others answering. Silhouetted by bright lights, a sea of faces came and went. Or maybe she was just fading in and out. She didn't know. Didn't care.

"OD. Alcohol. Acetaminophen and aspirin—approximately 62,000 milligrams each. Plus caffeine—16,000 milligrams. That's if she took the entire bottle."

"Ingested two to six hours ago."

"Vomiting?"

"No. But she was found in the shower. Could have gone down the drain."

"Two to four hours, maybe she's got a chance. Six? Shit."

"Gastric tube. See what we get. Marcus, take over."

Taylor heard people talking as they worked over her. Her

head was tilted back, her mouth open. A tube went down her throat, stopped. Her neck arched. Her body jerked.

"She's convulsing. Hold her down!"

Hands pressed against her shoulders, forehead. The tube went down again. She gagged again.

"The tube's too damn big! Sliced the lining of her throat. Christ, she's bleeding."

Another voice asked for her parents.

"They've been called. We got a guy out here who says he's her legal guardian."

Sam!

Taylor shook her head, trying to ask for him. Wanting him. Needing him to hold her hand and tell her it was going to be okay. But it came out as a garbled groan.

Someone squeezed her hand.

Sam?

A woman said, "It'll be all right, honey. Hang in there."

Taylor listened to a gurgling suction sound. The stomach pump was finally working, explained the woman who stroked a cool palm across Taylor's forehead.

Losing track of time, she drifted in a strange, peaceful haze until she heard her father's angry voice yelling at the doctor that it was all a mistake, an accident.

She opened her eyes. Instead of lights and faces hovering over her, she was looking down from the ceiling of the small curtained cubicle.

A loud beep sounded.

"Doctor, we're losing her."

"No!" shouted her father, lunging toward the table.

A nurse pulled him back as Taylor watched the medical team. Bells rang. Noises and voices from other parts of the trauma center filled the air.

Someone moved out of the way, opening her view of the person lying on the table in a bloodied white terry robe.

It was her own body!

Feeling as if she was being pulled downward from this vantage point, she resisted.

No! I won't go back!

As the doctors and nurses worked futilely, she left them and found herself in another room. The waiting room. Her dad and Sam stood together next to a wall.

"Why, Sam? What happened? What went wrong? You were supposed to be helping her!"

It wasn't his fault, Dad!

"I'm sorry, Joel," Sam said.

No, Sam! Don't apologize to him! This isn't your fault!

Sam didn't hear her. Instead, he just kept talking. "I just didn't see this coming."

"Why not?" her dad demanded. "You are the one who's supposed to be the expert!"

"Now is not the time or place to be fighting about Taylor."

"Like hell—"

"Stop right there." Sam held up his palm. He leaned in and spoke in a low, threatening voice. "If you or Nicole would quit thinking of yourselves, Taylor might not be in there right now! Both of you forgot your very own daughter's birthday, you son of a bitch."

"I had a business trip!" her dad practically yelled. "I can't just cancel important meetings for a birthday party. Nicole was supposed to—"

"You know damn well she didn't do a thing for Taylor." Sam shook his head. "The two of you are pathetic excuses for parents."

"You bastard. When my lawyers get done with you, you're going to kiss that goddamn ranch goodbye."

Stop it, both of you! I just wanted out. That's all. Dad, you didn't want me! Mom didn't want me. Nobody wanted me. It's not Sam's fault, it's yours!

As Taylor's mind filled with apologies for screwing up again, she saw the doctor approaching.

"Mr. Bradley? We are administering antiarrhythmic drugs to counter the negative effects of the medication on her heart. She's already suffered one seizure here, possibly previous ones before Mr. Kempton found her."

"But she is still alive, right?"

"Yes, but—"

"Don't tell me she's going to die. This was an accident. Just a cry for help. She only took aspirin, for God's sake. Just aspirin! Nobody dies from plain old aspirin."

"Vodka too," Sam said. "Although I don't know how she got a hold of it, or how much she drank before the bottle broke in the shower."

"But *aspirin?* Who the hell dies from aspirin? It's not like she couldn't have gotten her hands on something a hell of a lot stronger and deadlier. Hell, if she really meant to do herself in, she could've raided my medicine cabinet. She didn't mean to do this, I tell you. It *was* an accident!"

The doctor continued in his attempt to soften the blow of the attempted suicide. "Perhaps you're right, sir. She may have only done this as a cry for help, expecting to be found in time. However, even though it may take longer for aspirin to do the damage, believe me, it is just as lethal as any other drug overdose. I have seen it happen too many times, unfortunately."

~

MEGAN HEARD the devastating news in the middle of the night. Mario had phoned to tell her about Taylor. Knowing that it would be on every local broadcast by morning, he was calling everyone connected to the ranch.

"How's Sam?" she'd asked.

"Taking it really hard. He's blaming himself."

After jotting down the name of the hospital, Megan sat on the edge of her bed, and dialed her old home number to reach Stewart. After she explained everything to him, he promised to break the terrible news to Jason first thing in the morning.

"I'm going up there," she said.

"Do you think that's wise?" He sounded more concerned than she had expected. "The media will make another circus out of this. Perhaps you should lie low."

"I don't care anymore what people think of me. I want to see Taylor."

"Are you sure this isn't about Sam?" His question was not damning or spiteful, yet she couldn't answer him.

"Mario and the others are going as well. I know Jason will ask—"

"I said I'd handle Jason," he assured her.

Since they had learned the truth from Jason, Megan had insisted Stewart drop his custody demands, which he had been quick to do. They had already agreed to keep their son home from school until after the juvenile authorities dealt with Cameron, and after Stewart's attorney conducted a press conference regarding the resolution of the case.

"I thought the worst was over," she said, referring to the nightmare of their son's molestation. "What more could possibly happen?"

"Don't ask that kind of question. It only invites more trouble."

"You're not superstitious, Stew."

"No, I'm not. Then again, I'm not the same person I was before all this happened."

"Neither am I."

"Drive carefully, Megan. I'm worried about you."

"Don't be."

"I'll *always* be."

Megan clutched the phone tightly in her fingers. His voice was so kind and gentle. So much like the old Stewart. "I…"

"I know. I'm sorry. For everything. I wish—" He paused. "I wish I hadn't hurt you. I regret that, you know. Whether you believe me or not, I do love you. And I love you for giving me our son."

"Please, Stewart—" Her voice caught in her throat.

"Sorry… Again… Forgive me."

It was her turn to pause, not because she couldn't find it in her heart to forgive him but because she felt as if she was standing at the threshold. There had been so much pain. So much anger. Now…now was a turning point.

"Tell Jason I love him."

"I will."

~

TAYLOR WAS PUT on a respirator within a few hours. Shortly after another seizure, she slipped into a coma. Her life came to a standstill while the rest of the world went on as usual. Except Sam's camp. Despite the rally of supporters on his behalf, he closed the Flying K indefinitely. No one could blame him. He spent nearly every hour of the day waiting for Taylor to wake up, coaxing her, talking to her, playing her raucous music for her. Her parents no longer blamed him, but he continued to blame himself.

Further investigation of Cameron uncovered kiddie porn websites on his computer, as well as two other victims, one boy and one girl, who had been molested during their own grade-school years. There might have been others, but the two middle school kids were willing to testify in court. The day before the start of the Christmas holiday break, Cameron was taken into custody on the sidewalk in front of his high school.

~

THE FOLLOWING SATURDAY MORNING, nearly four weeks after Taylor's suicide attempt, Megan had started out the door for her weekly visit to the hospital when she found Griffin sitting on the curb in front of the bungalow. He asked to tag along. Of course she agreed to take him, especially since she knew how thrilled Jason would be. Even though she had to pick up her son at the "big house," Jason split his time between the two homes now. More of a typical divorced parents' arrangement.

Megan welcomed the distraction of the boys talking during the drive to the Valley. She was so tired lately that it was difficult to drag herself through an ordinary day, let alone manage the hours on the road. Stewart hounded her to visit the doctor. Mainly to get him off her back, she had scheduled an appointment for Monday afternoon.

In the waiting room at the hospital, she got up from her chair to greet Mario and suddenly felt light-headed.

"Are you okay?" He reached out to steady her.

"Just a little dizzy," she assured him, but then the room spun around her as her knees buckled.

She woke up to the sight of a nurse kneeling next to her. "Have you had previous fainting spells?"

"No." Feeling completely embarrassed, Megan glanced around, realizing she was lying on the floor of the waiting room. "I forgot to eat lunch, and I'm terribly tired. I was just having a little attack of low blood sugar. I'm sure of it."

Jason didn't look too convinced.

"I'm okay, sweetheart. Honest."

The nurse didn't look too sure either. Neither did Sam when he returned from Taylor's room with Griffin in tow. "Shouldn't she go to the emergency room? Doesn't someone need to do tests for something like this?"

"I'm fine," she answered, though the nurse seemed to be agreeing with Sam. Not surprisingly, for insurance reasons, they wanted to make sure she hadn't hit her head or done anything that the hospital could be liable for later.

Minutes later, waiting alone in the examination room surrounded by privacy curtains, Megan felt a cold chill on her lower back. She reached around to close the gap in the examination gown, then checked her watch, wondering how long she would have to wait for a doctor.

The freezing touch of a hand on her shoulder startled her. With a yelp, she jumped off the table and spun around. Her heart pounded in her chest.

Sam barged in between the slit in the two curtains, followed by two orderlies. "Are you all right?"

Standing right beside him, clear as day, was Taylor.

CHAPTER 20

The next day, Stewart stood behind the wet bar in the family room of his Naples home. Christmas was less than a week away, and the temperature outside was eighty-two degrees. He was hot and sweaty and thirsty, pouring himself a second drink.

With a hand towel draped around his neck, Maxwell sat on a stool, nursing a bourbon and water, looking as neat and tidy as ever, even though the two of them had just finished an afternoon playing a relentless game of tennis.

Except for them, the house was empty. Jason had gone to the bungalow for the rest of the weekend to be with his mother, who was resting quietly.

"She asked me what else could go wrong," Stewart said, adding a little more liquor to his own glass.

"Did you warn her not to tempt fate?"

"I did, though only because your own superstitions have rubbed off on me, my friend."

"It's tragic. About the girl, that is." Maxwell shook his head sadly. "How eerie too. Megan seeing her at practically the very moment that she passed away. It isn't any wonder Megan fainted from the shock."

"She says it was from low blood sugar."

"Ah, yes. Well, more than likely it was."

"I happen to know the real reason."

"And that is?"

"Megan is pregnant."

"You must be joking."

"She told me this morning." He took a drink, swallowed it, and added, "I've suspected it for at least a month. She acted the same way with Jason. She finally made an appointment for tomorrow afternoon, but her visit to the emergency room confirmed my hunch."

"And how do you feel about it?"

"How should I feel? I'm going to be a father again. It wasn't planned, but I'm happy. Give me a few more months and I'll have her agreeing to move back in with me."

"But that baby can't be yours!"

"I slept with her, Max."

"You what?"

"You heard me."

"Why, for God's sake?"

"One last hurrah, you might say."

"Good Lord, what were you thinking? No, don't even answer that. I don't want to know."

"Don't be jealous. Not now. You've put up with it all these years. This isn't like you, to get upset with me for sleeping with her one last time."

"I am absolutely not jealous. Shocked, perhaps. Disappointed in you. When did this happen?"

He shrugged. "September, I think. Or was it late August. Doesn't matter. She's far enough along with her pregnancy that the timing fits."

Glaring at Stewart, Maxwell set down his tumbler in a slow

and deliberate move. "There appears to be another man in her life. Sam Kempton would be more likely the father. Obviously."

"Obviously?" Stewart snorted in disbelief. "What *is* obvious is my wife and I have had our dirty laundry aired in public. The last thing I want right now is for TMZ to get a hold of this. We don't need it. Jason doesn't need it. I'm doing this for him. He has had one hell of a year."

"Now, Stewart—"

"No, Maxwell. Don't ask me to put Jason through the humiliation of some sleazy reporting that his mom is carrying the love child of her own boss. Oh, and let's not forget that this alleged affair occurred while he had a teenager under his roof. The same teenager who OD'd on a bottle of pills with a vodka chaser."

"Christ, you couldn't have written a novel with more bizarre plot twists. No editor would believe it, let alone buy it."

"Meanwhile, the tabloids will be laughing all the way to the bank."

"*Meanwhile,*" Maxwell said, "Megan comes back to you because she thinks this baby is yours. But recreating your cozy little All-American family is not going to reverse the fact that you have been outed. Whether you want to deal with that or not, don't ruin Megan's happiness too."

"What about Jason?"

"Hell, this will be a walk in the park for him after what he's already been through. Give him some credit. He's got as much survival tenacity as both his parents combined. We're the ones who've screwed up our lives. Why take him down with us?" Maxwell stated stoically, "I beg you, Stewart, don't go through with this horrible charade."

"Maxwell, you're the one who pushed me into marrying Megan in the first place. You're the one who taught me to lie and cover up who I am. Now you can stand there like a pompous ass and judge me for it?"

Maxwell looked pale and sadly distraught. "I regret the role I have played in hurting Megan and Jason. And you. Which is precisely why I can no longer be a party to your plan."

~

THE PRIVATE MEMORIAL service for Taylor was held at sea on Tuesday morning, two days before Christmas. It was small by comparison to most Hollywood standards. Only a hundred or so of the parents' closest friends and associates, give or take a few. Then there were the token few kids from Taylor's high school and, of course, the gang from the Flying K.

For the service, a luxurious yacht had been supplied by the head of one of the studios. Sam couldn't remember which one of the parents was affiliated with the executive, and didn't care. He only knew the few people from the ranch, and planned on meeting up with them in the parking lot of the Rainbow Marina in Long Beach.

Of course it was a media feeding frenzy. Every news station had sent a truck and crew. Police were directing traffic consisting primarily of limousines and high-dollar sedans.

Megan had come with Jason. Stewart too, which surprised Sam. The soon-to-be-ex-husband didn't act like he was headed to divorce court, not from the way he hovered attentively around Megan. She looked thinner. Fragile. It unnerved Sam to see her with Fisher. Sam should have been the one at her side, shielding her from the onslaught of reporters that raced toward the famous author and his family.

The boat arrived from its mooring in Newport, loaded its hundred-plus passengers, and slowly motored through the Long Beach Harbor, past the historic black-hulled Queen Mary at her permanent anchor, which drew eyes starboard to gaze at her.

Some man pointed to the white geodesic dome that had been built to display Howard Hughes's wooden airplane, Spruce Goose, that had since been dismantled and moved to Oregon. To a woman at his side, he explained, "For a while it was owned by Warner Brothers as the world's largest sound stage. But now it's a terminal for Carnival Cruise lines." He named a dozen movies that had been filmed inside, claiming several as his own projects. The woman was clearly impressed.

As the self-appointed tour guide rambled on, Sam wondered if the man and woman even knew Taylor Bradley, or if they were just along for the ride.

As the boat passed through the Queen's Gate opening in the breakwater, Sam had overheard enough conversations to figure out that the list of passengers was made up of primarily industry hotshots. He wondered how many deals would be made on a handshake within the next few hours. How many of them even cared why they were here other than to have been on the A-list of invites?

Shit. Only in LA would you find a funeral turned into a networking party.

Once under considerable speed on the open ocean, the yacht headed toward Catalina Island, twenty-six miles in the distance, then angled north midway into its route and cut its engines.

Away from the obnoxious reporters and prying eyes of the cameras, the somber ceremony was conducted by a woman minister dressed in a long denim skirt and heavy cable-knit sweater. On each side of her stood Taylor's mother and father, both of whom appeared shattered beyond measure. On a table in front of them sat a pink urn made of Himalayan sea salt holding the cremated remains of a lost adolescent. A white cardboard base kept it from tipping over as the boat gently rolled. The salt-tinged December breeze chilled the air as Joel leaned over the stern of the boat and lowered the urn into the choppy waters of the open channel. Then he lifted the Hawaiian lei from around his neck and gently tossed it on the ocean surface and turned away. Nicole repeated the same gesture, followed, one by one, by the rest of the mourners until there was a sea of color.

Seemingly out of nowhere, hundreds of small dolphins appeared in the midst of the poignant tribute. The enormous pod surrounded the yacht, churning the surface of the sea in a vast playground of leaps and dives that spread out at least a half mile in all directions.

"It's the super-pod of common dolphins," Griffin said, standing next to Sam. "I saw them on my first whale-watch in sixth grade. There must be five thousand out there right now. What a perfect send-off for Taylor."

"Yeah." Sam smiled. "She would've been stoked."

I am, Sam. This is totally cool.

At the sound of Taylor's voice, Sam whipped around, expecting to see her, yet knowing he was crazy to think such a thing. And, of course, there was no one there.

Griffin leaned in. "She's here."

He nodded, though he assumed the fifteen-year-old was speaking figuratively, not in the context of a real ghost. "Yeah, well, she had a strong spirit."

"Sam, don't think I'm crazy for saying this but I think Taylor is here. A while back, at your barbecue, I remember her saying that she really believed the ranch was haunted with some of the old actors who filmed those Westerns in the canyon. She said when she died, she'd come back to the Flying K..." His eyes grew bright with tears.

"She was just joking around as usual," Sam said, slinging his arm around Griff's shoulders. "I wouldn't take her seriously."

"But...maybe she knew back then that she was going to—" He stopped short of finishing his thought. "Maybe if I'd told you that she was talking about dying, you could've helped her before she really did it."

"Don't torture yourself with guilt." He squeezed the boy's shoulder reassuringly. "You couldn't have known, Griff. None of us knew."

~

MEGAN STOOD near the bow of the boat as it headed back to port. Her fingers wrapped around the rail, holding on tight for the occasional big swell. She welcomed the wind on her cheeks, praying the cold air would ease the nausea, as Stewart had said it would.

Her raw emotions were so close to the surface already. She hadn't handled the memorial service well at all. Hearing the final words of farewell to Taylor, watching the grieving parents, it had all been too much. She couldn't seem to stop crying, even though Jason's hand had squeezed hers in concern and reassurance. Stewart had moved closer too, slipping his arm around her waist to support her.

As soon as the service had concluded, the nausea had returned, prompting Stewart to lead her to the bow where, he'd assured her, the fresh sea air blowing against her face would be a sure remedy. It worked but not entirely. He left her alone while he went to inquire about a private cabin for her to lie down and rest.

"I was hoping to find you alone," Sam said, catching her in the most inopportune moment of blowing her nose.

"Oh!" She hurriedly disposed of the tissue into the pocket of her jacket. She knew this meeting was inevitable, but she had purposefully kept her distance, afraid to get too close, afraid he would somehow see her secret in her eyes. "Hello, Sam."

He dropped an elbow on the rail, leaning close to be heard over the wind. "Hello, yourself."

She smelled liquor on his breath, and her stomach lurched. He had fallen off the wagon. She could hardly blame him.

"I just spoke to Jason. He says you're sick."

"Only a little," she lied, knowing it was more than the motion of the boat that was making her ill. "Jason was getting a bit too fretful, so I asked him to hang out with Griffin for a while."

"It was nice of you to bring Griff."

"I may have had ulterior motives, I'm afraid. It helped Jason get through the ceremony. Griff has been like a big brother, especially since—" She remembered that Taylor had taken the overdose at the very same time that Sam had been helping her own family.

"How is Jason doing in therapy?"

"Very good. Thank you for referring us to Dr. Creel."

His quick nod acknowledged her gratitude. "And what about you?"

Her ignorance of Jason's painful ordeal would forever haunt her with shame and remorse. Another attack of emotional tears threatened, but she held them back. If she started, she might never stop. "I'm…managing to get through it."

"I'm glad." Sam took another drink from his glass.

"Sam, I know how you must be feeling about Taylor, but this isn't going to help." She nodded at the glass in his hand.

Silently turning away from her, he didn't answer. Instead he took another drink. She wondered if this was only his first glass, but strongly suspected it wasn't. Probably not even his second. He seemed a bit unsteady, more so than adjusting to the roll of the boat over a large swell. "Joel told me nothing is going to happen to Thorndike. No statutory rape charges. Nothing. It's too late now. With Taylor gone, she can't testify."

"I'm sorry, Sam. It's not right."

"No…no, it's not." He lifted his glass in a toast. "Welcome to the surreal world of Hollywood. Sleazy shit happens all the time."

She reached out to touch his shoulder, but stopped, afraid he would shrug her off. The tension beneath his heavy suede coat emanated from him in waves. With the liquor in him, she wasn't sure what to expect.

As if reading her thoughts, he turned back, only halfway, only enough for her to see the side of his face, drawn and tired. Propping his forearms on the rail, he held the tumbler between both hands.

"My brother Bill always talked about taking risks," he said. "Of making a positive difference, of not being afraid to trust in tomorrow. But look where it got him. Dying too young to make a bit of difference."

Drawn together in their grief, Sam confessed the relentless guilt over failing Taylor, not to mention her parents, no matter how self-absorbed. As her guardian, he had been responsible for her and he'd blown it.

"But you were helping Jason, remember? Not even white knights slaying dragons can be in two places at one time."

Either he didn't hear her gentle humor over the sound of the wind, or he chose not to listen to her. "All summer I was too wrapped up in the ranch to really give Taylor the attention she needed."

Too wrapped up in me, you mean. She held her tongue, all too aware of her own obsession with Sam while her son suffered alone with his secret.

"I found out from Nicole that Taylor had been seeing Thorndike. During her school lunch hours, mostly."

"How did she find out?"

"Taylor told her. Over the phone. That afternoon she took the pills. She was crying to her mom over that SOB running off to Vegas to marry someone else. The way she was crying and cussing, she sounded drunk to Nicole, which only pissed her off and made her hang up."

"You see, Sam? Not even her own mother saw what was coming."

"But I should have seen it! I'm trained to know the signs."

"What signs? She didn't say or do anything before this that would lead anyone to believe she'd swallow a bottle of pills."

"I'm willing to bet that Taylor never intended to commit suicide. If she had, she would've found something a hell of a lot stronger than aspirin. She knew I was coming home at any time. She wanted me to find her. She was just using it as a cry for help. But I didn't come home in time."

As they talked, Megan tried to convince Sam that he should be proud of his devotion to the girl. He had been like a father to her since her first summer at camp when she was five years old. And when things got tough, he was there for her, taking her in when her own parents washed their hands of her. He had given Taylor the laughter and memories of a home and family she'd never have known without him.

"You can't ask any more of yourself than that," she said.

With tear-filled eyes, Sam shook his head. "No, I'm exactly like my old man. He always put his ranch and his camp kids before his own family. When Taylor came to live with me, I thought it was my chance to prove to myself that I wasn't following in my dad's footsteps. To be honest, I'd even looked at this temporary guardianship as good practice for the day when I would have my own daughter." He looked at her. "That's not entirely true. Actually, I thought a lot about the day we would have our own daughter."

Touched deeply by his confession, Megan wanted to tell him about the baby. In her heart of hearts, she had wanted to believe that he was the father, not Stewart. But her almost nonexistent cycle left the date of conception under question. Considering the size of the fetus in the first sonogram, her doctor speculated a due date that coincided with her one and only time with Stewart.

Sam laughed bitterly, "Some joke, huh?"

"Excuse me? What joke?"

"For once I actually wanted to be a father, but losing Taylor proves that my parenting skills suck. Good thing Maryann didn't go through with her pregnancy."

Megan masked her shock. "You never mentioned this before."

"It wasn't a big deal. We had been dating only a few months so

I left the final decision to her. Ironically, after the wedding we couldn't do anything right to conceive a child."

"Did you resent Maryann's decision?"

"At the time, it seemed like the best solution. I was drinking —" He held up his nearly empty glass, giving it a little lift as if toasting himself. "And trying to juggle my counseling job, which made me a self-appointed authority against bringing unwanted children into this fucked-up world. Maryann agreed, especially since she was trying to get her own career off the ground. Neither of us was in the position to accept the responsibilities." He swirled the liquor in the bottom of his glass. "From the looks of things, I'm still not in a position after all these years."

"I disagree. You would be a wonderful father."

"Nope. Not true. I can't even make a marriage stick. No woman wants to be isolated up there in the sagebrush and mountains like a pioneer wife, not to mention that same second-fiddle business that my kid would face. I know from my own childhood that any kid of mine would get lost in the hordes of other camp kids. He'd be desperate for his parents' attention, and envious of the boys playing Little League while their parents watched from the stands."

"But I can't believe you would really let those things happen to your own son. Not after you went through it. Not when you know firsthand what it feels like. You love children. Right now, you're letting the alcohol do your talking."

"Maybe," he said, polishing off the drink, then looking her straight in the eye. "And maybe not."

What if he truly believed his drunken words? What if he had already written off fatherhood for the final time? Would it make a difference if he knew about the baby?

Perhaps if it was his. But it might not be.

She tried to ignore the inner voice, wanting to confess to Sam, wanting to believe he would embrace fatherhood if he was given another chance.

Even if she had proof of his paternity, there was still a possibility that she might not make it through this high-risk pregnancy with the IUD complications. What then? After his devastating loss of Taylor, how could he deal with losing his own child before it took its first breath?

Sam spoke, interrupting her painful thoughts. "I miss you, Megan."

Don't, Sam, her mind silently pleaded. But her heart answered, *I miss you too.*

He asked, "Have you thought any more about coming back to work for the weekend camps?"

"I'm afraid I can't do it." She saw the disappointment deepen in his eyes. Unable to tell him that the doctor wanted her to take extra precautions, she made up an excuse. "I took on some extra work at school. A play for the spring festival. I'll be swamped with auditions, rehearsals and weekend work-parties to build the set."

"I see."

Does he? she wondered. Or did he see right through her lie? Her own guilt settled heavily in the pit of her stomach like sour milk, escalating the nausea. "I'm sorry, Sam. I've got to find a bathroom before I get sick."

Darting toward the nearest cabin entrance, she bumped into Stewart coming out, unaware of Sam on her heels.

"I've got her," Stewart said, leading her inside as she glanced back to see Sam turn away and look out to sea.

TWENTY MINUTES LATER, lying on the bed of a large, elegant forward cabin, Megan felt like a wet rag that had been through the wringer. Stewart had held her head throughout her violent retching, then helped her to the bed, sitting next to her as he placed a cool washcloth on her forehead. It was a strange feeling to have him close, to see him acting as if the entire year had been nothing but a dream.

"I wish I could get you something for the nausea," he said, offering her a sip of ginger ale through a straw. "Maybe you should've gotten a patch from the doctor."

"No."

"Oh, yeah…the baby."

His words triggered a silent trickle of tears from her eyes. Until now she had been reticent to tell Stewart that he might not be the father. Not that she was afraid he would use her affair with Sam as an excuse to take Jason away from her, especially after everything their son had been through. Stewart had dropped the legal proceedings.

"No more tears now," he soothed. His hand slid to her stomach. Her weight loss over the past year had made her so thin that the roundness of her belly beneath her baggy shirt seemed more pronounced, even though she was only four months along. Fortunately, her long jacket had covered her shape. Stewart mistook her tears for worries about the baby. "I know you're scared about the IUD, but the doctor says he's delivered perfectly healthy babies despite those things being in there. It's going to be okay."

"I wish I was as sure as you."

He smiled. "And I'm just as sure that we're finally going to have that little girl you've always wanted."

"You never wanted another child." *Neither does Sam.* "And I'm not expecting you to raise this one. It's over between us. Go back to work. Go back to Maxwell."

"I've quit the force. I can't juggle two careers anymore. As for Maxwell…he's gone too."

"Why? What happened?" He looked surprised by her concern. "Did you expect me to be happy?"

"As a matter of fact, yes."

Seeing the side of him that she had once loved so deeply, she reached up and stroked his cheek. "There's been enough hurt and pain. I don't want to feel that way about you any longer. You are who you are, Stewart. It's not your fault. And it's not mine either."

"It was never yours."

"I know..." She cried, letting go of the past, of the pain. "Maybe I shouldn't have been so insistent on going through with this pregnancy."

"But you want this baby. You're just worried, that's all."

"Stewart, please..."

"I won't let you talk this way."

In a moment of inexplicable need to purge herself of the pain, she knew she had to tell Stewart the complete truth. About everything. All of it came tumbling out as if she had no more control of her words than she had of her own body.

After telling him about Sam, she added with firm conviction, "Don't think I went out looking for another man to get back at you for your affair. But I will not let you use this to get Jason from me."

"After everything he's been through, he needs both of us right now. I can't take him away from you." His dark eyes were filled with remorse. "I saw how much he worried about you during the service. I think it's time you told him about the baby."

"Do you think he'll be happy about the news?"

"I'm sure of it. I certainly was..." His voice trailed off, as if he remembered that his happiness might be short-lived if the child she carried was not really his own.

"I'm sorry. I don't know what else to say. If tests prove this baby is yours, I won't keep her from seeing you."

CHAPTER 21

Stewart saw Megan after her doctor's appointment when she came by the Naples house to pick up Jason. He'd known for weeks her doctor was growing more concerned with sonogram images of the precarious position of the IUD relative to the fetus.

"How are you doing?" he asked, greeting her at the door and leading her to the kitchen.

"I've been ordered off my feet."

He pulled up a chair from the breakfast table, and made her sit down before saying another word. "How much notice can you give the school?"

"None, apparently." Her hand tenderly stroked her round abdomen.

He knelt in front of her, gazing up at her. "May I?"

She nodded. He placed his hand beside hers, remembering the magic of feeling Jason move inside her. The years swept away, leaving him in a mist of memories. He had loved Megan more at that moment than any other time in their marriage. The image of his own son growing inside her had moved him to tears that day. Nothing had ever affected him so deeply. Nothing except the moment Jason was born.

A ripple of movement beneath his palm brought a smile to his face. He glanced up at Megan, seeing her own radiant smile.

"I've made so many mistakes. So much has happened in this past year that has forced me to take a long, hard look at myself. Dr. Creel recommended a therapist, and I've started to see him. I want to change," Stewart said.

"Really?" She cocked an eyebrow and he realized she may have misunderstood.

He shook his head. "I've been a self-centered ass for a long time. I never wanted to be like my dad, and I never thought what I was doing was anything like my dad. But I'm going to lose Jason if I keep going down this road. I want him to be proud of me, Meggie. And this baby too."

The corners of her mouth fell. "But what if she's not yours?"

"She? Is that your wishful thinking or did you get another sonogram?"

She nodded and looked down at her round belly, smoothing both hands over her blouse. "It's not one hundred percent, but the doctor is fairly certain it's a girl."

"I'm happy for you."

She gazed up into his eyes. "I should probably tell Sam but what if I do and blood tests prove you're the father, not him? I don't want to hurt him."

"You have to quit thinking in terms of 'if,' Megan. He should be here. He should be feeling the baby kick. He should be taking care of you now, especially considering the doctor's orders."

"No," she said, pushing herself up. "I need to go. Get Jason for me, will you?"

He rose to his feet, gently grabbing her shoulders. "I hate to say this to you but what you're doing to Sam is what I did to you."

Her eyes opened wide. "Hardly! This is not anywhere near the same thing."

"I kept the truth from you from the beginning of our relationship, telling myself I was protecting you. I didn't want to hurt you. Isn't that what you're doing now with Sam?"

"Yes...no! You're twisting it all around."

"I don't think so." He sighed. "If you aren't going to tell Sam, then let me help you move back here. Just until the baby arrives. No strings attached." He held up his hand. "I swear to you that I've changed, Meggie. This is not about getting my family back together again."

"I wish I could believe you."

"I still care about you. I always will. And I can't stand by while you struggle through this pregnancy all by yourself. Here at the house you'll have the elevator so you won't have to climb stairs. We still have the housekeeper so you won't have to clean. I can hire a cook too."

"Let me think about it," she said, then went to the bottom of the stairs and called out for Jason.

Within seconds, the stairwell was echoing with the sound of their son running down the carpeted steps.

"Did you say yes?" he asked her, then to his dad, "Did she say yes?"

She also glanced from one to the other. "In cahoots, you two?"

"Naw," Jason said, "But if we were living here, you could have Dad around, and maybe then I could, like, go see Griff and Sam and everybody up at the ranch some weekend."

Megan frowned slightly, then answered, "If you want to visit the ranch, you only need to ask. I'm sure your father would be willing to take you."

"But not for the whole weekend. Not if it means leaving you alone," he argued.

"I'm alone every other weekend when you stay here. There's no difference."

"Yes, there is." He turned away, terribly disappointed.

Stewart ruffled his hair. "You gave it your best shot, sport. Tell you what, I'll make a phone call, see if you can visit this weekend, and promise to check in on your mom."

"Cool."

~

ON FRIDAY NIGHT, Stewart took Jason to the Flying K, both of them promising Megan that they wouldn't breathe a word of her guarded condition to anyone. During the drive up the coast, Jason didn't quite understand why it was such a big deal to his mom, especially when he really wanted to tell Griffin that he was going to be a big brother too.

Stewart did his best to explain that Megan had her personal reasons to wait until the baby came before announcing its arrival. And it was only right that they respect her privacy. After the fiasco with the news media invading their family's lives and telling things to the whole world, Jason understood and agreed to keep quiet.

Stewart thought he had handled the sticky subject pretty well, even though he himself was not the least bit comfortable about keeping this important news from Sam Kempton. If there was anyone who was surprised by his sudden change of heart toward Sam, it was him. Something had come over him. Maybe it was the day Maxwell had so adamantly opposed him, issuing his ultimatum. Or maybe it was the day of the memorial service when he realized he couldn't go on living a life of lies.

After making sure Jason was all situated for the weekend, he headed back to the parking lot. Unfortunately, he didn't get away quite as easily as he'd hoped.

Before he reached his Corvette, Sam caught up to him.

"I want to know about Megan," he asked with a slight belligerence, as if Stewart was his rival. He wasn't, of course. Not anymore. Not ever, really.

The divorce papers were signed. She was free. But it wasn't his place to tell Sam those particular details.

"She's doing okay."

"Just 'okay'? What is that supposed to mean?"

"I'm in no position to speak for her. If you want to know anything, you'll have to call her. Better yet, drop by and see her sometime."

"It's not like I live in the neighborhood. Not like you do."

"You're right. What was I thinking?"

SAM STUDIED the expression on Stewart Fisher's face, sensing something wasn't quite as it seemed, sensing the man wanted to say more. He remembered the closeness between Megan and her estranged husband on the boat. Jealous of their intimate friendship, Sam wished he was the one, not Stewart, who lived near enough to drop in on her.

Ah hell, if he was perfectly honest with himself, he really didn't want to live anywhere but under the same roof with her. The past several weeks he had gone back to AA and stayed sober. Each day had been more than miserable for him. And not just because of his grief over Taylor. And not because of the interrupted nights of sleep when he thought Taylor was still in his house. Simple exhaustion had him seeing movement out of the corner of his eye, even in broad daylight. He'd turn, but nobody would be there. He told himself it couldn't be Taylor. She was gone. He wasn't crazy. He knew it. He also knew something else—

He missed Megan.

He wanted her back at the ranch, but it was apparent she didn't want to come back.

"I know she was supposed to be getting ready for some sort of big production," Sam said.

"Really? Is that what she said? A big production?"

"Yeah. It was going to take up all her time."

"More than she expected," Stewart said.

"Would you mind telling her that as soon as she gets through with it, she still has her old job waiting here for her?"

"I will, but...I wouldn't expect her to return too soon. This, uh, job is taking a lot out of her. She might not be back up to speed until the end of the school year."

"Good. Just in time for the summer session."

"Maybe you should call her about that," Stewart suggested. "You would be better at twisting her arm than I would. She doesn't exactly listen to me these days."

For a fleeting moment, Sam wondered if Stewart was actually trying to help him get together with Megan. But that couldn't be true. Not after everything he knew about Stewart's efforts to keep his family together. Not after seeing Stewart whisk Megan away from him on the deck of the yacht. No, it had to be nothing more than wishful thinking.

"Well then, I guess I'll just have to make a point of calling her sometime in the next few weeks," Sam said. "You'll be back here on Sunday about noon to pick up Jason?"

"Yes, noon. See you then."

Sam waited all of about ten minutes before calling Megan, using the excuse that he was making plans for the summer staff. If she turned him down too quickly, he would know it wasn't a heavy school schedule that was keeping her from coming back to the Flying K.

"I can't, Sam."

There. He had his answer. And his gut felt like he'd taken a direct punch. What more could he say?

"Sam? Are you there?"

"Yeah, I'm here. I'm just searching for something to say. But the only thing that comes to mind is, why?"

"It's not you, Sam. Please believe me. I...am seriously considering another career. In adolescent psychology. If I go through with it, I'll start classes this summer. But this doesn't mean I won't see you again. I planned to register Jason for the summer session."

"Interesting. His father didn't mention it when he was just here."

"I, uh, haven't discussed it with him yet. As I said, I'm only considering it."

"How is the play coming along?"

"Play? Oh, the *play*! Fine. Good. Could be better. You know how these things can be. I think I'll be holding my breath until that final curtain call." She sounded so bright and enthusiastic that he figured her life must be a hell of a lot better than Stewart implied. Perhaps there was a new man in her life that Stewart didn't know about. Or if he did, he did a good job of hiding it.

Angry with himself for foolishly holding out hope of having her back, Sam wished her luck with the play, said goodbye and headed out the office door. With this new monkey on his back, it was going to be one hell of a long weekend.

~

THE FIRST OF MARCH, Megan was six months pregnant and already as large as a house. Dr. Ames speculated she and Stewart would be taking home a twelve-pound future linebacker. Although he was well aware of the media exposure regarding their family, he assumed the baby was Stewart's, and she said nothing to the contrary.

Edema had complicated the already high-risk pregnancy, requiring frequent office visits to keep a close eye on her condition. She had been having false labor for over a month, but hadn't breathed a word of it to Stewart, who had become her self-appointed guardian.

Their relationship had changed since they had been brought

together to help Jason. The family therapy had led to healing of their personal lives as well. Realizing they would forever be linked together through their son, they both worked hard to get through their own issues with each other. There would still be more sessions, together and apart, but now Megan was letting go of the past so she could move forward.

Stewart was handling his new public identity with poise and dignity. For the most part, he had not been torn apart for hiding his sexual identity throughout the years. Most of his fellow police officers were supportive. As for the publisher of his novels, the word from his editor was that "any publicity is good publicity," and that book sales were up. Yet it would remain to be seen if sales figures would continue to rise, the true barometer that would affect publisher support.

By the middle of the month, Megan finally gave in to Stewart's suggestion to move back into the big house. Spending more time in bed, she couldn't cook for Jason when he stayed with her, often relying on Stewart to drop by with dinner.

After her first week back at home, she had spent the quiet Friday reading a novel, then glancing through magazines. Her restlessness was worse than most days. She had too much time to think about Sam. Too many times she had reached for her phone to tell him about the baby. Then her heart would start pounding in her chest so hard she thought she was having a panic attack. Maybe she was. But she couldn't tell him such news over the phone. She had decided to tell him but she kept putting it off.

Pacing the floor made her feel more tired than usual and caused her back to ache. Despite the pillows around her on the sofa, she couldn't make herself comfortable no matter how hard she tried.

It didn't help matters knowing that she could not even look forward to seeing Jason later in the afternoon and hearing about his day at school. Instead, he would be on his way to the ranch with Karen and Mario who would also be picking up Griffin along the way.

With a book deadline demanding his full attention, Stewart had arranged the camp weekend to keep Jason occupied and give Megan the peace and quiet that she didn't request. In deference to her secrecy about her pregnancy, however, he also arranged to meet the camp counselors at the school so that they would not need to visit the house, and risk seeing Megan. Not even Griffin knew about the baby. His visits with Jason took place at the other house.

While Stewart was taking Jason's gear to him at school, she settled in front of the television, surfing through the channels for an interesting program or movie to pass the hours. Stumbling across an afternoon talk show about teenage suicide, she was immediately drawn into the program.

Minutes before the end of the hour, Stewart found her sobbing, cussed under his breath, then reached for the remote control and clicked off the show. "Letting yourself get emotionally upset can't be good for the baby."

"Don't be a nag," she said, trying to laugh off her latest crying jag. "I cry over Hallmark commercials, for heaven's sake. Get used to it."

He grabbed a tissue from the box on the coffee table and handed it to her. "Before I get back to work, can I get you anything?"

"No, I'm fine. Quit hovering. You're making me nervous."

"I'll bring a dinner tray up for you at six. How's that?"

"I can manage to walk downstairs to the kitchen to eat."

"But the doctor said to keep you off your feet as much as possible."

"Go and write!" she commanded, waving him off. With her arm outstretched dramatically pointing to his office, she suddenly gasped and dropped her hand to her stomach.

"What's wrong?" He perched on the edge of the coffee table in front of her.

"I...I think I'm in labor." She grimaced.

"But it's too early."

"I know!" she snapped. "But this is different from the other ones."

"Other ones? Other *contractions*? Are you saying you've already been having contractions? For how long?"

"A month. But Dr. Ames called them false contractions. Nothing to be too concerned about."

"Why didn't you say anything?"

"Are you kidding? You're already acting like a mother hen. I didn't need any more hovering and checking on me every five minutes."

He grabbed the phone off a nearby end table and handed it to her. "Call Sam."

"It's not a good time to deal with him."

"If you're in labor, you need to tell him before you have this baby."

"Don't tell me what to do," she argued. "When you quit the force, I respected your decision. The least you can do is quit badgering me about when I decide to tell Sam about this baby."

"It's not the same situation, and you know it."

She winced, holding her breath as another pain swept over her.

"You're fighting it. Take a deep breath."

Glaring at him, she inhaled deeply, then blew out a long breath and pointed to the phone.

"Call Sam?" he asked.

"No!" She dropped her head back in exasperation. "Call Dr. Ames."

IN THE BACK seat of Karen's car, Jason didn't talk much to anybody during the long ride to the ranch. There was a bad car crash on the Santa Monica Freeway, with bloody people lying on the road and paramedics treating them and everything, so it took them four whole hours to get to camp instead of two. Sam wasn't too worried. At least he didn't act like it. Most everybody else came later than usual too. Except people coming from the Valley.

Friday night was always spent getting all the new groups settled into their different cabins. Weekend camp wasn't like summer camp with the counselors and CAs staying in the cabins with the kids. Instead, it was always scout groups and church youth groups who had their own chaperones. So the cool thing was that Jason and most all the other CAs and younger counselors got to sleep both nights in the Rec Hall on the sofas and the floor.

Mario and Karen slept at Sam's house though.

Jason was glad he didn't have to sleep there. He didn't much like going anywhere near the house anymore. When Karen parked her car up there that night, he was real quick to grab his gear out of the trunk and head back toward the Rec Hall with Griffin.

He glanced over his shoulder at the house. A shiver ran down his back. "Do you think she's really still here?" he asked.

"You've been listening to too many of Mario's ghost stories," Griffin said.

"But what if they aren't just stories?"

Griff didn't answer.

"I heard him talking to Karen. I heard him say he saw Taylor as real as you and me."

"I don't wanna talk about it." He shifted his backpack. "Hey, I got some good news. We got ourselves a place to live. For a little while anyway."

"Cool! Can I come and see it?"

"You better not. It's not exactly a good area, but at least I can go back to school now."

"You quit school? When?"

"Last fall. I had to work and help out."

"Wow, Griff. Don't you get in trouble for that? I mean, don't they, like, send somebody out to find you?"

"Not if they don't know where to look."

After dumping their gear in a storage room in the back of the Rec Hall, the two of them washed up before heading around to the back door of the kitchen to serve dinner along with the other CAs.

LATER THAT NIGHT, after all the different groups had eaten and done their Friday night games and then left for their cabins, Jason started thinking about his mom, and wondering if she was okay, and worrying about if maybe he should be home helping take care of her. His dad was so busy working on the book that sometimes he didn't remember what time it was.

Maybe if he just called home…but he couldn't do that unless he walked back down to the office in the dark. And he'd probably have to ask Sam for permission. And then Sam would want to know why. And Jase couldn't tell him about his mom and the baby.

He hated keeping secrets. He really, really hated it. He told his own secret, but he still couldn't tell nobody about his mom's secret or Griff's. Not even the therapist, who was a good friend of Sam's and would probably talk to him even if he said he wouldn't.

At least Griff wasn't living in the van anymore. That made Jase feel a little better. But it still didn't sound too good. How long was "a little while" anyways? A couple weeks maybe?

And then there was his mom.

After everything that was said about his dad in the newspapers, Jase got a long talk from his dad, then another one from his mom. He understood about his dad now. Well, sorta. He had a friend in his class with parents that were both women.

But what he didn't exactly understand was how his dad could be gay and still be a dad. That part was kind of confusing, especially now that his mom was having another baby.

Drifting off to sleep with his mom on his mind, Jason tossed and turned all night long until a nightmare woke him up. It was pitch black and he didn't know where he was.

Then he saw her!

Taylor was a few feet away, looking just as real as ever, just like Mario said. Wearing a black T-shirt and jeans, she had a sad smile on her face.

"Mom! Dad!"

"It's okay, Jase," Griffin said in the darkness, putting his hand on Jason's shoulder just as Taylor vanished.

"Did you see her, Griff?"

"Shh. You'll wake everybody else up."

Afraid to admit he was scared, Jase said, "I gotta go to the bathroom. Will you come with me?"

"Sure."

Slipping into jackets and shoes without socks, they left the Rec Hall through the side door and walked around the corner to the restrooms. Inside, with the light on, Jase felt like he could breathe again.

"I saw her. I saw Taylor."

"It was only a dream."

"No, she was really there." Jase hesitated, then finally answered, "I dunno. Maybe...I did have a dream about her. But that was before I woke up and saw her for real."

"What did she do in the dream?"

"She came to take my mom away with her."

"Whoa, that's heavy stuff. But it was just a nightmare. You know it's not really going to happen."

"What if it does?"

"It won't. I promise." Griff shifted nervously from one foot to the other. "She's gone, Jase. She isn't going to take your mom or hurt her or anything. Your mom's okay."

"But the baby—" He clamped his mouth shut.

"Wow, your mom's pregnant?"

Jase nodded. "I'm not supposed to tell."

"Why not?"

"I dunno. She just doesn't want anybody to know. But something's really wrong, and she can't work anymore, and she moved back into the big house with me and my dad. I wanted to call her tonight, but then I didn't have a good enough reason to tell Sam why and…"

"And so you had nightmares." Griff gently squeezed Jason's shoulder. "Tell you what—if you promise to go back to sleep, I'll promise to think up a good reason for you to call home tomorrow during the afternoon break, okay?"

Jason agreed, but the next day when he tried to call home, his dad answered and told him that his mom couldn't come to the phone 'cuz she was staying at the hospital for a few days.

"Something's really wrong," Jase said to Griff later in the Rec Hall when they were alone. "Dad said the baby almost came but the doctors stopped it. But she's got to be in bed until, like, June!"

Griffin did his best to convince him that everything was going to be fine. But when that didn't work, he tried to make him laugh by stuffing a pillow under his shirt, then acting like he was pregnant. He looked so stupid and funny that Jase couldn't help but crack up.

"Here's your mom trying to get on a horse," Griff said, throwing his leg over the back of the sofa. Turning to look back at Jason, he froze. Jase followed his gaze. Sam stood in the open doorway to the kitchen, watching them.

~

SAM HAD HEARD enough to realize the mocking impersonation of Megan was not entirely a joke. He came out of the kitchen as Griffin yanked the pillow out from under his shirt and ditched it behind the sofa.

"Is it true?" Sam asked Jason. "Is your mom having a baby?"

The boy stared at the toes of his shoes. His silence was answer enough.

A baby, thought Sam, his mind reeling.

He walked around the side of the sofa and sat down next to Jason. "She asked you not to tell me, didn't she?"

"Not just you. I wasn't s'posed to tell anybody. She's gonna be mad if she finds out."

Sam was getting pretty steamed himself, being nearly one hundred percent sure she was carrying his child. From what he knew about the sham of a marriage, he had to be the only man she had slept with. Damn her for hiding this from him. What could she have been thinking?

Then he remembered the last time he'd seen her. At the memorial service. With a drink in his hand.

Shit.

He had taken a nose dive into booze for two solid weeks afterward. It would've been a hell of a lot longer if Mario hadn't found him and called Maryann to come to the ranch and talk some sense into him. Somehow they had managed to sober him up enough to remember his staff depended upon him for their paychecks. So he had straightened up and returned to his weekly meetings.

Looking back through the alcoholic blur of the day of Taylor's service at sea, he couldn't blame Megan for cutting off all contact with him. He had as good as told her that he wasn't cut out for marriage or parenthood. And proved it by falling off the wagon. Now he needed to set things straight with her.

After a little bit of coaxing, Sam found out about Megan's premature labor. "Which hospital is she at?" he asked, trying to hide his own panic.

Jason shrugged. "I dunno. Dad says she's probably gonna be home by the time I get back."

"She can't expect to stay alone—"

"She's not. We all live in the big house now."

"That's just great," Sam grumbled, standing up.

"Uh-oh, I wasn't s'posed to tell you that either."

"It's okay. You shouldn't have been put in the middle of all this. I'm sorry that your mom felt that she needed to keep this from me. Don't worry. She won't be mad at you. I'll make sure of it."

The rest of the day dragged by so slowly that Sam would've sworn somebody had messed with the clocks. As soon as he'd heard about Megan, he had wanted to leave Karen in charge and hightail it to Long Beach. But he couldn't just take off. He had a camp to run, dammit. Besides, one of the parent-chaperones hinted that her group planned a special presentation to him. How could he not show up?

Here he was again—choosing the ranch over everything else important to him.

He tried to rationalize his decision, telling himself that he couldn't simply barge into Megan's hospital room and demand answers. Who knew what kind of effect that would have on her condition? Anything he needed to say could wait one more day.

Late that same night, he sat in his living room with Mario and Karen. Unwinding after the excruciatingly long day, they talked about the different sessions, about the CAs who were improving and those who were showing signs of burnout. Karen mentioned how well Jason seemed to be doing. Sam agreed, although his mind had wandered off into a different direction, not really hearing the rest of the conversation.

Mario teased, "You need to get laid."

"Grow up, Mario," Karen scolded half-heartedly.

"Hey, don't blame me. After all these years I know how to read this guy. He's distracted and grumpy. Time to call Maryann."

"In case you haven't noticed, moron, Sam hasn't seen her in months."

"Hel-lo? I *know* that. Why do you think I suggested it?"

Sam interjected. "Knock it off, you two. I am distracted, and maybe grumpy. But it's got nothing to do with sex. Then again, maybe it does."

"See?" Mario said, a smug glance at Karen.

"Ah, hell…" He raked his fingers through his hair. "I may as well get it out in the open. You're gonna find out soon enough anyway."

As Mario and Karen waited in silence, Sam leaned forward, rested his elbows on his knees, and gazed at the floor. "Megan is in the hospital. Premature labor. I have good reason to believe the baby is mine. Problem is, she hasn't gotten around to telling me. And right now I'm torn between staying put and going down there."

"Go," Karen said.

Mario didn't agree. "If she hasn't told you, she may not want you to come to the hospital."

"Yeah, I figured there's a good chance I'll make an ass of myself."

"So risk it," Karen insisted. "You have to, Sam. Go *now*. Before you change your mind."

Mario said, "It'll be midnight by the time he gets there. What good will that do?"

Sam nodded. "I know. Besides, Jason doesn't know the name of the hospital. She's supposed to be released tomorrow afternoon, so I figured I could see her if I took Jason home."

CHAPTER 22

*L*ate Sunday morning Griffin found out from Jason that Sam was taking the boy home, and that Sam had extended the same invitation to him. He tried to get out of it but couldn't think of anything to say. Whenever he rode with Karen and Mario, he always had an excuse to be dropped off at a gas station or the mall or something. They didn't seem to mind, but he knew Sam wouldn't let it go at that.

On the trip home, he had to tell Sam that his family had moved again. It was the fourth time since August that he had to make up another story to cover up the truth. He had to remember them all so he wouldn't screw up and repeat one of them.

"Our last landlord sold the house," he said. "It happened real fast, so we had to get an apartment for a few weeks."

"Your parents are sure having a bad run of luck with houses."

"Yeah, I guess. We won't have a phone, so you can still call my aunt if you want to get a hold of me."

When they reached the Long Beach Freeway, Griffin directed Sam to the downtown exit, then to a gas station where he said his dad would be picking him up. The van was waiting as they pulled up. Sam got out to say hello to his dad, but Griff didn't think it was that simple. He figured Sam was too smart to just let things be. After a few minutes, though, he just said goodbye and went on his way with Jason.

~

PULLING up to the curb in front of the villa-style house in Naples, Sam watched Stewart come out the door and down the steps. He appeared surprised initially, then wary. As Jason bounded out of the car, Sam switched off the engine and got out.

After Jason hugged his dad, the two men exchanged a somewhat formal greeting before Sam opened the trunk to get the boy's gear.

Stewart said, "What happened with Karen?"

"Nothing. I had some business down here, so I offered to bring Jason home."

"I see. Well, I won't keep you."

"Is Megan home?"

"No." Stewart did a pretty good job of acting puzzled, as if Megan still lived somewhere else.

"I know she's back," Sam stated. "And I know about the baby."

Stewart looked down at his son. "Jason?"

"I'm sorry, Dad. I just—"

"It's okay, Jase. Why don't you go inside now?"

Sam said, "Don't be angry with him."

"I'm not." He gave his son his full attention. "It's really all right. I'm actually glad you told him."

"You are?"

"Somebody certainly needed to," Stewart said. "Take your stuff up to your room now."

After the boy disappeared into the house, Sam expected Stewart wanted a chance to speak his mind before taking him to see Megan. Instead, he turned back around with a grave expression on his face.

"She really isn't here. She's at Memorial Hospital."

"Jason said she was coming home today."

"She didn't respond as well as the doctor had hoped. He's keeping her there indefinitely."

"Why?"

With a shake of his head, Stewart raised his hands. "It's not up to me to explain. You need to talk to Megan."

"I will." Sam nodded, pulling his phone from his pocket. "Memorial Hospital?"

"Long Beach Memorial."

"Got it. Thanks." Sam spoke into the phone, asking it for directions as he got back into his car, leaving Stewart standing on the sidewalk.

Entering her private room twenty minutes later, he stopped at the sight of her—eyes closed, one arm wrapped with a blood pressure cuff, the other with an IV tube. Wires snaked out from beneath the bedsheet to two heart monitors. One of them had to be for the baby. He looked at her rounded belly. His throat tightened with happiness mixed with fear. For her. For the baby.

He approached the side of the bed and gazed down at her face, softened with the dark cloud of hair draped across the white pillow. He touched her cheek, awakening her.

Unable to find words to speak, he watched her eyes widen with surprise, then something that looked like anger that flickered for a moment and fled, leaving behind a watchfulness, a waiting game, waiting for someone to speak.

In the awkward silence, Megan turned her gaze to her swollen stomach, smoothing her hand over the thermal blanket. "She seems to be hanging in there for the time being."

"A girl?" Sam asked.

Without looking at him, she nodded. "From the way she kicks, she's a tough little fighter."

"Like Taylor," he remarked unthinkingly. "I'm sorry. I shouldn't have said that. It just came out. She won't be anything like Taylor."

Touching his hand on the bed rail, she said, "Taylor had a great deal of good qualities in her. She was so sweet with the five-year-olds, and especially patient with Kelsey."

Smiling sadly at the memory, Sam nodded. "She had a great laugh too. I didn't realize how much I missed it this past year." He paused. "She was looking for something to make her happy again. She was so much more vulnerable than I ever imagined. And Thorndike took advantage of that. He led her to believe he was in love with her."

"Sex and love aren't the same thing."

"Sometimes it's hard to tell them apart, no matter how old you are."

She watched him intently for a long, silent moment. "Are we talking about her or us?"

"All of us, actually. Taylor wasn't much different from me, it seems. We both fell for people who couldn't love us back. Maybe she learned it from me. First it was Maryann, then you."

"But I...I did love you."

"*Did*, huh? You sure have a funny way of showing it." He shoved himself away from the rail, and walked several paces to the wall and back. Feeling ready to explode, he fought to control the tone of his voice, to keep himself calm, to keep from exploding. "I told myself it was my fault you wouldn't come back to the ranch. I thought it was Maryann all over again. She hated the dirt and dust. She hated the isolation. She hated my work."

"I'm not Maryann. Never was. Never will be. I wasn't born with a silver spoon in my mouth. If anything, I fit better into a dust-ridden cabin than a fancy trophy house in Naples. Stewart wanted that place, not me."

"Okay, so maybe you aren't Maryann. That doesn't explain why you cut me off without telling me something as important as this." He pointed at her belly. "That little girl is mine, dammit. I deserved to know!"

"I didn't say anything because I…before we…that is, I was with Stewart one last time."

"What? Why? After you found out about Maxwell?"

"I don't expect you to understand. It…it just happened. But it proved to both of us that there was nothing left of our marriage."

"So this is his baby?"

She winced and couldn't look him in the eyes. "I won't know until after the paternity tests."

"When were you going to get around to asking me to take one?"

Her head snapped up. "I kept trying to call you. I just couldn't, especially when there was such a big risk of losing her. I wanted to spare you the pain if I miscarried. Besides that, I didn't want you to feel obligated to marry me for the sake of our baby. I just got out of one marriage where I'd sacrificed myself and everything I used to be. I'm not about to make the same mistake twice."

"You're confusing independence with stubborn pride," he said, raising his voice.

"That's the pot calling the kettle black." She pulled her shoulders back. "Despite the image you project of yourself, you aren't really a rogue cowboy out on that remote ranch. But you're too proud to admit that you're using your self-imposed solitude to keep from getting emotionally involved with anyone who will abandon you again. Look at everyone in your life you loved—your parents, your brother, your wife, Taylor. If you knew about this baby and then lost her—"

She gasped in pain.

The shrill noise of the monitor's alarm filled the room, bringing a surly nurse rushing through the door, chastising both of them for doing whatever it was they were doing to set off the warning bell on the blood pressure machine.

"It's my fault," Megan said.

"No, it's mine."

"I don't care who's to blame," groused the nurse, "as long as it doesn't happen again."

After she left, the room felt silent. Sam went over to the window and looked out on the traffic on Atlantic Boulevard. It had started to drizzle and the streets were black with rain.

With his back to Megan, he asked quietly, "What's wrong with the baby?"

"Nothing is physically wrong with her."

He turned, leaning back on the ledge of the window, folding his arms over his chest. "Then why were you worried about a miscarriage?"

She explained the complications to him.

He listened, then asked, "What about you?"

"I…suppose I could lie and say I'm fine, but"—she lifted her arm to show her IV tube—"I wouldn't be here if I was, now would I? Dr. Ames is the best obstetrician though, and I have complete trust in him. Everything will be okay."

"It was pretty gutsy of you to face this alone," he said, "even if I totally disagree with your reasoning."

"I've wanted another baby for a long time, but that's not the reason I went ahead with this pregnancy. I wanted this baby because I'm hoping and praying she's yours."

He came over to the side of the bed and took her hand. "I want to be there when she's born. I know you're determined to be independent, so I won't say another word about tying you down with a marriage license. I just want to be a part of your life and this baby's life. Would that be okay with you?"

She hesitated, then nodded, her eyes brimming with tears.

~

"DON'T LET HER TAKE YOU!" Jason cried.

"Who?"

"Taylor!"

A shiver ran down Megan's spine. "Why on earth would you think such a thing?"

"I...I saw her, Mom. An' she won't leave. An' she wants you."

Megan had been home only a few days when Jason had darted into her room from across the hall, frightened from a nightmare, and needing the comfort of her arms around him.

Her six-day stay in the hospital had caused a major setback in Jason's progress. His first visit had been difficult with his anxiety over her condition. His second visit he had been quiet and withdrawn. By his third visit, Megan could no longer allow herself to remain in the hospital until the baby came. She had begged Dr. Ames to release her if she promised to stay in bed.

Sam had wanted her at the ranch where he would have a private nurse to care for her. But she couldn't go, not when it was too far away from her son as well as the hospital and Dr. Ames. Her health was too precarious. She had no other option but to return to the Naples house, a decision she soon realized had been the best for Jason. He had some of his old spunk back, yet still watched and worried over her as if they had reversed their roles.

But she wasn't ready for him to grow up quite yet. He had already done so in other ways. His childhood innocence had been stolen from him. The world was a darker place, with shadows and demons and nightmares that were real.

Now, though, when he came to her in the night to be held in her arms, she felt, for just this moment in time, that her son was a little boy again, that she alone could protect him from the bad things.

Leaning against the pillows with him in her arms, she tucked his head under her chin, lost in his own little boy scent of dust and sweat.

The poem *Little Boy Blue* drifted into her thoughts, and suddenly one line stood out—*And as he was dreaming an angel song awakened our Little Boy Blue...*

An angel? Taylor? Hardly. She mentally shook off the improbable connection her mind had made.

"You must have been dreaming, Jason," she said to her son cuddled against her.

"That's what Griff said too. But she's real, Mom."

"You've seen her before tonight?"

His head nodded vigorously under her chin. "She's waiting for something."

Awaiting the touch of the little hand, the smile of the little face...

The words echoed in her head, and again she tried to block the far-fetched notion that the poem had anything to do with her son's dreams. Or visions.

"She doesn't want me, Jase. I'm staying right here with you and the baby." *And Sam.*

As her son drifted off to sleep in the protection of her arms, the rhythm of the poetic words haunted her. What if it was Taylor who had awakened Jason? Megan had seen the girl at the hospital after she had died. What if she was lingering in their midst, lost between here and the afterlife, waiting as Jason had said, but not for Megan...

Awaiting the touch of the little hand, the smile of the little face...

What if the little hand, the little face was of her own little boy? What if Jason knew that Taylor had come for someone but didn't realize that someone was him?

No matter how irrational it seemed for a ghost to be after her child, she wanted to lash out against whatever evil was at their door again. Jason was seeing ghosts, and he believed something terrible was going to happen. She had to believe him. She had to protect him.

Feeling his heartbeat against her own chest, she slept fitfully. The baby moved, as restless as her mother.

Around midnight, Stewart checked on her, found Jason asleep in her bed, and carried him back to his own bed, despite her weak protests.

"He'll be fine. It's you I'm worried about. Get some sleep."

Megan didn't tell him their son was terrorized by a departed spirit. Stewart didn't believe such things, and would only fear their little boy was losing touch with reality and in need of more therapy.

An hour later, she tossed and turned, adjusting the body pillow to support the weight of the baby who kept pushing a tiny foot into the worst position for any comfort. Thinking of spending the next few weeks like this made her feel worse.

Unable to sleep, she got out of bed for another trip to the bathroom, and decided a few extra steps to Jason's room wouldn't be violating the doctor's orders. Not too much, anyway. She just needed to see for herself that her son was sleeping soundly. Then maybe she could too.

As she crossed the hallway, she saw a flicker of light in the back stairwell. Pausing at Jason's door, she glanced in, saw he was asleep, then turned toward the stairs.

"Stewart?" she whispered, moving at a slow waddle.

At the top step, she felt a cold chill down her spine as if an icy finger slid down her backbone. With a gasp of fright, she spun around.

As she lost her balance and grabbed desperately for the railing, she caught a glimpse of Taylor standing in the middle of the hallway, halfway between the two bedrooms.

"No! Not my son!" she cried. "Take me!"

Taylor turned, watching with a look of wide-eyed horror as Megan tumbled backward down the stairwell.

~

IN THE PREDAWN DARKNESS, Sam raced from Malibu to Memorial Hospital at speeds topping one hundred miles per hour. Met in the lobby by Stewart and Jason, he hugged the scared little boy.

"She didn't listen to me!" cried Jase. "I told her about Taylor, but it didn't help."

Stewart clarified. "He thinks Taylor is some sort of Angel of Death waiting to take his mother away."

Sam nodded in understanding, then looked at the boy. "I'm sure the doctors have more say-so than a spirit. And they're doing all they can to make sure your mom pulls through this okay."

"Jase, let's let Sam go see your mom," Stewart said, gently drawing his son to his side.

"Will they allow me?"

"I cleared it with Dr. Ames." The look in Stewart's eyes was enough without saying anything more in front of Jason. Someday, soon perhaps, the boy would learn the truth about the baby's father. For now, however, it was best to leave well enough alone.

Hurriedly approaching the doorway to Megan's room, Sam saw someone rush in, then out again. As he reached for the handle, the door flew open. He jumped back as Megan was being wheeled out of the room on a gurney.

"Where are you taking her?" he demanded, panic in his throat. He knew damn well where they were taking her. Falling in behind the medical entourage, he asked, "Is she awake? Can I talk to her?"

"She's out," answered someone.

Another asked, "Who are you? Where is her husband? Somebody notify the husband."

"Tell me what's going on? Dr. Ames? I'm Sam Kempton. The father. Fisher said he cleared things with you. If she's going into delivery, I want to be there."

A white-jacketed man dropped back from the group, and took Sam aside. "The fall caused the IUD to perforate the uterus. She's bleeding internally. We're doing an emergency C-section."

"Let me talk to her."

He shook his head. "She cracked the back of her skull in the fall, and has not regained consciousness. It won't make a difference to her if you are in the operating room or the waiting room. If you haven't had any preparation for this, which I doubt, you'll pass out in the middle of my surgery. I strongly advise you to wait with Stewart."

With that, the doctor took off after the rest of his team, leaving Sam standing in the middle of the hospital hallway, stunned and shattered.

~

MEGAN HEARD MUSIC. Soft, classical music. Rachmaninoff, she mused. The hauntingly beautiful concerto from the romantic film, Somewhere In Time. One of her favorites, she watched it at least once a year, always with tears and tissues over its bittersweet ending. Star-crossed lovers, separated by time, reunited in another life...

"Her BP's dropping! We're losing her!"

The concerto faded into the background as Megan became aware of the surgical noises. Machines humming. Instruments clicking. Doctors and nurses communicating.

Save my baby, she pleaded silently, unaware of physical pain, yet somehow knowing they were cutting into her body to take her little girl.

Megan felt as if she was floating on air and not lying on a surgical table. She rose weightless. She opened her eyes. The sterile operating room lay beneath her. From high above the table, she watched the doctor lift her child from her womb, and pass the lifeless form to another gowned and masked doctor.

As the medical team took immediate measures to save Megan's life, she hovered over the isolette where a specialist handled her premature daughter. Megan begged her to breathe, praying she would live. Seconds ticked by. Her baby seemed to be holding on, fighting for her life.

Megan followed the pediatric team out of the chaos of the operating room and through the doors marked Neonatal Intensive Care.

The passage of time seemed to ebb and flow as if distorted in a hazy fog. She saw glimpses of her life. Childhood. Parents. School. College. Stewart. Marriage. Childbirth. Jason. Motherhood. Teaching. Maxwell. Betrayal. Pain. Sam. Taylor.

Suddenly the teenager appeared in a black void of space before her—silent, melancholy. Megan knew in her heart the girl's feelings of complete and total loneliness as if they were her very own.

The darkness melted away like water running down the four walls of a room, revealing the sparsely furnished hospital waiting room where Stewart and Sam sat with Jason curled up between them, his head on his father's lap, his eyes closed. Taylor went over to them.

Remembering her son's words, Megan silently pleaded to the girl beside her, Don't take him, Taylor.

Jason opened his eyes, staring in utter fright. "Mom?" he whimpered.

Stewart hushed his son. "It's all right, Jase. Mom's not here, but I am. Try to sleep now."

Their boy bolted upright, mouth agape. His little body pressed back into the plastic seat.

Megan said to Taylor. "You're frightening him. Take me. We'll go. Right now." She leaned down to look her son in the eye. "I know you can see us, Jason. Don't be afraid. I'll love you forever, sweetheart."

He began to cry. Stewart pulled him onto his lap. Megan wanted so desperately to be the one to hold her son, to make the bad things go away. She couldn't. Not anymore.

"Tell your daddy I said goodbye. And tell Sam—" She turned to see Sam watching with deep concern as her son seemed to be losing control of his emotions, and not knowing why. "Tell Sam that I…said goodbye too."

~

TWENTY MINUTES after six in the morning, Dr. Ames entered the waiting room. Sam knew without seeing the man's grave expression that they had lost Megan. She was gone. He had already suspected that something terrible had happened as soon as Jason got hysterical about seeing the ghost of Taylor again. In some sort of mysterious way, the boy had also seen his mother right there in the waiting room. He said she had come to say goodbye.

Numb with shock and disbelief, Sam watched the doctor cross the room. Time slowed to a crawl as the man walked toward them. Jason turned away, burying his face in Stewart's chest, sobbing hard. For a fleeting moment, Sam envied the young boy, wishing he could do the same. He could drop to his knees in tearful prayer, but it would not bring her back.

No, he couldn't let himself fall apart now. He fought back his emotions, determined to lock them away until he could be alone with them. Only then would he allow himself to grieve for Megan.

As Dr. Ames approached, Sam stood, bracing himself for the official word. The man looked at Sam, then Stewart. "The baby's fine. A girl. Six pounds, seven ounces. Nice, good size for a preemie. Better than expected."

Sam glanced at Jason, who had stopped sobbing and sat listening, his face still turned away. Though he dreaded the renewed pain it would bring to the boy, he had to ask, "What about Megan?"

Dr. Ames studied his cuticles for a few seconds, then answered. "We had a…situation, but she's a fighter, I'll give her that. The next twenty-four hours are critical. I wish I could give you better news."

"Do you mean she's alive?" Sam asked, almost afraid to believe he'd heard the man correctly.

"Yes."

Jason jerked his head up. "Really? My mom's not dead?"

"No." Dr. Ames cocked one eyebrow, not too optimistically, as if he didn't want to say too much in front of the young boy. He scratched his jaw, speaking more to Stewart than anyone else. "She has successfully made it through surgery, but, as I said, she's not out of the woods yet. Not by a long shot."

Twelve hours passed. Megan hung on as Sam kept a bedside vigil, taking brief checks on the baby girl who might or might not be his daughter, but only through the viewing windows of the NICU. Compared to the other tiny newborns hooked up to the machines, she seemed more like a toddler about to walk out on her own two chubby legs. It was impossible to believe she came a month early.

The following day, Sam was still at the hospital when Stewart brought Jason to visit his unconscious mother and view his baby sister.

"You look like hell," Stewart said. "Why don't you take Jason back to our house, and catch a few hours of sleep in our guest room. I'll call if she wakes up."

"I can't leave."

After Jason innocently questioned Sam's decision to remain behind, the two men agreed that it was time to speak with the doctor about testing for paternity, knowing the real father would determine how they explained Sam's involvement. The results would take one to two days, so Stewart had to dance around Jason's questions until then.

Another twenty-four hours went by without much change in Megan, which worried Sam more than he was willing to admit. It was too soon after losing Taylor. He had held the same vigil for her too. Now he prayed almost continuously that the outcome would not be the same.

He ordered a dozen red roses with one pink bud for their daughter, and had them delivered to Megan's room. He read aloud from a book of baby names, discussing with her the ones that he liked but knew she would probably hate.

By ten o'clock the following morning, he had fallen asleep with his head resting on the bed. He awoke to the touch of her hand gently caressing his cheek.

His eyes opened to see her watching him. The corners of her mouth tilted up. "Hey there, lazybones," she said.

"Hey there, yourself." He turned his head to kiss the palm of her hand. "Decide to stay with us?"

"Funny you should put it that way." She gazed at him with a peculiar expression. "I did decide, Sam. I was given a choice, and I wanted to come back."

"I'm glad. No, more than glad. Ecstatic. Deliriously happy."

"You believe me?"

"Of course. Why wouldn't I?" He thought of Jason in the waiting room. "Did you see..."

"Taylor? Yes, I saw her. Jason saw her several times before, and thought she was going to take me away." She explained about the poem, adding, "Then I saw her at the house, and somehow believed that Taylor had come for my little boy. I was so upset and I lost my balance. That's when I fell."

Sam listened to Megan explain everything she had experienced during the surgery, including the minutes when she had technically died on the table. Dr. Ames had told him about it afterward, when Jason was not around. Her descriptions were uncanny for someone who was not supposed to be awake, let alone aware of the happenings in the operating room. She told him of her visit to the waiting area, of Jason's response, which Sam had witnessed firsthand.

"I still thought Taylor was there to take him, so I offered to go instead. But we weren't the reason she was still around."

"Something tells me you know why."

"It had to do with the baby, Sam."

"But she didn't take her."

Megan's eyes welled with tears as she shook her head. "No, she was waiting for her to be born. Like me, Taylor was given a choice. She chose to leave, but not until she saw for herself that our little girl made it through alive. Somehow she needed that happy ending, Sam, if not for her life, then for ours."

"You said our little girl. I think you should know Stewart and I requested paternity tests, but they aren't back yet. You can't know for sure if she's mine."

"Taylor knew."

~

LATER THAT AFTERNOON, their daughter was brought into the room in a portable enclosed isolette. Lying on the edge of her own hospital bed, Megan was able to reach through the arm holes and touch her little girl for the first time.

"She smiled," Sam said, looking over Megan's shoulder.

The nurse grinned. "I'm going to leave you three alone for a few minutes. Don't hesitate to hit your call button if you need anything."

Megan glanced back at Sam, grinning from ear to ear. "We have to name her."

He gazed at her, hesitant to voice his own choice.

"Taylor?" she asked, as if reading his mind.

"Do you really think—"

"How she chose to leave doesn't change my feelings about her. Besides, I feel like she's somehow responsible for pulling us through, playing guardian angel to our little girl."

"Taylor? An angel?"

Megan laughed. "I know, I know. I said those exact words, as I recall. But…she is, you know."

"Hard to picture her in wings." And yet Sam had always

known that Taylor had a heart of gold. "Still and all, she was the happiest when she was watching out for her little camp kids. I sort of like the idea of our own daughter under her watchful eye."

Megan looked back at their little girl. "Taylor it is, then."

Baby Taylor curled her fist around her mother's finger as Megan recited softly, "Awaiting the touch of the little hand, the smile of the little face."

EPILOGUE

Two years later, Megan watched Sam lift their daughter in the air and blow bubbles against her bare tummy. Taylor squealed in delight, followed by giggles that rippled into laughter among the guests of the birthday party. As the toddler playfully smacked a kiss on her daddy's cheek, thirteen-year-old Jason snapped a picture with his new phone.

Megan turned to see Stewart arriving with Maxwell. They had all come a long way in the past twenty-four months, much to Jason's delight. She offered the two men something to drink, but Maxwell suggested getting the beverages, discreetly leaving the two to a private conversation.

"Happy?" asked Megan, nodding at the wedding ring on Stewart's left hand.

"Extremely." He grinned. "You?"

"Extremely," she echoed.

"You're positively glowing."

"Not an original line for an author."

"Cliché or not, it describes you perfectly." He nodded toward the back door of the living room. "Take a walk with me?"

"A short one. I don't go too far these days."

He paused, frowning. "Are you okay?"

"Stop playing mother hen again. That's Sam's job now. This pregnancy is completely normal, except I'm twice as big as I was with Taylor. Only two weeks to go, thank God. Now I only wish this little guy would lighten up on the karate kicks."

"Are you sure it's not triplets?"

"Positive." She sighed, rubbing her tummy as she walked. "I'm getting too old for this."

"Hardly." He paused. "Besides, you always said you wanted to have eight children."

"I've scaled that wish list back to three. Junior, here, will be the last one. Sam and I have been seriously discussing the possibility of becoming foster parents."

"Won't leave much time for you to get that degree in psychology."

"Actually, I've enrolled at Pepperdine for the fall semester. Not full time though. It may take me ten years, but I'll make it happen." She reached around and rubbed her aching back.

"Maybe you shouldn't have taken on the task of such a big party."

"I have help, remember?"

The very same week Taylor had been born, Sam had hired Griffin's parents to work on the ranch—his mom as a cook and housekeeper, and his dad as foreman. The family lived in a small yet comfortable modular house on another part of the ranch, far enough away for their own privacy.

"Even Griffin's sister Annie has been great," Megan added. "She adores Taylor, and simply idolizes Jason."

"Appears to me you finally have yourself that big happy family," Stewart said, almost wistfully.

"I do." She reached out and gently touched Stewart's arm. "I'm grateful to have Jason living up here with all of us."

"He didn't need to be torn in two. He knows I love him, and

that I'm always here for him whenever he needs me. I suppose that's all that really matters. I still miss him though."

"I know…that's why it means so much to me."

Sam came up behind the two of them and slipped his arms around Megan. "Here you are! I've been looking frantically all over the ranch for you!"

"Liar," she laughed, then turned her head to the side to look up at the twinkle of good humor in his eyes. "I couldn't waddle fifty yards even if I wanted to right now. What's up? Do they need help in the kitchen?"

"Even if they did, I wouldn't come get you for it." He unconsciously rested his palms on her tummy, then said in a serious tone, "I got a call, sweetheart."

She placed her hands over his. "Ryan?"

"Yeah. He surfaced in Portland, Oregon. I promised his folks I'd go get him. But not until after the party's over."

"Is this the boy in the news?" Stewart asked Sam. "Weren't you his counselor at school?"

"Yeah. He's a good kid who got caught up with the wrong people. And a stepdad who allegedly kicked him out, although the mom has a different story."

"I've got a friend with a private jet," Stewart said. "It'll save you the long drive. Say the word and I'll make a phone call."

Sam stepped up beside her, leaving one arm around her waist. Gazing at her, he gingerly touched her belly. "Whatever it takes to get me back here as soon as possible, I'm all for it," he said, then turned to Stewart. "Make the call."

Reaching into his pocket, he looked puzzled. "I must've left my phone in the car."

"You? Forget your phone?" Megan teased.

He shrugged with that quirky, handsome half grin. "People change."

"Use mine." Sam pulled his out of his pocket and offered it to Stewart, who waved off.

"Thanks, but I only have the number in my contacts list. I'll be back in a bit."

Turning to Megan after Stewart was out of earshot, he asked her, "Are you sure this is okay with you?"

She nodded. "And if you have to bring Ryan home to live with us for a while, I'm okay with that too."

"You really are remarkable, you know?" He wrapped his arms around her and kissed her deeply. Until the baby kicked, startling him. "Hey!"

"He's pushing out the walls to make more room in there." She winced, then sighed an exhausted sigh.

"Maybe I shouldn't go to Portland."

"There's no reason to believe I'll go into labor while you are gone. Besides, I refuse to have this baby without you in the delivery room."

"But you couldn't stop it if—"

She cut off his argument with a deep, lingering kiss, then drew back and gazed into his eyes. "I won't go anywhere until you come back. I promise. Now get out of here. You have some dragons to slay."

~ THE END ~

WANT *to know more about Sue's books? Sign up for her "no spam" newsletter at* https://suephillipsauthor.com *and get a free book and the latest news!*

And don't stop here. Keep reading for an excerpt of Sue's bestselling time travel romance!

AUTHOR'S NOTE

This story was inspired by Jackie "Smokey" Armand, a young counselor at a youth camp that was located in Malibu, California for many years.

As a seasoned "camp kid," Jackie had become a CA by the time I attended my first weekend camp as a youth group leader. In addition to her statuesque, dark-haired beauty, there always seemed to be a sparkle of mischief in her eyes. In addition to her rapport with the children, she loved the ranch for the outdoors and the feeling of freedom. When I learned that her dream had been to work for the forest service (thus, the nickname), I understood her affinity with the wilderness—untamed yet peaceful.

At the age of twenty, Jackie was killed in an accident while riding on the back of her boyfriend's motorcycle at a time when she appeared to be happier than ever. Saddened that so many would never be touched by her laughter and free spirit, I wanted to capture the tough yet vulnerable Jackie, to somehow make her last forever. As often happens with writers, my mind began to weave that spirit of Jackie into a character with her own story. From this one spark of inspiration evolved Taylor, then the others with their own stories.

Jackie—may your colorful spirit live forever in the heart of this book.

~

Turn the page for an excerpt of Sue's bestselling Time-Travel Romance, MYSTIC MEMORIES.

"A wonderful time travel romance filled with adventure and page turning suspense." —Kristin Hannah/NYT Bestselling Author

"Don't pick up this book unless you plan to stay up all night..." —RT Book Reviews

MYSTIC MEMORIES EXCERPT

PROLOGUE

SPRING, 1815
CONNECTICUT SHORES

"TAKE whatever can be hauled by cargo wagon to my shipyard. I want it there at midnight Monday. No earlier—you understand?"

"Aye, sir."

"Do you swear on God's good name that no one else knows of this?" His lantern cast a flickering shadow across the deserted beach, illuminating the bow of the shipwrecked brig.

"Not a one, sir. She blowed up here last night during the storm. Full sails and all, sir. Thar weren't a soul aboard. Gone, all of them. The ship is cursed, she is. I heard old salts spinnin' yarns about her for years—mysterious deaths and vanishings of ship-mates. But never the whole crew before, sir."

"Enough! Do you think I haven't heard the rumors as well? Why in the devil's name do you think I want your work kept secret? I intend to use her piece by piece to repair other damaged vessels. Now that the blockade has been lifted, the demand for materials to build new ships has exceeded beyond my grasp. I cannot compete with the half-dozen other builders on the *Mystic* who have the means to meet the costs. Salvaging her is the answer to my prayers."

"Prayers, sir?"

"Indeed—I have needed a turn-of-the-luck for some time now. It appears to have happened."

"What if the curse she carried goes with these boards and timbers to the other ships? What then?"

"Nonsense. It is all nothing but superstition, my boy. I don't believe a bit of it. Mark my words—as long as no one knows that she's been used for repair, those fanciful rumors will stop. Not one of the ships to leave my dock will be haunted by the history of this ill-fated brig."

"No one will learn the truth from me, sir."

"Keep it that way and you will not need to be looking over your shoulder the rest of your life."

"Aye, sir."

"Monday, then. Midnight."

"Aye, sir. Have a safe ride back to Mystic, sir."

"I intend to." Extinguishing the lantern light, he turned to leave, then paused. "On the off chance anyone should happen by while you are working on her, it might be wise to destroy any evidence of her name."

"Consider it done, sir."

~

CHAPTER ONE

MARCH 1998
LONG BEACH, CALIFORNIA

"I need your help. My ten-year-old son is missing."

Cara Edwards studied the father of the young boy, her heart going out to Victor Charles in his desperate situation. He looked like a man on the brink of collapse, his emotions held only by a fine thread of control.

She already knew of the bizarre disappearance, as did anyone with a radio or television living anywhere on the continent during the past three months.

Fourth grader Andrew Charles of Huntington Beach had been with his class during an educational overnight experience aboard a nineteenth-century sailing ship, the *Mystic*. The following morning he was reported missing. No one, not even his fellow classmates, saw or heard anything unusual during the night. Nor had his body been washed ashore.

"I agreed to meet with you, Mr. Charles, but only to explain that I—" Her stomach tightened into a painful knot that she tried to ignore. It was extremely difficult to keep her objectivity in cases that were so gut-wrenching, such as this lost child. "I don't think I'm the person to solve this case. My brother never should have given you my phone number."

"You are a private investigator, right?"

"Yes, but—"

"And you are also psychic, right?"

She held up her palm to stop his interrogation. "I'm afraid you may have the wrong impression about me, sir. My brother has a tendency to misrepresent my… talents in that area. I don't deny I have a seemingly unique ability to be led in the right direction by a sixth sense. But I prefer not to advertise myself as a—"

"Psychic detective?"

She winced. "Is that how Frank put it?"

The man nodded with a bittersweet smile. She couldn't blame him for grasping at the last bit of hope Frank had thrown at him. If only Mr. Charles knew it was nothing more than a cruel joke by her older brother—a maneuver to get even with Cara. Frank had tried to humiliate her at their parents' anniversary party over the weekend, taunting her to offer her unique services to find the missing boy. She had sidestepped his barbs and he'd ended up looking like the fool. Now he'd paid her back by putting her in this awkward situation with Mr. Charles.

"Please don't turn me down." His blue eyes beseeched her. He reached inside his silk suit coat and withdrew a checkbook and pen. "Name your price."

She gently touched the sleeve of his jacket. "It isn't about the money. I simply don't believe I can do any more than the rest of your people have been doing for the last several weeks. I've seen the news reports. I know you've had at least one well-known psychic on this hunt."

"She didn't come up with any useful information."

"Nothing at all?"

He shook his head.

"Then what makes you think I can do any better?"

"Your brother said—"

"Frank had no business making claims that he himself doesn't believe. You see, Mr. Charles, my brother—in fact, my entire family—has never been able to conceptualize this phenomenon. Even I don't quite understand how or why I was born with an acute intuitive sense of knowing things, seeing things through my mind's eye. Once in a while it works in my favor to help a client. But I don't guarantee success."

"All I ask is for you to give it a chance."

Cara shook her head, turning away from the man to escape the desperation and anguish in his eyes. From press coverage, she knew he was in his mid-forties, but he looked ten years younger and closer to her own age of thirty-four. He had the boyish-blond good looks of a surfer who had made it big in the board-room. He was also married to an equally attractive woman who looked more like his sister than his spouse. The small, tight-knit family lived in Huntington Harbour with a moderate-size yacht tied to their private dock. Cara had caught a glimpse of the elegant waterfront home on the evening news. She had also seen the security force protecting the property from the reporters and cameramen camped outside on the doorstep—as well as anchored in the canal.

She glanced nervously toward the closed gate, expecting any one of those media maniacs to leap over the fence of the historic Rancho Los Cerritos, where she'd arranged this private meeting during the early-morning hours. Mr. Charles had managed to elude the news-hungry field reporters, but for how long?

As the two of them stood between their cars in the enclosed compound, Cara heard a sorrowful mourning dove. It seemed to echo the sentiments of the distraught father with a sad poignancy that tugged at her conscience.

Walking a few steps away, she ran her fingers through her close-cropped curls and released a sigh of frustration, her back to the man. "The last thing I want is to have my face flashed into every household in America, identifying me as a psychic investigator. I can forget about working undercover if I become known as 'that California Quack on TV.' " She hooked quotes in the air. "Without anonymity, I may as well kiss my business good-bye."

Mr. Charles came over and paused at her side, following her gaze toward the single gray bird perched high in the winter-bare branches of a sycamore. She noticed he'd put away the check-book and pen. His hands were stuffed into the pocket of his slacks. Earlier his face had been in shadow, but now, caught in the morning sunlight, it showed the ravages of this three-month nightmare.

"Do you have children, Ms. Edwards?"

"No."

"A husband?"

"I'm surprised you didn't do a thorough background check on me, if you don't mind my saying so."

"I don't. And I did."

"Then you already know the answers to these questions. Make your point."

"Your husband died six years ago on a hike in the mountains. You weren't with him. It was reported as an accident. But somehow you managed to dig up the truth and bring his murderer to trial…"

Cara tensed, feeling her fingernails dig into the palms of her clenched hands as her mind flashed images of those horrendous days following Mark's death. After seeing his killer brought to justice, she had been commended by one of the detectives, who had called her a "natural" at investigative work. Abandoning her well-planned future that had included Mark, she'd considered the police academy but chose to go it alone as a private investigator. Hiking and kayaking with Mark had given her not only physical endurance but also a sense of self-reliance, self-determination. She had also learned that an ordinary woman didn't attract attention. People didn't suspect a woman to be a down and dirty detective. They believed what they saw, whether she portrayed a homeless bag lady or an overzealous real estate agent. She was good at her line of work. Damn good. And proud of it. She liked to think Mark would've been proud of her too.

"…And with the exception of your brother," Mr. Charles solemnly concluded, "your family is somewhat embarrassed by your unusual abilities."

"*Somewhat* embarrassed? My mother is mortified. My father barely tolerant. And my kid sister wishes I would just act normal. What does normal look like anyway? I've never met a normal human being."

"In your line of work, I don't suppose you would."

"Not just in my line of work. Scratch the surface of anyone you know and you'll find secrets and neuroses no matter how well they are hidden."

"Yours being…?" He lifted one brow, pinning her with a knowing gaze, then answered his own question. "You're not comfortable in your own skin. Your special talent is a gift but also a curse. You went after your husband's murderer out of misplaced guilt because you didn't sense the danger before he was killed."

Cara felt her anger leap from the depths of a secret hell that had been sealed shut for nearly four years. "Is that your opinion or did you hire someone to dig it out of my shrink's private files?"

"In my business, I make a point of knowing who I'm dealing with. This is no different. My source tells me you keep a low profile but have an exceptional track record."

Flattery didn't take the sting out of his violation of her privacy. "You should have put your 'source' to better use—such as finding your son."

"Already done. He was the first man on it, Ms. Edwards. The news reports didn't exaggerate when they said Andrew vanished without a trace. Everyone on that ship on December twenty-second has passed every conceivable interrogation, including lie detector tests."

Cara watched as he walked to the trunk of his Mercedes sedan, opened it, and pulled out a baseball cap. He came back with it in his hands, worrying the bill.

"If you won't take the case, will you at least see if you can pick up something from his Anaheim Angels hat?"

"Did he wear it much?"

"Sometimes."

She would've preferred a ring or watch, something solid that wasn't washed frequently and that the boy wore most of the time. But she was willing to give it a try. She reached for the cap and held it for several moments in silence.

"Do you recall the last time you saw him wearing this?" she asked, unable to pick up anything but a feeling of contentedness. If nothing else, she sensed that Andrew Charles was a happy kid.

"I can't really remember. I've been rather distracted with my work the last several months…" His words trailed off with a tone of regret.

"I'm sorry, Mr. Charles. I wish I could help you." Her stomach clenched as she handed back the cap. She flinched.

"Are you ill?" The man leaned toward her as if she might need assistance.

"No, not really. Just a little reaction to something."

"I should have known you had a good reason to turn me down. I understand if you aren't feeling well."

"I only wish my brother would have consulted me before he called you. It could've saved us both a trip out here."

"I'm grateful for his desire to help."

She held out her hand. "Good-bye, Mr. Charles. I hope you find Andrew soon."

As the man accepted her handshake, Cara experienced a flash of images in her mind's eye. Unlike the posed head-shot of Andrew released to the media, these were snippets of the young boy through his father's eyes. Looking down on him, she saw his youthful face turned up in adoration.

No—I don't need this! I don't want to see him! Don't show me his face! Cara yanked her hand away, holding it protectively against her as if she'd been burned by a hot flame.

"Ms. Edwards? What's wrong?"

"I—" She cleared her throat, struggling to make her voice sound calmer than she felt. Why did she have to see the boy through his father's eyes? It was so much easier to turn down the case when the victim was only a black and white photo in a press release. Now…those youthful blue eyes would forever haunt her. "I saw your son."

"Where?!"

She shook her head. "It's not what you think. I didn't see him lying in a ditch. I saw your memories of him."

The man's shoulders sagged. "I guess I should be relieved you didn't see him dead."

"I'm sorry—" She cut off her words, realizing how much she seemed to repeat her apology. The knot in her stomach was tighter than ever. "You know, Mr. Charles, it's usually just plain old everyday investigative procedures that solve the case, not a paranormal camera lens in my head."

"I understand." He reached into his jacket again and brought out a small business card. "If you change your mind when you're feeling better, please call me. Anytime. Day or night."

Cara took the card, holding it in both hands as he drove away. She turned and walked into the restored adobe building where her Aunt Gaby worked in the visitors' information office. Her great-aunt had unlocked the gates to allow Cara and Mr. Charles the clandestine visit. Eighty-three-year-old Gabriella Salazar was a docent of the rancho during a retirement filled with activity. The small, white-haired woman was a sharp-minded historian with the strength and agility of most fifty-year-olds.

Aunt Gaby looked up from a pile of research books, pushing her glasses up from the end of her nose. "You look like you could use a sip of this. Here…"

Cara blindly accepted her aunt's personal cup of Yerba Santa. The holy herb was blended with mint and chamomile flowers to create a distinctively sweet flavor that soothed the senses before it even reached her upset stomach. Holding the stoneware mug in one hand and the silver-gray business card in the other, she propped one hip over the corner of the massive desk.

"I turned him down," she said, then grimaced at the sharp twinge in her abdomen. She sucked in a short breath and held it, waiting for the spasm to subside. Her own body badgered her as if, on a deep-down level, it knew the right answer and would not let up on her until she made the proper decision. But she had made the proper decision. Hadn't she?

"Perhaps you should have accepted."

"I don't need the notoriety."

"You will handle it with the utmost grace."

"You make it sound like I'm going to change my mind and take the case. I'm not."

"You will if you want to get rid of that bellyache."

"It's just a little indigestion."

Her aunt softly clicked her tongue in admonition. "This is your Aunt Gaby you're talking to, Cara—not your mother or father. When will you learn that I understand how these things work? Listen to your body. It's trying to tell you that something isn't right."

"Yeah, well, the only thing not quite right was last night's green peppers in my stir-fry."

Cara hated to admit that her aunt might be right...again. Gabriella Salazar had guided Cara through her childhood experiences when her parents had refused to believe the peculiar psychic revelations. Aunt Gaby had encouraged Cara to open up to her inexplicable insight, telling her stories of their ancestors who had similar abilities. Those same ancestors were part of a secret history no one else would acknowledge among the living descendants in her family— no one, that is, except Gabriella, Cara, and Cara's kid sister. Her own father was raised to believe in his singularly Latin heritage, which had been traced to the Spanish settlers of early California. Although her mother was half Italian, she also claimed that the other half of her bloodline was Hispanic. This was partially true. Only Aunt Gaby would talk of the Indians who became known by their mission names— Gabrielino and Luiseño. Only Aunt Gaby believed that the powers of the native people had been passed on through the generations who had denounced their blood ties to avoid persecution.

Her aunt flattened her palms on a scattered array of papers, levered herself to her feet, and leaned forward. "Cara, you must pay attention to what your soul already knows. You won't have a minute's peace until you do what you know is right."

Of all the women in her family, Cara resembled their matriarch, Gabriella, the most—in strong opinions as well as physical appearance. Both had light copper skin, a round face, and wide-set dark eyes. Both possessed the thick hair that held its own soft curls, though her aunt's had long since lost the deep brown-black color. In her youth, the woman had been as much in love with the physical challenges of outdoor life as Cara was. They were kindred spirits, the two of them. So it was no surprise that Aunt Gaby could dig right to the heart of the present situation.

"I realize how cold I must sound," Cara said. "I do care about the boy's safe return. I just don't think I can help."

"What if you can?"

"His father's had the best-of-the-best working for him for three months." Cara set the mug on the coaster beside her aunt's splayed fingers. With a shake of her head, she thought of the culprit who'd given her name to Mr. Charles. "What I would do to get my hands on Frank right now. My brother is a thirty-eight-year-old adolescent. It's his fault I'm in this mess."

"In it, are you?" Aunt Gaby's white brows arrowed upward, her eyes bright with amusement. "Why, only a moment ago you had washed your hands of it all."

"I'm not actually in this mess," she backpedaled, wishing her quick-witted aunt wasn't quite so fast at picking up a mere slip of the tongue. "It was just a figure of speech. I was in a mess. I've told Mr. Charles I'm out now."

Her abdomen knotted again. Cara tried to hide her discomfort.

"How is the pain?"

With a sigh of resignation, she grumbled, "Worse."

"See?"

"See what? I just need an antacid." Glancing around for her purse, she realized she'd left it in her car.

"Deny it all you want. Sooner or later you'll come around. That little boy is lost somewhere. And you won't be able to live with yourself if you don't do what you can to find him. Even if you come up empty-handed, you'll be no worse off than all the others who have tried and failed. But I guarantee you won't be hunting antacids anymore."

Absentmindedly, Cara fiddled with the business card in her hand, turning it over and over with the dexterity in her fingers she'd learned playing poker in college. She contemplated her aunt's advice. Maybe it wouldn't be so difficult to take a look around the ship. Maybe she could deal with the media attention. Maybe she wasn't giving enough credit to her own investigative abilities.

Aunt Gaby moved around the corner of the desk and slipped her arm around Cara's shoulders. "Stop being afraid of your psychic powers."

"I'm not afraid."

"Yes, you are." Gabriella spoke gently yet firmly. "You are also ashamed of them."

Cara tensed under the truth of her aunt's statements. Her own heated response surprised her. "Yes, I am embarrassed to admit I am different than most people. I'm afraid to be singled out by the reporters and labeled a weirdo, a freak. I don't know if I can ever truly let go of this fear."

"Then don't. Instead, you must allow yourself to feel the fear, experience it, embrace it…then do what you must do anyway. Let yourself be who you are."

The quiet words seemed to echo in the room, bouncing off the adobe walls as if blasted from a bugle. Cara couldn't deny the plainspoken reality. Acknowledging the challenge in her aunt's words, she looked down at the business card in her hand.

"Would you mind if I made a call?"

Grinning, Aunt Gaby gestured toward the desk phone with a wide sweep of her arm. "Be my guest."

~

WITH PERMISSION from the corporation that owned the *Mystic*, Mr. Charles arranged to take Cara aboard later that same morning. The hour-long drive south on the freeway took her onto Interstate 5 and past the exits for Laguna Beach and San Juan Capistrano before she finally turned off for the quieter Pacific Coast Highway. Within minutes she found Dana Point Harbor Drive and followed it north a short distance until it ended in a small parking lot at the base of steep bluffs near the Orange County Marine Institute. She cut the engine and hopped out of her eight-year-old Camry, activating the alarm with a remote on her key chain. The car chirped as she made her way through the full parking lot that served the congested marina.

Approaching the institute, Cara looked at the ship anchored several yards out in the water. The Mystic was smaller than she'd expected—about ninety to a hundred feet in length. As a meticulously restored nineteenth-century square-rigger, it looked as if it had been plucked from the pages of a history book. The dark wooden hulk was a sharp contrast to the sleek lines and bright colors of the contemporary pleasure boats moored in the east basin of the marina beyond the brig. It was hard to imagine that such a small ship plied the waters off California, let alone sailed the great distance around the tip of South America to New England. Though her school lessons were a bit foggy, she did remember the assigned reading of *Two Years Before the Mast*, recounting the experience of the author from whom the coastal community had taken its name.

"Ms. Edwards?"

She turned to see Victor Charles emerge from the front door of the building with a casually dressed gentleman at his side. He approached and introduced the other man. "This is Samuel Schermerhorn, director of the institute. He'll be taking us onto the ship."

The director offered a welcoming handshake. "I'm only too

happy to cooperate with the corporate owner and the Charleses, Ms. Edwards."

She shook his hand. "Please call me Cara."

"We would like to see this unfortunate incident resolved for everyone's peace of mind. I understand you're psychic."

Cara gave Mr. Charles a furtive glance of annoyance. "I assumed we had an agreement about divulging that information."

"To the press," Victor corrected pointedly. "Samuel isn't any more eager than you to have the newspapers exploit this ship as haunted. Such PR may have boosted the popularity of the Queen Mary, but it certainly wouldn't be an asset in this case."

Schermerhorn led them toward the dock. "Our primary focus is overnight visits for elementary students, usually in the nine- and ten-year-old age group. The idea of ghosts may be appealing at an amusement park or a historical building. But here we need the kids' attention on the reenactment of history and interaction with each other in problem-solving situations. Their imaginations are vivid enough without frightening horror stories to distract them. The word from parents has confirmed the opinion. Only recently have we been able to reopen the program, after the authorities ruled that our safety procedures were not at fault."

The three of them climbed down into a small powerboat, motored the short distance to the Mystic, and climbed the ladder to board her. Cara managed far easier in her jeans and running shoes than Victor did in his business clothes.

The deck was neat and orderly, with coils of thick ropes at the base of tall masts. The gray sky above was scored with lines and angles of rigging and cross timbers, the names of which Cara had forgotten from her school studies. The scents of the salty breeze and the old wood sparked her imagination with the danger and excitement of a more primitive era. An element of darkness and fear crept into her thoughts. She paid close attention to the sensation, seeking its source, waiting for something more to come to her. The feeling became like a black veil, obscuring shadowy thoughts and images that seemed to lie just beyond her mental grasp.

A gull flew past with a raucous "Scree—," effectively interrupting her concentration.

Turning to the director, Cara said slowly, "How old is this boat?"

"The actual brig," he corrected, "has been refurbished a number of times—the latest of which was in Connecticut at Mystic Seaport, hence her name. There probably isn't a single board on her that is original. I have the history of her in my files. It's spotty, at best."

"I'd like a copy when we're finished here."

The visit proved unproductive, which was as much a disappointment to the two men as it was to Cara. She didn't need special perception to read the expression on their faces. It was her own attitude of frustration that surprised her. Hadn't she expected to fail when she'd first met with Mr. Charles? Hadn't she told him she couldn't do it? Then why did it bother her so much that she'd been right?

A revelation came to her with such crystal clarity it startled her. She knew the answer to why she was bothered about being right…

Because her gut told her she'd been wrong.

TO ORDER A COPY OF MYSTIC MEMORIES, GO TO https://suephillipsauthor.com/books/mystic-memories/

ACKNOWLEDGMENTS

Special thank you to—

My long-time writing buddies—**Mindy Neff** and **Sandy Novy Chvostal**. I don't know how I could have made it through the years without your love, support and laughter. Thank you for pushing me to finish this book and for the many brainstorming sessions over the cover art. (Additional thanks, Sandy, for your Photoshop skills!)

Forever and always my "Big Sister"— **Jill Marie Landis**. Thank you for being one of the first readers of YOU OUGHTA KNOW many years ago and giving me great advice, especially the epilogue.

"Crazzy" **Craig Johnson**, owner of Wasewagan Camp & Retreat in Angelus Oaks, CA and Former Executive Director of Lazy "J" Ranch Camp in Malibu. CA. — Thank you for many fun weekends with my Scout troops that inspired this fictional story and characters. I wish I could remember the names of all your counselors and CAs so I could thank them, too.

Editor, **Julia Ganis** (www.JuliaEdits.com) — I'm so grateful to have your editing and proofreading skills to polish this book. You are an amazing editor!

Caroline Bégin, web developer at Creative Communication Solutions Ltd. (https://creativecs.ca/) — Thank you for redesigning my new website. You have the patience of a saint!

I couldn't have written this book without the help of family and friends keeping my spirits up — **Adrienne, Shawn, Abby & Charlie Fisher; Wes Phillips; Val Glass; Stacie Padilla; Gary & Jenny Liepitz; Gail Dawson; Shannon & Joe Vozar; Barbara Trznadel; Lyn Surnock; Roxanne Pitchford; Nancy Noble.**

ABOUT THE AUTHOR

SUE PHILLIPS spent much of her childhood in the shadow of the mystical Mt. Shasta in the Southern Cascade Mountains of California. Moving to Los Angeles, she majored in Journalism and enjoyed a stint as a DJ at her college radio station before marrying her husband, Don. With her daughter and son in school, she became a motivational therapist and exercise instructor for the Richard Simmons' Anatomy Asylum. While helping others achieve their dreams, she returned to college to pursue her own dream of becoming a writer. A class assignment grew into her first novel, DARK COVENANT, published two years later. Contracted under various pseudonyms by St. Martin's Press, Berkley/Jove Books and Harlequin Enterprises, she has since reissued her previous novels and now releases new work through Sweetbriar Creek Publishing Company. She is a member of Novelists, Inc., Women's Fiction Writers Association and the Alliance of Independent Authors.

For more information about Sue, please visit
https://suephillipsauthor.com
https://www.facebook.com/SuePhillipsAuthor
http://twitter.com/SuePhillips_
https://www.pinterest.com/SuePhillips_Author/